The Iron Brooch

Robert Kirk and the Fae

Yvonne Hendrie

Stairwell Books //

Published by Stairwell Books
161 Lowther Street
York, YO31 7LZ

www.stairwellbooks.co.uk
@stairwellbooks

The Iron Brooch © 2022 Yvonne Hendrie and Stairwell Books

All rights reserved. No part of this publication may be reproduced, stored in or introduced into a retrieval system, or transmitted, in any form, or by any means (electronic, mechanical, photocopying, recording, e-book or otherwise) without the prior written permission of the author.

The moral rights of the author have been asserted.

This is a work of fiction. Names, characters, businesses, places, events, locales, and incidents are either the products of the author's imagination or used in a fictitious manner. Any resemblance to actual persons, living or dead, or actual events is purely coincidental.

Cover art: Fiona Agnew

Paperback ISBN: 978-1-913432-54-6
eBook ISBN: 978-1-913432-49-2

Also by Yvonne Hendrie

The Water Bailiff's Daughter

Dedicated to Brian, with thanks for driving me round the Trossachs on the trail of Robert Kirk – and for being my loving companion on the cancer journey which followed soon after.

I would like to thank my good friend Paula Hamilton for once again reading a very raw first draft and giving me her encouragement; also my friend Fiona Agnew for grasping my vision of the iron brooch itself, and creating it for the cover. Most of this novel was written while I was shielding from Covid after treatments for breast cancer, and so I must thank our wonderful NHS and my local cancer charity, Ayrshire Cancer Support (which will benefit from the sale of this book), for their care and support during this unexpected chapter of my life. Yet again, I thank Rose Drew and Alan Gillott of Stairwell Books for their belief in this project, their support and encouragement.

Author's Note

"...love is strong as death,
passion fierce as the grave."
Song of Solomon 8:6

This is a work of speculative fiction, and all twentieth century characters are fictitious. It is based on the legend that Rev. Robert Kirk, author of "The Secret Commonwealth of Elves, Fauns and Fairies", was taken captive in Fairyland in 1692 because he revealed secrets about the fae creatures who inhabited the Trossachs region of Scotland; and on the rumour that during World War Two, a woman (who has never been identified) believed she could free him by giving birth in the Old Manse in Kirkton of Aberfoyle. Of the seventeenth century characters, Rev. Robert Kirk, Margaret Kirk, Robert Boyle (known as the Father of Chemistry), Viscountess Ranelagh, and some others alluded to in connection with them, were real people. To avoid spoilers, more information is given about them in a historical note at the end. Where facts are known, I have made every effort to be true to them, but a fantasy novel is, by definition, speculative.

Please note that Robert Kirk's manse is entirely fictional for the purposes of this story – the house in which he lived was replaced by another manse in the 1730s. I have adopted the spelling "fairy" in accordance with that used in his writings, rather than "faerie"; I prefer the latter, however, as it tends to distinguish the fae of Celtic myth from the tiny, mostly benevolent, winged creatures beloved of the Victorians and later generations. The Sith, or Sidhe, of Celtic myth and legend are a lot more complex, and their Fairyland is not necessarily the magical Otherworld in the sense we might understand nowadays.

Prologue

London, 23rd September, 1940

Brigid's footsteps didn't falter as she hurried through the blacked-out streets of London, her feet guiding her as if they had a life and memory of their own. Her heart fluttered with anticipation and her right hand trailed along whatever it encountered, walls cold after the coolest autumn day so far, wooden fences; where her fingers failed to find anything, she knew she was passing places where railings had been sacrificed to the war effort. Once she was clear of the warren of crowded streets where her in-laws lived and heading for the Thames, the waning moon hanging in the sky picked out silhouettes of well-known landmarks. Her pace quickened. Her destination loomed ahead of her now.

Brigid shivered, wishing she had taken time to dress properly, but she had acted on a whim. The heatwave of early September was a distant memory, lost in a haze of painful recollections. She hadn't been outdoors much lately, only moving from bedroom to Anderson shelter. She wouldn't even have done that if her sister-in-law hadn't dragged her from bed. Time moved on, but Brigid found it hard to move with it. She hadn't noticed London leaving summer behind. The family had taken to sleeping in the shelter now that the full force of the Blitz had broken on the city, but that night, instead of getting out of bed where she spent her days, and dressing warmly, Brigid had pushed her bare feet into shoes, pulled a coat over her nightdress, and slipped away. She heard her sister-in-law calling after her, heard too her mother-in-law's sharp remonstration and knew that Anne would have been ordered into the shelter. Nobody would follow her.

She was falling within the shadow of its walls now – walls which had driven fear into so many – the Tower of London. Yet as she immersed herself in its engulfing gloom, Brigid felt only relief that she had achieved her goal, the one conceived in her heart these past few weeks. She had returned to the sacred place she had found during her brief honeymoon when she and Will had explored the city hand in hand. In the midst of all the suffering and squalor of war, in the midst of a metropolis where the old places had been paved over for centuries, this was one hill where ancient forces were still at play. Didn't the ravens dwell here, near where the head of Bran the Blessed had been buried? Hadn't there been worship here long before the chapel of St. Peter ad Vincula was built? She had asked Anne to visit the library and bring her every book she could find, and she had fallen down rabbit holes of research which took her way back before the existence of London.

Brigid sank down on a patch of grass in the darkness and let its dampness seep through her. She didn't heed it. She sat so still and silent that a cat, inky as the night, detached itself from the shadows and poured its sinuous body around her, sniffing, nuzzling her back, unnoticed. Beneath her coat, pinned to her thin cotton nightdress, she felt the weight of her treasured brooch against her breast, rising and falling with the steady beat of her heart. Worries fell away from her. London fell away from her, slipped into a meaningless mist. There was only Brigid and the darkness and the ancient mound known as Tower Hill, where a sacred spring, long gone underground and forgotten, flowed for cleansing and healing. There was only Brigid and the coolness of her brooch against the heat of her body, its moulded ash leaves and thistles digging into her skin. She didn't hear the sirens, or the whine of approaching aircraft using the Thames as a pathway to the heart of the capital. She didn't see the sky light up around London as they struck their targets. She didn't hear or see or feel it when the mighty Tower took a direct hit, masonry exploding into the moon-washed sky.

#
Kirkton of Aberfoyle, Scotland. May 14th, 1692

Margaret begged Robert not to go. The birds had fallen silent despite the glorious May evening. There was that feeling in the air, the unsettling one which always kindled the far-away light in her husband's eyes and sent him wandering over the fields to Doon Hill. Such times were auspicious, he said – the veil between realms was thinner. She didn't doubt it, and that's what made her afraid.

The old festival of Beltane being a traditional time for sightings of the Sith – the elves, fauns and fairies said to inhabit Doon Hill – Robert had spent the last fortnight since the first of May prowling the hill in pursuit of them. He was exhausted and feverish, and had known no joy. Tonight, though, there was a sensation of the landscape holding its breath, poised. Margaret recognised such times from her childhood in Comrie. These were times when sensible people did not go wandering on fairy hills.

"Dinna go, Robert!" Margaret pleaded.

He stared at her with contempt, his face lit only by the fanatical gleam in his eyes. "They hold the answers," he said, "and they are reachable! Angels appear in visions but rarely these days and inhabit the heavens, but the Good People, the People of Peace, are here within the very earth upon which we walk! They have much to teach us!"

"Do they, though, Robert?" she asked. "Do they? Good grief, man, we know them tae be a race as flawed as any existing among humanity! How can they be betwixt man and angels when they steal womenfolk tae nurse their bairns, an' swap bonny babies in their cradles for their ain brats, an' harm livestock? We only call them the Good People so as no' tae offend them, because we fear them! Some of them are good, but not all of them, Robert, not all!" She was whispering as forcefully as she could. Walls had ears, especially here in Kirkton Manse.

"Silence, woman! You, a Campbell, have no right tae talk of flawed humanity or cast aspersions on beings ye dinna understand!"

Margaret shivered despite the warmth of the early summer air. Her husband had not always been like this. She cursed those clever men in London who had turned his head. She cursed the treachery of those who shared her maiden name in the travesty that had become known as the Massacre of Glencoe. She cursed the times in which they lived, when fear stalked the nation like a great mountain wildcat and neighbour turned against neighbour in the name of religion, or politics, or greed.

"I am not a Campbell!" she cried, as she had done so many times these past three months. "I am a Kirk, your wife, the mother of your son and with another child in my belly! If ye cannot show the respect due to me, at least consider our children!" As always, she wondered if he would have spoken thus to his first wife, her cousin, who had also been a Campbell. She knew he didn't love her as he had loved Isabel. Would the events of the last few months and years have conspired to make him turn on her?

"I am going to those who offer hope!" he said. He marched out of the manse, but she could see his steps were faltering before he had even reached the fields. His tall frame had grown gaunt and he stooped slightly, and his stride was not as long as it used to be. She feared for him. When the earth trembled as she had known it would, she sent Mac to look for him and was unsurprised by what he found. Others were summoned, and they carried his lifeless form back to the house where he had been born.

Chapter One

London, September 7th, 1940

Brigid closed the door of the outside toilet behind her. She leaned against it and took a deep breath, running her left index finger round the detail of the brooch she wore even although she was in her nightgown. She was confused and worried, and wished that Mam, who had given her the brooch to wear on her wedding day, was there to advise. She took the chamber pot she held in her trembling right hand to the outside tap and rinsed it thoroughly. Her mother-in-law was in the kitchen when she went back inside.

"Well, I'm glad to see you don't expect us to keep running with the pot," she said sharply. "Feeling better, I take it?"

"Yes, thank you," said Brigid. She couldn't talk to Brenda Watkins.

Brigid didn't know much about babies. She was an only child. She had known even less about making them until Will led the way, for her Irish Catholic mother wasn't about to tell her such things until her wedding day loomed, and her father had been adamant that would not be any time soon – and certainly not to Will Watkins. She was seventeen; there was plenty of time to find a better catch. A Cockney aircraft fitter? His daughter was a secretary and deserved more.

The night before her hastily-arranged wedding on August tenth, her mother, Mary MacKenzie, had looked at the floor, wringing her hands, and had said, "Well, there's nothing much I can tell you that you haven't found out already." Then she had fetched the old shoebox containing her few bits of jewellery. None of them had been bought for her – she had only ever been given the plain gold ring Brigid's father had slipped on her finger when they married. The box contained old jewellery which had been passed on to her husband amongst the modest belongings of a great aunt in Callander in Scotland who had died several years ago. "None of it's worth anything," she said, "but you must have something old and something borrowed – take a couple of things. Not that you need return the borrowed piece, of course. I don't have much use for any of it."

Brigid opened the box. She knew what was in it – she had played with the trinkets many times as a child. "I'll just take one, Mam, thank you," she said, choosing the black brooch, a circlet of moulded ash leaves and thistles, which had always enchanted her. "Anne is lending me a handbag for something borrowed. I can use it for my honeymoon tour of the city, too."

"I'm sorry I've nothing finer to give you," said Mary. "There are better bits in there than that old black brooch, though – but as you wish. It's your big day."

Brigid smiled. "It reminds me of you and Dad, Mam," she said. "The ash leaves for Ireland – the sacred tree – and the thistles for Scotland." Her smile faded. "Will Dad not relent, Mam?"

"No, child, you know he won't."

"You should stand up to him! You want to be at my wedding. You want to see your grandchild when he – or she – is born. You don't want me out of your life, Mam!" Brigid was choking on sobs.

Mary's eyes welled with tears, too. She enfolded her daughter in a hug which smelt of her husband's pipe tobacco, captured by her light cardigan as they sat by the unlit summer fire while she sewed and he read his paper. "He'll come round, lass, he'll come round. I know your father, and he will. Give it time."

Brigid tossed her ink-black curls with the confidence of youth. "It won't be like this for me and Will, not in our marriage!"

Mary's face coloured as if she had been slapped. "I hope for better for you in all things, Brigid," she said. "I always have."

Brigid had felt ashamed then, and held her mother tightly. "I'll miss you, Mam. And Dad. Both of you."

The next morning, very early, Will came to collect her as arranged. Walter MacKenzie had left for work even earlier, having said all he ever intended to say to his future son-in-law three weeks before. They were married in a ceremony attended only by Will's sister and mother late that afternoon, in London.

Now, almost a month later, Brigid went back up to the bedroom she and Will had shared during the two days' leave he had enjoyed from Biggin Hill, a rare treat in the midst of the Battle of Britain. He was an aircraftman at the base, keeping the RAF Spitfires in the air; he had gone on to work there after his placement on the production line at Castle Bromwich, where Walter MacKenzie worked and where Brigid was a typist. On August thirtieth, the airfield had come under heavy bombardment. Will was in a shelter which took a direct hit. He had died, along with forty others.

Brigid sat shakily on the bed. She could barely remember the funeral, except for Dad, his elderly face haggard with sympathy, saying she could come home now – they would look after her and the baby. Then her mother-in-law's parlour, where they had gathered for refreshments, had begun to blur and recede, and the concerned voices calling her name became muffled and distant; her father caught her before she hit the floor. When she came round, they helped her upstairs to bed and sent for a doctor. Afterwards, Mam explained that the blood on her underwear wasn't a good sign; she was too ill to travel back to Birmingham with them. She would have to stay in London for the baby's sake, for now, until they were sure the danger was past.

Now, eight days after Will's death, as she sat lost in thought, the sirens sounded. Startled, Brigid jumped and ran to the window, scanning the cloudless summer skies. Her sister-in-law Anne, sweating, threw the bedroom door open and shrieked that they had to get into the Anderson shelter. Brigid glanced around the room and grabbed a pile of books lying on the bedside table, and her torch. Anne shot her an incredulous look and rolled her eyes.

"Come on, Brigid!"

It was five o'clock on a scorching September day, no sign yet of autumn approaching. The sun blazed in a deep blue sky; there was nothing to be seen, and the sirens and calls and chatter of people running for shelter were surreal.

Brenda Watkins was already in the Anderson in the back yard. She looked at Brigid in disbelief as she clambered in with Anne, still in her nightgown, not even a dressing gown or a blanket, clutching a pile of books. "It's a good job some of us have our feet on the ground!" she said. She pointed to her wicker shopping basket. "I grabbed what I could from the larder. Hopefully, we'll get out soon, but you never know." She had spread blankets and cushions to make the shelter more comfortable.

Brigid sat down in a daze. She set her precious books on the bench beside her. They were her favourites, much read and always turned to in times of stress.

"I see you don't have a Bible among those," sniffed Brenda.

Brigid shrugged. "Dad's never encouraged it."

"No, well, you know my opinion on that. A mixed marriage is bad enough without the husband deciding he's an atheist."

"Mam raised me in the faith," said Brigid. "I went to a Catholic school. I know my Bible."

"You know your Catholic Bible," her mother-in-law sneered. "It's not the same. Watkins are Protestant. Anyway, like your mother before you, you prefer this nonsense." She nodded at the three books lying beside Brigid.

Brigid laid a protective hand on the cover of "The Lady of the Lake", by Sir Walter Scott. It and its companions – "The Secret Commonwealth of Elves, Fauns and Fairies", by Rev. Robert Kirk, and "The Celtic Twilight", by W.B. Yeats, transported her to other worlds and connected her to her parents' Celtic heritage. Although she had been born in Birmingham, her mother was Irish and her father was Scottish. Mary MacKenzie, with her tales of the fae creatures of her native land, had instilled in Brigid a love of folklore and fantasy. Since childhood, she had longed for the countryside, for hills and glens and streams of fresh water; she had always dreamed she would marry an Irish or Scottish farmer, without any notion how she was to meet one. Falling for Will had put paid to that, and now she was stuck in a stuffy air raid shelter in England's capital city.

She opened her mouth to defend her parents. They had taken plenty of flak for their mixed marriage, in their forties, a Scots Presbyterian turned atheist to a Roman Catholic. Their families took little to do with them; Brigid had never been to those romantic regions of which she dreamt, the places where her mother and father had been raised. She visited them through these books, and vowed to go herself one day. She was intrigued by the thought of landscapes shot through with magic, so beautiful and strange that people had really believed in a race of human-like creatures who inhabited the hollow hills and underground places. She wanted to believe in them herself; sometimes, she almost did, and although her mother laughed and said it was all nonsense, she had glimpsed a light in her eye that hinted otherwise.

Before Brigid could form her protestations, however, they heard the whine of aircraft followed by a series of thuds and bangs; the ground shook. There had been several false alarms regarding air raids, but there was no doubt that this time, it was real. They glanced at one another in fright; the bombing was near at hand, too close for comfort.

"The docklands!" cried Brenda. "They've come for the docklands!"

The bombardment went on for over an hour and a half. The two younger women were terrified, holding hands at the worst of the explosions, sweat running down their faces. Brigid had stomach cramps; she wrapped her arms around herself from time to time and her heart missed a beat when she caught her mother-in-law's eye, but the older woman said nothing. Brenda poured cups of the lemonade she had grabbed from the kitchen, and tried to tempt them with bits of cheese and pickles from a jar, and slabs of bread spread with precious butter, but they couldn't eat a bite.

When they emerged from the shelter, the sky was obscured by a pall of smoke hanging over the East End. Buildings blazed not far away. As they stood in the yard blinking, coughing on the acrid air, Anne glanced at the back of Brigid's nightgown and stifled a cry.

"You're bleeding, Brigid!"

Brenda looked and put her hand to her mouth. "Into the privy, love," she said, unusually gently for her. "Are you in much pain?"

Stifling her panic, Brigid didn't answer. Her mother-in-law stayed outside the door.

"Are you still bleeding, lovey, or was it just that bit?"

"There's more," she mumbled, miserable. She gasped and groaned as a particularly bad cramp seized her.

"Can you look in the pan, sweetie? Or let me in and I'll do it."

Brigid was mortified. She stood up and quickly pulled the chain on the overhead cistern. She heard a cry from Anne. Brenda spoke again.

"Did you pass it, pet?"

"Yes." She must have. She hadn't looked, afraid of what she might see. What did an unborn baby look like at four months?

"Come out and we'll get you cleaned up," said Brenda.

Brigid emerged ashen-faced and trembling. Brenda put an arm around her and said, "I feared as much. The bombing was enough to bring it on even if you hadn't risked miscarrying before it, God knows. I'm sorry. I lost my first one, too, but at least you weren't near term."

Brigid said nothing, her throat tight. She had begun to bleed in earnest that afternoon, which is why she had gone to the outside privy earlier. She had hoped she was wrong; she desperately wished she could hold the baby inside by sheer force of will. Since she had taken ill at the funeral a few days ago, she hadn't left her bedroom, the one she shared so very briefly with Will. Her in-laws helped her upstairs, helped her change out of her soiled nightdress and underwear, brought her water to wash and tea and toast; but they didn't have long before the second wave of bombers struck, and they had to run for shelter again.

#

Three weeks later, London was still under bombardment. The Luftwaffe came in waves every night without fail. The city was a smouldering wreck of burnt-out buildings. Brigid was still there. She had caught a tenacious summer cold and she was a wraith compared to the healthy bride who had gone there just six weeks ago, with appetite for neither food nor life itself. A doctor had again judged her too ill to travel back to Birmingham. Her infection and the miscarriage confined her to bed, but her mother-in-law's sympathy had been short-lived and she was impatient to see the back of her – especially now she carried no reminder of Will.

Brigid lay and relived the two days of married life they had been able to spend together over and over; in her mind, she traced again the paths they had walked as he showed her the sights of the city, but when her memory took them to the Tower of London, whose walls she had gazed at and *through*, probing with her mind – because she felt so much more than the Tower was to be found there – then she stopped, and obsessed, and thought about all the things she had read in the books Anne had borrowed for her from the library. She felt drawn to Tower Hill. It wasn't the ancient fortress itself; it was something she couldn't name. When she had stood there, she had become suddenly aware of the black brooch pinned to her dress, and as she clutched it, it seemed to give off its own heat. It was warmed by the sun, of course, she told herself, and yet... She desperately wanted to go home to Birmingham; she felt her strength returning and knew she would soon, but she had to go back to Tower Hill just once before she did.

She chose the night of twenty-third September. It wasn't planned – it was an impulse which drove her, quickening her blood and making her decide to elude the other women when the time came to decamp to the Anderson shelter. They slept down there every night now. She had just risen from her day's bed rest, clutching her brooch which had become a link to home and a talisman, when Tower Hill called her – a feeling that she had to go there. She couldn't waste a minute. She didn't even dress. Autumn had suddenly arrived and darkness fell quickly these nights, but Brigid slipped bare-legged into the street, fastening a coat over her nightdress. She walked like a person in a dream until she found her way there. She sank entranced on the sacred ground she had sought, and she didn't hear the planes or the bomb blasts or feel the earth shake when the Tower took a direct hit, because in her mind she wasn't there.

Only, in body, she was.

#

A nurse coming off duty next morning saw the figure in white down by the Thames. The girl – she thought she must be about thirteen – was wearing a tattered nightgown, covered in dirt and blood. She was barefoot, wandering near Tower Bridge, muddied and bleeding from her head. When the nurse approached and spoke, she looked through her as if she wasn't there. She didn't know her own name. The nurse summoned help and Brigid was taken to hospital, where Brenda Watkins, brought in by the police, identified her next day; she had reported her missing, and the description fitted. Although she looked like a slip of a girl, staff had noted a wedding ring: she was small and thin, light blue eyes, a head of curly black hair. The coat she had been wearing was nowhere to be seen, and neither were her underwear or shoes, but she had an old black brooch pinned to her nightgown.

Brigid looked through her mother-in-law as she did everyone else, as if she didn't know her. She said little, but when she did, she spoke of having seen another realm, of having sat between worlds and her spirit flying like a bird over the sacred mounds of Britain between Tower Hill and a place called Doon Hill in Scotland. She said she had to go there. She said was pregnant. Brenda told them of the miscarriage, and they judged her to be suffering from shock and concussion due to her head injury.

"She fills her mind with a lot of nonsense," Brenda said, "and this'll be it coming out now. I'll contact her parents. As soon as she's well enough to leave here, she'll have to go home to Birmingham. The girl's a liability. She's not the only one who's lost someone. It's no excuse for the way she's been behaving, lounging in bed and reading stupid books all day. Will was my son and she was carrying his child, but I had him far longer than she did!"

A week later, the MacKenzies arrived to collect her. Brigid was glad to go home, where her father assured her things would be as they used to be; they would forget all about the last few months. Brigid could have told him then that things would never be the same again, but no-one, not even her mother, would believe her until she could prove it.

Chapter Two

Birmingham, December 20th, 1940

Brigid heard her mother coming in the front door. She tensed, waiting for her to take off her coat and walk down the long hallway to the kitchen. Carrying on preparing the evening meal, her shoulders drooped as she remembered happier times when she had done this, the beloved daughter and not the burden she had become.

Mary MacKenzie came into the kitchen and donned her apron without meeting Brigid's eyes. "She'll be here at seven thirty, Jerry allowing," she said. "I told her I would be on the doorstep looking out, as long as your father has gone to the pub by then. If he changes his mind, I won't be there and she's not to come knocking."

"Thanks, Mam," Brigid replied. "No air raids for nights now. Maybe we'll be lucky." She smiled warmly.

Mrs. MacKenzie looked at her then. "I would say you're about the unluckiest lass there is," she said. Her soft Irish accent and those gentle eyes which wore their emotions so openly nearly floored Brigid.

The young woman squared her shoulders. "I've told you, Mam. I've told you what happened. I thought you would understand!"

"Your father always said I put too many fanciful notions in your head," her mother answered. "Of course, when you were born it was more the religion that bothered him, you being raised a Catholic because of me. But I never expected the old stories to influence you more than the Gospel, girl!"

Brigid fought back the tears stinging her eyes as the front door opened and they heard Walter MacKenzie's footsteps in the hallway. A moment later he appeared, blowing on his hands. "Something smells good," he said, glancing at his wife with a nod of his head. He walked over to Brigid and ruffled her curls. "Feeling better, wee one?" In the last few weeks, he had wiped out the fact that Will had ever been in their lives. He had his little girl back.

Annoyance replaced Brigid's sadness and helped keep the tears at bay. "Yes, thanks, Dad," she managed to say.

"Well that's good, because I have news that will please ye, lassie. Ye can have yer job back in the New Year. There'll be a vacancy. One o' the women is in the family way."

Brigid forced a smile. "Great news," she said. She didn't mean it; she didn't want to go back, and it was out of the question anyway. Her father would know that soon enough.

#

Later, Brigid lay on her bed waiting for their visitor to arrive. She didn't need this, for she knew. She had known since the night she was caught out in the Blitz. Mam insisted, though. Mam hoped Brigid would be proved wrong. She took deep breaths as she heard footsteps coming upstairs.

"Hello, Brigid," said the elderly woman ushered in by her mother. "My condolences on the loss of your husband, dear."

"Thank you, Mrs. White," replied Brigid.

"Now then, let me just warm my hands at the fire before we begin. I wore gloves, but the cold out there would penetrate anything. If there were no calendars, we would always know Midwinter was nearly upon us by the quality of the cold that suddenly descends." She held nimble fingers out to the glow of the fire Mary MacKenzie had insisted on kindling for the old lady's comfort. Those strong but gentle hands had brought Brigid and countless others into the world. The flames illuminated her white hair, worn in a bun as always, and cast a halo around it.

The examination began. Molly White was careful, smiling to put Brigid at ease. The lavender scent she wore had a calming effect on her patient, Brigid inhaling the comforting aroma, tension leaving her muscles, her mind less troubled. When Molly had done, she nodded to Mary, who sank on to a chair in the corner.

"How far?" she asked.

"Three months, I would say."

"I told you, Mam!" said Brigid.

"None of your nonsense, Brigid!" her mother snapped in reply.

Molly White covered Brigid and sat on the bed. "When did you lose your first baby, dear?"

"September seventh, a week after Will died. The day of the first bad bombing," gulped Brigid.

"And do you know when this one was conceived?"

Mary answered for her. "It's like I told you, Molly – she was caught out in the Blitz on twenty-third September. It's the only possibility. She was in her bed, ill, before, and in hospital after."

"I know it was that night," said Brigid. "I was on Tower Hill, but the Tower wasn't there…I went back to before it was built, before London existed, I think…"

"Hush, child, do we not have enough to bear?" her mother cried.

Mrs. White looked from one to the other and stood up. "Well, I'd best be on my way. I'll help as time goes on, of course."

"Thank you," said Brigid, "but the baby will be born elsewhere. I have to go to Scotland."

Molly glanced at Mary, who pursed her lips and shook her head at her daughter. She ushered Molly out, closing the door behind them. Molly paused at the front door. "She doesn't seem too perturbed about it, Mary."

"She wasn't bothered about the last one, either. She can be surprisingly unfazed, Brigid. Always been a bit of a dreamer."

"She wanted to marry her sweetheart before, so that's more understandable. But she doesn't seem to know how this pregnancy happened, yet she's happy about it. What was that she was starting to say, when you hushed her?"

"Oh," blustered Mary MacKenzie, "she's got some nonsense in her head about…I really can't repeat it…I blame myself. I brought her up with the old stories from my childhood in Ireland, and she took to reading books and…well, she's always been in her own world."

Mrs. White nodded thoughtfully. "Brigid's always had an innocence about her, Mary, and despite marriage and all that's happened, she still has." She paused, as if considering something. Then she shook her head to dismiss the idea that had flitted across her mind. "You know, I have a lifetime's experience of helping women in pregnancy and childbirth, in all sorts of circumstances. She believes whatever she's saying, whatever she's told herself. It's probably a way of coping, of covering up the pain and shame of what really happened that night. That's if she remembers at all, because of the bombing and her injuries. She might have been unconscious for a while, even when…you know…it happened. When the baby was conceived."

"Well, she won't live in dreamland much longer," said Brigid's mother. "Not when her father finds out."

"But it clearly isn't her fault," said Molly.

"Try telling my husband that." Mary's mouth was set in a grim line. She opened the door a crack, careful not to let the light spill out, and Molly White, the local woman who had as much wisdom as any qualified midwife, slipped away.

#

Mary MacKenzie sent Brigid to the matinee at the picture house the following afternoon, while she broke the news to her husband over a cup of tea in the kitchen. He stared at her in shock.

"No. No! That can't be right!"

"Molly White's examined her, Walter. There's no mistake."

"Three months? But Will was barely cold in his grave three months ago! I never thought…"

"Hush dear, don't be so hasty! There must be circumstances…"

"What kind of circumstances?"

"It can only have happened that night she was caught out in the Blitz. She ran away, remember? She had been ill in bed for three weeks before it. After that, she was in hospital until we went to bring her home."

"So she was out carryin' on that night?"

"No, Walter, no! Remember the state she was in? She was found wandering, all cuts and bruises, no shoes or coat or…other things. She couldn't even tell them her name. Don't you see, Walter?"

As her husband continued to gaze in consternation, Mary MacKenzie sighed. "I think somebody took advantage. She must have been unconscious for a while, or maybe she doesn't want to remember…"

Walter stood up then, hands gripping the tabletop. "You mean some man…forced himself on her?"

"It's the only explanation, Walter."

Mary could see it sickened him to contemplate this. It had been hard enough for him to accept that his little girl had been pregnant by Will Watkins. She held her breath. She had no idea what he would do.

"I'm goin' for a walk," he said, "tae clear ma head. Tae think. Tae decide how we'll handle this."

"Love, we'll have to help her, support her," said Mary, her eyes pleading.

"But there's nobody tae hold accountable for this!" Walter cried.

Mary placed her hand over one of his where it still gripped the table. "Which means that she needs us even more, Walter. And there's something else…she's convinced herself of some story. Molly White says it's to cover the memory. Maybe shock, or something." She didn't know how to continue. Anyway, she could tell from her husband's face that she had said enough for now, that he couldn't cope with any more.

He shrugged her hand away. "I'll have tae think."

She remained where she was until she heard the door shut behind him. Then she fetched a knife, knelt, rolled up the rug in front of the fireplace and prised up a floorboard. She pulled out a dusty tin box and began to count the money it contained.

\#

When Brigid returned from the cinema, she found her parents in the sitting room. Her father's cheeks were still flushed from his long walk. He couldn't meet her eyes.

"Come and sit down, Brigid," he said.

She obeyed, glancing at her mother, whose slight shrug indicated she didn't know what he was about to say any more than Brigid did.

Walter MacKenzie cleared his throat. "I'm saddened tae hear of yer predicament," he said. "Saddened. Disappointed. Angry. Angry that ye should be in this state again, Brigid."

Mary MacKenzie uttered a small cry, and he raised his hand to silence her.

"I don't know what ye were thinkin' of, runnin' away like that when it was time tae go tae the shelter. But I never really knew what ye were thinkin' when ye took up wi' William Watkins. I sometimes think I haven't known ye at all these past few months, since I learned what you and he had been up to. And now I hear ye've been at it again, wi' somebody else!"

The colour drained from Brigid's face. "I was not, Dad! I did not disrespect my Will's memory. Don't you, either!"

"Do not tell me what to do, girl!"

"Please!" her mother cried. "Walter, have pity! Did I not explain to you?"

"You did, Mary. And it is my opinion that she brought it on herself, runnin' away when she should have gone tae the shelter! She was askin' for trouble!"

Brigid stood up. "I couldn't help going to Tower Hill that night! It had been calling me since Will died. It was a special place to us, me especially. A holy place."

"What has religion to do with any of this?" Walter MacKenzie shouted. "Ye've never shown much interest in yer mother's faith that I've seen!"

"Tower Hill is one of the old places, Dad…a sacred place. Sacred before ever there was religion. Christian religion, anyway."

"God save us!" cried Mary MacKenzie, hastily crossing herself. "Brigid, this is no time for such talk!"

"Whatever are ye on about now?" Walter thumped the arm of his chair with the flat of his hand.

"I was not with any man!" Brigid protested. "It was like in *The Lady of the Lake!*"

"The what?" blustered Walter. "Is that somethin' aboot King Arthur? What's that got tae dae wi' it?"

"I tried to explain, Walter," said Mary hastily. "It's about memories, shock. Brigid, lass, that's enough for now!"

Brigid rounded on her mother. "Memories? Shock? What do you mean, Mam? I thought you of all people would believe me!" Her face was filled with the pain of betrayal.

"Well, will one of ye explain, please?" her father demanded.

Brigid turned to him. "In *The Lady of the Lake*, by your namesake and countryman Sir Walter Scott, there's a woman called Alice who becomes with child by a sort of spirit…a demon, maybe. No man is involved! Anyways, her son Brian the Hermit is a Druid, but I don't believe that of my child. Mine is a gift from the fae realm and I believe he has a special purpose."

Mary wrung her hands in despair as Walter's beleaguered brain sought to comprehend what his daughter was saying. Before he could utter a word in response, Brigid began reciting from the poem.

"All night, in this sad glen, the maid
Sate, shrouded in her mantle's shade:
- She said no shepherd sought her side,
No hunter's hand her snood untied;
Yet ne'er again to braid her hair
The virgin snood did Alice wear;
Gone was her maiden glee and sport,
Her maiden girdle all too short,
Nor sought she, from that fatal night,
Or holy church or blessed rite,
But locked her secret in her breast,

And died in travail, unconfessed."

Brigid's eyes were smouldering, her expression intense. When she had finished, she shrugged her shoulders and quickly added, "I'm not going to die in labour, though. And I won't lose this one. He's meant to be. He's special." She sat down again and hugged her knees, cheeks flushed, lost in reverie.

"What in God's name was all that about?" asked her father.

Mary held up a hand to placate him. "It's about a lass in the family way by a...a spirit, I suppose, like Brigid said. Walter, love, this is Brigid's way of...making sense of...what happened." Her eyes and voice pleaded understanding.

"Like a kind of virgin birth?" Walter asked, bewildered.

"Yes, but definitely not the Holy Spirit," Mary replied.

"Well, whatever it was, it was already too late for that wi' Brigid here!" cried Walter. "I've never heard such nonsense! I don't even accept it comin' from the Bible, so I'm certainly not listenin' tae clap-trap from a poem!" His face was puce with rage as he pointed a finger at his wife. "This is your doin', Mary MacKenzie! You an' yer religion an' yer stupid stories aboot fairies an' the like! Ye've been plantin' ideas in her head since she was born!"

Brigid sat placidly, unheeding of the conversation. "I was like Alice," she said, eyes far away. "She *watched a midnight fold, Built within a dreary glen, Where scattered lay the bones of men...* Just like me on Tower Hill. Yes, it's a place with a dark history, but different because it's sacred. An ancient holy place, a place of healing. Men made it dark and fearful. My baby won't be a Druid or a hermit. Dad, I have to go to Scotland, to Aberfoyle..."

Mary reached out and placed a restraining hand on her husband's arm. "Walter, please...can you not see she's sick? She needs help, understanding. She's been through an ordeal!"

Normal colour began to return to Walter's face. "She'll get it," he said. As Mary breathed a sigh of relief, he leant forward and tapped Brigid on the leg. "Look at me, Brigid!" Her eyes still seemed to be swimming far away, black pupils huge amidst the blue. "Brigid! Brigid!" His rising voice brought her attention to him at last. "The fact is, lass, ye're expectin' a bairn, yer husband's dead an' we don't know who the father is. That's what we have to deal with, no matter what ye have to say about how it happened. None of that matters now." Mary smiled encouragingly, and he took a deep breath. "On January third, ye will leave this house and take yerself tae a convent in London – one where unmarried women give birth. Yer mother can ask the priest for an address. Ye'll stay until yer time, then leave the child there for adoption. Then ye can come back, an' we'll never speak of it again."

Mary clutched her chest and cried out in protest. "Walter, no, I beg you – these places aren't always kind!"

"And couldn't she be doin' wi' some correction, some trainin' in obedience and morals? Where better tae get it?" yelled Walter. "I would rather she was religious than the nonsense she's just been spoutin'! I will not have shame brought upon this house again, Mary!"

Brigid continued to stare as if not quite with them, not in the room, not really knowing what had just been said.

#

Mary MacKenzie didn't go to chapel the following morning. Instead, she walked to clear her head before waiting opposite the church which Molly White attended. When Molly emerged, she hailed her from across the street.

Molly came bustling over, an understanding smile on her face. "How are things today, Mary?"

"Bad, Molly, bad. Walter intends to send our Brigid away to a home for unmarried mothers in the New Year. We're to put out the story that she's staying with her in-laws while working in the city. He'll have her back after the birth, but not the baby."

Molly drew in her breath. "He's a proud man, your husband. And she's the apple of his eye. I well remember the night I delivered her. This must hurt him terribly. I know how disappointed he was over her first pregnancy, and having to let her marry Will. He must be feeling confused and overwhelmed, Mary."

"I know that, but we need to put Brigid first before wounded pride or reputation! She's sick, Molly. In her mind, I mean. I couldn't bring myself to tell you the other night, but she thinks she's with child by some…magical means. I brought her up with legends from my homeland, and she never outgrew them. Her choice of books is still fairy stories, and these long poems full of fey maidens and what have you. She thinks she was in some sort of trance and was made pregnant. She thinks this child is a special gift."

Molly White looked startled. "Do you still know nothing of what actually happened?"

"No, but Walter thinks she was responsible for it nevertheless, because of her behaviour in taking herself off when she should have been in the shelter. She was found wandering by the Thames, barefoot in her nightgown. Something happened to the rest of her clothing. She wasn't wearing her – you know – undergarments." Her voice began to quaver.

"And Brigid still claims no memory?"

"She remembers sitting down on Tower Hill, then coming round in hospital. Those are her only real memories – the rest are dreams or hallucinations. Stuff about fairy hills from London to Scotland. The doctor said she was like somebody in a trance for a long time. The thing is, she keeps going distant on us, as if she would slip away in her mind again. She really isn't well."

Molly put a gloved hand to her chest. She frowned, then shook her head slightly as if to dispel whatever she had been thinking. "I don't know how to advise, Mary. It would be better for her to remain in familiar surroundings, I think. Would Walter listen to a doctor's opinion?"

Mary wrung her hands. "He thinks she'll be taken well care of in a convent home, and learn some lessons into the bargain," she said. "He's had no time for my religion, but suddenly it's going to come in handy." She paused and lowered her voice. "My sister died in one of those homes, Molly," she confided. "Walter doesn't know. It happened before we met. They work the girls hard and don't care how they suffer when their time comes. It's their punishment for sin."

Molly took a clean handkerchief from her bag and offered it to her friend. "I'm sorry to hear about your sister, Mary."

Mary dabbed her nose with the lavender-scented handkerchief and shook the tears from her eyes. "I'm sorry I troubled you, Molly."

"I don't mind, pet. But I don't know how to help you. It's a family matter." She placed her hand over Mary's and gave it a comforting squeeze, then turned to go. Mary didn't see the frown that darkened the midwife's brow, the shadow that passed over her face and made her look suddenly older.

Chapter Three

It was still dark, the morning of twenty-third December. Mary let Brigid sleep until Walter had gone to work, then she retrieved her money box from its hiding place under the kitchen floor and climbed the stairs to her daughter's bedroom. She opened the door slowly. Brigid turned in the bed, her face vaguely registering her mother's presence.

"Brigid, love – how are you?" Mary felt a pang as she looked at the pale features of her daughter. First thing in the morning, she still resembled the child she had been not that long ago. It was as Molly White said, she had always been an innocent sort of girl. She had been old enough to marry, but that state of affairs – and this new one – sat ill on her. Seventeen was still young, and Brigid seemed even younger.

"Fine, Mam. Just a bit sleepy. I woke earlier, couldn't get back over straight away."

Mary indicated the box in her hands. "I have a plan to help with this situation," she said. "I have some money I've been saving. Your father knows nothing about it. It's mine, from the sewing I take in. I want you to have it."

Brigid pulled herself up on to one elbow. "But we've always had to hand all our earnings over to him, Mam."

Words stuck in Mary's throat as she saw the puzzlement on Brigid's face, the sense of betrayal. Walter was her father after all, and she had never known her mother be disloyal, let alone disobedient. Despite the fact he wanted to send her away, he was still the father Brigid loved.

"It's like this, lass. Your father is a good man, and he's no different from any other in taking charge of everything, the money and all. He gives me enough to manage on. Enough for the necessities, and no more. When you came along, well…I didn't care that my clothes were plain and mended, but I wanted better for you. It is money I earn, after all, working my fingers to the bone and straining my eyes every night when I get a chance to sit down once the chores of the day are done. You wouldn't have had so many nice clothes, toys or books if I hadn't creamed some off. I only kept back some of what was mine, for you. I never spent a penny on myself."

Brigid bit her lip. "Oh Mam. I never knew!"

"Of course you didn't, my lamb. And you never would have, under other circumstances. When you married Will, I kept on saving for my grandchild. There's a decent amount there. I could never go daft and buy too much, or your father would have suspected." Seeing tears in Brigid's eyes, she began to choke on her words. "Don't think badly of me, love. It's not an easy world for us women. Men are in control, and even good ones like your Dad don't understand about a woman's needs, their own children's needs. Sometimes we have to look out for ourselves."

Brigid's cheeks flushed. "I'm not judging you, Mam. I'm sad it's like this for you and I never knew. I never noticed. I love you and Dad."

"Of course you do – and I love him, too." Mary looked at the floor. "I hoped you and Will would find a better way of managing things, though. You could have taken in bookkeeping the way I take in sewing. I think Will would have allowed you a bit of independence."

Brigid drew her knees up and rested her chin on them. "I never thought about it. Will turned my head and I just wanted to be married. But when I lay in bed ill after I lost the baby, I thought how I would like to come back here and work at the factory again, only in production, assembling Spitfires. Women are needed in jobs like that. That night I went to Tower Hill, it was a sort of goodbye to the place, to London. I was feeling stronger. I meant to leave and come home. I just had to visit my special place first. I don't know how to explain it, but I'd got a bit obsessed with it…I was drawn to it, Mam."

"If only you hadn't gone there, love, at a time like that!" Mary cried. "Of all the times you could have gone!"

"Hush, Mam!" Brigid begged. "I can't regret this baby. I thought you would believe me about what happened. I was being stupid to think that, wasn't I?"

Mary laid the box on the bed and blew into her handkerchief. "I would say you were being naïve, dear," she sniffed. "Naïve. There's nobody going to believe you, Brigid. Not about fae magic and the like. Now, you have this baby inside you no matter how it got there, and we have to do what's best. I want you to take this money and head back to London. Go to a part of the city well away from the Watkins. Find some respectable digs to tide you over, maybe a room and kitchen. Tell your landlord or landlady that you're a widow, bombed out of your home. Say your husband was a pilot – it'll earn more respect, take less explaining. Go and withdraw the money from Will's bank account – it's yours by right, and you'll need it. There's not a fortune in my secret tin here. You can be anonymous in London, and get the help you need. Attend chapel and take yourself to a Catholic hospital near your time – show them your marriage certificate, tell them you're a widow with no close family. They'll treat you kindly under those circumstances and help you bring the child into the world. And we'll see how you feel then."

Brigid was silent a few moments, trying to take in what her mother was saying. "But what are we supposed to tell Dad if I do this? And what about the baby when he's born?" she asked.

"We'll let your father think you've followed his instructions," Mary answered. "You'll be in London. You'll have obeyed him that far. You can write with a London postmark and make out you're in a home for unmarried mothers. Like I said, this buys us time to think, to make decisions. We've got six months. I'll work on him. But you must think on about your circumstances in case he won't bend, Brigid."

Brigid was silent.

"I'll put this back until you need it in January," said Mary, standing and lifting the box. "I'll keep adding to it, and send you more when I'm able."

"Where do you keep it hidden, Mam?" asked Brigid.

"Under the kitchen floor," said Mary. "There's a loose floorboard under the hearth rug." She left the room, closing the door behind her.

#

Mary was glad it was Monday, wash day. Hard work was just what she needed. Brigid would come to help and they could discuss matters further while they dealt with the week's laundry. She pulled on her coat and took a shovel of coals from the kitchen fire. She carried it at arm's length to the outhouse, turning her face away as the wind dislodged some hot ashes. She had already filled the copper boiler before going to see Brigid, so she shovelled the coals into the space beneath it and topped them with coke from the pile in the corner. Kneeling, she struck a few matches and threw them in; the coke took light, the coals kindled and flames sent shadows dancing on Mary's thin, deeply lined face and the brick walls around her. Then she returned to the kitchen and sorted the laundry. There was still no sign of Brigid. "Brigid!" she called. "Brigid!"

When she returned, the heat of the outhouse as the water began to boil was comforting on a freezing December day. She removed her coat and rolled up her sleeves, and taking the large wooden tongs in her hand, she began to lift articles of clothing one by one into the copper. Sighing as she added a meagre amount of "Sunlight" from her washing powder ration, she lifted the dolly stick and began to pound the clothes, agitating the water to foaming froth. Wiping stray suds from her arms, she returned to the house and put the kettle and some pans of water on to heat before carrying the tin bath outside. Where was that girl? She could do with her now. Mary wasn't getting any younger – she had married and given birth in her forties, and she was feeling the years that morning. "Brigid! Brigid!"

She hurried back and forwards with the kettle and pans, filling the tin bath tub, giving the copper a stir with the dolly stick, disentangling the clothes with the tongs. Then she set to work with soap and the wooden washboard in the tin bath, scrubbing the items too delicate to boil. They went through the mangle first while the copper continued to do its work. Mary's muscles, strengthened by farm work prior to her marriage, powered the handle efficiently. Her arms were red up to the elbow and her knees aching when she staggered back and forth to the washing line, hanging out the clothes. She called Brigid several times while doing all this, but her daughter didn't respond. Mary intended to give her a piece of her mind. She needn't think her condition excused her. They'd spent three months getting her back on her feet – she wouldn't allow her to take to her bed again.

Once everything had been hung, she returned to the kitchen and found two letters lying on the table, one directed to "Mam" and the other to "Mam and Dad". Her heart missed a beat. Fingers numb from wet clothes and cold wind, she fumbled to tear open the envelope addressed to her.

"*Dear Mam,*" she read, "*I've decided I must behave like an adult and leave now. I'll do as you say in the first instance, and go to London to collect Will's savings from the bank. I don't know how much is there. Therefore, I've taken the money from the box since you said it was for me. I can't presume on you and Dad any longer, and I can't bear to stay. Forgive me. I'm going to be a mother and I'm doing this for my child. I hope you, as a mother, can understand something of what I say. I will stay in London at first, but I intend to travel to Scotland as soon as I can. I'll write to you care of Mrs. White to let you know where I am. Please write back to me and let me know how you are and whether I should write to you and Dad both, and what I should say about my circumstances. We could let him go on thinking that I have obeyed his instructions, as you yourself said. I love you, Mam.*

Your daughter as always,

Brigid xx"

Mary groaned and lowered herself into a chair. She opened the second letter.

"*Dear Mam and Dad,*

I am truly sorry for the disappointment you feel in me, and the shame I have caused. Yet I must speak again of my innocence in this matter, and ask you to remember the innocence of my unborn child. I did not intend that this should happen and know only the truth I have told you, but the fact that it has happened after losing Will and our baby seems a wondrous blessing to me.

I cannot bear to remain in this house where my presence feels like a stain on your respectable lives. I will therefore do as you say, and find a Catholic home to take me in until the baby is born. It shouldn't be hard to find one, and takes away from Mam the burden of having to tell Father O'Dowd what has happened. Please believe me when I say that I am not leaving earlier than you said out of spite. I am going to be a mother and I have to learn to stand on my own two feet. I take responsibility for myself and my child. I love you both very much.

Your affectionate daughter,

Brigid xx"

Mary brushed aside the tears streaming down her face and blew her nose. She put the second letter back in the envelope. She picked up the first one again, mouthing "Scotland!" in despair, then crumpled it and threw it into the fire. She laid her head on her folded arms and wept.

#

Brigid had felt like a thief as she located the loose floorboard, prised it up and took the money. She washed and dressed quickly, threw some clothes and treasured belongings into an old carpet bag and wrote her letters, hearing her mother calling her, her voice becoming sharper each time. As she placed the letters on the table, she saw steam rising from the outhouse and glanced round the kitchen, taking in every detail. This was the heart of the home. She had bathed in front of the fire in the old tin bath since she was tiny. The family had shared so much around the work-scored table. She wasn't sure if she would see it again. Brigid choked back her sadness and scuttled to the hallway to grab her bag and coat.

Molly White lived a few streets away. Brigid was relieved when she opened the door at her knocking.

"Come in, dear," she said.

Brigid blinked in surprise. Few people were invited across the threshold in Mrs. White's house. It was a topic of speculation among the local women, wondering what it might be like. Mrs. White was highly regarded in the neighbourhood, placed on a pedestal by those who sought her services. She charged fair fees and did a professional job, and many grown men and women were in the world who might otherwise have perished during a bad birth, and their mothers too. She maintained a distance, though, guarding her privacy and giving little away. Brigid smiled and stepped inside. The house smelt pleasantly of lavender.

"Let's go through to the kitchen – it's warmer than the parlour," the old lady said.

Brigid felt as if she had stepped back in time. It wasn't like a city dwelling. Molly still cooked on a Victorian range embedded into a capacious chimney breast. On a blackened beam above the range hung horse brasses and bunches of dried herbs and flowers. It occurred to Brigid that she had no idea how old Mrs. White actually was. She had always seemed elderly to her. She had never known her hair any colour other than white; but despite the laughter lines which creased around her cornflower eyes and small gentle mouth, her skin was milky smooth and hadn't aged further as the years went on. Brigid had never heard anybody mention Mr. White, nor any family there might have been.

"Sit yourself down, dear," said Molly. "Would you like a cup of tea to warm you?"

"No thank you," said Brigid. "I have to be on my way. I'm going to catch a train to London, and you know how unreliable trains are these days."

"Are you leaving home, then?"

Brigid removed her woollen mittens and toyed with her wedding ring. "Dad said I had to leave on January third, but I can't bear to stay, things being as they are. Mam doesn't want me to go to a convent home like he does. She had some money for me that Dad knows nothing about. It'll help me stand on my own two feet, and that's what I intend to do. I don't like disobeying my father, and I don't like leaving earlier than he said, but I have to. I just have to."

Molly White said nothing, but her eyes softened and she reached out and laid a gentle hand on Brigid's wrist. Brigid felt a warmth creep up her arm and into her heart. Her shoulders relaxed and she smiled.

"I'm not usually brave like this."

"You've been very brave this year," said Molly. "You married and moved to London, and went to live with Will's family. You've dealt with your losses and you're dealing with this situation. You are brave."

"I have a favour to ask of you, Mrs. White," said Brigid, emboldened by this speech. "If you would rather not be involved, I understand and will think again. Mam doesn't know that I'm going today. I've left her a note. I just wondered if I might send a letter for her here, to let her know where I am and what my plans are?"

Molly squeezed her arm. "Of course, my dear. You can rely on me."

"Thank you." Brigid took the old lady's hand and stood. "I really had better get going."

"May I bless the baby?" asked Molly. "It won't be me who brings the little mite into the world after all."

Brigid shrugged, surprised and slightly embarrassed, and unbuttoned her coat. Molly placed her hand on her still-flat stomach and closed her eyes. The warmth Brigid had known in her arm was nothing to the heat which seeped into her now, gently trickling through all her veins and nerve-endings until Brigid tingled with energy and resolve. She stood taller, her eyes brighter. For a moment, she felt like confiding everything in Molly, but there was no time – and anyway, the old lady might think she was mad and try to stop her going.

Molly opened her eyes. "Blessings on you and the baby," she said. "All will be well."

Brigid began to button her coat. "I hate to say it, but I think Mam hopes I might lose him. She said if I went to London, it would buy us time."

"I'm sure she doesn't ill-wish you or the baby – not Mary," said Molly. "A mother has to hold a lot in balance, pleasing different people, solving problems, being practical. You'll find out soon enough how difficult being a parent can be."

At the door, Brigid turned and thanked the woman who had delivered her into the world, wondering if she would ever meet her again. She saw

Molly's eyes settle suddenly on the old brooch on her lapel; a brief frown creased the midwife's brow, but her smile didn't falter.

#

Brigid had never travelled alone in her life. There had always been her parents, and later Will, to take care of her. In any case, she had hardly ever been out of Birmingham before her marriage. When a London-bound train finally arrived, there was a massive crush of passengers surging to get on board, and standing room only. Brigid placed her bag between her legs and tried to lean against a wall in a carriage corridor. Every time the train stopped, and that was often, passengers were jolted forwards and fell back with the momentum, cursing mildly, banging into each other, apologising. At one point, there was a delay while precedence on the line was given to a supply train packed with essential goods. By the time the train reached Euston Station, the journey had taken three times as long as Brigid expected. She had eventually gained a seat, but was weary and stiff from being squashed up against the filthy window of the compartment.

Dusting herself down and rubbing pins and needles from her limbs, Brigid emerged into the streets of London for the first time since her parents had collected her from the hospital in October. The afternoon was wearing on. She was hungry, it was cold, and she had no idea how to set about looking for lodgings. She knew she would have to stay in London until she had been to the bank, and it was nearly Christmas. Once she had collected Will's savings, their savings, she then had to make plans for Scotland. She might have to stay here for a couple of weeks. The need for food and warmth drew her to one of the new Communal Feeding Centres, where she parted with a small amount of money for sausage and mash swimming in rich gravy. Wrinkling her nose at the dubious looking pudding of jam tart, with pastry made from the dreaded National Flour, she asked instead for a double helping of custard and a cup of tea. As the waitress set it in front of her, Brigid asked how to go about looking for somewhere to stay. The woman told her of a shop nearby which had adverts in its window.

Brigid fastened her coat and set out again into the grey streets. She located the shop, a newsagent on a corner, and her courage faltered as the enormity of what she had to do hit her. Her fingers drifted to the brooch she wore on her lapel, her black iron brooch, gently brushing it for comfort. There were various adverts, mostly for rooms, or even just a bed in a shared room. Some mentioned shared cooking facilities on a landing. Adverts for anything even a little grander – a room and kitchen, as Mam had suggested – were too expensive. She hadn't had time to count Mam's money yet, but she knew there wasn't a great deal there – not in terms of financing her plans for the next few months – if you could call them plans. The fact was, she intended to give birth in Scotland, although she didn't quite know how. She didn't even know why, except that the vision she had experienced on Tower Hill, three months ago to this very day, had shown her sacred hills from here to Aberfoyle in Scotland, and she believed it was a journey she had to make. Her spirit had flown over the landscape like a bird, and she had conceived the child she carried within her now.

She shuddered as she contemplated the adverts. Mam could have had no idea of London prices when she told her what to do. Brigid was used to humble but comfortable family homes. The idea of sharing anything with strangers was disconcerting. She pulled out a notebook and stood with pen poised, but her shoulders slumped in despair. She was overwhelmed. Shaking her head in frustration and giving way to panic, she shoved her stationery back in her bag and retraced her steps towards the station. She was going to travel by tube.

Some time later, she emerged from Tower Hill Underground Station and shakily directed her feet to the spot where she had sunk down on the damp earth three months ago. Daylight was fading. Work had begun on repairing the bomb damage to the Tower. Brigid concentrated hard, trying to remember that night, striving to recall the explosion. Many hours were missing from her life, but of this she was sure – she had not felt the blast, for she had been elsewhere. Her injuries would say otherwise, and the fact that she had been found wandering in ignorance of who she was and where she was in the morning, but Brigid maintained that in spirit at least, she had somehow fallen out of time, out of London as it was in 1940. She shivered and placed a hand over her stomach. It was too late to look for digs now. She became aware of her brooch, grasping it for courage and guidance. Brief thoughts of a hotel flitted through her mind and were dismissed as she suddenly knew what she had to do. She headed back to the tube station, where queues were forming for the safe place it offered those who had no yard for their own air raid shelters.

Chapter Four

Kirton of Aberfoyle, Midsummer's Eve 1688
Robert read the letter out to Margaret that morning, his heart full at the message it contained.

"Who would have thought," he asked her, tears in his eyes, "that a laddie born an' bred in Kirkton would be summoned tae London tae confer wi' one o' the mightiest minds o' the age?"

"You have one o' the mightiest minds I've ever known, Robert," Margaret replied. She didn't say it to flatter her husband. It was true. He held degrees from St. Andrews and Edinburgh universities, and had been ordained to his first parish before the age of twenty. He was a scholar, a fine linguist. No doubt Robert Boyle recognised that from his work on the Gaelic Psalter a few years earlier. He had become the person responsible for the Highland distribution of the Bedell Bible which the great Irishman had financed, and now he was to improve it for his Highland countrymen by translating it from Irish into Scots Gaelic. Margaret knew that this Robert Boyle was a great man of science with a zeal for promoting the Gospel. He would be a good influence on Robert, hopefully taking his mind off those other matters which often engaged him overmuch.

Robert folded the letter. "If I am to supervise this new translation," he said, "I may be away for quite some time."

"If tis needful, so be it," smiled Margaret. "It is God's will." Secretly, her heart sank at his obvious enthusiasm. Robert would not miss her, that she knew. He was a man devoted to his parish work and his studies. She had long known he found more comfort in his books and more interesting distraction in visiting among his flock than he did with her. He even preferred being out alone, climbing Doon Hill of a *summer's evening, to her company. If she suggested she go with him, he politely declined her presence.*

Had he permitted Isabel to accompany him around Balquidder? Isabel had lain eight years in the kirkyard of his first parish now, with "Love and Life" engraved by Robert's own hand on the stone above her, and on the bell he had bequeathed for the church there. It was said he hadn't looked at a woman before he met her, too intent on his books and "investigations"- he had interviewed parishioners who claimed to have had experiences of the fae in the thin air surrounding Balquidder, and had filled books with copious notes. He did the same in Kirkton, but here he went further, for this was where he had been born, and he claimed to have had his own experiences of the inhabitants of that Otherworld. Middle-aged now, he was seeking them again. He walked out on summer and winter evenings alike in search of the Sith, the Good People, the People of Peace, or whatever names they were given. Margaret shuddered. If Robert Boyle took him away from her, at least he would take him away from this unhealthy pursuit, too.

When her husband said he would go out that eve on the longest day of the year, she wasn't surprised. Midsummer was an auspicious time, when the veil between worlds might be pulled aside. She wondered if he would walk Doon Hill until dawn – Elsie, their maid, had let slip that he had done that every year since his return to the manse where he had been born when his father was minister here. His treatment of her since their marriage last harvest tide didn't lead her to hope otherwise. Yet a sudden surge of rebellion took hold of her. Was she not still a bride? And one not yet with child, whose husband was going to be away for many months…

"'Tis an auspicious eve for many things, I believe, Robert," she said, sidling up to him and laying her hand on his shoulder. "I hope ye will return tae me early."

The startled look on his face and the stiffening of his back made her drop her arm. His face blanched before a red stain spread from below his neckerchief and infused his cheeks. "Are ye suggestin' we desport ourselves like heathens?" he asked.

"Not at all," she blundered, "it's just that…"

"There will be no more of this unchristian behaviour, Margaret!" he said. "I am deeply shocked!"

"Of course, Robert, I…I'm sorry…it's just that ye like the old ways…"

"Because I have belief in the things of old does not mean I partake of the old ways," he said.

"No. No, of course not." Now it was Margaret's turn to burn with shame. There was no more Christian man than her husband. To use Midsummer's Eve as an excuse to behave like a milkmaid towards a stable boy was inexcusable. Yet they were man and wife...Margaret was confused.

"We must be careful in our speech and approach to the matters which I investigate," he said, more softly.

Margaret let out a long breath. She understood him now. How remiss of her. There must be no taint of irreligion. Such things might lead to an accusation of witchcraft. There were those among Robert's colleagues who disdained his *"investigations"*.

"Of course, Robert. I am so sorry!"

"I'll likely be gone all night," he said. *"This eve I go to Balquidder."*

She stared at him. He could not meet her eyes. In a rush, she understood that he expected to be in London over Christmas, so would visit his old church tonight instead. Isabel had died on Christmas Day 1680. He visited her grave, not on the anniversary itself when he had to observe the birthday of Our Lord with his flock, but on the shortest day of the year just before it, if the snows allowed the journey. This she had learned to her shock and dismay last Midwinter's Eve, when he had held a lonely prayer vigil in the freezing church at Balquidder until dawn. She had thought it excessive in a widower of seven years, and demeaning to herself, his bride of but a few months. Now she knew the full truth of it.

He was a hypocrite. For all his talk of disdaining heathen ways, he was going in search of Isabel. *"Love and Life"*: he had engraved it on her headstone with his own hand, and had it inscribed on the church bell he had bequeathed. Isabel was his true love, and still the biggest influence in his life. He was eliciting the help of the fae to find her again, even if only for a ghostly glimpse, at this time when the veil between worlds was thin, as it was at Midwinter. Margaret had admired her older cousin, even as she had secretly nurtured a longing for her husband. It had been the realisation of her greatest dream to be noticed by him at last. But he was bound to Isabel still. He would rather linger in a cold kirk in hopes of seeing a wraith, than share the warmth of their marriage bed. At Midwinter, he had returned to her chilled, ashen and disappointed. He was going to try again.

A worm of bitter jealousy entered Margaret's heart.

Chapter Five

At first, Brigid wondered if she should have gone to a hotel after all. She had enough money for a modest guest house for a couple of nights, although she was loath to fritter it away. At the thought of it, packed beneath her clothes, she stuffed her carpet bag more securely under her legs. It would have been a cheap bed and breakfast, and she would probably have ended up in a shelter anyway, she told herself; but this place was hell on earth. She had changed in a toilet, putting on extra clothes below her coat, and pulling socks over the precious nylons she had bought in the summer for her wedding day, but she was still cold. Despite that, when women from the Women's Royal Voluntary Service came around serving tea, she declined because she didn't want to visit the toilet any more than was necessary. She was aware from the smell that not everyone was bothering to try to reach the toilets. The indignity appalled her. The tiled wall at her back was freezing and she was grateful that her bag raised her legs off the damp platform. Other people were better prepared with blankets, but Brigid didn't own any. There were some make-shift bunk beds in one part, but all had been claimed before she got there. The platform seethed with people, and those later than she had been flooded down on to the rail tracks.

The noise of families chattering grated on her ears. There was raucous laughter at times, some outbursts of song. Surely, they would quieten as the night wore on? She borrowed a newspaper. It was a distraction and gave her a purpose; the adverts for accommodation, however, were just as discouraging as those in the corner shop. When she came across one about a room in Aberfoyle, though, she forgot her discomforts entirely. Eyes wide and crystal-blue with concentration, she read that there was a room available at the manse in Kirkton of Aberfoyle, Scotland, for a young woman who was willing to work for board and lodging. The incumbent clergyman was away serving as an army chaplain, and his wife required help with the house and garden and their five children.

Brigid dived into her bag and retrieved her copy of "The Secret Commonwealth of Elves, Fauns and Fairies" by Robert Kirk. She couldn't believe it! This was the house where Sir Walter Scott had written "The Lady of the Lake", and learned of Kirk's manuscript, bringing it to public notice. She didn't hesitate. She took out her writing pad and wrote a letter of application. Lacking any permanent address, she gave her Birmingham one. She would let Mam know via Mrs. White that she was expecting a reply, once she had somewhere to live in London – she would remain in the city until she heard from the minister's wife, this Mrs. MacKendrick. Although she had been appalled at her mother's advice that she should lie about when her husband had been killed and what his occupation had been, several lies now tripped off her pen with ease. Somehow, it was easier to lie in writing. She wanted the room in Kirkton Manse so badly. She hesitated when she thought about the two character references required, but finished by saying that they would follow. She would think of something. Maybe Molly White would provide one. Surely, in line with her vision of hills from here to Aberfoyle, this was meant to be?

Drained but content in a wondering, excited way, she settled herself, legs over her carpet bag, her mind beginning to drift immediately. The noise of the underground station receded to nothing, and deep darkness engulfed her. Yet Brigid wasn't asleep. She was suddenly alert to a greater truth about her surroundings. She was in the bowels of the earth at Tower Hill, three months to the night that she had sat on the damp grass above ground at a spot close to here. The same mood began to claim her, and Brigid sank down into it. The noise of other people sheltering from the Blitz and the chill of her concrete and tiled surroundings melted away; and she was floating in darkness again, going back to an older place, before London, a sacred place with a holy spring where ravens perched on bare-branched Midwinter trees.

Brigid's spirit had been claimed again, and she was a child out of time in the womb of the earth. She was in London, but Scotland was calling; she sensed the other realm hidden beneath the world as she knew it, the maze of passages and hills and thin places between the worlds. She was destined for Doon Hill; she would go to Aberfoyle, and give birth. For some reason, that was where her baby had to be born. That was the guidance she had received, and now her way there had opened before her.

#

Doreen Johnstone had been watching the girl for hours. People watching was what she did to while away the night. It was hard for anybody to sleep in the Underground, overcrowded, cold and smelly as it was, but when your husband was on Air Raid Precaution duty, it was impossible. The girl had attracted her attention first of all by the fact she seemed to be alone, although so young. She was barely more than a child, slight of build and with a mop of black curls. She looked ill at ease and exhausted as she tried to settle herself against a wall, upright and crammed between two noisy families. Her obvious discomfort piqued Doreen's attention, and she noted the hand which lay protectively over her belly much of the time. Doreen pursed her lips knowingly. Then, when the girl asked a man if she might borrow his newspaper, she saw the wedding ring. Doreen blinked in surprise. She didn't look old enough to be married. It must have been a shotgun affair, for certain.

Doreen watched as the girl turned the pages, a weary look on her face. Her legs were slung over the top of a carpet bag. That was odd, too, thought Doreen; it was a travelling bag, too large for overnight needs. Suddenly, the girl froze as she turned a page. Her eyes flared wide and Doreen noticed how startlingly blue they were, like those light blue Ceylon sapphires she had seen in shop windows up West. The girl bit her lip, delved into her bag and pulled out a thin book. Doreen couldn't see what it was. The girl glanced from the book to the newspaper and smiled. She took out a pad and a pen and began to write furiously. She frowned with concentration as she worked, and seemed satisfied but exhausted when she had finished. She fished out an envelope, addressed it and applied a stamp. Then she handed the newspaper back with thanks, put her writing materials away, and leaned back against the wall. She closed her eyes and sat motionless, legs over the bag. If she slept like that, thought Doreen, she would be stiff and sore come morning, especially in her condition.

The man to whom the newspaper belonged laid it aside. Doreen, who was lying curled among strangers nearer the tracks, pushed up on one elbow and reached out for it. "May I?" The man nodded, his eyes glazed with lack of sleep. The girl hadn't refolded the paper well. It opened at the last page she had read. There were a few adverts for accommodation, among them one about some house in Scotland; she couldn't see what had caused her to become so excited. An idea began to form in Doreen's mind, and it occupied her for the rest of the long, uncomfortable night.

#

Hours later, when the crowds around her began to stir and stretch weary limbs, Brigid returned to her surroundings slowly. She didn't know where she was at first, but it wasn't like three months ago – she was well aware of who she was, and of her predicament. Her back ached and her legs were numb, and she knew she had slipped away again and been held fast in some space between worlds, a happening which she could neither help nor hinder. As she tried to push herself up, a woman appeared in front of her.

"Need a hand, lovey?"

She had a sharp-featured face with skin stretched over prominent cheekbones, and a wide, reassuring smile. Despite a night spent on the platform, her hair was well coiffed and she wore make-up and an expensive coat.

"I'm fine, thank you," said Brigid.

The woman leaned closer. "Just thought you might be sore. This isn't the best place for someone in your condition, is it, dearie?"

Brigid was taken aback. The woman noticed her surprise.

"Oh, it's not showing," she whispered, "at least, not under all those layers you're wearing. Another woman just knows, picks up the signs. Feminine intuition."

Brigid smiled warily. "It wasn't very comfortable," she said.

"Off home now then, are we?"

Brigid sighed. "Actually, I'm looking for lodgings."

Doreen Johnstone looked shocked. "On Christmas Eve? Where is your husband, your family, chick?"

Brigid swallowed. "My husband was killed." That much was true; she didn't have to give any more details.

Doreen's face fell. "You poor lamb. I am sorry. No other relatives?"

"My father...well, he didn't approve of my husband." That also wasn't too far from the truth, but Brigid bit her lip. She should just have said "No", or "Not here".

"You might be hard put to find anyone to take you in today," Doreen said. "People have made plans at this time of year, maybe family staying in the rooms they would rent out." She hesitated a moment. "Tell you what – we've got a spare room, me and Fred. Not that we usually take in lodgers, but you would be welcome...if you like."

"Oh!" Brigid couldn't believe her luck. This was obviously a respectable woman, and it would save her a lot of wearisome searching and possibly even having to spend Christmas in the Underground. "If you're sure..."

"Of course I am, lovey," said Doreen. "We can't have you wandering round like Mary, finding no room at the inn, now can we?" she said. "Not on Christmas Eve!" She picked up Brigid's bag with her free hand, her own in the other, and they joined the crowds surging towards the escalators.

#

Doreen lived in a neat red-brick terrace not too far away. She led Brigid down a back lane and into a small yard, where a hen house stood in an enclosure. "We gave up the Anderson shelter to make room for chickens," Doreen explained. "My husband's on Air Raid Precaution duty such a lot, and I prefer the company down the tube station. When all those farm hens were killed off this year – when the feed ran out – I couldn't stand the egg shortage. No egg rations here, dear – stay with us and you and baby will get all the protein you need!"

They went into the house. The kitchen was small and practical rather than homely, but it was spotlessly clean. They passed through into a dim hallway with a staircase, the bannisters made from dark, polished wood. Doreen stopped and smiled. "Perhaps I should show you the other rooms before you decide if you want to stay." She opened a door into a dining room with French windows looking on to the yard. "The view's usually better," she sighed. "Flowers and that. But it's winter, and there's a war on. Anyway, the chickens are better to look at than the Anderson was."

"It's lovely," said Brigid, who wasn't used to a dining room and had never seen French windows, except in films.

Doreen smiled proudly and led her back into the hallway, where she opened another door. Weak morning light flooded a beautiful room which was decorated for Christmas; no tree as yet, but a few seasonal ornaments were dotted around the room and some greenery twined around mirror and picture frames. "Fred picked the holly and ivy at work. He's a cemetery caretaker," she said.

"A gravedigger?" asked Brigid.

"Oh, there's a lot more to it than that," sniffed Doreen. "My Fred's more of a supervisor. It's a responsible job."

She led the way upstairs. The doors to two rooms were open; Brigid glimpsed a double bed in one, bookcases and a table with a sewing machine on top of it in the other, much smaller one. Doreen opened a third door. "This is yours, if you want it," she said.

Brigid entered a room better than any she had ever seen. It was as if Doreen had been expecting a Christmas guest. The bed was made, draped with a luxurious bedspread which matched the curtains. The heavy furniture was polished like everything else in the house. On the dressing table, a mirror, brush and comb gleamed silver on a lace cloth, and china dishes waited to receive jewellery and trinkets.

"It's as if it was just waiting for me," whispered Brigid. She hadn't meant to say it out loud.

"I believe it has been." Doreen patted her shoulder. "I think you could probably do with a sleep in a nice warm bed. You can freshen up if you like…we have an indoor privy, it's the door we passed on the half-landing on the way up. Just a sink and toilet, I'm afraid, but better than going outside. Now, would you like some tea and toast before you snuggle down?"

Brigid thanked her and Doreen said she would bring a tray.

"Er…Mrs. Johnstone, what is the rent?" she asked awkwardly. She wondered how long it would take to receive a reply from the minister's wife in Aberfoyle, and if she could afford such a grand room even for a couple of weeks.

Doreen smiled sympathetically. "Don't go worrying about that now, love," she replied. "Tell you what – be our guest for Christmas. Let me know the day after Boxing Day if you want to stay, and we'll come to an arrangement."

"Really, that's too kind…I couldn't impose like that…" Brigid knew she wouldn't be a long-term lodger, but it was Christmas Eve and this was too nice a place to lose.

"Nonsense! What kind of Christians would we be if we couldn't take a young woman in at Christmas? A war widow, too, and expecting."

Brigid sank into the eiderdown of the bed in wonder, relaxed and relieved. Surely, this too was meant to be. She was right about her special baby, and the powers which walked between worlds, the ones which had summoned her, were taking care of them both on their way to Scotland.

#

An odour of pipe smoke tickled her nostrils when she woke hours later, as light was fading over London. The silhouette of a man leaned over her, features indistinguishable in the dimness of the room. Brigid, disorientated, whimpered slightly.

"Don't be scared, Miss," said a voice, masculine but gentle. "I'm Fred, Doreen's husband. Just came to check on our guest." He walked over to the window and drew the blackouts beneath the floral chintz curtains before switching on the light. He was a small middle-aged man with hazel eyes which seemed too large for his wrinkled face. "We would have lit a fire in here if we'd been expecting a guest," he said, "but since you're snug as a bug in there already, we'll spare the coal if you don't mind. The rations don't go far. We like to keep a hearty blaze in the parlour."

Brigid rubbed her eyes and sat up. She had a confused memory of her mother waking her. Had that been only yesterday morning? "Mr. Johnstone?" she said. "Pleased to meet you." The polite greeting sounded strange in the circumstances, as she lay in his spare bed. "It's so kind of you and your wife…" she blustered. "I hope you don't object to her bringing me here…"

"Of course not!" he said. "Welcome. There'll be some tea on the go soon, then we'd best get to the tube station."

"Oh…"

"Can't risk staying here, and we gave up the yard to the chickens, see. No shelter to make a sudden dash. I'll be with you tonight. I'm off duty." He smiled and left the room on slipper-shod feet, pipe in hand.

#

Doreen was in the kitchen preparing sandwiches to take to the Underground for supper.

"What delights do we have to look forward to tonight, my love?" asked Fred.

"Egg, as always," beamed Doreen, "and a carrot mixture from a war recipe. Not sure it's up to much, but it's a change anyway. Well, what do you think of our lodger?"

"She's a china doll," Fred replied. "Are you sure that wedding ring's genuine?"

"She doesn't seem the deceptive type to me," mused Doreen, "but there's been a fall-out with her family. I intend to get it out of her, the whole story."

"No doubt you will, my love. No doubt you will."

Doreen began frying sausages and eggs.

\#

Brigid appeared just as Doreen was setting the table. The smell of cooking had wafted upstairs and reminded her that she hadn't eaten since that morning. She had slept the sleep of the exhausted but relieved – deep and dreamless, like a healing draught.

"Hello, lovey," smiled Doreen. "You pull up a chair and make yourself at home."

Fred sat at the head of the table with the women on either side of him. Conversation was polite and restrained. The food, washed down with scalding tea, was filling and welcome.

"Your hens lay marvellous eggs," said Brigid.

"Best I've tasted," said Fred. "Reckon I'll go on keeping 'em after the war."

"I've not had many at all lately," said Brigid.

Silence fell again.

Doreen took a gulp of tea and smiled. "So, when is the little one due, dearie?"

"June," Brigid replied.

"I knew you couldn't be far on. It can't be long since you lost your husband, then, you poor darling."

Brigid swallowed and kept her eyes on her plate. "October."

"Killed in action?" asked Fred. "What did he do?"

Brigid looked up and saw the keen interest in his eyes. Mam had told her to say her husband was a pilot. The lie stuck in Brigid's throat. Ground crew were every bit as important – they didn't get the credit they deserved for keeping the RAF flying. Yet to say he had been a pilot would impress people and mean no more awkward questions. She wouldn't know how to answer if they probed where, when and how her aircraftman husband had died in October, for he was killed in August.

"He was a pilot," she said.

Doreen paused, her knife and fork poised. "Did he know, dear? About the baby?"

"No."

Doreen sighed and shook her head. "Had you been married long?"

"No…er…not even three months."

"I bet you had just turned sixteen, ay? Got married as soon as you could. What made your father give his permission, if he didn't approve of your choice like you said?"

Brigid faltered. She was digging herself into a hole under Doreen's interrogation. "He just…gave in eventually," she said weakly. "I'll be eighteen in February. On St. Brigid's Day. That's where I get my name." She reached for her cup and took a swallow.

Fred stared at her. "You barely look fourteen," he said. He stared appraisingly. "Thirteen for certain, I would have said. Hey, Dor, our girl would have been fourteen by now."

Doreen set her knife and fork down and glared at her husband. "I'm well aware of that."

Minutes passed. Cutlery clinked off china plates and tea was sipped. Brigid didn't know what to say. They had lost a child. Were there others, living? Doreen must be in her forties and Fred even older, so they might be grown up and left home, maybe serving somewhere, maybe married. She hadn't noticed any photographs, though.

"Well," said Doreen, her teacup tinkling in its saucer as her hand shook slightly, "it'll be time for the night quarters soon. You'll be more comfortable tonight, lovey, we've made sure of that."

"I had a word with my mate on the tickets," Fred explained. "He's reserved a bunk for us. They're not great, but better than the ground."

"Oh!" exclaimed Brigid, "That's too kind!"

"Not at all," said Doreen. "We have to take good care of you and baby. First, though, since it's Christmas Eve, I refuse to leave this house without a bit of tradition!"

Fred rose and pulled Doreen's chair back as she stood. "After you, m'lady," he said.

She led the way to the parlour, where a Christmas tree now stood in the corner near the fireplace. Smouldering coals burned low in the grate. Fred flicked the switch for the fairy lights, and their multicoloured glow reflected from bright baubles hanging on the tree's branches. There was greenery forming a garland on the mantelpiece, and together with the tree it filled the room with outdoor scents. Brigid gasped in wonder. They stood in silent appreciation for a few seconds before Doreen lit the lamp on top of the piano. She seated herself and flexed her fingers.

"Our guest shall choose the first carol," she beamed. "What'll it be, poppet?"

The excitement of youth and new experiences bubbled up in Brigid. They had never made much of Christmas at home. It was a religious festival to her mother, and didn't figure greatly in her father's Scots' Presbyterian upbringing; even less so once he lost his faith. She had never celebrated it in a grotto like this.

"Hark the Herald Angels Sing!" she replied.

#

Twenty minutes later, they were on their way to Tower Hill Tube Station, laden with blankets, food and flasks to make the night more comfortable. Brigid had packed her blankets inside her carpet bag, empty now of her clothes, but with her mother's money safely stashed at the bottom of it; she had even taken the precaution of slitting the lining of the bag and hiding the money in there. She couldn't leave it behind and risk losing it in an air raid.

As promised, there was a bunk waiting for them. Doreen proposed she and Brigid should go top-to-tail when it came time to sleep. Considering many slept in single file along the side of the rail tracks, somebody else's feet almost touching their heads as they lay, it wasn't such a great hardship. They made up the thin mattress as best they could and settled to while away the time. Someone had brought a Christmas tree down to the platform, lights and all, but the mood was sombre. An elderly man attempted to get some carol singing going, and people joined in with forced jollity for a while. Then the family groups settled to their own conversations.

"You've not told us much about yourself," Doreen remarked to Brigid. "You've been too busy sleeping, of course!"

Brigid blushed. "I'm sorry about that," she said. "I didn't mean to be rude. I didn't get much sleep last night."

Doreen frowned. "You looked as if you were well away."

"No," said Brigid, "not really…I was sort of half and half." She wondered if the other world which seemed to claim her spirit in this place would come for her again tonight. She would fight it, she decided. It left her vulnerable, and she felt exhausted when she came out of it. Yet it wasn't without benevolence, and felt totally natural, this inexplicable slipping away into timelessness. Brigid frowned as she tried to imagine what it meant.

"Well?" Doreen prompted gently. "Tell us a bit about yourself – where you come from and all that. I can't place your accent."

"I was born in Birmingham, but Mam's Irish and Dad's Scottish and I've ended up sounding like this," said Brigid. It was true that she didn't have a Brummie accent, or any kind of accent you could name. "Dad works at Castle Bromwich, making Spitfires. I worked there, too, in the office, until I married."

"Doreen said there's been an estrangement between you and your parents," said Fred.

Brigid twisted her wedding ring. "That's right," she replied.

"What did they have against your husband, dearie?" asked Doreen, eyes avid for information.

Brigid took a steadying breath. "They thought he was a bit cheeky and I was too young," she said. "That's all."

Doreen and Fred exchanged a glance. "Do they know about the baby?" Doreen's voice trembled slightly.

Brigid frowned, her eyes on the ground. "I made my bed the day I married Will, and I'll lie in it," she said.

"But do they know?" pressed Doreen. "Did you go back to them when you lost your husband?"

Brigid thought hard. Mam had told her to say she had been bombed out of her home and had no close family, but it wasn't so easy when you were under the searchlight, and she had already given herself away about her family. "Yes," she said. "And yes, they know. Things weren't the same at home. I couldn't stay there."

Doreen and Fred exchanged glances again. "What about your bloke's folks?" asked Fred. "No joy there?"

"Most definitely not," Brigid replied, her voice diminishing with the effort of this awkward conversation.

It seemed to satisfy them. Doreen patted Brigid's hand and smiled her usual wide-mouthed grin, lipstick perfect and blonde curls bobbing, and Fred picked up his newspaper. Brigid swung her legs on to the bottom bunk and closed her eyes. She thought of the other item which was in her bag as well as the money – the application for the position in Aberfoyle, which she hadn't managed to post because she had slept so long. She felt sick when she thought of the lies she had told in the letter, and the ones she had added to them since.

Sighing, she tucked her blankets around her. Despite the fact she had slept most of the day, she felt as if she needed more. She was deeply exhausted. She began to drift away, but tonight her dreams were normal and her sleep refreshing. When she came to hours later, she was top-to-tail with Doreen Johnstone while Fred Johnstone sat on the ground, his soulful eyes on her face. She closed her eyelids again quickly to ward him off, placing a hand over her belly, where her mysterious child grew in the darkness of her womb.

Chapter Six

Pall *Mall*,
London.
The *thirty-first October, 1688*

My Dearest Wife,
Forgive my not having written to you before now. I have had much to see and learn besides the tasks with which I am charged in translating the Bible into our native tongue. Our own dear Edinburgh cannot compare with the sights of London! It is so vast, so advanced! I find myself lodged most agreeably with Mr. Boyle and his sister the Viscountess, in grand surroundings such as I never thought to dwell amongst in all my life. I have a room in which to sleep and work, and the use of the library. Mr. Boyle occasionally invites me into his laboratory, where I have observed some of his experiments and learned his methods. He is a quiet and modest man for all his brilliance, not blessed with good health.

Of Lady Ranelagh the Viscountess I see little, although I have been invited to dine in company on two evenings. Such grandeur in the dress and manners of the guests present! I felt quite the country yokel. The first time, I'm ashamed to say, I stared at the dark-skinned persons who waited at table. I find it painful to use the word "slaves", yet such they were. Such they are. We have discussed this, my dear, and you know my unease on the subject, which you share. My host noticed my interest.

Next day, he called me to his study, where a young negro was waiting. At Mr. Boyle's bidding, he bared his arm for me and I touched his flesh. It feels like ours. Mr. Boyle bid him remove his wig, and I ran my hand over his hair, so very different in texture from any I have known. I could barely look at his eyes – so large, so dark, and so blank. They were quite devoid of expression as we examined him and discussed him. His face was immobile, a mask. As you know, Mr. Boyle is involved in many areas of research, and he has done work on the subject of these negroes. It was a commonly held belief that their skin colour was due to the strength of the sun in their native lands, but his research has proved otherwise – it is inherited. Therefore, they do differ from us.

I ventured to press him as far as politeness allowed on his views on slavery. "My dear Kirk," he said, "do you not feel the peacefulness which comes from your pipe after a hard day's work? Does your mouth not water at the sugared delicacies my sister serves her guests?" Of course, I had to admit to these things. "Tobacco and sugar are of such benefit to the family of man," he said, "that God has ordained these indigents work under our direction to harvest them and bring them where they may be used to their fullest potential." He explained that many people took to pipe smoking during the Great Plague to combat its airborne infection. It saved lives, he said. I must confess that in relation to the slave trade I still felt most uneasy at this, although I have never questioned my pipe or the small commodities of sugar we use in our much less affluent household.

"The indigents – these native people born with dark skins – belong also to the family of man of which you speak, Sir, do they not?" I asked. "But of course," he replied. "God created them as he created us, and I do not hold with the view that they are of a different human family – but he ordained different purposes for those with dark skins." I glanced at the slave, who stared steadfastly at the picture rail, his eyes still great blank pools. I dared say no more; I didn't know what to say. My host discerned my discomfort but mistook the cause.

"Fear not, Kirk," he said. "My sister only keeps those who have denounced their heathen, savage ways and converted to Christianity." He bid the man recite The Lord's Prayer, which he did with a heavily accented deep voice and a fierceness of expression which took my breath away. His eyes came to life, fire blazed in their midst; I saw his teeth, large and whiter than any I have ever seen. It was as if he had been animated by the words of Our Lord, and I think in this Mr. Boyle is correct – it is our duty to bring these creatures to faith. He further informed me that he had tried, though without success, to press for legislation granting better conditions to those slaves who had converted. I must say, I think honouring Our Lord appeared to give the slave some semblance of the divine spark - maybe even a soul.

My dear, I admit this incident vexed me and caused me a bout of homesickness. For all London's magnificence, I miss Kirkton, our simple lives and our humble abode. Autumn will be turning to winter sooner there than in this southerly place; I picture Doon Hill frost-kissed already. On this All Hallows Eve especially, I turn my thoughts to my favourite haunts and know that the veil will be thinner, and I not there to investigate. However, it is the Gospel of our Lord which calls me for now, and I am here to ensure my flock, and others far and wide over our beloved Gaeldom, may have it in our own dear tongue.

I pray you are well and send my love.
Your husband,
Robert Kirk.

#

Margaret laid the letter down. Robert had departed for London six weeks previously, and she had been longing to hear from him. She leaned on the table and closed her eyes, massaging them with her knuckles to clear the confusion and misery that had settled upon her. A memory flitted across her mind, of the visit of a butterfly collector to her father's house when she was a child. He brought as a gift nine of the beautiful creatures pinned on black velvet within a silver frame. She hated to see them, devoid of life, displayed like that. He had told her that some of his catches he kept for the purposes of scientific research, dissecting them to study their parts and composition. She had seen him prowling around the grounds with a net, and had gone out and been deliberately boisterous to scare the butterflies away.

Her horror at the thought of ripped wings returned, and merged somehow with black flesh, which she was certain hurt and bled red like any human being. She hoped her Robert would not be corrupted by the ways of high and mighty people and the grandeur of London. Despite his forty-four years and his great intellect, he retained a certain innocence, almost naivety. His head, when not in his books, was in the clouds. He exasperated her at times, but she would not have him changed. She had wanted his mind taking off certain paths of thought, but not for it to be led down worse ones.

When she opened her eyes, blinking, she saw through the morning room window Doon Hill rising above the river in the distance. She shivered. She had grown up among the hills at Comrie, hills which had shuddered sometimes and where stars had fallen from the sky; she had in her possession two lumps of rock which had fallen from the heavens. Her family had seen a star trailing flames one sharp winter's night when all the stars were blazing lanterns in the black velvet of the sky. Their falling neighbour had eclipsed them, a ball of fire as it hurtled towards the gardens and exploded in a mass of orange flames and sparks. They had just descended from the carriage after a Christmas visit to a neighbour, and they stood shocked and afraid; but Father had heard of such things, and said it was a good luck gift. In the light of next morning, they searched and found pieces of the shooting star, three large boulders and a few fragments. Margaret's mother and brothers were disappointed at the lumps of iron, which is all they were; they had expected silver or gold. Margaret marvelled at iron falling from the heavens, though, iron which had blazed as it did in the village forge as the smith worked at his trade. She had always been fascinated by the smithy and the marvels the smith conjured with metal. Her father gave her the two lumps she desired, and sent the rest to a scientific friend in Edinburgh. The butterfly collector had been interested in her possessions to the point of covetousness. She had hidden them well after that.

People spoke of the atmosphere around her old family home, and there were plenty of stories of the magic of those hills and the hidden peoples who dwelt there; yet they were nothing compared with this Doon Hill and the tales she had heard tell, especially those told by Robert. The hill itself was low and insignificant; it only stood out because the landscape in that direction was otherwise flat, there by the river. She cast her mind back to Balquidder and her few visits there when Isabel had been alive; Robert said even wilder things of that place.

She felt like rising and slamming the shutters upon Doon Hill. Her husband spoke of no longing for her in the midst of his homesickness. He spoke of the hill. His work, his flock, his investigations into the fae all came before her. She jumped as two figures loomed into view, approaching the house; her friends come to call. She composed herself, so that when the maid showed them in she could answer their enquiries with eyes glowing with pride.

"Ah yes, ye have called at just the right time, for I have heard from Mr. Kirk this very morn! He has a fine room, dines sometimes with Viscountess Ranelagh, and works closely with the great Mr. Boyle. He is an honoured guest, and treated as an equal."

An image of the slave with his blank eyes came to her as she said that; staring at the picture rail as Robert pressed the flesh of his arm. Her pride in her husband had acquired a dark shadow. She hid it behind a hospitable smile, pouring tea for her visitors.

"Do you have any sugar?" asked Mistress Brown, the younger of the two ladies. She had recently returned from a stay in Edinburgh, and now delighted in being the upholder of every latest fashion and whim. The taking of sugar in tea had not yet reached Kirkton Manse.

"I'll have Elsie bring some," said Margaret, her smile faltering. She did not own a bowl for it. The maid looked at her in bewilderment when she gave her order. Excusing herself, Margaret went to the kitchen and chipped some sugar shards off the small cone she had there, and placed them in a miniature ornamental pewter quaich. Her hand trembled as she considered the journey this precious commodity had made to her table, and she looked at it as she never had before.

Chapter Seven

Christmas Day was pleasant and relaxed. There was chicken for dinner, to Brigid's delight and surprise. It was a long time since she had tasted any. When Fred said it was one of their own, killed by his own two hands for the occasion, she went a little pale; she was a city girl after all, although Mam had spoken of life on the farm enough for her to know that livestock were not pets. She thought of Scotland and the terms of the tenancy for that room in the Manse – work in lieu of paying rent, some of it with livestock – and she said she was interested in learning about caring for the birds. Fred said he would gladly teach her.

They went into the parlour after dinner, which was a midday meal, and Brigid saw three gifts had been laid under the tree. She didn't expect that one was for her, but it was. Doreen made a point of presenting it to her first.

"Thank you so much!" said Brigid, blushing. "But I have nothing for either of you. I'm so sorry. You really shouldn't have."

"We didn't expect anything from you," smiled Doreen. "You didn't know you were going to be here. It isn't much. You know how things are, nothing worth buying in the shops. Open it carefully – I want to try to save the wrapping paper to use next year, if this dratted war isn't over."

It was a bar of scented soap. "It's lovely. So thoughtful, thank you."

"We can get the tin bath in front of the fire for you some time soon," said Fred. "Bet you could do with a nice soak. After the war, I intend to turn the boxroom into a proper bathroom. The last people put that privy in the cupboard halfway up the stairs. I'll do a better job."

Doreen looked at him fondly. "Not much my Fred can't turn his hand to. Here, darling, open yours."

It was a gardening book. "Just what I need," said Fred. "That's the next job, come springtime – plant up some veg in the space left in the yard. No flowers this year, my love, sorry – we've all got to make sacrifices."

Doreen unwrapped her gift, two pairs of knitted stockings which Fred had paid a local woman to do for him. They were wrapped round a bar of soap identical to Brigid's. Brigid could see that Doreen wasn't taken with them, although she thanked him and tried to hide it. "They smell lovely from the soap," she managed to say.

"I thought they'd be good for down the tube station," said Fred, pleased with himself, "keep you warm".

Brigid chuckled to herself. Doreen kept warm with the finest blankets in her linen cupboard, as she had discovered last night. She was a silk stocking woman, and there would be no compromising because of the war if Doreen Johnstone could help it.

Doreen looked wistful. "There's been no bombing for nights now," she said. "At least, not here. Couldn't we chance it tonight? Spend Christmas Night round the fire. Brigid could even have that bath before bed."

Fred hesitated. Then, "No," he said, "definitely not. We're not taking any risks. Don't look at me like that, Doreen! You ain't seen the sights I've seen." He indicated Brigid. "There are *four* of us to think of."

Brigid smiled, pleasantly surprised by the reference to the baby. Her hand, as it did so often now, strayed to her belly. Doreen gazed at her.

"Right enough, Fred," she conceded. "Right enough. No risks."

#

Boxing Day passed in a similar manner to Christmas Day. They played Dominoes and Fred taught Brigid card games. She went out with him when he tended the chickens. Doreen told her to help herself to magazines, so she spent some time in the box room, browsing their bookcases, which were full of old novels as well as piles of magazines. Most of the classics were represented. When she returned with a Thomas Hardy novel, "Tess of the D'Urbervilles", Doreen screwed up her face.

"The books were my father's," she explained. "Great reader, he was. Never took to it myself, not novels like that anyway. The odd bit of romance, maybe."

"It's a wonderful library," Brigid enthused.

"Well, I can't wait to see a bathroom in there," said Fred. "It'll be a reading room for my newspaper!"

They all laughed.

"Consider the books yours," said Doreen.

Brigid stared at her.

"We'll only be turfing them out after the war, when Fred gets to work on the new bathroom, if we don't use them as fuel for the fire before that."

"Thank you," said Brigid, wincing at the thought of all those volumes going up in smoke, and feeling awkward at the fact they obviously expected her to stay for a long time.

They went to the tube station as usual. Brigid slept well again. She felt relieved not to have any more experiences of drifting away to other times and places. A niggling voice inside asked if she hadn't just imagined it after all. She allowed herself to sink into the security of her new-found situation. Who would have thought that she would be blessed like this, to find digs in a lovely home with such good people? She had enjoyed the nicest couple of days she'd had in a long time, and the best Christmas she had ever known.

As she awoke refreshed and actually looking forward to the day ahead, Brigid chewed her lip and thought about her circumstances. Maybe she should stay with the Johnstones, at least for a while. She thought of Robert Kirk and the room in his old manse; in the cold light of day, did she really have any chance of being taken on to work there? The baby wasn't showing yet, but it would soon – what then? How could she just place herself among a strange family as an employee in her condition, and then expect to be permitted to stay and give birth? Logic warred in her mind with the things she had experienced, the visions she had seen…they had seemed so real, but…Brigid gave herself a shake.

The only reality of which she could be sure was the baby in her womb. Anybody else in her position would grasp what the Johnstones had to offer without thinking twice. It was a miracle that Doreen had noticed her in the Underground. Maybe this was what was meant to be. Brigid made up her mind – she would follow her head and do what was best for her baby, not her heart and questionable intuition which told her to do something wild and irrational. In the afterglow of Christmas, with good food inside her and comfortable surroundings, Brigid had begun to question what had really happened on Tower Hill.

#

At breakfast next morning, Brigid took a breath and said, "You wanted a decision today – on whether or not I want to stay. Well, I love it here. I would like to stay, but I'm worried about the rent, you see." Her cheeks flushed. She desperately hoped they could come to terms which would suit them all. She needed to save as much money as she could, and given the rents being charged for far inferior accommodation, she had cause to worry.

Doreen paused as she poured a cup of tea. Fred looked to his wife to speak. Brigid glanced from one to the other. Doreen cleared her throat, finished pouring and placed the teapot back on its stand. She named a sum of money.

Brigid's eyes opened wide in surprise. It was less than she had seen advertised for a room with shared facilities, and here her meals and laundry would be included – although she would hand over her ration book, of course, and help in the house. "Are you sure?" she said. "That's really very generous!" She calculated rapidly in her head. She could easily afford it for a while. Anyway, Mam had said she would send more when she could, and there was still Will's money to claim from the bank.

Doreen took a sip of tea and put her cup down. "We were thinking maybe you don't have much, dear," she said gently. "Newly married, widowed so soon and all that."

"I have some savings," said Brigid.

Doreen smiled. "They won't last forever, though, will they?"

"My mother is helping me. She promised she would send me more when she was able," said Brigid. "I promise the rent will be paid. And I still have to claim my husband's savings from the bank."

"We trust you, don't we, Fred?" said Doreen. "But what about long term? Those savings won't last, and you've a baby on the way. What do you plan to do?"

Brigid looked at what was left of her boiled egg, aware of their eyes on her. "I'm finding it hard to think far ahead," she said. "I suppose…I suppose I hope Dad might have me back. Me and the baby both."

Doreen folded her hands and leaned towards her. "Is that likely, chick? It sounds as if there's been a serious falling out. A young girl like you, expecting her first baby, arriving in London two days before Christmas? A young widow, and her husband a war hero, no matter what your father thought of him!"

Brigid couldn't fight back the tears which began to spill out of her eyes. "I don't know," she said. "I don't know what will happen to us."

"Well, it's a disgrace, the way you've been treated," said Doreen. "Fred and I want you to know that you've a home with us. You're a smart girl – you worked in an office, you said? You'll need to find work again, of course, once the little one's here, get a steady income. I'll be more than happy to care for the baby. Isn't that right, Fred?"

"Whatever you say, my love," said Fred. "Whatever you say."

Brigid tried not to show the mixed emotions overwhelming her. It was a perfect solution to all her problems, something she could never have hoped for, and yet… "Thank you," she said. "You're the kindest people I've ever met." She rose from the table, seeking time to think. "I'll just go and freshen up, if you'll excuse me."

#

When she left the room, Fred turned to his wife. "What kind of people are they, turning her out when she's carrying their grandchild? Just because they didn't like her husband?"

Doreen's face hardened. "There's more to it than that," she said. "Her father could have stopped them marrying, since she isn't twenty-one. I reckon he found out they'd been carrying on, and married her off quickly just in case she was pregnant."

"But she wasn't," said Fred, "not then. So why turn her out now?"

"Well, he didn't actually do that, according to her. She left of her own accord because things were difficult. Independent little madam despite appearances, I'll give her that."

"So there's a chance of reconciliation?"

"Let's hope not," said Doreen.

"Don't get attached, Dor," said Fred, sighing. "She's a little stunner. She'll have another fella in no time, kiddie or no kiddie."

Doreen shot him a look. "She needs protecting, Fred. We have to make sure nobody else takes advantage, like her husband obviously did."

Fred shrugged his shoulders and lifted his newspaper.

#

Brigid had paused to enter the toilet on the half-landing where the stairs turned. The dining room door was open. Overhearing the Johnstones' conversation, she frowned. She slipped inside and shut the door quietly, leaning her back against it, unsettled by what she had just heard. Brigid hated the need to lie, afraid she would trip herself up at some point – but they would turn her out if they discovered that she had conceived the baby after her husband's death, and that she had lost the one that was his, that had been the reason for their marriage. A wave of homesickness and grief washed over her; it was all too much at times. She had taken to wearing her mother's brooch every day, as a reminder of home. She lifted her right hand now and grasped it where it lay against her sweater.

Suddenly, her blood seemed to drain to her feet. She fell forward against the wash-hand basin, gripping it, fighting the weakness in her limbs, failing and sliding to the floor. There was a time of inky blackness, then it cleared, slowly, like a substance swirling and dissolving in a bottle. It transformed into a whirl of white and Brigid beheld, as if she was peering into a snow globe, a ruined church with a wooded hill beyond.

A wintry landscape was laid out below her; and there was a whisper inside her head, telling her this place was her heart's desire. Her spirit soared into the scene as once it had flown over the sacred hills of Britain; she spiralled down to a grave beside the roofless ruin. A sudden gust of wind cleared the flakes settling on the recumbent stone. Brigid beheld the name "Robertus Kirk", part of the Latin inscription there. This was her destiny, whispered a voice whirling with the wind and the snowflakes. She should not fight it, it insisted. The voice was chill, ice at its heart, commanding. Brigid shivered, yet her heart burned with longing.

#

Some time later, Brigid lay in bed distressed at Doreen's close observation of the doctor's examination. It had been bad enough to endure this with Mam and Mrs. White. She had thanked her landlady for fetching the doctor, had tried to convey with her manner that she could go now, but Doreen had not taken the hint.

The doctor straightened up. "Both mother and child appear to be in excellent health," he said. "Is this your first pregnancy, Mrs. Watkins?"

Brigid nodded, hating the need to deny the existence of her lost baby, Will's child.

"I see no cause for concern," smiled the doctor.

"But we found her out cold behind the privy door!" cried Doreen. "It was a struggle to get in to help her, when she didn't come back to the table and we realised something was up!"

"Mrs. Watkins seems to have suffered a faint," said the doctor. "It's not unusual. She didn't bang her head or do herself any mischief when she fell to the floor." He hesitated. "I gather from Mrs. Johnstone that there has been some distress in your life recently, my dear?"

Brigid nodded again and turned her head away.

"I suggest bed rest for today, and I'll leave a sedative, enough for a week. Two pills at bedtime." He turned to Doreen. "You say you met in the tube station? Do you not have a shelter in the yard?"

Doreen shook her head. "Gave it up for chickens," she said. "No room for both."

"It's not the best place for her," said the doctor. "Not that anywhere but her own bed is, and the same for all of us. But she would be better in the close company of those she knows, rather than being exposed to strangers and all the noise and germs down there."

Brigid bit her lip and kept her head averted. She didn't know the Johnstones, not really, kind as they had been – they had only just met.

The doctor touched her gently on the shoulder. "Stay in bed for today, young lady," he said. "I'm sure you'll be well cared for."

Brigid looked up into his kindly, grave face and acknowledged his words with a weak smile and muttered thanks. Doreen saw him out. A few minutes later, the bedroom door opened and Fred entered. He approached the bed soundlessly on his slippered feet and stood looking down at her.

"You gave us a fright there, girl."

"I'm sorry. Just one of those things. I'm fine. Sorry to have put you out, Mr. Johnstone."

"No need for any of that," he smiled. "You're one of the family now. We look after our own. Call me Fred. Uncle Fred, if that feels better."

"Thank you, Mr…Fred. Uncle Fred." Neither option sounded right to Brigid. She would have preferred to stick with Mr. Johnstone.

Doreen appeared, popping her head round the door. "Alright, chick? Now, you get your head down and rest, like the doctor said. Fred, come away and leave her in peace!"

Brigid pulled the covers up and hunched her body away from them. Doreen closed the door, but she could hear them out on the landing.

"We'll have to get rid of the chickens and put the Anderson back up," Doreen said.

"Are you joking?" cried Fred. "The trouble I've gone to…my chickens…"

"Best for her and baby!" said Doreen firmly.

"She's young and healthy! She'll get over it, she'll be fine!" Fred replied.

"We can't take any chances, Fred Johnstone! You said so yourself!"

"I was just being nice…Dor, love, don't you think you're getting too involved?"

"Don't you see, Fred? This is our chance!"

Their voices tailed away as they descended the stairs. Brigid lay tense and wakeful beneath the covers.

Chapter Eight

They insisted Brigid stay in bed for three days, only allowing her to rise and dress in order to go to the tube station to spend the night. Nothing Brigid said would persuade them otherwise. They showered her with kindness and concern, bringing her the best food they could obtain. The eggs stopped, though. Hammering from the yard alerted her to the fact the hens had gone, and the Anderson shelter was going back up.

It reminded Brigid of those awful weeks after she lost Will and their baby. She had been content to lie in bed at that time. There seemed little else she could do, weak and overcome with grief as she was, and Brenda and Anne mostly left her to it, so she had peace at least. There was none of that to be had here, with Doreen and Fred. Doreen sang as she did her household chores, popping in every half hour to see if she wanted anything. Saying she would like to get out of bed for some fresh air brought a kind rebuke; not until the Anderson was ready, said Doreen. It was taxing enough to go to the Underground at night – she had to save her strength for that. Fred came and sat on her bed when he returned from work. He held her hand as if she was a frail invalid. It took resolve not to grab it away from him, and bury every part of herself beneath the covers.

The pills the doctor had left knocked her out cold. She knew nothing of what went on in the Underground that night of the twenty-seventh, and she had to be helped home the following morning, supported by Fred as her feet stumbled. She refused to take the tablets the next night, instinct telling her they couldn't be good for the baby. Doreen was adamant – did she think she knew more than the doctor? Brigid's feeling about it was so strong that she only pretended to take the tablets, holding them in her mouth until Doreen wasn't looking. She slipped them into her coat pocket and made a mental note to act as if she had taken them.

The Luftwaffe returned on the twenty-ninth. Brigid and Doreen emerged from Tower Hill tube station at dawn to find London smouldering, choking under clouds of dust. It had been bombarded for nearly ten hours. Doreen was frantic about Fred, who had been on duty. They arrived home to find him sitting in the house, ashen and trembling. He had never known a night like it – the city ablaze, such destruction, so many deaths. Doreen took the kettle out to the standpipe set up on the street, because the water main had been hit. Brigid went to her room to write to her mother.

"Dear Mam," she wrote, *"I am sorry for not being in touch a couple of days sooner, but I am anxious to let you know that I am safe and well after this terrible night for London. I want to catch the post so you will get this as soon as possible, so I won't say too much at present.*

I have found a lovely room in a pleasant house at the above address. I am the only lodger and all my meals are provided. Mr. and Mrs. Johnstone are a friendly and caring couple in their middle years. It is only the three of us here. The rent is very reasonable."

Brigid paused and sucked her pen. It sounded fine, yet it didn't convey the many shades of truth. Her room was delightful, the house was beautiful, the Johnstones were kindness itself; but the thought of her shabby, threadbare home in Birmingham brought a tightness to her throat and chest. She would have swapped it for this place of shining perfection any day. The smell of beeswax and whatever else Doreen lavished on the house was beginning to cloy. The incessant chatter of her hosts, their expectations, their concern for her condition, left her feeling she could barely breathe at times. She looked back at her letter. There was no way to convey any of that, and no way she should.

"I am well and happy here for now," she continued, *"but of course, I miss you and Dad terribly. Please write and tell me how you both are, and what I should say*

of my whereabouts in a future letter to you both. I shall write regularly. Christmas and settling in kept me busy at first. I spent Christmas here, and we had a nice time."

Brigid thought guiltily of the succulent chicken she had enjoyed. She felt a pang that it had been a merrier Christmas than any she had known back home. New Year's Eve was tomorrow, though, and that was Walter MacKenzie's night. He was a Scot who loved Hogmanay, and was at his happiest and most amiable. They used to have friends and neighbours round, a real party, as he boasted that he would show these Sassenachs how to see out the old year and welcome the new. She wondered if they would go ahead without her this year.

"I do hope you will enjoy your traditional Hogmanay gathering tomorrow night. I shall think of you. I will be with you in spirit at midnight."

Blinded by tears, Brigid signed her name and took the envelopes and stamps from her carpet bag. She had paid Doreen a week's rent from the money secreted in its lining, saying she would have to go to the bank before she could pay more. She couldn't have the Johnstones knowing how much she had hidden. She hoped it would put an end to their insistence on her staying in bed all day, but Doreen had said there was no hurry. She would take a walk today, though, if only to the nearest post box.

As she pushed the banknotes in her bag more securely inside the lining, the sharp corner of the other letter she had written a few days ago jabbed her hand. She hadn't destroyed her application for the post in Aberfoyle, despite her decision not to go ahead with it, to remain here in London. The things she had seen when she "fainted" in the toilet and her growing sense of claustrophobia with the Johnstones had caused her to hesitate. She was at war with herself again, her head and her intuition. The first told her to stay. The latter told her she was not meant to be here – she had to give birth in Scotland, in the house where the books she loved had been written. Why, she had no idea. Her head argued that this was a ridiculous notion, but her intuition refused to be silent… She took the letter from its hiding place and pondered what to do. Time was of the essence. She slipped it into her handbag with the letter to her parents, and headed downstairs to put her coat on.

Doreen met her as she walked into the kitchen, pulling on her mittens. "And where do you think you're going, young lady?"

"I've written to my Mam," said Brigid. "I have to let her know that I'm alright after last night. I want to catch the post so she'll get it as soon as possible."

"I'll take it for you, chick," said Doreen. "You have to go back to bed and rest."

"I slept fine," said Brigid. "The pills make me." She was more of an actress than she would have thought possible, both at feigning sleep and stumbling a little as if drugged in the morning. In fact, she hadn't slept well. She was weary of lying in bed all day, her young limbs and mind starved of fresh air and exercise. They had to let her out soon.

Fred appeared behind her. "Nobody that's been laid up unwell should be out wandering those streets this morning! Anyway, you'd be lucky to find a pillar box left standing. Did you notice the lampposts, melted by the heat, bending over? I can't see the post running as normal, not today."

As Brigid hesitated, Doreen repeated her offer. "I'll take it to the nearest Post Office I can find open," she said, "and you get to bed this instant! You must think of the baby."

"I feel as if I need some fresh air, though," said Brigid. Her voice had a pleading tone.

"You had enough of that walking home from the tube," Doreen countered. "Anyway, you could hardly call the air fresh – it's full of dust and fumes. Not good for you or baby!"

Brigid sighed. They had a point. She shrugged and acquiesced. As she drew the letter to Birmingham from her handbag, Doreen glanced in and spotted the other.

"Two letters? You have been busy."

Her nosiness irritated Brigid. "The other isn't important," she said. "It's one I wrote a few days ago, not urgent." She didn't want the Johnstones to know anything about it.

"I'll take them both," said Doreen. "Seems silly to post one and not the other."

Brigid shrugged and gave a dismissive shake of her head. "It can wait."

There was an awkward silence as Doreen continued to stare at her. Fred asked if that cup of tea was coming any time soon; he had had a hard night, in case they had forgotten. They didn't heed him. Doreen smiled, a tight grin which didn't reach her eyes. "Give me both letters, chick. There's a good girl."

Brigid gave in and pulled the letter to Aberfoyle from her bag.

Doreen read the address. "Scotland, ay? Who's this Mrs. MacKendrick?"

Brigid wasn't going to admit to her plans. "My Dad's Scottish, as I told you," she replied. "We keep in touch with relatives."

Doreen's eyes never left hers. "Thought they might take you in, did you?"

"It's just season's greetings," said Brigid. "I wrote it before Christmas, but never got round to posting it because I came here and fell asleep all day. I would have written another eventually, but you may as well take this one. I'm sure they'll understand."

"Are they likely to invite you to live with them?" Her eyes and tone were keen.

Brigid felt uneasy. "I doubt that very much."

"I'll take them straight away," said Doreen, shifting suddenly, making for the hallway to get her coat.

"I suppose I'll have to get that bloody tea myself," moaned Fred.

#

Doreen hurried away from the house, the letters in her handbag. She was so preoccupied that the scenes of destruction she passed didn't affect her as they normally would have done. She made for the Rest Centre where her friend Pat Simmons volunteered, helping those who had emerged from shelters to find they had been bombed out of their homes. It was teeming, overflowing with people being fed and accepting bundles of donated clothing with quiet thanks, in a stupor as they struggled to comprehend all they had lost. Doreen barely noticed them. She located Pat, busy with a tea urn.

"Can you help me, Pat?" she asked without preamble, rushing up to her.

"Oh, Dor, not you an' all!" her friend cried.

"No, it's not that," said Doreen, shaking her head. "We're fine, house is fine. I need to steam open a letter."

"Can you not do that at home?" asked Pat.

"It's awkward," Doreen replied.

Pat took in her pale face and wild eyes. "You don't suspect your Fred of being up to no good, do you? Not Fred, surely!"

"No! Nothing like that. Look – we took in a young widow before Christmas. Looking for digs, no references. It's a letter she's written, seems a bit shifty about it – I just want to check she's all she says she is."

Pat busied herself with the urn. "There are plenty of kettles in the kitchen. Help yourself. You can't be too careful these days."

"Thanks, Pat." Doreen left the hall and took the corridor down to the kitchen. She knew her way around because this had been her school as a child, and then the place where she had worked as a dinner lady before she married Fred. The pupils who came here had all been evacuated, hence the council had made it a Rest Centre. The kitchen was steam-filled and noisy as a crowd of volunteers cooked breakfast. Doreen ignored them and fetched a spare kettle. She found an empty gas ring and set it to boil. It seemed to take an age. People glanced at her, and she told them she had Pat's permission. Everybody knew and respected Pat Simmons. Finally, she held the letter to the spout with a pair of tongs and watched as it opened. She carried it away and sought an empty classroom, removing the letter and reading hungrily.

A smile spread across her face as she read, and the tension left her shoulders. Silly little chit! She remembered now the advert in the paper the night before Christmas Eve, Brigid's sudden burst of enthusiasm as she scribbled in the writing pad. Imagine thinking she had a chance of that! In her condition! Not that she mentioned it, of course. Doreen almost laughed out loud; almost, but not quite. It showed Brigid wasn't as innocent as she seemed. She was a little fibber. She even lied about her age, saying she was twenty. Doreen frowned; she had been on the way to post this application – it showed that she wasn't as grateful to be with them as she let on. It might be worth taking a look at the other letter. She pulled it out and noted the address, "Mrs. Mary MacKenzie, c/o Mrs. M. White". Matters between her and her father must be really bad if she couldn't write to her mother at her own address.

Doreen hurried back up the corridor and commandeered the kettle and gas ring again. Back in the classroom, she read the letter and reflected. Brigid had naught but good to say of her and Fred, but she sniffed at the *"happy here for now"*, and wondered what she meant by asking her mother what she should say of her whereabouts in a future letter. There was more to Brigid Watkins than met the eye. She would need watching. Doreen found some glue and sealed up the letter to Mary MacKenzie. She put both letters back in her bag, waved her thanks to Pat in the assembly hall before she left, and headed down to the Thames.

She took the letters out and held up the one to the minister's wife at the manse in Aberfoyle, dangling it over the river and letting it go. A gust of wind carried it away out of sight, down the Thames towards the sea. "Doing her a favour," she chuckled. Doreen considered the other letter and held it lightly between finger and thumb. "I suppose I'd better take this one to the Post Office now," she said. She didn't move, though. A fierce flurry of wind took the envelope from her hand and sent it swirling after the first. "Oops," said Doreen. She smiled. "It's for the best." She stuck her chin in the air and turned towards home.

Chapter Nine

Molly White had spent Christmas alone, as usual. She had neither family nor friends; she didn't encourage intimacy. Oh, there were those like Mary MacKenzie who considered themselves her friends out of long acquaintance, but they didn't really know her. She only let people see what they needed to see. Part of that, of course, was doing what was considered respectable for a midwife, and that meant going to church. She had paid her dues on Christmas Eve and Morning. It was no hardship; she liked the singing and the atmosphere. It gave her the only companionship she had over the season, unless her services were called upon, but it was enough. She had been content to sit by her range, think and dream.

Mostly, and unusually for Molly, she had thought about herself. She felt the cold in her bones keenly this winter. She had served long in this place, and in other places before that, and the aches she felt, the exhaustion, the fact she was slower and not thinking as clearly as she used to, all led her to the conclusion that she should retire soon. When she returned home from a birthing and shut her door behind her these days, sagging in relief, letting her weary flesh droop, the sight that greeted her in the mirror told her everything she needed to know.

Why, then, had this problem of Brigid Watkins arisen now? This was the second matter she pondered this Christmastide. She must have missed the signs when she examined Brigid and spoke with her, even although the young woman had tried to tell her, hastily hushed by her mother. She hadn't pushed Mary for answers that night. It was only two days later, when she had come to her in distress, that the truth had hit home.

Molly had burned a summoning concoction of herbs to call Brigid to her, but had been surprised to learn that she was leaving Birmingham that very day. She had done what she could, laying hands on the child beneath Brigid's young flesh to bless and protect. There was little more she could do if she chose to have the baby elsewhere. Molly wanted to retire as soon as was feasible anyway, and waiting to deliver this baby would only have held her back. Yet she couldn't stop thinking about Brigid. It was many, many years since she had come across such a conception, and how would Brigid fare? Would she be sent a suitable midwife?

Molly cast a handful of herbs and pine cones into the fire in the range. Her one companion in life, a striped ginger Tom called Seamus, stalked up to her then and dropped a dead bird at her feet. "Thank you my dear, just in time," she said. She threw the bird on the fire also. Seamus hissed and she set a bowl of his favourite food in front of him. "Fair exchange." She turned her attention to the flames, muttering, asking for guidance in the matter of Brigid Watkins and her child. As the bird burned, so her spirit flew in search of Brigid.

#

The Anderson Shelter was ready by New Year's Eve. Fred called Doreen and Brigid out to look at it, smirking and winking. Doreen sniffed and followed him into the yard. She had been in a terrible mood since yesterday. Fred threw open the door and invited them to enter, bowing dramatically. Descending behind Doreen, Brigid giggled as she saw Fred's attempts to cheer up the bleak interior. He had taken some old Christmas decorations and festooned the low ceiling, the colourful paper chains hanging down so Doreen had to duck beneath them.

"We can celebrate New Year in style, my love!" he enthused.

Doreen shook her head. "I'm surprised an ARP warden doesn't know a fire hazard when he sees one!" she cried. "Fred Johnstone, sometimes you don't have the sense you were born with! Anyway," she added, "after the other night, I'm not so sure."

Fred stared at her. "Not so sure of what?"

"About this shelter. I mean, if the house took a direct hit and came down on the yard, would it really save us? We might suffocate before they could dig us out." She shuddered.

"They would know where to dig, where to look, sweetheart. And anyway, that's not to say it would ever happen."

Doreen avoided his gaze. "I'm going down the Underground as usual."

Fred's mouth fell open. "You're what?"

"You heard."

"Bleedin' hell, Dor! The work I've done – my chickens are gone, my back's breaking…!"

"There's no need for that language, Fred Johnstone!" Doreen looked at Brigid, who stood awkwardly between them in the small space. "Do you think you could go to your room and give us a few minutes, miss?"

Brigid blanched at her harsh tone. "Of course," she said. She squeezed past Fred and went back into the house.

#

Up in her room, with its gleaming furniture and pretty china trinkets, Brigid sat dejectedly on the bed. The night of the twenty-ninth to thirtieth December had been dubbed the Second Great Fire of London. Everybody was subdued as they approached New Year 1941. Doreen had been short-tempered ever since returning from posting the letters yesterday. She had always struck Brigid as the nervous type, despite her broad smiles and bluff and bluster, and Brigid supposed the sight of the city yesterday had been too much for her. She thought of Birmingham and sighed. She was homesick, thoughts of this year's events lurking around her like shadows.

Pulling her carpet bag out of the wardrobe, she took her mother's savings from their hiding place at the bottom. If they were to shelter in the Anderson from now on – if Fred managed to persuade Doreen – she couldn't very well take the bag in with her. What was she to do with the money? She examined the lining of her coat, thinking about cutting it so she could insert the money in there, spreading the notes out to flatten them – would she rustle too much when she moved, she wondered?

Brigid tensed as she heard footsteps on the landing outside her room. She shoved the wad of notes under her pillows just in time, before the door handle turned and Fred walked in. Brigid bristled, wanting to tell him that he should knock. She was a paying guest, after all; but her low rent and the kindness they had shown made her feel she had few real rights.

Fred sat down heavily on the bed beside her. "She won."

"Do we have to go back to the Underground then?"

"Yip."

"I'm sorry."

"Not your fault."

"But you wouldn't have built the Anderson again if it wasn't for me, would you?"

Fred sighed. "True. So, be a good girl and do as she says. As we say. We'll take care of you."

Brigid swallowed. "I never meant to be a burden, you know. I only wanted a room until I got myself together…"

"Yeah, but things are decided now, ain't they, girl? You're staying here and Dor will look after the baby while you get a job." He reached for her hand. "We'll be like a proper family. You're the kid we might have had if things had worked out."

"But I'm not," said Brigid. "I have my family in Birmingham."

"And look how much good they've been to you!" He squeezed her hand. "You stick with us. Now, Her Majesty down there says you're to get to bed. That's what she sent me to tell you."

"But why?"

"Because the doctor says you need rest. Because we're going back to the tube station rather than the peace and quiet of our own shelter."

"But I'm fine!" protested Brigid.

"No arguments!" Fred scolded. "Like I said, do as we say."

She pulled her hand away. He stood and, reaching down, placed his index finger under her chin and tilted it up. His nail was sharp against her tender skin.

"Brigid," he said, "you might as well learn now that only one person is allowed to be moody or have a temper in this house. Anybody else dances to her tune. Now be a good girl." He left and closed the door.

Brigid swallowed. She thought of her letter winging its way to Scotland – to Robert Kirk's old house near Doon Hill where she was meant to go. It was all too much to be a coincidence. She only had to bide her time. Somehow, it would work out.

#

A couple of hours later, Doreen and Brigid made their way to the tube station. Fred had been called out on duty at the last minute to cover for another ARP warden who was ill. Doreen walked briskly, shoulders tense and eyes downcast. She had little conversation. They descended into the bowels of Tower Hill. As their decision to go there had been taken late, they were unable to get a bunk. An uncomfortable night lay ahead. Doreen had brought some magazines. Brigid had finished "Tess of the D'Ubervilles" that afternoon when she was supposed to be resting. It had left her melancholy, but she didn't mind that when it was induced by a book. She had chosen "The Mayor of Casterbridge" from the box room, and was already aghast at Henshaw selling his wife and child. However, no sooner had she begun to read than she was paralyzed by a dreadful realisation: she had forgotten to retrieve the money from under her pillows after Fred left her room that afternoon. Brigid kept her eyes on her book while her mind worked frantically. She had to go back for the money, but how could she get away from Doreen? Her heart was racing and her hands began to shake.

Doreen glanced up from her magazine. "You alright?"

Brigid didn't look at her. "Fine."

"You sure? You look a bit green around the gills."

Brigid flicked her eyes briefly at her landlady. "I suppose it's only to be expected from time to time."

Doreen sighed and set down the magazine. "I'm watching you, you know, Brigid. I want to know everything that's going on with you."

Brigid shrugged, trying to stop her hands trembling. "I have no secrets." She bit her lip; stupid thing to say. Doreen's eyes were burning into her.

"I hope not. Only sometimes, I suspect you're not being straight with me. Right now, young lady, you look as if you've got a guilty conscience."

Brigid stared at her then in genuine surprise. How could Doreen know anything? She blinked, dismissing the thought. There was no way she knew a thing, and especially not concerning the money stuffed beneath the starched, spotless bed linen in her shining guest room. Brigid thought quickly. "It's this book," she lied. "Books get to me. I really feel them, you know?" That much was true.

"No," said Doreen. "I don't know. If that's what reading stuff like that does for you, I'll stick with my kind of thing. My father was a misery, that's all I can say. Didn't do him much good." She picked up her magazine and settled down again.

#

The hours passed slowly. Brigid turned pages mechanically, not taking in a word. Doreen alternated between riffling through magazines and staring at the people around them. Unlike previous nights, though, she didn't share her observations with Brigid. Her landlady's comments on the activities, dress and behaviour of their fellow shelter seekers were sometimes amusing, sometimes barbed and caustic. Brigid had long since realised she herself must have been watched by Doreen Johnstone. What exactly had she been thinking? She had detected the pregnancy, after all, even although it wasn't showing yet. She remembered Fred's words about them being a proper family. The money below the pillows never left her mind.

The time came for supper. Doreen unpacked the sandwiches and handed Brigid a bottle of water and a cup along with her pills from the doctor. She watched to make sure she took them, before turning her attention to the large thermos. Brigid quickly flicked the pills from the side of her gum with her tongue, catching them in her hand and transferring them to her pocket as she had done every night. When Doreen handed her a cup of tea, a course of action came to her. Did she dare? She weighed up the risks. The fear of losing the money weighed more heavily than anything.

Doreen's cup sat beside her on the cold stone of the platform. It was one of her best; they did things properly when they came down here, even although bombs might be falling above. Brigid tried to be careful; just the merest nudge with her knee as she pretended to make herself more comfortable, and the cup went over, rolling out of its saucer.

"Oh!" she cried. "I'm sorry, Doreen!"

"Heaven's sake! That's my mother's china. It better not be chipped!" Doreen picked up the cup and examined it.

Brigid sighed with relief that it wasn't damaged, wiping up the spill with a handkerchief. "Here," she said, "give it to me and I'll pour you another." She set the cup down at her other side. She took the flask and turned away from her landlady. She poured the tea and slipped one pill into it. Remembering the effect two had had on her, she was afraid to put them both in. She added a teaspoon of sugar from the small bag Doreen had brought, and stirred well, praying the pill would dissolve, hoping the sugar would disguise the taste.

"That's enough stirring! Give it here," said Doreen. "You've nearly damaged it as it is, without scraping the glaze off!"

Brigid passed the tea over and waited, hands cupped around the warmth of her own beverage to stop them shaking.

#

It didn't take long before Doreen began to grow drowsy. She remarked that things must be catching up with her. She tried to fight it, shuffling herself awake, yawning, stretching, rubbing her neck. Finally, she slumped back against the wall and slid down the tiles, mouth open. Brigid put a pillow behind her head and arranged a blanket over her, slipping her hand in Doreen's coat pocket and taking the house keys. Then she left, picking her way around the people on the crowded platform. When Brigid reached the escalator, she gaped in horror. She knew she would have to climb it, that it wouldn't be working, but she didn't expect to find people camping on it. Yet there they were, the latecomers who hadn't been able to find places on the platforms or even the rails. Some were chatting and playing cards, others reading, and some were asleep, stretched out along the steps.

"Excuse me, excuse me," murmured Brigid, beginning to climb, doing her best not to step on anybody as she fought her way over and among them.

"Oi!" cried one man. "Where do you think you're going?"

Other voices began to join in.

"Is she headed out?"

"Bloody lunatic!"

"Don't go out there!"

Near the top, a woman grabbed her ankle. "Jerry's giving us hell again! I just managed to get in on time. You can't go out there now!"

Brigid stared at her. She became aware of explosions not far away. She hadn't thought to grab her gas mask.

"I have to go. It's important!" she said, shaking the woman off. She darted up the steps for the exit and felt the rush of cold night air as she gained street level. Outside, London was burning again, nearer at hand than was safe. At least it lit her way. Brigid ran through the streets. Heart pounding, lungs bursting, she arrived at her lodgings; her knees almost gave way with relief when she saw the street was undamaged. As blasts continued, Brigid fumbled in her pocket for the front door key and let herself in. Wasting no time, she stumbled upstairs in the dark and into her room. Flicking the light on, she dived at the bed and seized the money from under the pillows, unbuttoning her coat, pulling up her clothing and stuffing the banknotes inside her underwear, her bra and liberty bodice bulging with it, then her panties. Then Brigid heard a noise.

She froze, thinking she must have imagined it; but no, it was unmistakeable. Somebody was downstairs, walking from the kitchen to the hallway. Brigid stayed very still. It must be Fred, on a break from his duties. He had come in the back door. It had never occurred to her that he might come home in the course of a night. Maybe he was going to use the toilet.

Brigid tiptoed over to the light switch, flicked it off and pushed the door until it was almost closed. She stood with her back against it, breathing hard.

"We'll go upstairs," said Fred.

Brigid gasped and clapped a hand over her mouth. Another voice, female, sounded from below.

"You've got a shelter, mister. Couldn't we go in there?"

"And who do you think might be in my shelter?"

It was Fred, but it didn't sound like Fred. His voice was hard, authoritative.

"Sorry, I never thought."

"If you wanted a safe billet, doll, you've landed the wrong punter. Now, upstairs!"

The female voice said: "Won't your wife know if we use your room? What if she comes out of the shelter?"

"We're not going to use our room," Fred replied, "and she won't disturb us."

Brigid nearly cried out. Legs shaking, she felt her way round the wall until she came to the large wardrobe; opening the door, she slipped inside, pushing herself right to the back and into a corner, and she pulled the door behind her. It was still open a crack, but there was nothing she could do about it. She made herself as small as she could, hugging her knees.

Fred entered the room and switched on the light. Behind him came a dark-haired woman, slightly-built; Brigid caught sight of her painted face, startled to see that beneath the lipstick and rouge she looked little more than a child.

"Is this your daughter's room?" she asked, looking around.

Fred Johnstone dealt her a blow with the back of his hand. She landed sprawling on the bed. He hauled her off it and flung her to the floor. "Wait there!" he said.

He left the room. Brigid, her breath coming in ragged gasps she was afraid the girl would hear, listened as he opened the linen cupboard. He returned holding an old sheet, one of the ones he kept there for decorating and other dirty jobs. He didn't look at the girl, rubbing her reddened cheek on the floor where he had flung her, as he folded it and laid it carefully over Brigid's bed. Then he helped the young prostitute to her feet.

"You're not here to ask questions," he said. "Now, let's get down to what we came here for. You just do as you're told, there's a good girl."

Brigid's head began to swim. She thought she was going to be sick. She leaned forward, her head between her knees, and clamped her arms tightly around herself until they ached, as the sound of bedsprings and Fred's grunts filled the air, against the background of explosions, sirens and shouts that was London beyond her room – a room which she would never think beautiful again.

Mercifully, the noises from the bed didn't last long. A loud groan from Fred ended it. Brigid raised her head and peered through the crack. Seeing the girl and Fred pulling on their clothes, the childish slenderness of her body and his belly overhanging his groin, she closed her eyes and pressed the heels of her hands into them. She heard coins tinkling, and footsteps scurrying to the door, then a creak close at hand. She opened her eyes and stifled a gasp. Light had spilled into the wardrobe; there was a familiar smell, too. Pipe tobacco. Fred Johnstone's arm came into the wardrobe and his fingers began fumbling their way among the few skirts and dresses hanging there. They were at the other end of the rail under which she hunkered, terrified, her fist in her mouth lest she cry out.

After a few seconds, Fred withdrew his arm and pushed the door shut. Brigid was plunged into darkness. She dared to breathe again, straining her ears. She heard a drawer being opened, then another. He was going through her belongings. The pipe smoke he had exhaled while examining her clothes was trapped in the wardrobe with her; Brigid fought hard not to cough.

Suddenly, he spoke: "Next time, I'll get her to wear her clothes. Her, or whichever one I pick up. The more like our little lodger, the better."

Tears of terror leaked from Brigid's eyes. She was trembling so much she was certain the wardrobe must be shaking, too. He sounded like himself now, like the Fred she thought she knew, not as he had done with the girl. It made his words even more frightening. There was still a crack of light entering via the hinges on the wardrobe door, but it went out, and Brigid heard the sound of the bedroom door closing. She didn't dare move in case he knew she was there and was tricking her into giving herself up; but after a few minutes, she realised she had to take the risk. She pushed open the door and peered out.

As far as she could tell in the total darkness of the blackout, he had gone. Brigid eased herself into the room. She felt her way towards the light switch and flipped it with a hand still violently trembling. The room flared into light. It was empty. Brigid fell back against the wall, breathing deeply. Her bed was tidy and unrumpled, the sheet they had used gone. She forced herself to open her drawers – all was in order. There were no signs anyone had been there, except for the lingering odour of Fred's pipe. Brigid glanced at the clock on the mantelpiece. There were less than two hours left of 1940. She had to get back to the tube station.

The sounds of the Blitz from outside still pervaded. Brigid opened the bedroom door just enough to peer out and listen; the house was silent. It was only then that a fact unregistered at the time struck her – Fred had not been wearing his ARP uniform. He was not on duty after all. He had lied about that. He might still be around. There was nothing for it – she had to risk it. She removed her shoes and held them as she crept along the landing and tip-toed quickly downstairs. The house was in total darkness – he must have gone, unless he was behind the closed door of his and Doreen's room, or the toilet; or he might be in the Anderson, of course. Brigid gained the front door and opened it carefully, closing it as if it was china which could shatter. Then she ran in stocking soles until she was round the corner, where she stopped to put her shoes back on cold, numb feet and check that the money was secure under her clothes. She rested against a wall for a few minutes, drained by everything that had happened; but anxiety made adrenaline kick in, and she bolted for the Underground station.

#

Chapter Ten

Pall *Mall,*
London
The twenty-seventh day of November, 1688
My dearest Wife,

 I thank you for your letter and assure you that I am safe and well. The strife has not touched us here in Pall Mall, although you are right to be concerned at the rioting all over this land of England since William of Orange landed in Devon at the beginning of the month. It has vexed my heart sorely, as you know all religious conflict does. The fact so many of our brethren in the Highlands are of the Catholic faith and loyal to King James is indeed worrying. Perhaps by the time you read this letter, word will already have reached you that the King rode back to London in retreat yesterday. It seems that William of Orange will have the victory, but I bid you be of good cheer – I gather he cares as little about differences in the way churches govern themselves as I do, and I do not think we Episcopalians are in danger.

 As for Mr. Boyle and the Viscountess, they are Anglicans and so fear nothing should this William and his wife Mary come to the throne, and I am safe as a guest in their house. In any case, Mr. Boyle is, like me, adept at paying court to both sides in a dispute. It was thus that he was unmolested by the Civil War, and lest that sound dishonourable, let me assure you it was with the best of intent – it was in order that nothing should stop the advancement of his scientific endeavours. In the same manner, my dear, my endeavours for the Gospel and for my flock – indeed for all my countrymen in the Highlands – are the guiding principle of my life. I shall pay my dues to whichever monarch prevails and continue my mild middling stance in all matters of church governance, as I did when I signed the Test Act back in 1681; in short, I shall do whatever is needful for my work of translation and distribution of the Bible in our native Gaelic to continue, and for the care of my flock.

I have a belief that the things which unite us in Gaeldom are stronger than the divisions of religion. We hold in common the pure love of our land – the beauty of our hills and glens, our lofty mountains and deep, cool lochs. Furthermore, we all of us know of that other kingdom, or should I say commonwealth, of beings who rank higher than mortals in God's creation, yet lower than the angels of Heaven. They favour us by making their abode within our beloved land itself, and I begin to think they hold answers to many of our problems. Indeed, it will gladden your heart to know that I have found common ground on these matters with none other than Mr. Boyle. You may have heard that a race akin to the Sith are also known in his native Ireland, and Mr. Boyle is well acquainted with their exploits.

I continue in awe of Mr. Boyle! Such a heart for Science and the Gospel! He stands against the rising tide of atheism in our day and emboldens me to do likewise. This, my dear, is our real enemy, rather than religious differences – that there are those who deny the very existence of God. Mr. Boyle believes in the scientific observation of nature in order to prove it is God's creation; thus he believes that Science and Religion may be mutually supportive. It is from this that I have had the most marvellous idea. My investigations into the Good People, which hitherto have been for my own interest, shall henceforth take the nature of RESEARCH with a view to publication. Those accounts I have already collected, and the interviews I conduct in future, together with my own experiences, shall be recorded in a scientific paper. I shall prove that the Sith do indeed dwell in our land, and thus prove how much more wondrous is God's creation than many realise; how can they doubt the existence of a Creator when such marvels are revealed?

My dear Margaret, I have had cause to wonder if they are here also, even in the midst of this grand city. That a race of them dwells in rural areas of England and Wales I am in no doubt, for many are the tales similar to the Scottish and Irish accounts of them, although the creatures go by other names; but here in London there is a hill upon which is built the mighty Tower of London, that ancient fortress of which all have heard. There are rumours that the Tower was founded upon much older edifices, and that indeed the hill itself was once a place of heathen worship before any human hand laid down a stone to build. That interested me given the history of my own dear Balquidder.

I went to this Tower Hill and I had the sensation that the air is indeed thin to those who have the gift of recognising it. I thought to conduct some research there, but was warned away by Viscountess Ranelagh, for fear of bringing suspicion of witchcraft upon her house. She said that we have enough trouble concerning religion and politics to deal with at present, and she is a most learned lady. Indeed, I revere her as much as I do her brother! She has long campaigned for religious freedom and was most vociferous in her attempts to influence both the government and the unfortunate Charles the First in their disputes. She is a grand lady late in years, yet she retains her intellect and interest in all things.

You may have noticed earlier that I referred to the land of fairy as "that other kingdom, or should I say commonwealth". It is Lady Ranelagh who has made me consider the change in my thinking. Her brother Boyle believes in an Empire of Man. I have written to you of his views on the slave trade – he believes that the manufacture of sugar and tobacco, in which indigents have been put to their greatest use, is proof of God's creation of this Empire, in which all are placed in hierarchy. Lady Ranelagh is uneasy with this view (as am I); she was a believer in republic at one time, although she later modified that idea. However, her political reasoning caused me to consider my use of the word "kingdom" in reference to that other race of which we know, those dwellers in our hills, and it strikes me that the evidence I have gathered points to a commonwealth rather than a kingdom. There are many types of creature, of which elves, fauns and fairies are but a few, and they are bound by their wish to coexist for the common good. Thus do they deserve their title of "the People of Peace". If only we could end our divisions, religious and political, and live likewise!

I am disappointed to say that Lady Ranelagh has no opinion on the Sith, or any other kindred race, despite her upbringing in Ireland. She says we have many more pressing concerns in this world without considering the subterranean existence of another. Indeed, she has become concerned at her brother's collecting reports of supernatural experiences, and has persuaded him not to include them in a work he has planned. She says it is a matter of discretion. He has bowed to her request, although it causes him to be all the more encouraging of my endeavours.

I would like to conduct research into the environs of the Tower of London; I believe the fae are present there. As Lady Ranelagh's guest, however, I could not proceed when she requested me to cease my interest. But imagine it, my dear Margaret! Hidden peoples within our hills from one end of this isle to the other, and across the sea in the

Emerald Isle, and our Good Lord alone knows where else – for He created them all! Therefore be of good cheer and fear not, dearest wife.

Your affectionate husband,
Robert Kirk

\#

Margaret Kirk dropped the letter on the table next to her cup and shook her head in disbelief. The fool! Her husband was too clever for his own good – his mind ever on philosophical matters and naïve about the things of the world. This William of Orange might well care little about church governance himself, but certain Protestants had taken his imminent victory as a sign to begin persecution of Catholics. Episcopalians were already regarded with suspicion in Scotland, and Catholics barely tolerated; of course there would be trouble! Yet here he was gabbling about the fae again. Times were dangerous enough – the Sith should be left well alone. She had thought Robert Boyle would be a positive influence – first the slave, and now this. She reached for paper and pen.

"Husband dearest, I am glad to hear you have a sensible counsellor in Viscountess Ranelagh, and I beseech you to listen to her and put all such matters out of your head. Robert, there is a current of unrest here, and real fear as to how this situation may unfold. I do not share your belief that we Episcopalians shall be spared – we have overmuch in common with our Catholic brethren, as you yourself recognise. We share more with them than with the Presbyterians who rule our land. Please come home, Robert. Your flock needs you here. Your family needs you. Please consider the son of your first marriage – Colin needs you. I need you."

\#

Chapter Eleven

Brigid helped Doreen cook a roast chicken dinner with one of the culled hens on New Year's Day. It was a midday meal, as Christmas Dinner had been. Brigid went quietly about her tasks, preoccupied with processing her thoughts on the rollercoaster of the past week. Doreen was also subdued that morning. She had slept the whole night in the tube station, even when New Year greetings had been exchanged by those around them at midnight; she felt muddle-headed, she said. Brigid dreaded to think of the state she herself might have been in by now had she not deceived her about taking the pills. If there was one thing she knew, it was that she had to keep her head clear in this house, because she had to work out how to get away from it as soon as possible.

They mostly ate in silence. Fred looked from one woman to the other and eventually suggested they should have baths that afternoon; they both looked a bit peaky. He would bring the tin bath and fetch and carry the water to the parlour.

Doreen patted his arm. "You are a love. Brigid can go first, quick dip, then I can stay in longer. I feel like a nice long soak in front of the fire."

Brigid forced a smile. She had avoided Fred as much as possible and was finding it hard to look at him. "I'm not fussed about a bath," she said. "Thanks for the offer, though."

Doreen studied her. "Fred's right, you do look peaky and tired. Do you think the pills are wearing off, now you're used to them?"

"Yes," said Brigid, "but not to worry. I only have two doses left. It wouldn't be good for me or the baby to keep on taking them."

"Doctor said that, did he?" asked Doreen. "I don't recall that."

"Well, no," admitted Brigid. "But he would only give me a week's supply for good reason."

Doreen scooped a forkful of potato. "Fair enough. You can go and rest in your room while I have my bath."

Fred's over-large eyes were on Brigid, great hazel-flecked pools of concern in his weathered face. "Sure you don't want one, girl? It would do you good."

"No thank you," she said.

After they had cleared away the dishes and had a cup of tea, Fred fetched the bath and Brigid heaved a sigh of relief and went upstairs. She closed the bedroom door behind her and looked at the wooden-backed chair in front of the dressing table. In a film once, she had seen such a chair wedged beneath a door handle to stop anyone entering. If she did that, though, and Fred tried to open the door, he would know what she had done; it would alert him to the fact she wanted to keep him out, that she had some reason not to trust him. For now, she would let it be. Doreen was directly below her in the bath, in front of the parlour fire; what could he possibly do?

Brigid went to the bottom of the pile of books on the chest of drawers, and removed "The Secret Commonwealth of Elves, Fauns and Fairies", by Rev. Robert Kirk. It was a 1933 edition she had first borrowed from the library, before her mother bought a volume for her because she took it out so many times. Brigid wanted to check what was written about the second sight; was it this that she was experiencing when she drifted away from this world – something which a Victorian introduction to the book called telepathy? Since her experience in the toilet the day after Boxing Day, she had abandoned her doubts. Something or somebody wanted her to see these things.

Was it telepathy with Robert Kirk? Was he himself calling out to her? She remembered her glimpse of his grave. She tried to recall the whispering voice she had heard, but all she could remember was the chill in its tone; she couldn't be certain if it had been male or female. She knew the legend, of course – that Kirk had not really died, but had been taken captive by the fae inhabitants of Doon Hill as punishment for the things he had revealed about them. Some said his coffin was empty, merely weighted for the funeral, others said the fae had conjured his double to be carried down from the hillside and buried in the kirkyard. To keep her mind off other matters, she set about reading the slim volume again. She was undisturbed. Whatever else he was doing, Fred didn't venture near her room that afternoon.

By the end of the book, knowledge had come to Brigid; she knew, not that she had ever really doubted it, that her baby was special. Even although he was adamant that the second sight was not normally gifted to women, there was a connection between her and Robert Kirk. She had to go to Aberfoyle, whether she had a reply from the minister's wife, or not. In fact, she couldn't afford to wait for one.

#

The following day, Brigid reminded her landlady that her rent was due; she had only paid one week. She would have to visit the bank where Will had kept his savings. Doreen studied her as she spoke. The woman still wasn't as warm towards her as she had been at first, but her mood had thawed.

"I'll come with you," said Doreen. "We'll go tomorrow."

Brigid forced a bright smile. "It would be lovely to have your company," she said, "but I'd rather go and sort things out today. New Year, new start and all that."

Doreen's eyes didn't leave her face. "There's no hurry," she said, after a long pause. "The second, the third, what difference does it make? Tomorrow, like I said. And we'll take a month's rent this time."

Brigid was afraid her landlady would see the panic which seized her at these words. She maintained her smiling demeanour. "I can just as easily go now and sort it all out," she shrugged.

Doreen turned her attention back to her magazine. "Tomorrow," she repeated.

Brigid backed down. She didn't know what else to do. The last thing she needed was for Doreen to be with her, and she certainly didn't want to hand over a month's rent. She had no intention of staying there that long. She excused herself and headed upstairs. At the turn in the staircase, she stopped and listened to the voices below.

"Why are you asking monthly rent now?" asked Fred.

"Because I don't trust her," Doreen replied. She sighed. "I wasn't going to tell you, but…she's not as keen to be here as she lets on. That letter to Scotland was an application for a job as a live-in help. Work in lieu of rent."

Brigid clapped her hand over her mouth and grabbed the bannister to steady herself.

"How do you know that?" asked Fred.

"Steamed it open, didn't I? Looked guilty as hell, she did, when I saw that envelope. I knew something was going on."

"She might not get it, though."

"She definitely won't. I chucked it, not that she stood a chance anyway."

"What's the problem, then?"

"Don't you see? If it's not there, it'll be somewhere else. She doesn't intend to stay here. I'm making sure she's financially strapped so she can't take off!"

Brigid held her breath. There was a pause, then Fred said, "But we can't force her to stay."

"I am not letting this chance of being a proper family go, Fred Johnstone! I'll do everything in my power to keep her here."

Another pause. "I told you not to get too involved," said Fred.

"And you're not?" said his wife. "I've seen the way you look at her!"

"Like what?" asked Fred sharply.

"Like you've found your little girl," Doreen replied.

Brigid crept into the toilet and, for the first time in her pregnancy, vomited into the white porcelain bowl.

#

The two women set out for the East End next morning. Brigid's brain was still fomenting schemes to be rid of Doreen, but none seemed viable. When they reached the bank, she said she might be some time, as she would have to meet with the bank manager regarding transferring her savings. She hoped Doreen would say she would look at the street markets or something, anything; but the woman said she would accompany Brigid to the meeting. They entered the building. Brigid made her request and then found the courage to square up to her.

"Doreen, this is mine and Will's business," she asserted. "You didn't even know him. Out of respect to my late husband, I have to do this alone."

The clerk had returned, and he picked up their conversation. "Excuse me," he said, "The Manager will see you now, Mrs. Watkins. I'm afraid you'll have to wait here, Madam," he added with an inclination of the head to Doreen. "Client confidentiality. I do apologise."

Doreen sniffed, pursed her lips and retreated stiffly to the row of chairs in the corner. As the clerk ushered Brigid into his boss's office, she thanked him. "My pleasure, Mrs. Watkins. Family friend, is she?"

"Landlady," whispered Brigid. "For the time being."

In the safety of the office, she withdrew all the money and closed the account. It wasn't a great sum, as she had expected. She crammed it into her handbag. Some of her mother's money was in there, some was padding out her bra, and the rest she had pushed inside the lining of her coat, spreading it out. She was taking no chances now. She told the bank manager that she was leaving London.

"Where are you bound, Mrs. Watkins?"

"Scotland," she said. Somehow, she would manage it, although she hadn't yet planned how and wasn't even sure as to why.

Her mission at the bank over without Doreen's interference, Brigid breathed a little easier, but she still couldn't relax. She was near the area where Will's family lived; it was their bank, too. With a large dose of denial fuelled by youthly optimism, she told herself it would be a huge coincidence; but still she was wary. She could have explained herself away – maybe saying she was on her way to visit them after the bank – but having Doreen in tow would complicate matters. Still, as she reasoned, it was unlikely to happen. To round the corner and see Will's mother and sister, therefore, threw her into confusion. For a moment, she wondered if she could escape their notice, but Anne caught sight of her and her face lit up with delight.

"Brigid! Oh look, Ma, it's Brigid!"

Brenda Watkins' face showed less pleasure at meeting her late son's wife. "Hello, Brigid," she said. "Happy New Year to you. Hope you're feeling better."

"Yes, thank you," mumbled Brigid. "Happy New Year to you, too." She wondered if she could get off with introducing Doreen as a friend rather than as her landlady. The Watkins women were glancing at her with curiosity. Doreen looked as if she should have been shopping up West, well dressed and perfectly coiffed as always. "This is…er…" she started.

"Mrs. Doreen Johnstone," said Doreen, nodding tight-lipped to Mrs. Watkins. "I'm Brigid's landlady."

Brigid gulped as she recalled the picture she had painted for the Johnstones, of her uncaring relatives who weren't interested in Will's widow or her condition.

"Mrs. Brenda Watkins, and this is my daughter Anne," said her mother-in-law. "Landlady, did you say?"

"Have you moved back to London?" asked Anne, frowning. "Why didn't you come to us? I've missed you!"

Brigid blushed to the roots of her hair, trying to find words to get herself out of this.

"Hmmph!" said Doreen. "When her own won't have her, what else was the girl to do but seek lodgings?"

"That's not strictly true!" gasped Brigid.

"As good as!" cried Doreen. "Your father making life impossible, and this lot not caring tuppence for you!" She indicated the Watkins women with a sneer.

"What are you talking about?" snapped Brenda. "Her father dotes on her! True, we might not have seen eye to eye all the time, but she's family – my Anne here thinks of her as a sister, and she's welcome any time!" She turned to Brigid again. "Not good enough for you now, are we? And

I don't need to ask what you've been doing here - clearing out our Will's money that should have gone to the one who raised him!"

"Well!" cried Doreen. "No wonder she didn't come to you if you would take what your son left for his widow and unborn child!"

"Excuse me?" said Brenda Watkins. "Not that it's any of your business, but they were only married five minutes and the little mite didn't see the light of day, so why should she get it? I'm a widow, too!"

Brigid grabbed Doreen's arm. She tried to speak; she wanted to pull her away before anything else was said, but her throat constricted and she could barely move for the horror gripping her.

Doreen shook her off, frowning. "What do you mean, the child didn't see the light of day? I thought this was your first baby, Brigid?"

Three pairs of inquisitive eyes bore down upon her. Brigid looked from one to the other, desperately trying to think what to say. Her mother-in-law's mouth fell open as the meaning of Doreen's words struck.

"Are you pregnant?"

"Of course she is!" said Doreen.

Anne Watkins stared at Brigid in disbelief. "Well, she shouldn't be," she said.

Brenda Watkins raised an accusatory finger. "You lost our Will's child a week after he died!" she cried. "Whose is this? And how far on are you?"

"It's not what you think!" Brigid's voice came out as a strained whisper.

Doreen shook her head to clear it. "Would somebody mind telling me what's going on?"

"You've taken in a lying little tart, that's what!" hissed Mrs. Watkins. "She lost my Will's baby on the first day of the Blitz – I was there! If she's pregnant now, it's nothing to do with our Will – he's been dead four months!"

"It's not what you think!" Brigid repeated, tears in her eyes and pleading in her voice.

Doreen grabbed her upper arm. "Come along, Brigid," she said, "let's not be having a scene in the street!" She began to steer her away.

"Oi!" yelled Brenda. "You're surely not going to take her part, a respectable woman like you! You should throw her out on her ear!"

Anne had begun to cry. "How could you, Brigid?"

Doreen ignored them. "Keep walking. We'll talk about this in a civilised manner back home."

They had travelled by bus, but Doreen hailed a cab when one chanced to come along. She pushed Brigid in the door when they reached their destination, then seized her by the shoulders and bundled her into the parlour. "Explain yourself!" she demanded.

"It really isn't what you think!" said Brigid. The journey back had given her time to consider. "I'll never be able to make you believe that, though, and I understand, truly I do. So I'll just pack my things and go." It might be the best thing that had happened. It didn't matter that she had nowhere to go; she would find somewhere. It was enough now just to be able to get away, to have an excuse.

"Not so fast!" said Doreen. "You've spun me lies for over a week. I took you in on Christmas Eve out of Christian charity, and this is how you repay me!"

"I'm sorry," said Brigid. "I really am. But I couldn't tell you the truth."

"You can bloody well start now, missy!"

Brigid opened her mouth to speak, but what she had said a moment ago was true; she couldn't tell this woman the truth, not as she understood it. Look where it had got her with her own parents. She gulped.

"I was very unwell after I lost Will," she began. "We married because I was expecting. He was killed and yes, I lost our baby. Then I was laid up with a terrible cold. Near the end of September, I got caught out in the Blitz. I've no memory of that night. When they found me, I was down by the Thames, wandering around. I didn't know who I was or where I was. I was injured and I had lost some of my clothes and my shoes." Bare facts; how could she make anybody else believe the rest? "I found I was pregnant after that."

"Tell me straight – were you out meeting a man?"

"No! It was less than a month after I lost Will and our baby. I had been in bed, ill. I was in my nightgown! I just got up and…wandered off. I don't know what happened, I don't remember anything."

Doreen regarded her in silence for a few seconds. They had been standing, but in a calmer tone of voice she told Brigid to sit. "I suppose your father flung you out, then? I noticed that letter to your mother was addressed care of somebody else."

Brigid blinked in surprise; Doreen's nosiness was infuriating. She hadn't considered the address on the letter when she had handed it over. Had Doreen steamed it open, too, along with the letter to Aberfoyle? She swallowed her fears and decided on total honesty.

"I told the truth when I said I left because things were difficult. Dad didn't throw me out just before Christmas. He wanted me to go to a home for unmarried mothers, a convent home. I was supposed to go today, as it happens. He said he would have me back, but not the baby. I didn't want to give up my baby. I ran away. I left word for Mam with her friend. She's the one I sent the letter to." She was desperate to ask if that letter had been posted, but of course, she didn't dare; she only knew of the fate of the other by eavesdropping.

Doreen sighed. Her face gave nothing away. "You have got yourself in a pickle, haven't you? No point making it worse by taking off from here. I'd be obliged if you would go to your room while I think things over."

Brigid swallowed. "I think it's best if I leave."

Doreen gave the ghost of a smile. "Well, as it happens, I don't."

#

Upstairs, Brigid moved stealthily, opening drawers slowly lest Doreen catch the sounds of their creaking and guess what she was up to. She was not going to stay here, no matter what Doreen said, no matter how accepting she might appear to be. Brigid shuddered as she packed garments she knew Fred had touched. When she had finished, she walked downstairs and tapped on the parlour door before entering.

Doreen had lit the fire and sat staring into it. She turned distractedly, but her unfocused gaze snapped to attention when she saw Brigid standing there still wearing her coat and carrying her carpet bag. "Where do you think you're going?"

Brigid raised her chin and squared her shoulders. "I'm leaving. It's for the best, for all of us. You've been terribly kind, and I'm more than grateful. If you would just tell me what I owe you, and give me back my ration book, we'll settle up and I'll be on my way."

Doreen's eyes narrowed. She rose and brushed past Brigid as she left the room. "Wait here."

Brigid sighed with relief. A few minutes more and she could leave. She heard Doreen's footsteps in the kitchen. Then she heard the sound of the key turning in the back door. Doreen's footsteps returned along the hallway and went beyond the parlour. Brigid's heart missed a beat as she heard the key turn in the front door also. She rushed into the hallway.

Doreen's flushed face was triumphant as she pocketed the key. "You're not going anywhere," she said. "Not now, not any time soon."

Chapter Twelve

"Dear Mother,

I wrote to you the day before New Year's Eve, but I think my letter may have been lost in the post, as that was nearly a month ago and you haven't replied. Well, I have more news now, and it is excellent. The lovely couple with whom I have found lodgings, Doreen and Fred Johnstone, have agreed to adopt the baby. They have longed for a child and I can fulfil their wish. In return, they will care for me until the birth, and indeed, have already been doing so.

Their house shines like a new pin thanks to Doreen's housekeeping skills, and Fred has a responsible job with the council and is an Air Raid Precaution Warden. I have a beautiful, comfortable room, fit for a princess. I have been keeping well, but one night when I had a fainting turn, they sent for the doctor straight away. It was just one of those things, and I and the baby continue well. We spend our nights safely in an Anderson shelter, so you need not worry on that score. I help Doreen around the house and am reading my way through her late father's library of books. She is making new clothes for me, as the baby has begun to show.

I hope that this news will please you and that you will feel able to pass it on to Father. I hope for full reconciliation so that I may return to Birmingham once the baby is born and safely in Doreen's care. I'm sure Father will see that this is a much better solution than giving birth in a convent home, because I know the people who will be raising my child and I am happy for them to have him or her. I hope you are both well and hope to hear from you soon."

Doreen hesitated and Brigid glanced up at her, pen poised. It was Doreen's best fountain pen. "Sign it the way you normally would," she said, turning away.

Brigid put the nib to the paper and scratched "With love and very best wishes, B." Hopefully, Doreen wouldn't remember the stylistic details of the letter she had steamed open a few weeks ago. Brigid knew now that it had never reached its destination.

Doreen read over the letter she had dictated and handed her an envelope. "Address it and I'll post it today. Send it to that other woman, like you said you would."

"Like the one you threw in the river?" asked Brigid, lip curled.

Doreen ignored her remark. 'I just hope they don't want to visit," she sniffed. "It's more likely than if you had been in a home. I'll have to think how to put them off."

"It'll be a wonder if they haven't been contacting the Catholic homes looking for me already!" cried Brigid. "They must be worried sick – I left a month ago!"

Doreen stared at her a moment. "Maybe it would be better if they thought you were…lost to them forever. They might think you've been killed in an air raid. You could start again, a new life, no ties. Me and Fred'll give you some money when you leave here, you know that, and you've got your savings. You'll be able to get an office job again. You won't need them."

Brigid clenched her fist around the pen and banged the table. The nib broke and ink blotted Doreen's white cloth. "Are you totally insane?"

"Now look what you've done! My good cloth! My pen!"

Doreen removed her sewing machine to the sideboard, along with the maternity dress she had just finished making. As she whipped the tablecloth away, Brigid stood and grabbed the letter. Her skirt was held closed by her large kilt pin, the button no longer able to meet the buttonhole. She stalked out of the room and upstairs to her bedroom.

#

She was still there two hours later, curled on the bed listening to the hum of high-pitched chatter from downstairs, when Fred walked in. She didn't turn round, not even her head. He sat down beside her, his back against hers.

"Well, it's all a bit bizarre, isn't it? Can't say I'm too happy with this latest myself."

Brigid didn't reply. She remained motionless. She would give no acknowledgement of his presence.

"Listen, I've been thinking. There's another way round all this." He cleared his throat. "You know I'm fond of you. I could find somewhere for you to live, after…Some place decent. Me and the kiddie, we could visit. I would make sure you got to see the mite."

Brigid's eyes fell on the letter lying beside her on the bed. She swallowed and forced herself to face him. "Would you post this for me?" Seeing his hesitation, she said quickly, "Doreen dictated it. Only, I think she's had second thoughts about sending it. But my parents have to know I'm alive and well, Fred. Whatever happens after, they have to know that."

He nodded. "You'll think about what I said?"

She held his gaze. "Yes. Post it now, please, before she drags you in down there."

He smiled. "And you'll think about…other things?" He ran his hand down the length of her arm.

Brigid swung her legs round quickly, nearly knocking him off the bed. She smoothed her hand over her skirt, showing the little bump there. "Have some pity, Fred! And some patience."

"But…?"

"Yes."

He stood. The pupils of his eyes were dilating, drinking her in, his irises turning black with desire. She wondered if he had ever looked so hungrily at his wife.

"Go, before she knows you're here!"

He smiled, a grin of wolfish delight, and left the room on his little feet, quiet, always quiet. Brigid shuddered and fell back upon her pillows. She heard the front door closing. A moment later, the noise from the parlour increased as Doreen opened the door and called, "Fred? Was that you?"

A waft of laughter and cigarette smoke, punctuated by the tinkling of teacups in saucers, preceded her up the stairs. She burst into Brigid's room, her hand on her heart as she saw that the young woman was still where she should be.

"Thought I'd got away, did you?" Brigid mocked.

"Must have been Fred. Didn't even know he was in the house." Doreen was wearing the maternity dress she had been sewing earlier.

"He came to see me," said Brigid, "and he's gone to post my letter. I asked him to, in case you conveniently lost it, or let it blow away, maybe."

Doreen's eyes narrowed. "You're getting too lippy, girl," she said. "Don't think your condition means I can't give you a slap."

Brigid smirked. "I've already lost one baby, remember? No risks, Doreen."

The older woman pursed her lips. "You stay here and keep quiet. When Fred comes back, my friends want to congratulate the father-to-be." She shut the door firmly behind her.

Brigid had heard her discussing a lock with Fred yesterday. Nothing surprised her now. She jumped as she heard Fred returning from posting the letter. He was drawn into the parlour immediately, where shrieks of delight issued from Doreen's friends assembled there. The tea party had been arranged to announce her pregnancy, at the age of forty-four, and fourteen years after the only child she had managed to conceive had died in her cot aged two months. Not long afterwards, Brigid listened to the farewells as the visitors left. When the front door closed behind the last one, she rose and opened her bedroom door. Going downstairs, she heard Fred and Doreen speaking.

"I'm not sure we can pull this off, love. I wish you hadn't done this today."

"Well, we can't take it back now. It's done. I want this baby to be ours, Fred."

"But Brigid might have been persuaded to hand it over anyway, if you had carried on being good to her. At first, I thought you wanted both of them – her and the littl'un. She could have been like our Rosa."

"She's nothing like Rosa would have been! She was fair like me and you."

"You know what I mean." There was a pause, then: "The kid's not likely to look like us, either."

"You never know. We don't know about the father, since she claims to remember nothing. It might work out."

"But what if it's got a crop of curly dark hair like her?"

"There's always bleach. Blonde curls like me."

Brigid gasped and put her hand to her stomach. As she kept telling herself, nothing should shock her now. Reaching the bottom of the stairs, she jumped as a knock came at the front door. Doreen appeared and shooed her back upstairs. She heard a voice say, "Telegram", and a moment later Doreen was calling to Fred that her brother-in-law had been killed, and she would have to go to her sister.

#

Doreen's sister lived in a hamlet near Durham. She planned to spend a week with her, leaving the next day. Her excitement at the tea party dissolved into a fluster of preparations. As they ate supper before she and Brigid headed to the Anderson shelter, she told Brigid not to get any ideas, that they had made a bargain. She ordered Fred to watch her.

"I know you don't like going to the Anderson unless the air raid warning goes, but when you're not on duty, you'll have to. Every night. And you'll have to fit a padlock on the outside for when you're on duty – lock her in. Don't trust her at all. She ran off from her mother-in-law's place when she should have been heading for the shelter."

Fred glanced at Brigid. "I'll take good care of her."

They had been using the Anderson ever since Doreen had forced Brigid to make the arrangement to live with them and bear her child in secret while Doreen faked a pregnancy. They told the neighbours Brigid had moved on, and she had to remain hidden. They kept the doors locked. She and Doreen slept in the shelter each night, creeping out under cover of darkness. Fred kept to his own bed when not on ARP duty, unless the sirens sounded.

Brigid thought frantically. "If you're going to put a lock on the door anyway," she said coolly, sipping her tea, "there's no need for Fred to join me in the shelter unless he has to."

"Oh yes…"

"I don't mind…"

Husband and wife spoke over each other. Fred deferred to Doreen, a pulse in his neck the only betrayal of tension.

"We have to make sure you're well for the baby's sake," said Doreen, "so he'll be in there with you when he can. When you're on duty, Fred, you can always pop back and look in when you get the chance."

Brigid shrugged as if it didn't matter one way or the other. Fred sighed and smiled and assured them both that he had everyone's interests at heart, the baby, Brigid and Doreen. Brigid took another sip of tea and knew that she couldn't delay any longer.

#

Doreen departed early next morning, not long after Fred left for work. She locked the front and back doors from the outside. It was no more than Brigid had expected. If she was to make her escape before Fred returned, it would have to be by breaking a window and climbing out, with all the risks that entailed. She had another plan. If it didn't work, she would chance the window tomorrow and hope to keep him at bay tonight.

Doreen had left her a list of jobs to do. The house had to be kept in the manner she expected, as long as Brigid took rests for sake of the baby. The first thing Brigid did was find her ration book, then she packed her bag in preparation. After that, she got on with household tasks to keep herself busy, and made a package of sandwiches to put in her bag. She rested in the afternoon, forcing herself to breathe deeply and clear her mind.

Fred's evening meal was on the table for him when he came in from work. She served him cordially enough, quelling the tremor in her hands as she wondered if he would make a move on her before she could act. They always drank tea in the parlour afterwards, so she made it and prepared the tray while he lit the fire. She carried it through, set out his cup on the side table next to his chair, and began pouring. He caught her wrist.

"There's no need for either of us to go to the shelter," he said. "Not unless we need to, like you said. We can stay in our own bed unless Jerry comes calling."

"That's tempting," she said.

He let go of her wrist and she put the tea pot down.

"You not having any?"

"I've gone right off it. It's one of those pregnancy things – it happens to a lot of women."

Fred frowned, remembering. "Oh yes. I recall now that Dor did an' all. She went off tea and coffee. Not that it would take being pregnant to put anybody off the coffee we get these days." He drained his first cup quickly as was his habit and helped himself to more. "You sure you don't want any?"

It was one of the last coherent things he said. As he slurped from his cup and nibbled on his biscuit, his mouth became slack and his speech slurred. He dribbled tea, and pieces of food fell from his lips. He knocked his cup off the side table and when he bent clumsily to retrieve it, he slid off the chair and knelt on the floor, swaying, before slumping sideways. He lay with his mouth open, eyes closed.

Brigid wasted no time in taking the back door keys from his trouser pocket. Then she donned her coat and grabbed her bag. She was certain there was a night train to Scotland, and she intended to be on it. She had put all of her secret stash of unused pills in the teapot, and she hoped it would be enough to knock Fred Johnstone out cold until well into the next day.

Chapter Thirteen

Molly White was dozing beside the range. January had been a busy month for births. She had been called from her bed several nights in a row. Anybody who saw her now, at this moment, would have been shocked. A network of grooves had appeared on her smooth cheeks, and there were hollows around her eyes. Her flesh seemed to have shrunk. Her hands, resting in her lap, were bony appendages with scaled skin stretched tight. Even her hair was thinner in its bun. She leaned back, her mouth falling open to reveal yellow teeth. She drew a long, rattling breath.

Something clattered through the letterbox and landed with a soft thud. It was enough to rouse Molly, whose midwife senses were always alert. People rarely had to rap on her door twice before she sprang into action, neat and twinkling and reassuring. Now, however, she had to take a moment before pushing herself out of the chair. Her normal work was enough to exhaust her these days without the exertions to which she had been putting herself in the interests of Brigid Watkins. Like most of her kind, Molly chose not to dabble overmuch in magic, especially with her centuries of experience. She had integrated well with this world. There was magic enough in her skills with mother and child, helped by her knowledge of herbal lore; she reserved the use of some powers for her own preservation.

Molly had long ago chosen to pass through the veil between worlds, and to redress the horror many of her kind felt at the long history of abductions by those of her race who stole human mothers to breastfeed their young, or swapped babes when they didn't appeal and left a fairy brat, a changeling, in the cradle of a human child. She belonged to the Ancient Order of Fae Midwives. Her long life – fae lived to greater ages than humans – had been spent in posting after posting, moving on from place to place down through the ages. She took from each posting the full essence of what she had learned, but few memories. Those were barred by the mysterious Order so that midwives never looked back, never yearned for attachments long gone, never wallowed either in triumph or regrets. All their energy had to be focused in the present, on the posting with which they had been entrusted.

Molly's recent exhaustion was a sign that all this was about to come to an end. She would be called into retirement soon, and if it wasn't for Brigid Watkins, she would accept it gladly. Yet when had there last been a case like Brigid's? She wasn't at all sure she had ever been involved in the case of a child brought about by fae conception, although she knew it happened, of course, when an ancient elemental spirit became attached to a human female. She couldn't remember. It bothered her. Brigid bothered her – she would need help, special help, but she had disappeared in London. The promised letter to her mother had never come. Then, finally, a nasty one from her mother-in-law had. Mary MacKenzie had confessed all to her husband then, and they were frantic with worry. She had to help them. This morning she had succeeded in drawing to her a letter which should have taken longer to arrive. It was addressed to Mary MacKenzie c/o her address, but she opened it anyway. The contents left her puzzled, then worried.

It was now early evening, so when she saw two letters lying on her doormat, she knew her efforts had produced more fruit. They hadn't been delivered by the Royal Mail, not at this time of day. She picked them up. Sure enough, they bore no postmarks, their stamps never having been franked. Molly sniffed, frowning over the distinct whiff of…what was it? River. They smelt of river. One was for Mary care of Molly's address, while the other had been meant to go somewhere in Scotland. She carried them through to the kitchen and settled again beside the range. The one from Brigid to her mother was reassuring as far as it went, except that it had been written a month ago. The other was dated the day before Christmas Eve and was an application for a job as a live-in help; Brigid had lied in a way Molly wouldn't have believed possible of her. She obviously had a great fancy to go there, to Scotland. Taken together, these letters didn't make much sense. The job application caused a niggle somewhere in the back of Molly's tired mind. She frowned and shook her head as if to dislodge a fly from her hair. More strands of it fell from her white bun, thin and lank. She sighed.

Molly rose and went round her kitchen, snipping pieces off bunches of dried herbs hanging from the pulley most people used for drying clothes, opening jars and mixing pinches of whatever they contained with the herbs and with foul-smelling liquid from two black stoppered bottles. She drank the mixture in one draught, gasping and retching afterwards, lowering herself back into her chair and flinging wide the door of the range. Then she leaned forward until her face was so close to the fire that it would have scorched any normal person. Instead, the glow lit her fragile skin and began to smooth the creases; the heat entered her body and met with the potion, filling her with strength and vigour.

When she was satisfied that the transformation was complete, she closed the range door and collected her coat and scarf from a peg on the wall. She twinkled at her reflection in the hall mirror, her teeth white as ice, skin smooth, hair full and shining in its perfect updo. Then she picked up the letters and placed them in her bag, donned her gloves, and headed out into the night. Ten minutes later, she was knocking on the MacKenzies' front door. Mary answered, surprised to see her there at this time of night, but knowing why she had come.

"Oh, Molly, hello. Do come in. I'm afraid we have no news to give you, though."

"Thank you, Mary. Nothing at all?"

"Come in. He'll tell you himself."

Mary led the way to the sitting room, where Walter rose to his feet, folding his newspaper. He was thinner than Molly had ever known him, his face gaunt.

"Ah, Molly. Good evening."

"Hello, Walter. I hear you had no luck."

Mary plumped a cushion and motioned for Molly to sit. She sat and waited for Walter to speak.

"They're not certain o' her name," he said. "The shock o' the news drove it oot o' their heads. It might have been Dora, they think, or maybe Doreen, but no recollection of a surname. A respectable, well-dressed woman, early forties, was all they could say for sure."

Molly sighed. "It must have been hard for you."

Walter sagged. "It would have been harder for Mary. I'm glad I insisted on going alone. They never did like oor Brigid. Well, Will's mother didn't. His sister's as bad against her now, though."

"Were they able to set your mind at rest that Brigid is well?"

Walter smiled weakly. "Oh aye. She looked well, and her landlady stood by her, whisked her away in a taxi even although it was obvious she had lied tae her." He rubbed a weary hand down his face. "I just hope the woman's got fond of her an' forgave her, didna throw her oot. I visited six Catholic homes, just in case, but she wasnae in any o' them. I had nae time tae dae mair."

Molly let a beat fall. They all stared at the fire crackling in the grate, its distraction filling the silence. Then she took a deep breath.

"I received a package today," she said. "In it was a letter written two days ago, and also two others which appear to have been lost in the post."

The MacKenzies turned to stare at her, faces blank, uncomprehending.

"It was too late for me to bring them to you, Walter. I knew you would be on your way by the time I got them. They're from Brigid. I hoped you would find her today, that she would be here with you now." *And if she was, thought Molly, I wouldn't be.* She had hoped, but she had a feeling that Brigid would be elusive. She could give them some positive news now, but even so…she wasn't sure Brigid would be so easily found. She paused, mulling over how best to explain.

Mary clapped both hands to her mouth, and Walter started out of the chair.

"Is she alright?" he gasped. "Where is she?"

"She's well," Molly replied, "I'm sure she's as well as when Brenda Watkins saw her…but there's no easy way to say this…something is far wrong." She took the letters from her bag. "Before I show you them, let me explain."

Mary and Walter glanced hungrily at the letters, but Molly kept them firmly in her grip.

"One was written the day she arrived in London," she said. "She gives her home address on it, so she couldn't have found anywhere to stay by then. It's an application for a job as a live-in help somewhere in Scotland. But I'll tell you more about that in a minute."

"How come she sent it to you?" asked Mary.

"It wasn't meant to come to me, Mary. It's been lost, along with the second letter written a few days later, just before New Year. That one was for you and was addressed to me as we arranged, and somehow the application ended up with it, in the same envelope the Royal Mail eventually got to me." She looked away as she said the last bit. "I'll read your one out, shall I?" she added quickly to divert awkward speculation. "Forgive me for opening it, but I was desperate for news of her whereabouts, like you, but when I looked at the clock I knew Walter would have been on his way to London long ago. I hoped he might find her without these."

As Molly White read aloud Brigid's letter of December thirtieth, emotions flitted rapidly across the faces of her parents. When she had finished, Walter remarked that she did indeed sound well and happy at that time – before later events. They had been horrified to receive a letter from Brigid's mother-in-law last week, in which Brenda Watkins said that she had at first decided not to write to them to express her disgust at Brigid, but the thought of her betrayal of Will, hardly cold in his grave, had pierced her to the heart, and she hoped Walter and Mary would never have their deceitful daughter back. Walter had managed to get a day off work to head to London to try to trace Brigid; alarmed at having received no word from her, Mary had eventually told him the truth about her savings and Brigid's departure. The letter they had received from Mrs. Watkins was the only clue they had as to where she might be. Now they had an address!

Mary was uneasy about Brigid's tone, however. She thought the girl was holding something back, she said; she couldn't put her finger on it.

"I agree with you," said Molly. "I think she was homesick, despite her brave words. Her whole aim is to reassure you. London took a terrible hammering the night before she wrote this."

"But she's with good people who are taking care of her," said Walter. "That's something, at least. And now we know where she is, we can go and bring her home!"

Molly sighed. "I'll read you her next letter, written two days ago. I'll be interested to know what you think of it."

As she began to read, both parents, who had been leaning forward the better to catch every word, stiffened and sat straighter in their chairs. They glanced at each other when she had finished.

"It disnae sound as if the same person wrote those letters," muttered Walter, frowning.

"The same person didn't!" cried Mary. "That second one wasn't written by Brigid! None of it is her style, and she would never sign herself that way! She calls us Mam and Dad, not Mother and Father!"

Molly handed one letter to Mary and the other to Walter. "It's the same handwriting, but the same person definitely didn't compose both these letters. I can only guess that the second one has been dictated by her landlady. The references to the house make me think it's more likely to be her than her husband."

"But why?" asked Walter, flabbergasted. "Why would anybody do that?"

"The answer, I think, is in the letter itself," Molly replied. "She desperately wants Brigid's baby. Brigid may not actually be willing to give the child to them."

"So…?" began Mary, at a loss.

"I think they're forcing her to stay," Molly said gently.

"How can they do that?" asked Walter. "She can walk out the door at any time, surely!"

Molly chose her words carefully. "They may have deprived her of means," she said. "They may have taken her money, or her papers. They may be keeping her locked in."

"This is monstrous!" cried Walter.

Molly took out the third letter. "This arrived with the other two. It's the application for the live-in help's position in Scotland."

Walter waved it away. "That doesn't matter now. She's always had fantasies aboot Scotland and Ireland, always the dreamer – how did she expect tae land a job in her condition?" He turned to his wife. "Mary, I want you with me this time. We've got the address – we need to arrive unexpectedly and find oot exactly what's goin' on!"

"Quite," said Molly. She had thought it her duty to bring the application to their attention, but Walter was right – it was irrelevant. Molly slipped the letter back into her bag. "Don't panic – remember that if they want the baby, they have to take care of Brigid. I'm sure they're treating her well," she said.

#

Little did Walter know that he had been looking for his daughter on the very day she had been plotting her escape. Brigid wasn't to know that, either. She was intent on rescuing herself, and she reckoned heading for home would not be an answer to her dilemma. When she closed the door for the final time on the Johnstone's house, she walked quickly while looking out for a taxi – they were becoming increasingly elusive these days. Hailing one down eventually, she asked the driver which station the night train to Scotland departed from.

"That'll be the Paddy?" the man asked.

"The Paddy?"

"The Irish mail train," he said. "It leaves at nine, I think, plenty of time."

"I'm going to a place called Aberfoyle," said Brigid. "Do you know if it will take me there?"

The driver shrugged. "Sorry miss, I don't know where it stops. Best check at the station. You want to go to Euston, then?"

"Yes. Thank you," said Brigid, settling back for the journey.

She queued for her ticket at Euston under posters reminding passengers that war needs came first and there were likely to be delays. She was tired already, and knew she was in for a long, uncomfortable night even if they didn't encounter any. She asked if the train for Scotland stopped at Aberfoyle. The ticket clerk, tired and harassed, checked the timetables and said she would have to change at Glasgow.

Brigid hung around the station anxiously, despite knowing that Fred couldn't possibly recover in time to catch up with her even if he had any idea where she was. She drank a few cups of tea and made her way to the platform as soon as the train was boarding, half an hour before the journey. She located the Third Class carriages. A few passengers had taken their places already. Brigid selected a compartment where two elderly ladies dressed in tweeds sat either side of the window, its blackout blind firmly pulled down. They were half-asleep. As she sank into the sprung seat, a rustling noise issued from her coat and they stirred and stared at her.

"Sorry," said Brigid, flushing.

"Have ye got it lined with newspaper for warmth?" asked the woman opposite.

"Yes," lied Brigid, thinking of the banknotes concealed in the lining. She remembered reading the tip about newspaper.

"We all have to do what we can these days." The woman smiled kindly enough, and closed her eyes.

Brigid was satisfied that they wouldn't trouble her with chatter or questions. They were Scottish, their accents different to her father's, their air of reserve similar. Had Molly received her letter and passed it on to her mother yet? It was probably far too soon. At the time Doreen dictated it, she had hoped they would realise it wasn't hers. She would have to write again as soon as she had secured an address in Scotland. She supposed she would have to book into a hotel or boarding house first. At least prices wouldn't be as high as they were in London.

The compartment filled. Brigid was soon squashed against her elderly neighbour by a giant of a middle-aged man, gathering her rustling coat around her against the encroaching chill of the January night. The train pulled out almost on time. Brigid was weary. She dozed to the swaying rhythm and was jolted awake as they stopped at stations. The corridor outside the compartment began to crowd with people who couldn't find seats.

Brigid pictured the train with its lights shielded against view from above, ploughing northwards through the night. It was disorientating. It occurred to her that she was like her baby, being carried in a dark confined space. She hastily dismissed the thought, afraid that it would lead to her drifting away to who knew where or when. Feeling her eyelids drooping and knowing she needed sleep, Brigid had to give in and hope for the best. She wondered when they would cross the border, knowing that somewhere out there in the night before they did, she would be passing close to where Doreen slept with her bereaved sister.

#

After many hours of fitful sleep and strange dreams – although, thankfully, they *were* only dreams – Brigid woke abruptly as a shouted announcement sounded down the corridor: "Change here for Glasgow!" She started up and stared around her.

"We have to change?" she asked.

"If ye're goin' tae Glesga, aye," said the man next to her.

"I have to go there to change for somewhere else. I thought this train stopped at Glasgow!"

"Nae such luck," shrugged the man. "This train's bound for Stranraer tae catch the boat for Ireland."

Brigid rose stiffly and lifted her carpet bag from the luggage rack. A couple of minutes later, she was standing outside on the open platform of a small country station. It was still dark, the ground was slippery with frost, and a chill wind carried the tang of salt sea air.

Chapter Fourteen

Mary filled a flask and packed it in a bag with the sandwiches she had prepared for the journey. They were heading for the station before it was even light, determined to catch the earliest available train to London, as Walter had done only yesterday. He came into the kitchen and picked up the provisions.

"Ready, Mary?"

She turned to face him. "One thing, Walter." She took a breath. "We're bringing back Brigid and her baby – when the little mite is born, he or she stays. We're not having any dealings with these people in London again. Neither they, nor anybody, will take Brigid's child away from her." Her eyes were fierce.

Walter coloured to the tips of his ears, his expression pained. He sighed, conceding. "I give you my word, Mary."

Mary clutched his hand in silent thanks, and they made for the front door.

#

More than twenty passengers alighted at the little station with Brigid. They headed for the wooden building on the platform and crammed into its tiny waiting room. There weren't enough seats. A young soldier gave up his place for her and cheerfully stretched his long legs out on the floor in front of her. She sat down gratefully and asked where they were. There were no signs, of course – they had been removed in case of enemy spies.

"Dunragit," came the reply.

"And where is that?" she asked.

"Scotland," he answered, "the south west. Galloway."

Brigid was none the wiser. "Is it far to Glasgow? Do you know when there will be a train?"

"Your guess is as good as mine," he shrugged. "If we make good time, it'll tak a couple o' hoors tae get there."

Day began to dawn and there was still no sign of a train. Brigid ate the sandwiches she had brought from London and held her head under the tap in the toilets to gulp some water. The air in the waiting room was thick with a pall of cigarette smoke. Gazing out of the window, she saw, on the other side of the tracks, fields stretching down to the sea, which glimmered icy blue. After a while she stood and picked up her carpet bag, stepping around people on the floor.

"Someone is welcome to my seat," she said. "I'm going out for fresh air."

"Ye might be oot there a while. Dinna freeze yersel', lassie!" winked a sailor lounging near the door. He rose and followed her out of the waiting room.

"Smoke?" he asked, offering her an open packet.

Brigid shook her head. "I don't, thanks, not really. Just now and again."

He shrugged and smiled, cupping his hand against the icy breeze as he lit up. "Where are ye bound? Can I keep ye company?"

Brigid coloured as she realised she was being chatted up. "I'm going to the place where I want my baby to be born," she said.

The sailor's eyes widened. "Nae bother," he shrugged. "Good luck."

They had reached the edge of the station building and could see up a country road to a straggle of houses not far away.

"Well, would ye look at that!" he cried.

Brigid followed his gaze. A painted, covered wagon drawn by a horse was coming down the lane.

"A gypsy caravan!" said the sailor.

"A vardo!" cried Brigid, who had heard of them from her mother.

The heavy-set mare plodded to the station, where a middle-aged man reined her in and jumped down. His companion, a youngish woman with a shock of fair hair falling from the back of a colourful headscarf, handed him a battered leather bag and jumped to the ground holding a strange wicker basket which she had been carrying on her knee.

"She's nae gypsy!" the sailor muttered, his eyes keen.

Brigid took in the woman's unfashionable long skirt and ancient boots. She kept her eyes on her as she walked away from the sailor to the nearest bench, breathing in the chilly air, so refreshing after the waiting room and the long, restless night on the train. She drew her coat around her, but she didn't mind the cold. The thin covering of frost was already thawing in the sunlight falling on the tarmac.

The woman from the vardo climbed the steps to the platform and waved at her companion.

"Dinna forget!" he yelled.

"I'll stay in touch, Johnny Fa," she called back, "but dinna wait for me!"

"Ah, ye'll be back in nae time, beggin' tae marry me!" he retorted, a wicked grin playing about his lips.

Brigid smiled wryly as the sailor stamped out his fag end and melted back into the waiting room. The woman shook her head fondly, but her expression was grave as she walked past Brigid to the last bench at the end of the platform. As she did so, the basket in her left hand, held by a thick leather strap, shook of its own accord and a strange cry came from inside. Brigid jumped. The woman kept walking, setting the basket and her bag at her feet when she sat, tossing her head back and inhaling the sharp salted scent of the sea. Whatever was in the basket was not at peace, however, for it scuffled inside and more odd noises issued forth; deep, strangled croaks and clicks. Brigid couldn't help staring.

The woman tutted. "Hush, you!" she hissed. "What's got you in a flap?" She glanced round and locked eyes with Brigid. She looked away, speaking again to the occupant of the basket. "No! Whatever it is, no!" The basket began to move of its own accord with the struggles of the creature within, and it juddered in the direction of Brigid's bench. The woman sighed and looked back at Brigid.

"It's a bird," she said. "My…pet, for want o' a better word. But not exactly."

Brigid stared at the basket. "Don't you have a cage for it?"

"He's never been caged in his life!" retorted the woman. She glanced away. "Sometimes I've had tae tether him, but not for a while…This is just tae keep him safe for the journey. He's never been on a train. Neither have I." She folded her arms over her patched old coat and stared ahead. The basket was still edging its way towards Brigid, a series of clicks coming from within.

"What kind of bird is he?" Brigid asked. "May I see?"

The woman looked appraisingly at Brigid. "He seems determined on it, although I don't know why," she said. She glanced at the station building. "Come over here," she said, "away from prying eyes."

She dragged the basket back as Brigid walked over and sat beside her. Bending, she unbuckled the straps and lifted the lid slightly. A beady black eye stared at Brigid, and a powerful bill stuck out and emitted a triumphant "Gwah!"

"A crow!" cried Brigid.

The woman shut the lid. "He won't appreciate that," she laughed. "He's a raven. Rab is his name, a wise and proud bird."

"Wow! Imagine having a raven for a pet!"

"As I said, he's not exactly that," said the woman. "He's more like a partner in crime." An irritated clicking came from the basket. "He tries tae keep me on the straight and narrow," she laughed. The morning sun caught the silver-gold of her hair, falling over her shoulders in spiral curls. Her face was tanned and creased around her eyes and mouth. "I'm Megan," she said. "Now, tell me about yourself, since Rab here seems sae interested in ye!"

Brigid opened her mouth and closed it again, suddenly wanting to retreat to her bench near the station building, if not further away. Why did she attract the attention of strange women? Not that Doreen Johnstone had been strange at first, but respectable appearances had masked the truth. This woman, with her gypsy scarf and tumbling blonde hair and a raven in a basket was definitely odd.

The expression in the woman's eyes changed. "Oh, I'm sorry!" she said. "We're a bit of a double act, me and Rab. I'm a fortune teller, an' he often selects my customers an' brings them tae me. I didna mean tae pry, no' really. But…well…he's sensed somethin' aboot ye."

Brigid stared at her. "You don't look like a fortune teller."

"Well, it's not what I was born to," smiled the woman. "Can we start again? I'm Megan, like I said. I'm not lookin' for money! I'm just following Rab's lead."

"I'm not going to tell you anything," said Brigid, raising her chin. "If you have the gift, if you have something to tell me, please continue." Her look was challenging. She wasn't sure she believed in predicting the future, and by her own admission, Megan wasn't even a gypsy born. She pulled off her right mitten and stuck her hand out towards her, palm upwards.

Megan shook her head. "I dinna need that." Her eyes roved over Brigid, taking all of her in. "You're pregnant."

Brigid laughed. "Almost anybody could tell that!" Her coat, when she sat, strained a little at the seams these days.

Megan didn't respond. She was busy staring into Brigid's eyes. "But there's more. You're caught up in somethin' ye dinna understand. Ye're runnin' away frae danger an' at the same time runnin' towards more."

The hairs on the back of Brigid's neck began to bristle. Could this woman know what had happened? Did she really have the gift?

"I know fae when I see it," Megan continued. "There are shades of other worlds around you, Brigid. Ye walk between them, between the worlds. No – ye fall between them. Ye canna control it. Somethin' is controlin' you."

Brigid's heart skipped a beat. "I had to get away from a bad situation – it was my choice, I managed it myself!" She had been surprised at her own daring, proud of it. She wondered if Fred was coming round yet. He would feel as if he had the biggest hangover of all time. It would be a while before he could function, and he would search for her before admitting to Doreen that Brigid had escaped. She was miles away. She had ensured her safety, and that of her child. She was heading for their destiny – even if she didn't know where she was going to sleep tonight.

"Oh, I've known what that's like," said Megan. "I'm on the move because of similar…the man that brought me, he wants tae marry me. But I'm not sure. I've decided tae dae ma bit for the war effort while I think on it. I'm goin' tae Ayr tae sign up for the Women's Land Army! An' I hope to be sent where I have some unfinished business tae see tae, somethin' I didna handle well. I think maybe we have things in common, Brigid."

"I wish you well," said Brigid, cold, polite. Megan's sharing of confidences wasn't going to encourage her. She was giving nothing away. She knew Megan's sort was good at building on personal information to make predictions and give advice.

Megan smiled wryly. "I'm no great shakes at fortune tellin'. It was somethin' I stumbled into while gettin' away frae somethin' else. I'm good at makin' a mess o' things."

Brigid raised her chin. "And you think I'm doing the same."

Megan stared at her intently. "I don't know for sure. I'm bein' straight with ye, Brigid. I have some gifts. I know about other worlds. I know that sometimes ways open between them. I know there are some who can pass between worlds at will, and others who stumble through by chance, and others who are called through. I can see you've been called. I don't need tae hear yer story."

"So what do you want with me?" Brigid's heart was beginning to pound under the scrutiny of Megan's blue-grey eyes. They were mesmerising. The expression in them shifted like the sea.

"Every sense I have is tellin' me tae warn you tae be careful. Ye don't know what ye're dealin' with, Brigid. Be careful who ye trust."

"I've learned that lesson, and I am," said Brigid.

#

It was early afternoon when the MacKenzies reached London. As the train drew into the city, they felt a rush of adrenaline at being within easy reach of their daughter; they headed straight for a taxi rank, the

Johnstone's address clutched in Walter's hand. It took a while to obtain a cab, but finally they did, settling on the back seat and reading the address out to the driver.

The man hesitated. "That part took a pounding last night, mister," he said, "but I'll run you there. Just warning you."

Mary's hand flew to her mouth. Walter patted her leg reassuringly. "I'm sure it'll be fine," he said. "Brigid wrote that they slept in an Anderson, remember."

Nothing could have prepared them for the sight that met their eyes as they drove through the area where the Johnstone's house stood – had stood. The driver turned into a debris-strewn road, rubble piled high on either side.

"I'm sorry," he said. He stopped and opened his window, calling to a policeman on the corner. "Which one was number twenty-six?"

#

The train for Glasgow finally pulled into Dunragit Station amidst great sighing clouds of steam, grey against the clear blue of the sky. Brigid managed to find a window seat. She barely acknowledged Megan as she sat down beside her. Could the woman not take a hint? She averted her head and gazed out of the window as the view changed from rolling green hills and fields to a coastal vista with islands on the horizon. They stopped frequently at tiny stations where all sorts of people climbed aboard; children travelling to school a couple of stops further on, smartly dressed people heading to work, women going shopping. It was enchantingly rural and different from anything Brigid had ever known. Her attention was drawn by a small island shaped like a currant bun, sitting in the sea in sun-drenched isolation.

Megan suddenly spoke. "Have ye never seen it before?"

"No," she said. "I've not been in these parts. I thought maybe you knew that." She couldn't resist the dig.

Megan ignored her tone. "It's called Ailsa Craig. I grew up on the coast near here." Her bird gave a croak and she shushed him as the other occupants of the compartment stared. The pet carrier was on her knee. She opened it a crack and slipped in some nuts from her pocket. "He knows we're near his old home. How did ye end up in Dunragit, Brigid?" she asked.

Brigid continued to stare out of the window. "I was on a night train from London, and we had to change there for Glasgow." Her tone was distracted now. "It's such a strange sort of island! It looks like a hill stuck in the middle of the sea. You could imagine magical creatures living inside it." Brigid turned round, forgetting herself in her wonder. "Can't you feel it, too?"

Megan stared at her. "It's also known as the Fairy Isle, or Fairy Rock," she said, adding in a whisper: "And you're right, Brigid. Not all fae dwellings or portals are on land. Not all fairy hills in these mystical isles are landlocked. I know about such things," said Megan. Her voice was barely audible now. "Take care."

A short time later, the train pulled into a much grander station, with a fine red sandstone hotel dominating the station buildings. It was obviously a larger town.

"This is Ayr," said Megan, rising. "This is where the next part of my life begins. Good luck, Brigid." Her raven emitted an enormous "Gwah!" which caused the other passengers to jump, and Megan jostled her way awkwardly out of the compartment, Rab's basket held aloft, her bag bumping into the backs of her long-skirted legs.

Brigid sat back with a sigh and tried to shrug Megan's presence off. She was glad the woman had gone. The train continued on its way, meeting a few delays as it left the coast behind and neared Glasgow. It was late morning when they arrived at Glasgow Central after a grim crawl through grey urban sprawl, the wastelands on the edge of any city. As a landscape, it was much more familiar to Brigid than the rolling hills and sea vistas of the south-west, which had been delightful. The station echoed with whistles and the roaring and clanking of trains. The light was strange; glancing up, Brigid saw a black roof, then realised it was a huge expanse of glass which had been painted, no doubt for blackout purposes. She enquired about the train to Aberfoyle and learned that she had to change stations, and also wait a while. Wearily, Brigid took herself out into the streets of Glasgow to find somewhere to eat before making her way to Queen Street Station.

#

Mary and Walter MacKenzie stared in horror at the pile of rubble which had been their daughter's lodgings. A policeman was trying to persuade them to go to a Rest Centre and await news there. He had explained to them that the first thing the fire and rescue services had done was to remove the rubble which had fallen on the back yards where the shelters were; but the Anderson at number twenty-six had been empty. The neighbours had gone to the Rest Centre, he told them; maybe their daughter and the couple who owned the house had gone away for the night, he suggested. There would have been plenty of warning to get to the shelter if they had been there.

Men picked their way over the wreckage of the houses, carefully shifting what they could, searching among the rubble. A weary-looking ARP warden appeared, a King Charles Spaniel on a lead. He unfastened the lead and gave the dog a pat and a shove.

"Go on, boy, see if you can find Fred!" He turned and spoke to the policeman. "I've checked, and he wasn't on duty last night," he said. "Maybe him and the missus decided to chance it. Charlie here"- he pointed to the dog sniffing over the ruins – "liked Fred. He loved animals, you know. His wife was too houseproud to let him have a dog. He might be able to sniff him out…"

Walter MacKenzie interrupted. "Our daughter was lodging with the Johnstones. I'm sure she wouldn't have taken the risk of not going to a shelter!" Even as he said it, though, he remembered a crucial night when she had done just that. He dismissed the thought; she would never have risked it again, especially not with a baby to consider.

The man looked thoughtfully at Walter. "The girl moved on," he said. "My wife is – was – friendly with Fred's Doreen." He put his hand to his mouth as a thought struck him. "She was in the family way again after all these years! What a tragedy!"

Mary frowned. "I don't think so," she said. "It's our Brigid who's expecting."

"Is she?" said the man. "I wouldn't know about that. Never met her, and don't think the wife did, either. But she definitely moved on. My Moira was here just the day before yesterday – Doreen had a tea party to tell her friends the good news. Four months gone, she was." He shook his head sadly.

"But Brigid is four months…" Mary began.

Walter held up a hand. "Wait, wait," he said. "We received a letter yesterday, written by Brigid the day before."

The ARP Warden made a face. "That was fast post for these times," he remarked.

"Never mind that," said Walter. In fact, it hadn't occurred to him, or Mary, in their relief. "It was written in this house, or what used to be this house!"

The policeman and the warden gazed at them, their expressions glazed. It had been a long night. Suddenly, there was excited barking. Charlie the spaniel was trying to dig. Men rushed over and began heaving bricks and masonry out of the way. Fred's friend hurried to join them. After twenty minutes' hard graft, they stopped and stared, turned to where the policeman stood with the MacKenzies, and shook their heads.

#

The policeman ushered Mary and Walter to a table in the Rest Centre and went to fetch them some tea. They watched as he spoke to the woman who seemed to be in charge. They turned and glanced their way. The woman called to a colleague to take over from her and walked towards them with the policeman, holding a tray with four cups, milk and sugar.

"Mr. and Mrs. MacKenzie, this is Mrs. Simmons – she's a friend of Doreen Johnstone."

Pat Simmons sat down nervously. "I'm sorry for your circumstances," she said. "I was just telling Sergeant Wilcox that I met Doreen yesterday. She was on her way to the station to catch a train to Durham to be with her sister, who's just been widowed. I don't know where your daughter went, but she left Doreen's house a few weeks ago." She paused, hand to her throat. "Somebody will have to tell Doreen what's happened!"

"I'll arrange for our Durham colleagues to be contacted forthwith," said the policeman. "Can you provide us with any more information about Brigid Watkins, though? Do you know why she might have left?"

"But she didn't!" Walter protested. "We have the letter…"

The sergeant held up his hand in a gentle silencing motion. "Is there anything you can tell us?"

Pat Simmons hesitated. "Well, Doreen…she came here and asked to borrow a kettle to steam open a letter. Said she had just taken a young widow in and wasn't sure of her…wanted to check she was all she said she was."

"And?"

"That's all I know. I was busy."

"When was this?"

"The morning of thirtieth December – I remember because of the dreadful night before."

"Do you have any idea who the letter was from?"

"It was one the young woman had written, as far as I remember," said Pat.

Walter and Mary glanced at each other, horrified. The sergeant misinterpreted their meaning.

"I know what a ghastly breach of privacy that was," he said.

They kept quiet. They knew Brigid must have given herself away in that letter; it would have been the one to Mary, via Molly White. It must have made her landlady suspicious. Yet they knew she hadn't thrown Brigid out as a result – not then, and not even later, after they had met the Watkins women outside the bank. She had been at the Johnstone's house until two days ago.

Pat's embarrassment and discomfort were obvious. Hand shaking, she began to sort out the tea things, pushing cups towards the MacKenzies and urging them to help themselves to milk and sugar.

"You're not in any trouble, Mrs. Simmons," the sergeant continued, kindly. "Please think. Is there anything else you can tell us? Did Mrs. Johnstone say anything about the letter, and what did she do when she had read it?"

Pat took a sip of tea. "I sent her to the kitchen to use a kettle. I didn't see her again until she waved goodbye to me before leaving. We didn't speak. This place was even busier than today, you remember what the bombing was like that night… I'm sorry I can't be of more help. But really," she said, looking directly at Mary, "your daughter was no longer staying there. I was round at Doreen's just a couple of days ago, at the tea party to announce her news. So that's good, isn't it? Your daughter's out there somewhere."

Walter slapped the table, exasperated. "But I keep trying to tell everybody – Brigid wrote to us from that house the very day of this tea party you mention!"

Pat shrugged. "Well, I was there, as I say, and there was no sign of her. I swear."

Sergeant Wilcox spooned sugar into his cup. "Thank you for your help, Mrs. Simmons," he said. "We won't keep you any longer. Do bear in mind that you would be advised not to help any individuals to tamper with the Royal Mail again."

Pat flushed at his words and stood shakily. "I hope you find your daughter," she mumbled, before scurrying away.

"But this letter…" Walter began.

"Walter," said Mary, "we have to tell everything."

Chapter Fifteen

Brigid felt better after a hot meal, and she seated herself on the train to Aberfoyle with a sense of anticipation. The end of her journey was in sight, although what awaited her there, she had no idea. As the train chugged beyond Glasgow, leaving Scotland's industrial heartland behind, the scenery became increasingly rural and more rugged, frosted at lower levels and snowy in the heights. It was entirely different to the south-west corner of the country which had enchanted Brigid that morning – stark in places, hills and mountains rearing. As they steamed into station after station and travelled further north, something more than the chill in the late January air made her shiver. This landscape was breathtaking, yet somehow overwhelming. She thought of Sir Walter Scott and "The Lady of the Lake", of his dramatic descriptions of the region she was entering; of beauty and grandeur, yet with a vastness which was overpowering.

The closer the train came to Aberfoyle, the more Brigid's confidence deserted her. With the optimism of youth and the conviction she had a mission, she had expected to feel exhilarated. Her father had been born in these parts, in Callander; she had thought it would be like a homecoming to arrive in the Trossachs of Scotland, that area between the Lowlands and the Highlands which was abundant in beauty and beloved of writers and artists. Instead, she felt apprehensive. Megan's words of warning came back to her, and she couldn't so easily shake them off now, as the train slowed to a halt at Aberfoyle Station late in the afternoon.

Her limbs were stiff as she climbed out and took in her surroundings; a long, low station building, forested hills and rocky crags beyond. The train departed and Brigid stood there as the steam cleared. Now she could see what was on the other side of the tracks – a river which glowed in the light of the sinking sun, and beyond that, the mound of a low, dark hill. The platform was clearing, the few people who had alighted with her looking purposeful as they hurried on their way. A chill wind crept up from the river. Brigid shivered. She had to find somewhere to stay.

The elderly station master was standing nearby, talking to a striking young woman Brigid had noticed boarding at Glasgow. She wore her sleek black hair short, cut almost like a man's; her brown eyes were large in a strong-boned face, and her lips full. There was a foreign air about her, her skin tone quite dark. As Brigid approached, though, she could hear that her accent was Scottish, and very like her father's – she must be a native. The station master turned and looked at her enquiringly.

"Can I help ye, miss?"

Brigid swallowed. "I'm looking for somewhere to stay," she said. "Could you direct me to a guest house, or anybody who has a room to let?"

The woman spoke. "You'll be lucky at this time o' year – there's no' much open, an' the military are billeted in what is." She stabbed her finger at the station master's tie. "There's more goin' on around here than anybody lets on. Is that not right, Mr. Brown? All these mysterious trains in the middle o' the night!"

"Now, now, Ria!" the old man winked. "Ye've tried tae get information oot o' me before, an' ye know ye're wastin' yer time!" He puffed out his chest and turned to Brigid. "She's right, though, miss…I'm strugglin' tae think…" His words tailed off at Brigid's panic-stricken look.

The woman called Ria noticed it, too. "It's no' the best time tae arrive withoot makin' plans," she said. "What are ye here for?"

Brigid opened her mouth, but had no idea what to say. "My father comes from these parts," she blurted. "A long time ago. I fancied a visit."

They were staring at her with curiosity. Ria spoke again. "Are ye in some kind o' trouble? Ye seem very young tae be pitchin' up here alone!"

"I'm a married woman!" Brigid protested. "Widowed. And in the family way, as it happens."

The station master's eyes showed both surprise and sympathy. "We've no room tae spare or I would take ye in myself, Mrs...?"

"Watkins," said Brigid. "Brigid Watkins."

He looked appealingly at Ria, whose eyes widened in a clear message. She would not take this stranger in. She sighed.

"I'll take ye tae my cousin's wife. Waifs an' strays are her job."

At that moment, the ground beneath them shook, just for a few seconds. Brigid looked around, puzzled, expecting to see a train approaching, but there was nothing; there had been no sound.

"That's not happened for a while!" said Mr. Brown.

"What was it?" asked Brigid.

"An earth tremor," he replied.

"Like an earthquake?" Brigid asked.

Ria laughed. "Nothin' sae dramatic, although they've had them at Comrie. Small ones. We're near the fault line that makes the Highlands high and the Lowlands low. The ground shifts at times. But ye're right, Mr. Brown, it's not happened for a long time."

Brigid stared around her and gasped. "Where...?" she started, but stopped. For a moment, it was as if the station had disappeared. She had glimpsed a small hamlet of strange-looking houses; curved, low-pitched thatched roofs, resembling upturned boats in their shape.

"What's wrong?" asked Ria. "Ye look as if ye've seen a ghost!"

"Nothing," said Brigid, who was doubting her own eyes; the scene had been so fleeting, she must have imagined it. "I'm just tired."

Ria stared at her. "Fit tae walk, are ye?" she asked. "It's no' far."

Brigid's attention snapped back. She was being taken to someone who made waifs and strays their concern. She wasn't entirely happy about that, but there seemed to be no alternative on offer.

"Yes, I'm fine," she said. "Your cousin's wife…are you sure she won't mind?"

Ria laughed. "It goes wi' the territory. She signed up for it when she married my cousin. He's the minister o' Kirkton, although he's an army chaplain these days. She'll not exactly be delighted tae meet ye, but she does her duty."

Brigid blinked. Minister's wife…Kirkton…army chaplain…She was being taken to Kirkton Manse! She was going to the house in which Rev. Robert Kirk had been born, and later lived as minister of the parish; where he wrote the very book she had in her bag; where Sir Walter Scott had been shown the manuscript and brought it to public attention when he visited over a century later, where he had written "The Lady of the Lake"! Brigid's spirits soared. She glanced behind her at the mound of the wooded hill beyond the river, and knew without a doubt that she was in the presence of Doon Hill. Colour crept into her cold cheeks. She barely registered that Ria was still talking until she heard Robert Kirk's name mentioned.

"…not one o' the Robert Kirk crowd, she wouldna be keen…"

"Sorry?" asked Brigid. "I was miles away."

"I was saying," frowned Ria, "that as long as ye're not one o' the Robert Kirk crowd, she'll no' turn ye away."

"What do you mean?" asked Brigid.

"One o' her husband's predecessors is a bit famous…"

"Or infamous!" laughed the station master.

"Aye, too true! Well, if ye haven't heard o' him, all the better. Ignore anythin' ye do hear. Susan gets sick o' tourists an' strange sorts turnin' up lookin' for information."

The glow which had suffused Brigid's cheeks faded away. She forced a smile and prepared to follow Ria, thanking Mr. Brown as they turned to go. Daylight was fading fast as they walked briskly along the pathway outside the station. When they came to the end of it, Brigid was surprised that Ria turned left; she had made to turn right, in the direction of what appeared to be the town.

"Kirton's this way," said Ria. "We call that bit the Clachan, an' the Kirkton is over the river."

Brigid nodded. She was going to Kirkton Manse, of course, but she hadn't realised it was a distinct place. It began to make sense as they crossed the bridge and she saw, to her left, the walls of a graveyard dominated at one end by a ruined church. Away across the wintry fields, Doon Hill hunkered in the twilight. She had seen this place when she had collapsed in the Johnstone's toilet just after Christmas, although it had been snowing in her vision; her spirit had soared above it like a bird, swirling with the snowflakes. She had to bite her lip to stop herself from grinning. It was just as well that waifs and strays were the business of a clergy wife; she was going where she was meant to be. It was all falling into place.

"Is your cousin's church elsewhere?" she asked Ria. "I can only see a ruin."

"Aye – the Victorians built a new one in the Clachan, but they kept the manse here. Tom and Susan are Episcopalian. Most folks here are Church of Scotland. I dinna bother wi' any o' it."

"How old is the ruined church?" asked Brigid.

Ria shrugged. "Georgian, I think," she said. "There was another one here before it, though. There are some very old graves at that end o' the kirkyard."

Brigid smiled to herself. Indeed there were, and one of them was Rev. Robert Kirk's, although legend stated that he wasn't in it, but captive in the Otherworld which existed inside the brooding bulk of Doon Hill. She was disappointed that the old church wasn't the one in which he and his father had served. As they drew nearer the manse, though, glimpsed behind the bare branches of a row of trees which screened the front garden, she smiled to see that it was very old indeed. It was a large house, its whitewashed walls standing out against the encroaching dusk under a grey-slated roof. At one end, a gable faced the road at a right angle to the rest of the building, and two attic windows nestled beneath a high stack of chimney pots.

They walked up a curving driveway to the front entrance, where a low porch in the angle formed by the gable looked like a later addition to the house. "I usually go roon' the back," said Ria, "but she'll insist on a visitor comin' in the front door – even if ye are a waif an' stray. Mind, if she decided ye were a tramp, she would direct ye tae the tradesman's entrance."

Brigid suppressed her joy at seeing Robert Kirk's former home, and braced herself to meet Mrs. MacKendrick, who sounded formidable. She was glad now that Doreen had thrown her job application into the Thames – it would never have withstood the scrutiny of this woman. If, by some miracle, she had sent for her, *she* would never have withstood her scrutiny.

Ria raised the robust thistle-shaped knocker on the storm door of the porch and hammered vigorously, then she stepped inside, opened the inner door and called, "Susan! Susan!"

Footsteps sounded from the stone hallway within, and a tall, elegant woman appeared. Her auburn hair was held back from her pale oval face by a jewelled clasp; her complexion was flawless, her eyes green as a cat's. She was holding a cigarette, and her long legs were clad in wide, draping trousers.

"I heard you hammering the door down!" she said. Her accent was English, clipped, upper class. "Why have you come to the front…?" Spying Brigid behind Ria, she stared at her, then back at Ria, perfect eyebrows arched questioningly.

"This one pitched up at the station, same train as me," Ria said, nodding towards Brigid. "Needs somewhere tae stay. She's pregnant."

Brigid bridled at Ria's abrupt introduction. She stepped forward. "I'm Mrs. Watkins," she said pointedly. "Brigid Watkins. I came here without making any plans for accommodation, and when I asked, I was advised there was probably none to be had. Ria kindly suggested you might be able to put me up. I would be very grateful. I can pay." She clutched her carpet bag with both hands, heart beating wildly. This woman before her was not what she had expected, not at all. Brigid had expected to see a woman in tweeds like those on the train from London, although younger of course; but Susan MacKendrick looked neither tweedy nor old enough to have five children.

"Good evening, Mrs. Watkins," said Susan MacKendrick. "Well, you'd better come in, if you really have nowhere else to go. Payment won't be necessary. Christian charity is the duty of the Church, after all."

Brigid's cheeks burned with shame and anger at such a cold welcome. "Then I will make a donation to your husband's church," she said. At that moment, if there had been any other option, anywhere else she could have gone, she would have walked away – Robert Kirk's manse or not. In their different ways, these were two of the rudest women she had ever met. As she stood there in the doorway, she felt a prickling over her heart, where her iron brooch was pinned to her blouse beneath the layers she had donned to keep warm. A confusing sensation of homesickness combined with strength and determination flooded her. The brooch was her mother's gift to her but also an inheritance from her father's great aunt, who had come from these parts. It was her talisman. She acknowledged the feeling and took a steadying breath as it passed over her. The brooch had made itself felt before. She didn't know what the connection was, but she was meant to be here, in Scotland, in this very house – and deep down, she had known it for weeks, ever since she had seen the advert.

Susan MacKendrick eyed her with more interest. Her lips twitched as if amused. "That won't be necessary, although welcome should you wish to do so. I've had a long day and I'm tired, Mrs. Watkins. Please do come in." She stood aside to let her pass and spoke to Ria. "I'm just about to start preparing the evening meal, if you'd like to stay?"

"Thanks, but I'll head home."

"Did your business go well?"

"Aye, all settled. It's all mine now!"

"Good. You deserve it. See you soon, Ria."

Brigid thanked Ria for her trouble. She had gone out of her way, after all, even if grudgingly. Susan MacKendrick indicated that she should hang her coat on the stand in the hallway, and she did so reluctantly, aware of the money concealed in it.

"If you'd care to join us in here," said her hostess, showing her into an untidy sitting room, "I'll make you a cup of tea and get on with some cooking."

As she walked into the room, five heads gathered around the fireplace turned to look at her. "Hello," said Brigid.

"My children," smiled Susan, with the first warmth Brigid had seen in her eyes. "They can introduce themselves. No doubt they'll entertain you. They're a little excited by the earth tremor." She left, closing the door behind her.

Brigid caught sight of herself in the mirror over the mantelpiece. Her curly hair was always on the wild side, but now it was a bush. She glanced down at her grubby knee-length socks, worn for warmth. What a picture she must present! She had been travelling since yesterday evening and had only splashed water on her face in station toilets. No wonder Ria had described her so disparagingly. She smiled at the children, who were studying her with shy curiosity. They were all very close in age, one little more than a baby. Brigid needed to use the toilet. She wanted to freshen up. "I just need to speak to your mother," she said. "I'll come back and we can introduce ourselves." She left the room and followed the smell of cooked vegetables to the kitchen, where she found Susan MacKendrick grey from head to toe with a dusting of National Flour.

"Mrs. MacKendrick, might I use your facilities?"

The woman looked up. "I forgot to put my apron on, and the damned bag burst!" she said. "And I also forgot to put the kettle on. Sorry. I had the veg all prepared for Woolton Pie. I'm not the best with this awful pastry, or what passes for it these days."

Brigid smiled. "It's not the best time to have an unexpected guest," she said, "when you're planning on making something you're not expert at."

"I'm not expert at anything!" cried Susan MacKendrick.

It suddenly occurred to Brigid that there didn't appear to be anyone else in the house. Was there any chance the minister's wife had not managed to fill the position she had advertised? "I need to freshen up," she said. "Travelling since yesterday, you know, practical clothes for the journey…but I'm not bad with pastry, if you would like some help with dinner."

"What? Oh, you mean tea. I've forgotten what dinner is – a nice affair around eight o'clock, no? They call lunch dinnertime here, and what we're about to eat is tea, like children in the nursery. Later, and less formally, I would call it supper."

Brigid tried to hide her amusement. "Where is your home?" she asked. "I mean, where do you come from?"

"It's one and the same thing," Mrs. MacKendrick replied. "My home will always be London. Fell for the charms of the assistant minister at our family church, didn't I? Bit of teenage rebellion, truth be told, not the catch my family expected…never dreamed we would end up here in the back of beyond. Then no sooner have we arrived than he buggers off to be an army chaplain!"

"You have your hands full," Brigid observed, her tone sympathetic.

"You don't know the half of it!" said her host. She sighed and dusted off her hands. "Look, I was rude when you arrived. I'm sorry. I'm not a natural at being Lady of the Manse, as they call me here. Can we start again? Please call me Susan, Brigid."

"Thank you, Susan. I'm sorry to have turned up like this, and I am grateful."

Susan MacKendrick shook her head. "You poor thing. Where have you come from?"

"London."

"Well, isn't that a coincidence? My home town. Shocking journey, though, and you in the family way. Forgive my appalling manners – of course you must want to use the facilities." She turned to the sink and began running her hands under the tap. "Come with me. I'll have to make up a bed for you, and the room will be cold. There are some logs outside – once this is on to bake, I'll set a fire and…"

"I can do all that!" Brigid interrupted. "If you just show me the way to the toilet and the room I'm to have, then I'll get the pie done for you. Leave out the bedding and I'll see to it and the fire."

Susan smiled. "What a helpful girl. Sorry, young woman! You really don't look old enough to be married."

"Widowed," said Brigid.

"Oh, I am sorry!"

Brigid shrugged. She didn't want to get into this conversation now, not until she had time to think about it. "Thank you. Let's make a start!"

"Follow me," said Susan, "but I'll see to the bedroom. Freshen up, then stay here in the warm and cook the meal. You would be doing me an enormous favour."

A mixture of hunger and curiosity about their mother's guest drove the MacKendrick children to the kitchen while Brigid was working. There were two girls and three boys, all aged between eighteen months and eight years. The eldest, Katie and Simon, were twins. Brigid didn't have much experience with children, but she chatted to them and found small tasks for the older ones to do, while their mother was busy preparing her room. She thought again about her application, how foolish it had been, and yet…the position hadn't been filled…

Susan reappeared and settled herself beside the kitchen fire, her youngest on her knee, a cigarette in her hand and a glass of sherry by her side. "I'll just make the most of having someone to cook for us!" she laughed. "I keep this for special occasions! I'll pour one for you, shall I?"

"Don't waste it on me," smiled Brigid. "Another time, maybe. Don't you have any household help?" she asked, keeping her eyes fixed on the pot she was stirring. "It can't be easy, this big house and five children, and still being expected to do parish duties."

Susan sighed. "I could have a local woman, or girl, come in if I chose," she said. "In fact, the parishioners would be livid if they knew I had advertised for a Londoner to live in, in preference to any help available here."

Brigid kept stirring. "Why did you want someone from London instead of a local?"

"A clergy house is a goldfish bowl," she said. "The last thing I need is someone from the parish coming in here, seeing how we live. Anyway, I…I rather hoped for some company from home. I thought there might be some suitable young woman who would like to get away from the city, especially now."

"And there wasn't?"

"None of the applicants met my requirements."

Brigid took a deep breath, her eyes still averted. "Would anyone other than a London girl do?" she asked.

"I liked the idea of having someone live in," said Susan, "so I thought it might as well be someone I could relate to. Someone from home."

It had never occurred to Brigid as odd that a Scottish minister's wife should advertise in a London newspaper. "I've lived in London," she said, turning to face her. "My husband was a Londoner. And the truth is, I have nowhere to go."

Their eyes met and Susan looked at her appraisingly. "We'll talk once the children are in bed," she said, drawing on her cigarette.

Chapter Sixteen

Pall Mall,
London.
The twenty-seventh December, 1688
My Dear Margaret,

The year will have turned by the time you receive this, and therefore I bid you New Year greetings and hope the birthday of Our Lord has been pleasantly observed by the locum who took my place. My thoughts are with you and my son, and of course with his mother who lies buried in Balquidder – your cousin, and loved by us both, therefore I know I am not being an insensitive husband in mentioning her. I daresay Colin has little memory of her and that with every year we are married, he thinks only of you as his mother. I thank you for your concern for him, but I am convinced that your care of him will be sufficient to quell any worries he may have. Do not become hysterical, my dear. Continue your charitable duties in the parish and assure our people that all is well. Remain calm for their sakes – do not inflame any fears they may have.

There has been little change here since last I wrote, and therefore I see no need to return before the completion of the work to which God has called me. We live in tumultuous times, it is true, and you may have heard by now that King James has escaped the capital, leaving the way clear for William of Orange and his wife Mary; but here in Pall Mall, we keep our heads down and continue with the greater good which is our work for the Gospel in our beloved Highland homeland. This will be of more benefit to my flock, and our brethren throughout Gaeldom, than my speedy return. It is my belief that such an action would only serve to increase alarm, when I do not think there is cause for it.

In addition, I find that my influence here is broadening and my research may be of importance to the nation. Yes, Margaret, you read that correctly! I was invited to dine last week with Rev. Edward Stillingfleet, who like me and Mr. Boyle is a seventh son. He was interested to hear my views on the heightened awareness often conferred on seventh sons, namely the Second Sight. As you know, I am so blessed, or I would not have seen the things which I have regarding the inhabitants of the fae commonwealth; but Mr. Boyle, much as he would wish it, does not have this gift. Rev. Stillingfleet is a lauded preacher and writer with a distinguished career. Perhaps because of that same discretion in such matters which Lady Ranelagh asked of her brother, he refused to be drawn on his own experiences; my guess is that he has had them, but does not admit to them. He ventured the opinion that occult phenomena such as the Second Sight entail the danger of contact with the Devil on the part of those who indulge in them, and are therefore sinful. It is my belief that he suppresses the gift in himself, therefore, either out of genuine fear for his soul, or fear for his reputation; for he is an ambitious man.

When he said this of the occult, I thought perhaps he intended either to chastise or warn me, or both. Then, however, he mentioned Mr. Samuel Pepys, a notable man here in London (although I might also add, a man of some notoriety). This Mr. Pepys is a Member of Parliament and holds the post of Secretary of the Admiralty. He is a member of the Royal Society, that body of men devoted to science of which Mr. Boyle was a founding father. Certain members (such as Mr. Boyle, as we know) are interested in so-called occult phenomena, believing they exist as part of nature and should be researched as they may have usefulness. My dear, Mr. Pepys believes Second Sight may be of use in the defence of the realm!

I knew then that the reason I had been invited to dine with the Stillingfleets was to encourage my own research into the phenomenon! Rev. Stillingfleet might say what he thought appropriate to his station, but he was tipping me the wink and telling me to continue with my endeavours. To ease any qualms he might have, I put forward my theory that what appears to us now to be supernatural, or preternatural, will one day be proven to be entirely natural. There is far, far more to God's creation than we know. As if to confirm the direction her husband was giving me, Mrs. Stillingfleet, who had remained politely silent during this part of our discussion, suddenly spoke saying she would be most interested to read my conclusions on the subject; no doubt the great man had instructed his lady beforehand to give the encouragement he himself felt unable to give in his position.

Therefore, my dear, you see that I *must* remain in London. Firstly, I *must* finish the work on the Gaelic Bible which I have begun, and secondly, I *must* continue to meet with influential men. I am learning so much from Mr. Boyle, I am in the confidence of men like Rev. Stillingfleet, and who knows, this Mr. Pepys M.P., Secretary of the Admiralty, may wish to meet with me also. My research is now, as I say, of importance to the nation, as well as to the upholding of the Gospel and faith itself in these dark days.

But fear not, gentle Margaret! I cannot continue my research into Second Sight and the Secret Commonwealth of those various creatures known to us until I return to my own dear land, and since I have been entrusted with this great work, I will not be in London indefinitely. The Lord Himself shall send me home to continue His purposes at the time of His choosing; meanwhile, I must be His obedient servant and concentrate on the Gaelic Bible, and you must be patient and accepting of my absence.

My fond love to Colin, and to you, dear wife.

Your husband,

Robert Kirk

#

Margaret let the hand holding the letter fall into her lap, and she sat back in her chair, stunned.

Chapter Seventeen

Walter MacKenzie helped his wife to her feet, shame and fatigue eating into him. They hadn't expected to have to stay overnight, and the Underground had been the only option. They had slept – when they could manage it – slumped upright in a cramped, damp corner, and Mary seemed to have aged ten years since yesterday. Now, he feared today's news would finally break them, but they would cling to any shred of hope remaining. The police had managed to trace Doreen Johnstone to her sister's house near Durham, and had confirmed that Brigid wasn't with her. She had been in such a state of shock that she had simply looked blank when the young woman was mentioned, Sergeant Wilcox had told them; and given her condition, the officers hadn't thought it a good idea to press her. He refused to comment when Mary reminded him that Doreen Johnstone was most certainly not pregnant; they had told him the whole story and shown him both letters. "We have to keep an open mind," was all he had said.

They made their way out on to the streets and found a hotel serving breakfasts. Neither felt like eating, but Walter insisted on it. It passed some time while they were waiting, engaged their minds and their hands as they drank scalding tea and cut up their food, forcing it into their mouths. They used the hotel facilities to freshen up as best they could, and headed for the police station Sergeant Wilcox had named last night, to see if there was any more news.

He met them himself. "Mrs. Johnstone will be returning to London today to make arrangements for the funeral," he said. "We intend to question her. We're as anxious as you are to hear any word of your daughter."

That sounded better than yesterday's attitude. "Do ye believe us now?" Walter asked.

Sergeant Wilcox seemed to be considering his words. "The men have been working at clearing the rubble since daybreak. There is no sign of your daughter." He didn't say "of her body" – he didn't have to; if she was in the house, that's all there would have been left to find.

"But where else would she be?" asked Mary. "The letter…"

"Is it possible she may have gone out for the evening, or to stay overnight? Didn't she have friends she might have gone to? She had lived in London for a time following her marriage, after all."

"She never mentioned any," said Mary, "and she would have. I tell you, that letter may be in her handwriting, but she didn't write it!"

"Hush now, Mary," said Walter. "Maybe she had recently made new friends. She could still be alive. We have to hang on to that."

Mary's eyes filled with tears. "It's her birthday," she said. "St. Brigid's Day. She might be a widow and pregnant, but she's only eighteen!"

The policeman glanced sympathetically and cleared his throat. "Mrs. Johnstone and her sister caught the night train. They're coming here once they've visited the site of the house."

Mary and Walter glanced at each other. "Should we wait or come back, Sergeant?" asked Walter.

"It's up to you."

"Maybe a walk would kill the time better," said Mary.

They left the station, and they didn't have to think twice about where they were heading. They turned their footsteps in the direction of Fred and Doreen Johnstone's house; or at least, of where it had stood.

#

Far away, in Scotland, Brigid woke to the sound of chickens clucking and calling. She started up in panic, thinking herself back in her room at the Johnstones'; but the weak morning light illuminated the high ceiling and spacious proportions of her new abode – the wallpaper which came from another era, the furniture scarred with time and use which didn't shine as Doreen's bedroom suite had done. She heaved a sigh of relief and fell back on her pillows. London was a world away.

She smiled as she remembered that it was February first, St. Brigid's Day, her birthday. At that very moment, she felt a fluttering low in her abdomen, like butterfly wings. "Hello, little one," she said, touching the place where her baby lay beneath her rounding flesh. It was the first movement she had felt. She eased herself out of bed and over to the window. She couldn't see for the frost patterns which feathered it like fancy glass; her breath misted in the air. Pulling her dressing gown around her, she picked up her toiletries bag and made her way to the bathroom along the hallway. It was a cold, cavernous room into which a toilet, bath and sink had been fitted at some time in the last couple of decades, she guessed. The water which dribbled into the washbasin was lukewarm, but she felt fresher and returned to her room to dress warmly before going downstairs. The family was gathered in the kitchen, Susan doling lumpy porridge into bowls while Katie and Simon toasted bread on long forks in front of the fire.

"Good morning," she said.

"Good morning, Brigid," Susan replied.

"What would you like me to do?" she asked. She had secured her place. It hadn't been too difficult, but Susan MacKendrick was no fool. She had speared Brigid with a steely look as soon as the children were bedded down the night before, and had demanded to know the truth. Pregnant young widows didn't travel hundreds of miles in the dead of winter, in wartime, without good reason. Brigid told her the bare bones of the truth; a child conceived when she had been injured in an air raid, no memory of what had happened; her father unwilling for her to keep it; a landlady who had wanted to steal her unborn baby, and her husband, a predatory landlord, who had held her captive. She simply said she had managed to escape when Fred dozed off; no need for too much detail. She had always wanted to come to Scotland, to the Trossachs, where her father had been born. She had found her way here rather than to Callander; best to admit no special interest in Aberfoyle, after what Ria had said.

She told Susan about her shotgun wedding and the miscarriage. She didn't say why she had gone to Tower Hill that fateful night, or about the strange experiences she had had then and afterwards. She left Susan to draw her own conclusions about the child she now carried – she knew she would think what everybody else did. It was all believable, and she intuited that Susan MacKendrick wasn't a typical clergy wife who would judge. She had offered herself as household help in return for board and lodging, just as Susan's advert, which of course she didn't mention, had stated.

Susan had been appalled at her story, at how much she had endured in the past few months. "You should have gone back to your parents after what happened with those wicked people!" she said. "They would be horrified! Your father surely wouldn't deny you a roof over your head after that?"

"He would still insist on me giving birth in a home, one where they take away your baby," shrugged Brigid.

"But you're married! Well, you were. Could you not say the baby was your husband's?"

"That was Mam's plan, but it would only have worked when my time came – and at a Catholic hospital, not one of their convent homes. Dad just won't let me keep the baby, Susan, and I want my baby."

Susan had paced the floor for long minutes, smoking, deep in thought. "You have to sort this out with your parents, Brigid," she said finally. "You can stay here meanwhile, and help me out. But there are five children in this house already, and much as I love them and sympathise with your plight, I don't need another! I might end up looking after you and your child! What I need is someone to help take care of mine!"

Brigid had agreed with the confidence of youth and the certainty that she was meant to be here. She intended to make herself indispensable. It shouldn't be too hard – look at Susan, struggling; look how far she, Brigid, had come in being able to cope. She was eighteen today and treading on sacred ground. She felt invincible.

"The first thing you can do after breakfast," said Susan now, "is clear up the dishes and clean the kitchen. Then go to the Post Office and send your parents a telegram – just letting them know where you are, and that you're safe and well. I'll point you in the right direction. You can write in more detail later, to start resolving this issue. Take some time to yourself after that. I want you to take care of the children this afternoon while I ride my horse."

Brigid agreed. She had fully intended to let her folks know what had happened in London and where she now was, but when she did, she was going to omit any mention of coming home. She would inform them that she had found a respectable place to stay, and employment. That would do for now. Dad wouldn't want her back, and Mam would just be relieved she was safe. She wondered if they had ever looked for her, and if Mam had told Dad about her deception in looking for digs rather than going to a convent. She knew they would receive that letter dictated by Doreen soon, so she wanted them to know her latest news as soon as possible.

Breakfast was a lively affair, with the children providing distraction. When she had finished her chores, she grabbed her rustling coat from its peg in the hallway – she must remember to take her money out of the lining – pulled it on with a thrill of anticipation, and paused in the porch to take a deep breath of sharp wintry air. A thick frost lay over everything; the hills glistened in the strengthening sun and the sky was light blue. She could see the ruined church which had succeeded the one where Robert Kirk had ministered, and – joy of joys! – she could see the wooded mound of Doon Hill, fabled place of fairy fame. She was living in Aberfoyle, in the house where Sir Walter Scott had stayed while writing "The Lady of the Lake", where he had heard about Kirk's manuscript and brought it to public notice. This first of February, her eighteenth birthday, the day of the saint for whom she was named and of the goddess who had preceded her in myth, was a morning shot through with golden threads of magic. Brigid had to stop herself breaking into a skip as she headed down the slippery path into the lane, where snowdrops uncurled dripping heads as the sun released them from frozen torpor.

#

One of the Metropolitan's few female police officers had been dispatched to meet Doreen Johnstone and her sister and take them to the site of the house. Doreen's appearance had suffered after a night of tearful travelling. Her makeup had worn off and run in places, and her hair was untidy. She stood in front of the wreckage of her home and ran her fingers through her curls, then she opened her handbag and began to reapply lipstick.

Jess, her sister, put an arm around her. "Doreen, love, are you sure you're okay?"

"Fred likes me with my lipstick," she replied.

"But love, Fred is…he isn't here to see you."

Doreen turned round to look at her sister as if she didn't understand her words. The lipstick and compact mirror fell from her hands and she staggered backwards.

The policewoman steadied her and cleared her throat. "You've seen everything there is to see, Mrs. Johnstone," she said. "Perhaps we should proceed to the station…" Her words trailed off as she became aware of someone rushing at them, someone who pushed between herself and Doreen.

"Mrs. Johnstone?" The woman's Irish accent was soft, but her voice insistent.

Doreen didn't heed her, didn't appear to hear.

Jess answered. "Who's asking?" Her tone made it clear that her sister was in no state for intrusions.

"Where's my daughter?" cried Mary MacKenzie. "And are you really pregnant, because I don't think you are!"

"How dare you…!" cried Jess.

Doreen raised her gaze from the ground as if pulling herself back from far away. She focused on Mary. "My baby!" she whispered hoarsely. "My poor baby!"

"There is no baby!" yelled Mary, and before anybody could stop her, she grabbed the front of Doreen's coat and began to tear at the buttons.

"Madam, stop! Step back!" the police constable ordered.

Jess grabbed Doreen and tried to pull her away, and Walter took hold of his wife's shoulders.

"Mary, leave her be!" he cried. "This isn't the way!"

Stunned, Doreen belatedly tried to fight her off, but Mary had hauled up her sweater and was pulling something out of her skirt. She jerked it away in triumph. It was a homemade cushion of sorts, moulded to fit around Doreen's middle. She pushed it at the policewoman, a savage look on her face.

Walter spoke first. "What have you done with our daughter? Where is she? Where was she when this happened?" He indicated the bomb site.

The police officer stared at the cushion. "I think we should all go to the station and discuss this properly…"

"But my baby!" wailed Doreen, rising panic in her voice.

Jess's mouth had fallen open in shock. She gave herself a shake. "Doreen, love, I think we have to do what the police constable says…"

"It'll be dead!" Doreen sobbed. "It'll be dead with her and Fred if they didn't go to the shelter! Why didn't they go to the shelter?"

"Did you have her tied up or locked in?" cried Mary. "She was your prisoner! Where in the house was she being kept?"

Doreen broke free of the group and headed for the rubble of her home, screaming for Fred.

#

Brigid followed Susan's directions into the Clachan of Aberfoyle and found the small Post Office. The middle-aged Post Mistress could barely conceal her curiosity as she dictated her telegram – DISREGARD LAST LETTER (STOP) WELL AND IN ABERFOYLE (STOP) WILL WRITE WITH DETAILS (STOP) BRIGID

"Where are ye staying?" asked the woman. The thick lenses of her glasses made her look like an owl.

"At Kirkton Manse," Brigid replied.

"And what brings ye here?"

Brigid hesitated. "I'm helping Mrs. MacKendrick," she said.

"Oh – that's nice. She's no' the type tae cope wi' a manse an' all they bairns. Very fancy for these parts. This goin' tae Birmingham, then? Is that where ye come from?"

"Yes," said Brigid.

"Are ye related tae the minister's wife?"

"No."

The Post Mistress gazed at her expectantly, waiting for further information. She sucked in her cheeks as Brigid remained silent, and gave her a sideways glance from head to toe as she turned to fetch her change. When she held it out, Brigid took it in her left hand to display her wedding ring. She exited thankfully and headed back towards Kirkton. The small town and its shops which Susan had assumed would interest Brigid, held no interest at all. She followed the road back towards the river, where pockets of ice lingered in shadows on the banks. It was so quiet she could hear the dripping of things thawing. It was the only sound. Everything else was still. Not even a bird sang. Crossing the bridge, she followed the kirkyard wall as she had yesterday, but this morning she entered the gates, her pulse quickening with anticipation.

She picked her way over the rough, frozen grass, winding between gravestones which grew more ancient and crumbling the nearer she came to the ruined church. Robert Kirk's grave was within the shadow of its walls, she knew, facing Doon Hill. She found it near one of the corners, and gazed enraptured at the recumbent stone with its frosted mossed Latin inscription that she had so long dreamt of seeing. Her brooch, pinned to her coat lapel today, caught the pure light of the morning sun with a gleam which drew Brigid's eye; she looked down. Despite its iron blackness, every ash leaf and thistle stood out in stark relief. It was a beautiful piece of jewellery, made more so somehow by the light of the land in which it had been forged, for it had belonged to her great great aunt who had lived in Callander.

As Brigid pondered this thought, the earth suddenly trembled as it had last night; some loose masonry fell from the ruined church. It lasted only seconds. Not a leaf on any of the evergreens was shaken from its bough. Fast on its tail, a blast of wintry air coiled around the kirkyard. It came from the east, where Doon Hill dominated the view, Robert Kirk's grave facing it. Brigid shivered and, puzzled, followed an impulse to turn within its icy coil. She found herself looking at Kirkton Manse, her new home. However, the trees which screened the front garden were no longer there, and three faces peered from the windows. Two were framed by the attic windows of the jutting gable, high up under the chimney stack, and one was in a room below them which she knew to be Susan's bedroom. She was too far away to make out any features, but one of the faces in the attic was dark. Aware she was suddenly in shadow, she glanced behind her and saw not a ruin, but an ancient church – fully built, yet bearing no resemblance to the ruined shell beside which she had been standing. It was not that church restored, but another entirely. It was momentary. She blinked and it was gone. The Georgian ruin was back. The manse half-hid behind its bare-boughed trees again. There was nobody at any of the windows. The wind had departed, too.

"Hello," said a voice to her left.

Brigid jumped and saw an old woman leaning up against a headstone, her arms folded and a smile on her face. At first, she wondered if she was really there. The woman seemed unperturbed, as if she had felt neither the earth tremor nor the icy blast. Brigid's manners deserted her.

"How long have you been there?" she asked.

"Long enough," said the woman.

#

Sergeant Wilcox entered the interview room and took a seat. "Well," he said, "that was a fine way to behave! If Mrs. Johnstone *had* been in the family way, you could have been charged."

"But she wasn't. She isn't expecting. How long would it have taken the police to get round to investigating that?" asked Mary.

Walter took her hand. "I agree with my wife," he said. "It was her word against ours, and would you have done anythin' tae gainsay her? Now, tell me what you intend to do to find our daughter!"

Sergeant Wilcox folded his hands and leaned forward. "We've put the word out around all the Underground shelters in case she heads to one. We'll keep an eye on the train and bus stations, since you say she has money and could travel. But she's an adult and, well – she's a needle in a very big haystack. We think she'll end up back in Birmingham. We're sure she wasn't in the house, although we're having the rubble searched again as we speak – but it looks as if she left at some point after Mrs. Johnstone went to Durham. She would want to get right away before Mr. Johnstone woke from…whatever it was. We assume he fell asleep because inebriated, and missed the air raid warning, although his wife says he wasn't given to drink – but since she was away, he may have indulged. I think your daughter's probably headed home at this very minute, if not there already."

Walter squeezed Mary's hand. "I think he's right, love."

Mary was rigid with tension. "And what about her – that woman? Does she get charged with imprisoning Brigid?"

"We can't prove anything except that she faked a pregnancy," said the policeman, "and that isn't a crime."

"But have you questioned her? Has she admitted to keeping Brigid locked in, or whatever they did with her?" Mary pressed.

Sergeant Wilcox sighed. "Doreen Johnstone can't admit to anything," he replied. "She's in a psychiatric hospital, heavily drugged and unable to speak. We'll question her again when we're able, but…"

"I want justice for Brigid!" cried Mary.

Walter put an arm around her shoulders. "That won't help us find her," he said. "We need tae concentrate on that, an' forget this sick woman. She's lost her man. She's paid the price. She can't have been in her right mind in the first place. Forget her. She doesn't know where Brigid is. The sergeant's right – let's go home an' hope she's there, or wait for her tae turn up. Brigid's alive, Mary, that's the important thing."

Sergeant Wilcox nodded gratefully.

#

"Did you feel it?" asked Brigid, eyes wide with shock. The old woman was still leaning against the gravestone.

"The earth tremor? Aye."

"And the blast of wind?"

"Such things happen, Sassenach." The crone's eyes sparkled with mischief, as if she was enjoying Brigid's discomfort.

"What things?"

"More than we can ever understand. Ye'll need my help, lassie."

Brigid stared at her. She was dressed in threadbare tweeds, a faded scarf on her head and gnarled fingers curling from filthy fingerless gloves. Megan flitted across her mind, the woman with the raven - her warning about danger and being careful who she trusted. Her elation had evaporated, carried away by the shifting of the earth and the icy blast from Doon Hill. Earth tremors happened – Ria had explained that. Sudden winds occurred all the time. Yet Brigid had seen strange houses after the tremor last night, although she had dismissed it as her tired imagination. She wasn't tired now. She knew what she had just seen.

"What do you mean? You don't even know me!"

The old crone laughed. "Calm doon, lass. Ye're carryin'. I have eyes in my head."

It took Brigid a moment to understand what she meant – she had noticed she was pregnant, carrying a child. She shrugged, trying to sound casual. "I don't need any help, thanks. I'm fine."

"Ye will when yer time comes. An' maybe before that. I'm Agnes Clay, the midwife hereaboots."

Brigid glanced at her arthritic fingers. Her nails were dirty. She thought of Molly White, of her cleanliness and neatness and the scent of lavender which surrounded her. Surely, even in an out-of-the-way place like this, a woman such as Agnes Clay could not pass for a midwife?

"Did you see anything different just now?" she asked, still captive to her vision.

"Times and places have many layers," Agnes replied. "Sometimes things get stirred up." She unfolded her arms and pushed herself stiffly away from the headstone. "I'd best be on my way. We'll meet again."

Brigid watched Agnes Clay hobbling over the frozen graveyard. It occurred to her that she hadn't asked her name; how did she seem to know her, and that she had come to stay? She shivered, suddenly chilled to the marrow. She hurried back towards the manse, remembering this time to use the back door as Susan had told her. At the rear of the house, she found herself in a yard where chickens pecked and clucked. There were some ramshackle outhouses, but also a large stable which had been kept in good condition. Part of it had been turned into a garage, although no car was in it. The other half housed Susan's horse. The top half of the stable door was open, and Brigid recognised Ria's voice. She walked over and leaned inside.

Ria was holding one of the horse's rear hooves while Susan caressed the animal's muzzle. They both looked up.

"Here she is, the wee English lassie," said Ria, "lookin' as if she's seen a ghost again!"

"Did you feel the tremor?" asked Brigid. "Another one!"

"Aye. Things are restless," said Ria. Her glance fell on Brigid's brooch and a look of curiosity crossed her face. She quickly turned her attention back to the horse.

"Two tremors in such a short space of time!" Susan exclaimed. "I've only known one before last night, in all the time I've been here. Katie and Simon are pulling the study apart looking for geology books. You might check on the younger children, please, Brigid, see if they're alright now. They were a bit scared. I said they could all have their sweet ration."

Ria laughed. "The bairns are scared? She's scared!"

Brigid flushed at being the object of Ria's disdain yet again. "I'm not scared!" she cried. It was true. The word she would use was *disturbed*. She had been disturbed by several things. "The post mistress was nosy," she said. "Then I met this old woman called Agnes Clay…" She remembered just in time what Ria had said about Susan's dislike of "the

Robert Kirk crowd". She wouldn't say she had been visiting his grave. If they had seen her from the manse, fair enough…but she knew none of those faces at the windows belonged to the present occupants of the house. She had glimpsed the manse, but not in the present time. Yesterday, she had briefly seen the Clachan as it was hundreds of years ago, a cluster of boat-shaped hovels. She understood that now. She couldn't tell anybody any of these things. Yet she had a feeling Agnes Clay knew.

Susan sighed and rolled her eyes. "Mrs. Monteith is a gossipy old trout! And Agnes Clay is an old bat. I won't have her in the house, much as she thinks she has a right."

Ria dropped the horse's hoof and straightened up, hands on hips. "Aren't you two English gossips havin' a fine time puttin' doon the locals?" she said.

Susan ignored her kinswoman. "It's a small town, Brigid," she said. "Not a lot happens, usually. There's more going on with the war these days, but any new arrival attracts attention. There are few people who won't be curious about you, I'm afraid."

"Agnes Clay saw that I was expecting. The post mistress did, too, but Agnes Clay said she was the midwife and I would need her. I could hardly believe it!"

"No, neither could I, when I arrived pregnant with the twins," said Susan. "I've never had anything to do with her. I got a doctor in each time. You won't need her, because you won't be here," she added decisively. "Did you telegraph your parents?"

"Yes."

"Good. Make sure you write to them today or tomorrow, to catch Monday's post."

Brigid turned to go. She didn't know what else to say.

Ria spoke. "Auld Agnes has done a fine job o' bringin' bairns intae the world for as long as I can remember," she said. "She delivered me an' my brother. Ye shouldn't judge somebody just for bein' a bit different!"

Susan pursed her lips. "I judge her indifference to cleanliness as being unseemly in a midwife," she said, "as you very well know. Added to which, she is decidedly odd, but I would be prepared to overlook that if I had confidence in her professional abilities."

It occurred to Brigid that Ria herself was different. Today she was wearing a boiler suit. She had rolled up the sleeves, revealing surprisingly muscular forearms.

Ria shrugged. "The shoe's cracked," she said. "I can fit a new one this afternoon if ye bring her over."

As Brigid blinked in surprise, Susan said, with a hint of pride, "Ria's our local blacksmith, don't you know. She made that fine door knocker which heralded your arrival yesterday."

"Oh!" Brigid exclaimed. "That's wonderful! A woman blacksmith! Gosh!"

Ria's face remained expressionless, as if it was no great matter. "Following in my father's footsteps, God rest his soul," she said. "My brother was never interested. Loves the Navy. He intends tae stay in once the war's over, so everything's been signed over tae me. That's what I was doin' in Glasgow."

"Congratulations!" said Brigid. "Condolences on your father, though." She turned to leave again.

"Brigid?" said Susan.

"Yes?"

"This is a small town. Word gets around, even if you're here only a short time. The baby…it's your husband's, agreed? It's best all round if everybody thinks that."

Brigid blushed fiercely.

"Ye mean it's not?" asked Ria, looking shocked yet highly amused. "The wee widow's been back in the field?"

"Ria!" snapped Susan. "Go and see to the children and put the kettle on, Brigid dear. I'll explain to Ria. She's not a gossip. We can trust her."

Brigid choked back hot tears and headed for the house. Megan's warnings reverberated inside her head.

#

In Birmingham that morning, Molly White performed her usual toilette with the herbs and the potions and the fire. It was becoming a strain, a ridiculous strain. She was a walking bag of bones! She couldn't carry on with her life's work much longer. She thought about the MacKenzies. She had gone to their house last night, very late, in the hope that they would be back, and Brigid with them. She didn't understand the significance of her unborn child or why Brigid had been chosen, but she was prepared to bring the baby into the world before her retirement. She could hang on for five more months. The fact that the MacKenzies weren't back was worrying. Still, it was wartime – train services were all over the place. Something was niggling at her, though – something from that sixth sense which used to be so acute, but which was diminishing. It bothered her all day, like a fly buzzing around her head, only to zoom away when she tried to catch it.

As she sat down mid-afternoon with a cup of tea, she opened the range door and concentrated hard. She sighed and shook her head; no, she couldn't make the connections. Just then, there was a sharp rap at the door. She opened it to find a telegram boy standing there. Anybody else's heart would have skipped a beat, but she had nobody to lose. All these years, all these lifetimes, all these babies, and nobody to lose; it was rather sad. She took the telegram and read it. It was from Walter. They had been delayed in London. They hadn't found Brigid. They would explain later. She frowned. She had felt in her bones that something was wrong.

"Any reply, Mrs. White?" the telegram boy asked.

She forced a smile. "No, Timothy, thank you," she said. "I'll just get my purse." She knew the lad – she had delivered him fifteen years ago. He looked smart in his uniform. When she returned, he was studying the address on his next delivery. He dropped it as he reached for his tip, and Molly picked it up. She stared at it. It was for the MacKenzies.

"Well, there's a coincidence," she said, although she didn't really believe in coincidences. "My telegram was from them. They're not here – they've been delayed in London." She nodded at the telegram addressed to them. "This could contain important information that they really need." She stared at the boy appealingly.

He swallowed. "I can't give it to you, Mrs. White," he said.

"Do you remember their Brigid?" she asked.

He did. Boys didn't forget Brigid. He nodded.

"She may be in some trouble, Timothy," said the old lady. "Nothing that's her fault. She needs help. This could be vital information."

She could see that he was wavering. She opened her purse and fumbled for more coins. The lad's face flushed and he stood to attention.

"You can have it because it's you, Mrs. White, he said, "because everybody trusts you. But I don't want extra money. I only want to help Brigid."

"Good lad," she said. "Thank you, Timothy. You'll go far."

"I'll take my route past the MacKenzies' house so that I'm away for the right amount of time," he said, "and we must never tell a soul, except the MacKenzies."

"You have my word, Timothy. Thank you."

He turned to his bicycle. "I hope it helps Brigid."

Molly closed the door and carried both telegrams inside. Every sense was tingling, even that sixth one that had been drowsy of late. When she read Brigid's words, the pieces began to fall into place. She remembered the job application which she had mysteriously managed to draw to her. She recalled Brigid's brooch. Memories long whitewashed as century succeeded century began to swim to the surface of her mind. Her hand began to tremble as the shock caused her flesh to shrink back into its creases and hollows, and pain flooded every crack of her ancient body.

#

Kirkton of Aberfoyle, February 1st, 1689

Margaret stepped out of the door of the manse and breathed in the scents of morning. Birds were singing, heralding the change in the air. Spring was a long way off, but the frost wasn't so thick today and it hadn't snowed for a week. She drew her cloak closer and smiled as she trod down the path to the lane, intending to walk by the river as far as Doon Hill. She could never quite bring herself to climb it alone; the tales

Robert told of the place made her wary, although she would gladly have gone with him had he ever encouraged her. She hadn't heard from him since his letter at the end of the year, nor had she replied. Several times, she had set out her writing materials but had given up, not knowing what to say. They were growing apart before they had had a chance to grow close, thanks to this stay in London which had made matters worse instead of better.

Margaret reprimanded herself. The sun was shining, the season was turning, and she wouldn't allow herself to dwell on her worries today. She had a plan for dealing with them, a ritual of her own devising which she had carried out before at times of stress. She drew from a pouch attached to her belt a great number of small fragments of paper which she scattered above the river. Here they called it the Avon Dhu, but further downstream it became the mighty Forth which spilled eventually into the Firth of Forth. She walked along as she scattered yet more of the parchment petals, most of them landing in the water after dancing on the eddying breeze.

"Carry them away, Avon Dhu," she whispered, imagining their journey and feeling the burden lifting from her shoulders as Robert's shredded words drifted away from her, sodden and worthless, their passing observed by nodding snowdrops on the riverbank.

She walked on after they had all fluttered and floated on their long journey to the sea, feeling light of heart and a little giddy at this private act of rebellion. The path leading to Doon Hill was in front of her before she realised it. She looked up to the hill's summit, which wasn't very high; it was such an insignificant hill. Yet so many tales were told of it. Margaret shuddered, but at the same moment felt a steely resolve enter her veins. She would climb the hill. She would face her fears. Nobody who lived in these parts scorned belief in the fae, as many lowlanders now did in this modern age of science; Robert's fragmented words would be borne past places where folk would think he was a madman. Margaret only doubted his sanity in pursuing the creatures for whom mounds like this Doon Hill were entrances to their secret world.

Well, she wasn't seeking them. She wanted nothing to do with them. She merely wished to take in the view from the summit on the fairest day the year had yet offered. She started up the path and was soon amongst the trees, their bare boughs like the beams of a great roof above her head, supporting the winter-washed blue of the sky. When she felt the atmosphere change, she put it down to her imagination; yet somewhere a memory stirred and she paused for a moment, looking around. There was no breeze here away from the river, and everything was still. Not a branch, not a twig, stirred; the undergrowth on either side of the path was devoid of all movement, as if time had been suspended; no birds sang or fluttered from branch to branch now. The earth trembled just as she had remembered what this state of torpor, this sudden silence and suspension of life and time, heralded. It wasn't much of a tremor, and it would have been felt more keenly indoors – she knew this from her childhood in Comrie, where the ground often shook and items fell from shelves in her family home. Here, in the woods, where it had been so still, the trees shook for a few seconds, most noticeably the slender trunks of fairly young silver birch a few yards away. As soon as it was over, the birds began to sing again.

Margaret's feet faltered only slightly, but her heart beat wildly. She stretched out her arm and steadied herself against the solid trunk of an ancient oak. It was said that this was no time to be caught upon a fairy hill. She turned round to run back down the pathway when she realised she wasn't alone. A young woman stood beneath a nearby ash tree, snowdrops clustered round her feet, staring at her. Margaret put her hand to her throat and clutched her cloak. She would have to pass the woman, but she didn't want to look at her or engage with her in any way at all – for who knew what she might be, after the earth had trembled on Doon Hill? Margaret began to walk quickly on shaking legs, eyes downcast, fixed on the pathway.

"Good day," said the woman. "It's fine out, isn't it? Always a good sign when it's bright and clear on St. Brigid's Day."

At mention of the saint's name, Margaret slowed and looked at the woman. The creatures of the hill took little to do with saints' days. She was young and slender, hair so fair it was almost white, loosely bound in a plait hanging down her back to her waist. But she was solid, face round and cheerful, her skirt a muted shade of brown with a clean apron over it, and a plaid wrapped around her shoulders; apart from that skein of hair, there was nothing fae about her. Margaret stopped, feeling a little ashamed; she might have insulted someone new to the parish in her mistaken fear.

"Good morning," she said.

The young woman came closer, and Margaret detected the scent of lavender. Perhaps she had sewn some dried flowers into her hems, she thought, or carried them in her pouch. She had heard no news of any newcomers, let alone such a gentle beauty as this who would have been noted and caused much talk.

"It's Margaret, isn't it?"

Not Mistress Kirk. Not even "the minister's wife." The woman was gazing into Margaret's eyes, and although Margaret realised now that she had been duped, the scent of lavender grew stronger and she felt drowsy as she stared back into the cornflower eyes of her new acquaintance. Her feet refused to move. She was rooted like a tree.

"There's no need to fear," said the fae woman. "I am one of the kind who seeks to help mortals. You've been sent to me, Margaret. My powers drew you into my knowing and I will help you. I know of your troubles." She drew a bottle from the pouch at her waist – a fine glass bottle such as a noblewoman would own – and she anointed Margaret's forehead with its contents, a sweet-smelling emerald-hued oil which began to trickle down her face. Margaret, unable to raise her hands to wipe it, managed to purse her lips closed as the liquid found its way to them.

"No – don't resist," smiled the woman. "Let it linger on your lips, on your tongue, smooth and warm and sweeter than sugar. Swallow it. I promise you, Margaret, it will give you your heart's desire."

She couldn't fight it. Her lips parted and she admitted the delicious drops, licking her lips when they had gone and all that remained were the silver trails they had made upon her face in their journey to her mouth, from her forehead down either side of her nose, like angel's tears.

"Who are you? What are you?" she asked. "How do you know my name and my heart's desire?"

"I am one who has passed through the veil," replied the woman. "I have ways of seeing and knowing, and my aim is to help those whom others of my world would harm. You would call me wise woman or midwife. In giving you your heart's desire, I seek to save your husband from great danger. You know this danger of which I speak. Be a good wife to him when he returns; let not your heart be hardened. The child which is your heart's desire could be his salvation."

"Could be?" asked Margaret.

"I can help you conceive, then you must make of it what you are able. I can assure you of the child's safe delivery. A boy. Bind your husband to yourself and your son and keep him home."

"Do you also know of his first wife in the kirkyard at Balquidder?"

"Aye. As I say, keep him home — what is bone under cold stone to flesh in a warm bed? Believe in yourself, Margaret."

"I am not as beautiful as was she, nor have I the same sweet nature. I am not as good."

"You have your own beauty and strengths, Margaret. Discover them. Own them. You are enough."

The woman stepped away and began to walk through the undergrowth. Margaret noted that the ground was trampled beneath her feet, as beneath any mortal's.

"What is your name?" she called after her. "May I seek you again?"

The woman paused and turned. "You may. Whisper my name thrice under the ash, and return next day at the same time. My name is Molly."

She continued on her way and was soon lost to view. Margaret turned and ran for the open ground beside the river as fast as her legs would carry her.

#

Dusk was falling when Brigid managed to gain some time to herself and slip away from the manse. She had found looking after five children for several hours entertaining, but exhausting. At least it had taken her mind off the natives of Aberfoyle, and she had dismissed the incidents which had upset her earlier. Frost was settling on the fields again as she followed the course of the Avon Dhu towards Doon Hill, snowdrops closed against the cold and curled to face the night. The air tingled, penetrating her skin where it was exposed like pinpricks of icy needles. Where the sun had sunk below the horizon, the sky was pink-streaked against deepening shades of blue, and the river breathed mist into the shadows. When she reached the foot of the hill, it was too late to climb it; she was disappointed, but reminded herself that she would have plenty of opportunities.

She ventured up the pathway a little, just to sample the atmosphere, standing for a moment beneath the boughs of a great ash tree, leaning against the girth of its enormous trunk. She almost wished something would happen, but it didn't; not really. No trembling of the earth and seeing things as they once were. Nothing but a sound like a sigh which seemed to come from the trees, from the undergrowth, from the hill itself; a sigh of something within nature and yet outside it, a sigh that was almost a gasp of triumph. Brigid shivered slightly – she was where she was meant to be, but she still had no idea why. The sun set on St. Brigid's Day, her birthday unacknowledged by any save herself that year.

Chapter Eighteen

Mary and Walter MacKenzie – and Molly White – waited impatiently for Brigid's promised letter to arrive. Her parents' relief at the telegram was tempered by concern – where was she living, with whom? Why had she taken herself all the way up there? What were her plans? Fragments of memories came back to them – that she had said the baby had to be born in Scotland; Molly also reminded them of the job application, which she had burned since it seemed irrelevant, a flight of fancy. They had put Brigid's notions down to her state of mind following all the trauma she had known – her husband's death, the miscarriage, being injured in the Blitz and finding herself pregnant again – and they couldn't imagine that she was any better now, after running away and falling into the clutches of a deranged woman like Doreen Johnstone. Mary and Walter were determined that however happily she might think herself situated, they were going to fetch her home.

Molly listened to them, nodded and reserved her judgment. With the flood of memories which had overwhelmed her and left her gasping for breath, she recognised the significance of the job application Brigid had made. Aberfoyle. Kirkton Manse. A minister's wife. Molly knew this place, this house. It would be another woman, a different minister's wife, of course. Two hundred and fifty years had passed since she had dealings with the inhabitants of Kirkton Manse. She wouldn't have remembered at all if it hadn't been for Brigid and the barriers of magic and time that Molly had forced open in her efforts to find her. Yet since she had, it must have significance, and she was involved, like it or not. No matter how exhausted she felt, how much she longed to slink away into retirement, she was involved.

She still didn't know how all the pieces fitted, but the strange conception of Brigid's child on an ancient sacred mound, her claims about it and her determination to go to Scotland to give birth…and to that place, that house…Molly could only conclude that great matters were unfolding between the worlds. Brigid had been chosen for some purpose known only to those forces which were active in her life, whatever they might be. Molly couldn't imagine how they had found her on Tower Hill, and led her to live in the shadow of Doon Hill; not that the mound by the Avon Dhu cast a shadow as far as Kirkton Manse; not in a physical sense, anyway.

When Mary arrived at the door with Brigid's letter, she invited her in, right to the back of the house, to the kitchen where her daughter had stood a few weeks earlier. She saw the look of wonder and heard her intake of breath.

"It's like visiting the wise woman back home in Ireland!"

Molly smiled. "Sit down, Mary. We need to talk. But first, let's hear what Brigid has to say."

As she read her letter, Molly nodded in approval that the young woman had wisely omitted to mention any supernatural influences. She had been brutally honest about Doreen and Fred Johnstone, and the danger in which she had found herself from both – and also about how she had escaped. Her flight to Scotland, she explained, was an urge to get as far away from London as she could, to somewhere she had always dreamed of going. She wrote of her circumstances and said she hoped to persuade Mrs. MacKendrick to let her stay. She said she felt safe in Aberfoyle, where she was sure the Johnstones couldn't trace her, and she begged that they would understand.

Molly finished reading and looked at Mary. "This must have been very difficult for you to read, although the main thing is that she's well. How has Walter taken it?"

"Well, he's relieved, of course," Mary replied. "Relieved that she's safe, and also that her nonsense seems to have stopped – no talk about

The Lady of the Lake and having to give birth in Scotland because the baby's special. But he wants us to go and get her as soon as possible. It's ridiculous to think she can stay there for long – the minister's wife has five children of her own! And of course," she added, "he's really cut up about that evil man's intentions towards her. Especially after what must have happened on Tower Hill, when she was taken advantage of – raped. I can hardly say the word. He just wants her home where he knows he can protect her."

Molly took a deep breath, considering. She thought of the two letters which her magic had drawn to her, letters which the wind had carried over a river – probably the Thames – one of them the application for a household help at Kirkton Manse. She guessed that one of the Johnstones had disposed of those letters after reading them; but Fred was dead and Doreen was in hospital, and likely to require treatment for a long time. The loss of her husband had come on top of behaviour which revealed how damaged she had been for years, since the death of her only child. Molly sighed.

"Brigid isn't in any danger from the Johnstones, we know that," she said, "but she doesn't. And she admits to drugging Fred Johnstone in order to escape. Nobody would blame her for doing what she had to do. But Mary – she may have killed him. That's a lot of tablets. He might have been dead before the bomb hit. We'll never know, but…"

"He got what he deserved!" cried Mary. "How many others had he treated like that lass he picked up on the streets? Or innocent young women going about their business? Who knows what he's done! And nobody can prove Brigid harmed him in any way. Walter and I know what you're thinking – we intend to tell her to keep quiet about it! But nothing would ever be proved anyway."

"I'm thinking of Brigid's wellbeing," said Molly. "I don't think we should tell her he's dead. Of course she should keep quiet about what she did, and I'm perfectly sure she will – she's a sensible young woman. But she'll think maybe she caused his death, and that's an awful thing to live with even if the man deserved it. It could be harmful to her and the baby, set her back."

Mary frowned. "So what do we do, then? We can make her come home anyway, but she would feel better, I'm sure, if she knew the Johnstones were no threat."

Molly sighed. "I've sensed, Mary, that what you called Brigid's nonsense – about the fae and all that – isn't such nonsense to you as to your husband." She also sensed that the days of them making Brigid do anything were over, but she didn't say that.

Mary shifted and looked away. "I was a country girl from Ireland, Molly. Such beliefs are mother's milk there. Things happen. Oh, belief is dying away now in this modern age, or at least people say it is – but things still happen. They happen, Molly. There are places where they say the air is thin between worlds – that there's more than one world. Times when it's thinner, too…"

Molly reached out and took her hand. "I know, Mary, I know. I have something to tell you." She began at Aberfoyle in 1689. She had no memory of her postings in between then and arriving in Birmingham many years ago, but she told Mary what she was and what she knew of Aberfoyle and Kirkton Manse.

When she had finished, Mary sat and stared at her friend as if she should have known – as if she had always known there was something about her. People's thoughts and memories concerning Molly White were vague, their perceptions hazy. When you tried to think about how long you had known her, and that she hadn't really changed, your thoughts scattered and you didn't dwell on it. "So Brigid's baby," she said now, realisation dawning, "is special, as she claims? And she's where she's meant to be, like she said?"

"Yes."

"How on earth am I supposed to explain this to Walter?"

"We'll have to work together on this, Mary. I'll tell him the shock of Fred Johnstone's death and Brigid's implication in it could be detrimental to her fragile mental health. You'll have to tell the police something – say she turned up at relatives in Scotland, that she escaped the house when Fred was drunk. They're not going to pursue the matter further, with his wife in a psychiatric hospital. Also, Brigid's had one miscarriage at around the same stage as this pregnancy, and we might risk bringing on another one if we put stress on her now. I'll suggest she should be left in ignorance in the place where she feels safe, until the baby is delivered. I have to be the one to do that, Mary, and I want you with me. We have to go to Aberfoyle for the birth."

#

It was more than two weeks before Brigid had a reply from her parents. With each day that passed, she felt a little freer, relieved that they hadn't seen fit to charge up to Scotland and demand she accompany them home. When the letter arrived saying they understood – expressing how horrified they were at what had happened to her, and that they wanted her to be well and happy above everything – she was pleasantly surprised. Now she had to think what she should tell Susan.

They had become friends. Brigid was working hard. The manse was in a mess and downright dirty in places, and she had taken it upon herself to begin sorting it. She had created order out of a chaos of toys, books and papers, and set about washing down walls and panelling, skirting boards and furniture. She dusted and polished and was working her way from bottom to top, from the kitchen to the public rooms at the front and up the stairs to the bedrooms where she and the children slept, and Susan's room, and the unused ones. As she worked, she imagined Robert Kirk in these rooms. She wondered if he had used the same study, if his bedroom had been the one which Susan and her husband had chosen. She imagined him and his wife entertaining guests – it would have been his second one, wouldn't it? He had left his first wife buried in Balquidder. Sometimes she had to stop herself thinking this way. She had a feeling of being watched at times when she was alone, and she told herself it was her imagination for dwelling on former occupants too much. At least there were no more eerie earth tremors with their accompanying effect of catapulting her momentarily into the past.

She was aided by the snow, which fell thickly, cocooning her in her new home. The older children, Katie, Simon and Laura, trudged back and forth to school regardless, and the playtime larks with snowballs and snowmen combined with the effort of going and returning rendered them exhausted and much earlier in bed than usual. Brigid and Susan enjoyed cosy chats in front of the fire in the evenings. She was careful never to mention Robert Kirk, but each morning, she opened her curtains and gazed across the kirkyard to his grave, then up and over the fields where the Avon Dhu, which meant "black river" coursed between cotton-wool banks of snow to Doon Hill, snow clad and sparkling against a bleached blue sky. At times when blizzards swirled in, she remembered what she had seen when she had heard the icy voice in the Johnstones' bathroom, and she felt a little dizzy and anxious, disorientated by the whirling white wonderland which gave glimpses of Robert Kirk's grave before sweeping it away and revealing Doon Hill, only to snatch it as if it wasn't really there, a fragment of another world. She kept her precious books hidden in her carpet bag, where she had once again concealed her money in the lining.

She was as honest as she could be with Susan when the letter from Birmingham arrived. She didn't mention it until they were alone, then explained how she felt about being as far as possible from the Johnstones, and that her parents, although they wanted her to come home, had agreed to respect her wishes.

Susan smiled. "Well, I'm glad your father's had a change of heart, at least," she said.

"I don't know whether it's a total change," shrugged Brigid. "I'm not at all sure he would let me keep the baby. But he seems to care more about me than he did a couple of months ago."

"I'm sure he loves you, Brigid. You're a lovely young woman and you've made yourself very useful here." Susan sighed. "I'm not altogether certain about you staying, though. I mean, how long would it be for? And another baby in the house, and me probably ending up looking after the two of you for a while as well as my own! It's not what I expected of a live-in help, Brigid."

Brigid still didn't know exactly why she had been summoned to Kirkton Manse, why things had fallen into place to bring her here. All she knew was that this was where her baby was meant to be born.

Sometimes, alone in her bed, where it was safe, she concentrated hard, hoping to hear the voice again, hoping for a vision to show her why this was her destiny, but nothing came. "My Mam, and her friend the midwife who delivered me, want to come for the birth," she said. "They intend to rent a cottage," she added quickly. "I suppose they'll expect me to go home with them in due course." She couldn't imagine that she would go with them now, though. Surely her child was meant to be raised here, in the land of his birth, for some special purpose?

"But would you feel any safer from the Johnstones then, with a new baby? Surely, if there's any threat from them at all, it would be then? And you've said yourself, you don't know what your father intends for the child."

Brigid shrugged. It would all work out somehow. "Please may I stay meanwhile, Susan? That Doreen's mad, crazed, and he does everything she says. And he knows I know what he is, and he might come after me to try to make me keep quiet, who knows…I don't want to risk losing this baby. Now, I mean, in pregnancy, as well as after." Her clear blue eyes were honest and pleading.

Susan hesitated. "Alright. But I'm not making any long-term promises. We'll see how things go."

"Thank you! I can't thank you enough." Brigid suppressed a slight shiver of trepidation as she wondered exactly what the baby's birth would visit upon Kirkton Manse and her unsuspecting friend.

#

It was mid-March before spring showed any signs of coming. By then the blizzards had become showers of hail, sleet and driving rain, and weeks of wearying slush which froze anew each night into blackened treachery to life and limb. It was a relief to see the sun shining and beginning to conquer. On the first day when pavements and roads were almost clear and there was a little warmth in the air, the older children disappeared to run wild like animals allowed out to pasture. They frolicked around the glebe for a while – the piece of land allocated to the minister on which to keep livestock in days gone by, now used only by Susan's docile mare, Cherry – but after a while, they were nowhere to be seen. Susan asked Brigid to go and look for them.

She headed past the kirkyard and crossed the bridge over the river to the Clachan, calling their names and stopping to ask a local couple if they had seen them. Throughout the weeks of bad weather, she had regularly donned boots borrowed from Susan, newspaper padding out the toes as they were too big for her, and she had trudged this way on errands. She was becoming known to the townsfolk, and her story had gone round the place like wildfire – or at least, the version of it she could tell. Despite their reserve, the people were well-disposed to the pregnant young widow. The couple now told her they had seen Katie at Ria's smithy. Brigid had never been there. They hadn't seen much of Ria during the snows, and Brigid had been glad of that. She sensed that the woman resented her in some way. She followed the directions she was given and heard the sounds of metal being hammered before she turned the corner down the lane where the smithy was situated. When she came to the open door, she gasped at the sight of Ria, glistening with sweat as she worked at a large glowing implement on the anvil. The forge lit her from the side, making shadows of the hollows of her face and accentuating her strong cheekbones and brows. She was smudged with dirt and looked more exotic than ever, like some goddess from a creation myth of far-flung lands. The spell was broken the minute she looked up, hammer poised, and spoke.

"If it's no' the wee war widow! Ye'll be lookin' for the imp that's drinkin' milk in ma kitchen."

"Hello, Ria. I'm looking for two imps – the twins."

"I've got Katie here," she said. "I'll give her a shout." She pulled off her gauntlets and wiped her hands on the sturdy protective apron she wore over her boiler suit, which was half-unzipped, the top hanging from her waist, sleeves trailing the beaten earth floor.

Brigid followed her out to the small cottage which adjoined the smithy, but Ria stalked in the door and didn't invite her to follow. She reappeared with Katie a few minutes later.

"Any idea where your brother is?" she asked.

"I think him an' his pals went tae torment Auld Agnes," the girl replied. Her tone was matter-of-fact; she was neither telling tales nor fazed by the information she imparted.

Ria noticed Brigid's hesitation with amusement. "It's a sport for the bairns," she grinned. "Aye has been. Nae malice in it, an' nae offence taken by Agnes."

Brigid stared at her – Ria had been enraged at her and Susan for gossiping about the old crone. Ria's attention had wandered, though. She was gazing keenly at Brigid's iron brooch, worn today on the lapel of her coat.

"That's an interestin' piece o' jewellery ye have there."

"Thank you. It belonged to my great-great-aunt."

"Aye, it looks like an antique. I reckon it was old long afore she had it, though. Yer father is frae these parts, I think ye said?"

"Callander," Brigid replied.

"And is that where his great-aunt lived?"

"I think so."

"Do ye know anythin' aboot the brooch?"

Brigid shrugged. "No."

Ria regarded her intently. "How dae ye keep it in that condition?"

"It's always been that way," said Brigid. It had never even occurred to her that the piece showed no signs of age. "It wasn't worn for years. My mother kept it in a box with other bits and pieces."

Ria stepped forward and ran her index finger over the thistles and ash leaves. She drew back suddenly as if she had had a shock. "Do ye really know nothin' aboot this?" she asked.

Once again, Brigid felt the discomfort of being under Ria's questioning; those dark eyes which penetrated while giving nothing away. "No," she said. It was true as far as it went. She knew nothing of the brooch's history beyond the fact it had belonged to her great-great-aunt. She couldn't begin to explain to anybody, least of all Ria, that it felt like some sort of talisman, that at times it seemed to have a life of its own. She smiled wanly at the blacksmith and thanked her for fetching Katie, and they set off together, Ria staring after them.

Katie said Auld Agnes lived near Doon Hill, and Brigid sighed at having to trek a long way in a totally different direction. The fields were still too muddy for a short cut – she would have to pass the manse and go round by the road once they were over the river and back in the Kirkton. She was now almost six months pregnant and, although fit and well, she was heavier and beginning to feel the strain. Katie said she would show her the way, or she might get lost. Brigid was glad of that – she hadn't encountered Agnes Clay since the episode on her birthday in the kirkyard, and she was keen to avoid the old crone if possible. She sent Katie in to tell her mother what was happening while she ploughed on past Kirkton Manse. The girl caught up with her and they walked companionably towards the wooded mound of the hill, which had eluded Brigid while wrapped in deepest winter. She would have preferred her second venture there not to be an errand which involved Auld Agnes.

Despite Susan detesting the unkempt midwife, her children knew Agnes Clay well – everybody did, apparently – and Katie became more eager the closer they approached to her dwelling.

"We sometimes come up here for dares," she said confidingly. "That's what Simon will be up to."

"What kind of dares?" Brigid asked.

"Oh, knockin' on her door and runnin', leavin' stuff for her tae find."

"I won't ask what kind of stuff," said Brigid. "I think you're being unkind to an old lady. She lives alone in a lonely place." She shivered slightly as she spoke. The wooded slopes ahead had a darkening effect on the day. They had slipped into the hill's shadow as they walked. Then she saw it – an old railway carriage.

"That's where Agnes lives," said Katie.

It was unkempt, like its owner, rusting in places and with a general air of neglect. There was no sign of Simon or his friends. Katie disappeared round the back, where a burn rushed downhill through trees, flushed with snow melt. Brigid paused a moment at the bottom of a set of wooden steps leading up to the carriage door; she took a deep breath and climbed them, bracing herself to knock. She rapped loudly to cover her nervousness. There was no reply. She knocked again. And again. Something moved at the side of her vision; she glanced at the window with its dirty net curtains. She was sure they had twitched. Agnes was home, she just wasn't answering.

Brigid climbed back down the steps and stood staring at the carriage, thinking about calling out to the old woman. Suddenly, there were cries and whoops and Katie reappeared, crashing through the trees with a noisy gang of boys in tow. The children began to caper around the carriage and crawl underneath it, banging on the underside.

"Stop that!" cried Brigid. "You'll get filthy!" In fact, they couldn't have got much dirtier than they already were. She called Katie and Simon to her and turned to go. However, the door of the railway carriage opened with a loud whine, and Agnes stood framed in the doorway, a tattered shawl around her shoulders.

"Can I offer ye a cup o' tea, Mrs. Watkins? We'll have tae have a wee chat – ye're gettin' big! Yer mistress had the doctor in tae deliver her brood, but she'll no' pay that kind o' money for the hired help." She raised a gnarled hand and pointed at the children. "You're welcome tae come in, but no' them!"

Katie and Simon reacted to her scowl with raucous laughter. Brigid took a deep breath. The woman made her skin crawl. "Thank you, but I've been sent to fetch Simon home, and I'll have to get on." She could have told her that the midwife who had delivered her would be coming with her mother, but she intended to divulge as little to Auld Agnes as possible. She hadn't wanted to hear the things the strange woman Megan with the raven had said to her on the train, but she remembered her warning.

"As ye like it," said Agnes. "I'll be seein' ye, Brigid Watkins. I'll be seein' ye."

Her eyes sparkled and her mouth twitched, whether with amusement or malice, Brigid couldn't tell. She shuddered and called on the twins to follow her.

Chapter Nineteen

A few weeks later, Brigid woke with the glow of late spring sunshine suffusing her room. She had long ago taken to sleeping with the blackout curtains open once she had extinguished the light for the night, enjoying the fierce brightness of the stars and the knowledge of Doon Hill lying below them with its secrets. She had climbed right to the top by this time, and stood beneath the great tree called the Minister's Pine, but nothing had happened. She hoped lying open to the night might lead to more experiences which would explain exactly why she had been summoned to this house, but nothing had occurred so far, and the earth too had been quiet, no tremors since St. Brigid's Day.

A gleam on her bedside table caught her eye, and she glanced at her brooch lying there. It was beautiful in the dawn light, thistles and ash leaves showing every detail. Brigid was about to try to go back to sleep for a while when she saw the dress she had left hanging on the wardrobe door, ready to wear today. It was a maternity cast-off of Susan's which her friend had given her last night. She had been wearing Susan's maternity clothes for some time now; all they needed were the hems and sleeves taking up, and they were of such fine quality, pre-war items sent by her mother from London.

This was the first dress for the new season coming in, the season in which Brigid's baby would be born. He – she was still adamant about that – was due at Midsummer, some seven weeks hence, and she was becoming ungainly and increasingly easily tired. Susan had stopped raising the subject of her going home. Brigid kept up her duties well and asked nothing of her. She had mentioned that she might like to go somewhere out of town today – she hadn't explored anywhere much and the time to do so was limited now. Susan had given her the maternity frock to wear, a romantic flowing cotton in cream sprigged with embroidered pink roses. Brigid had never worn anything so fine in her life. As a ripple of excitement ran through her, the baby stirred and punched and kicked. She looked under the covers and laughed as a fist-shaped lump protruded from the mound of her belly.

She stroked the little body she could clearly feel beneath her stretched flesh. "You're ready for a change of scene, too, aren't you?" she said. It was now May Day. When Susan had asked about her plans, Brigid vaguely said she would hop on a bus out into the countryside somewhere. Susan hadn't enquired further and Brigid had been glad. She knew exactly where she was going. She pushed herself out of bed and walked over to the window. She gasped, at first thinking she was seeing into the past again.

Beyond the kirkyard, where the warming Avon Dhu breathed mist over the fields, there were figures in white, running barefoot through the wet grass. The rising sun shone through their flimsy gowns, nightdresses by the look of them, illuminating their legs and the curves of their bodies as they stooped down to the ground, some actually kneeling in the dew. They all ran their hands through the grass there by the river, where the hawthorn was beginning to flower, and lifted them to their faces. There were giggles, and loud gasps of cold, and when they rose they skipped and danced like children back towards the road. The illusion of timelessness was shattered when they retrieved boots and coats from the fence and donned them, shivering.

Brigid recognised some of the faces – all girls and young women from the Clachan, some of them members of Rev. MacKendrick's small Episcopal Church which she attended with Susan each Sunday. She smiled. Obviously, some of the old ways lingered despite the modern era and the prevalence of the Presbyterian church in these parts, for others among the village maidens were from strict Church of Scotland families who would disdain such superstition. They were washing their faces in the May Day dew to replenish their beauty. She sighed. It might have been pleasant to join them, but her great belly prevented that in more ways than one.

#

Kirkton Manse, May 1ˢᵗ, 1689
Margaret woke early and knew that she was victorious – she was certain that she was carrying Robert's child, even although they had only lain together last night. The bud of his seed was unfurling within her as surely as the hawthorn on the river bank was bursting into flower. She thought of the maidens of the Clachan and the Kirkton out there even now, washing their faces in the May Day dew beside the Avon Dhu.

Robert had returned from London two weeks ago. She had written to him after meeting with the wise woman Molly, but had kept from him the news that many of his Episcopalian brethren and their families were being driven from their homes. She did not want to be accused of exaggeration again, to alienate him further. Her tone had been warm, her news confined to his son Colin and household matters. He had written back saying he would be home once he had recovered from a slight cold and fever he had suffered. Lady Ranelagh had treated him with her own remedies; not kitchen ones such as you might expect, but medicines concocted with the help of her brother's scientific equipment. She kept two recipe books, he said, one such as all women kept for herbal remedies and such like, and one for these more experimental medicines. She made discoveries, but was careful to share her ideas via the men she knew, using their names, giving them the credit, as was fitting to her sex and station in life. Margaret wondered about that – it seemed galling always having to be in the shadow of men, to hide behind them because that was what society dictated.

She no longer argued with Robert, though. Her aim was to be a good wife and not vex him – she had to bear the child which could, as Molly had said, be his salvation. It had come as a shock to him, therefore, when he arrived home to find that friends and neighbours among the clergy had been driven from their churches and homes by Presbyterians bent on eradicating them for the slightest reason, for the least sympathy with popery. Margaret had ceased to be afraid that this was the danger facing Robert, because she had well understood Molly's meaning – he was in more danger from the fae he was provoking with his "research", than from his fellow man, and so it proved. Robert's middling stance, his pleasing of all persuasions, his scholarship and reputation saved them from homelessness.

He couldn't be glad of that as she could, however, as he wept for this scourging of his beloved Gaeldom. His Catholic friends were suffering worst, of course, and there was a growing feeling of militancy amongst even the mildest of them. The Kirks dwelt where the Lowlands met the Highlands, almost on the dividing line, where the land began to rise and sometimes shifted as if to remind people of that fact. It was restless territory. This land was everything to Robert and to many others, a place set apart, with its own beliefs and ways; the lines were being drawn not only between England and Scotland, where many rejected the rule of this William of Orange and his wife Mary, but also between the Highlands and Lowlands.

Thus it was that domestic matters and the wiles of a young wife not seen for eight months had failed to have any attraction for Robert at first. Margaret, despairing, had sought Molly under the ash tree near the foot of Doon Hill and had acquired a potion to add to his wine last night, the ancient Beltane Eve. She was determined to keep him from wandering on Doon Hill, with the air so thin, and she had succeeded. She had been horrified at first when, under the effects of the potion, Robert's tongue had loosened and he had begun to speak of Beltane at Balquidder, of the fires on the hill above the church and the herds of cattle and sheep driven among them for fertility, and the dancing and revelry. Och, he had said, it was what the folk had always done and it was important to understand the people and join with them as far as you could. He admitted they still acted thus at Samhain, too, carrying burning boughs from the fires to kindle their cottage hearths to ensure blessings of warmth and light. Sometimes Robert scared her.

When the love potion had burned through every vein in his body, however, his eyes blazed only for her, and the heat of their bodies had joined right there in the parlour on the hearth rug. He had carried her to bed afterwards for more of the same; she had felt, at last, like the bride she should have been nearly a year ago. She turned now and gazed at him as the first beams of the May Day dawn gilded his face; he looked younger than his forty-five years. He had put on weight in London, and it suited him. Margaret couldn't help stretching forth her finger and tracing his profile.

He woke and gazed at her drowsily, eyes warm. "Isabel," he whispered.

#

It was a longer journey than Brigid thought, the bus stopping in all sorts of out-of-the-way places, but she marvelled at the scenery as they skirted the shores of vast lochs and travelled up and down hill. She cricked her neck at towering crags and thought of Sir Walter Scott and her favourite book – had they driven past Loch Katrine, she wondered? Had they passed near the setting of "The Lady of the Lake" and the haunted heights of Ben Venue? It was indeed a beautiful landscape, but it still overwhelmed her as it had on the train in January. She wondered what she would make of the true wilderness of the Highlands – the Trossachs region, she had read, was a gentle introduction.

She felt frustrated suddenly at the thought of all the weeks she had been here without venturing beyond Aberfoyle. It had been enough just to be there at first, cocooned by the snows, then to get to know the Kirkton and the Clachan and to walk by the Avon Dhu to Doon Hill in her spare time. She didn't make a habit of visiting Robert Kirk's grave lest she arouse suspicion, and she hadn't told Susan where she was bound today, but it seemed important to visit before the baby was born. The birth was looming into reality with frightening speed, and she didn't know what would happen after it. Balquidder was a big part of Robert Kirk's story, and although she hadn't felt any sixth sense calling her here as she had to Tower Hill or Aberfoyle – whatever it was beyond the veil having fallen silent for many weeks – she wanted to visit for her own interest.

She had told the bus driver that it was the ruined church she was interested in, and he dropped her at the road end of the steep hill leading up to both the ruined kirk and its Victorian replacement. Brigid began to walk up, the tranquillity after the noise and jarring of the bus soothing to her soul and her sore back. It was an enchanting spot. Unlike at Kirkton of Aberfoyle, the ruined church here was the one in which Rev. Robert Kirk had ministered for twenty-one years, from 1664 until 1685. It was a graceful shell with the frames of some gothic windows intact; ivy clambered up and through them and the interior of the church sheltered shrubbery bearing the young green shoots of springtime. All around the secluded graveyard, there were trees bursting into leaf. The only sounds were birdsong and water flowing somewhere nearby. Brigid picked her way across the grass, squinting up against the sunlight at the little open belfry above the doorless entrance. It was empty. She knew

Robert Kirk had bequeathed a bell to the church, on which he had paid to have some significant words inscribed – words which he had also engraved on his wife's headstone. She glanced towards the Victorian church, higher up the hill – perhaps they had taken the bell there.

A grave near the doorway caught her eye – looking closely, she saw that it belonged to Rob Roy MacGregor. She recalled that Sir Walter Scott had written about him, a sort of Robin Hood character, but it wasn't a book she had read. She carried on picking her way among the graves, now in sunlight, now in dappled shadow, a slight breeze riffling her curls and lifting the hem of her frock so that it flowed around her. Brigid was enjoying herself. It occurred to her it was the first time she had felt truly free in months, maybe since she had set out with such determination to reach Tower Hill that fateful night. She wore a beautiful dress rather than a nightgown today, though, and she was in control of her destiny – at least, as far as she could see. She lived in Aberfoyle and her son would be born where he was meant to be.

After a short time, she found what she was looking for – the grave of Isabel, Robert Kirk's first wife. They hadn't been married long, she knew. Isabel had died on Christmas Day 1680 and they had a young son, facts which struck Brigid as terribly sad. The headstone was low and insignificant, easily overlooked, the writing obscured by lichen and erosion. Unlike her husband's memorial, this was the original stone. The handsome recumbent one laid over Robert's grave was a later piece, added when his legend began to become famous. Brigid bent and peered at the inscription. It was believed that the grieving husband had engraved it in the stone with his own hand. It was almost indecipherable, but Brigid knew it contained the words "Love and Life" – the same words on the bell he had bequeathed to the church.

Suddenly, she thought of another grave – her own young husband's, Will's grave, which she hadn't visited since his funeral. She had been unable to, prevented by illness and then by the events which had taken over her life. A wave of grief and guilt washed over her. Dealing with the circumstances in which she had found herself had blocked memories of Will much of the time – it felt like another life, their courtship and marriage, and sometimes seemed unreal. Now, here, more than anywhere else, she felt a kinship with Robert Kirk. It wasn't to do with his book or their shared belief in a fae realm - it was about the man himself, his love, his loss. The bones of someone he had loved dearly lay beneath her feet. She reached out to touch the words on the stone, to trace them with her finger; but the minute she did so, it was as if the world jolted and she was flung backwards.

Brigid landed a few feet away. It ran through her mind that there must have been a powerful earth tremor, and so she wasn't surprised that she should see into the past; but what she saw made her recoil in terror. Looking around, she thought to seek the shelter of the ruins, but there were none. There was no church, ruined or otherwise, and it was night. There was only the hillside itself, and higher up, beyond where the Victorian church should have been, it was ablaze. Bonfires burned all the way up the hill, and dark figures of people and beasts capered among them. The air rang with shouts and the banging of drums. Worse than all this, however, was the feeling of anger which crashed down upon her; not her anger, but that of another, a fury in the air itself which threatened to choke her more than the acrid smoke drifting down the slope.

As with other times she had glimpsed the past, it was over in a moment. She found herself lying on the grass two yards from Isabel Kirk's grave. Her hand went immediately to her stomach.

"Would ye like me tae check the bairn?"

Shocked, Brigid looked up and saw Agnes Clay standing over her. "What are you doing here?"

Agnes shrugged. "It's a free country. Also, I happen tae come frae here."

Brigid made a move to get to her feet, and Agnes stepped forward to help her. Brigid flinched. "I'm fine, thanks. I can manage." She glanced at the grass and saw her brooch lying there. How had that happened? It had a strong clasp and she had pinned it firmly to the light cardigan she wore over Susan's dress. She retrieved it and fastened it back in place. When she looked at Agnes, her eyes were on the brooch with a detached kind of interest.

"The ground didna shake, ye know," the woman said. "Not this time."

Brigid's mouth went dry. What force had thrown her backwards, then?

"Ye need my help in more ways than one," said Agnes.

Brigid dusted herself down. "Do you make a habit of hanging around graveyards?"

"Ha! You obviously do. Pot, kettle, black, my dear."

Brigid's fingers curled into fists. "You know nothing about me or my life!"

"I know life and death get mixed up and that death isn't as final as it might seem, wee Sassenach."

Her eyes had that peculiar sparkle of mischief or malice again; maybe it was both. At that moment, though, at that very moment, Brigid suddenly understood why she had been summoned to Scotland. It was as if the veil had been swept back and she was at last allowed to know. The knowledge washed over her in a flood and nearly knocked her off her feet again. Could Agnes see into her mind? To protect herself, this knowledge, from the old crone, Brigid took to her heels and rushed downhill across the grass, heading for the road. Near the bottom, she took a tumble and sprawled on her face on the tarmac.

An elderly man riding a bicycle narrowly avoided her. He jumped off and threw his bike aside. "Are ye alright, miss?"

Brigid pushed herself up to her knees, hand on her belly. She felt the baby move. Glancing over her shoulder, she saw no sign of Agnes. "I think so," she said.

The man took note of her condition and spoke again. "Good. Let me help you up."

He placed a hand under her elbow and put his arm around her waist. When Brigid tried to stand, a sharp pain shot through her left ankle.

"Steady, steady," he said.

He guided her, limping, over to a wall and she leaned against it. Brigid noticed that he was wearing a clerical collar.

"Let's have a wee look." He examined her foot and asked her to try moving it this way and that. "I think it's just a sprain," he said, "but bad enough. And not good to fall in your condition. Why were ye running, lass?"

"I was hoping to catch a bus," Brigid lied.

"Well, I live close by, and I think ye should come with me and get a cold flannel on that ankle, and have a cup o' tea first," he said.

Brigid had no idea when the next bus was due. She had planned to walk into the village when she was ready to go, enquire there and look around while waiting. Now she couldn't do that, not right away. She nodded weakly and said thank you.

The minister of Balquidder, for such he turned out to be, put his bicycle safely on the grass verge and helped her to her feet. The manse was nearby, but it was still hard going with a sprained ankle. It was rather a grand house, with an air of refinement Kirkton Manse lacked. Once Rev. McGill, as he introduced himself, had helped her into his study and fetched a wet flannel for her ankle, then two cups of tea and biscuits, she asked if it was the original manse.

"Oh no," he said. "This one's Georgian. It falls in between the dates of the two kirks here." He took a sip of tea. "There have been even earlier buildings on the hill there, ye know," he said. "In fact, worship in this glen goes back four thousand years."

Brigid blinked and stared, remembering the sensation she had felt on Tower Hill – the knowledge that something had been worshipped there long before the Christian God. She swallowed and asked tentatively, "Is this what might be considered a thin place, Reverend?"

He chuckled. His face was open and good-natured. "Indeed," he said. "There are all sorts of legends attached to Balquidder. People past and present claim tae have had experiences o' various kinds. The hill on which the churches stand was the Hill o' Fire, where the Beltane and Samhain fires were lit. Old Celtic festivals, ye know, old beliefs. It was an important site. St. Angus brought Christianity here in the eighth century and is buried where the ruined kirk stands. What is your business here, if I may be sae nosy? Rob Roy's grave, I'm guessin' – romantic notions bred by readin' Sir Walter Scott!" His smile was warm.

Brigid hesitated, the memory of what she had seen when she had been flung backwards still vivid in her mind. He had just explained her vision. "It was Isabel Kirk's grave I was visiting," she said. "I'm interested in one of your predecessors."

His smile faded. "Ah yes, the Fairy Minister." He frowned. "Robert Kirk gave great insights into the folklore an' beliefs o' his time," he said, "and that's valuable history. But he was responsible for so much more. He was a great scholar, a linguist. He translated the first Gaelic Bible, which was funded by Robert Boyle, the founding father o' the science o' chemistry. He was well read an' a big influence in these parts, but all the legends that sprang up – him captive in Fairyland, or even in the big pine tree on top o' Doon Hill – they've buried the things o' real significance that he achieved."

Brigid smiled and shrugged lightly, as if it didn't really matter. "You don't believe the legends, then?"

"No," he said. "He's as dead as any in the kirkyard."

Brigid took a steadying sip of tea. "But rising from the dead – or maybe not being dead in the first place – is Biblical, isn't it?"

The old man smiled benignly. "It's best tae keep faith simple," he said. "Jesus rose from the dead. Before that, he raised his friend Lazarus and a girl who he said had just been sleeping. Nobody else could have done these things. The dead in Christ go to Heaven, and that's where the good Robert Kirk is." His eyes shone with certainty.

Brigid smiled politely and nibbled her biscuit. She almost envied him. Rev. McGill wouldn't be bothered by the demons haunting her, she guessed. The thought startled her. Was that what they were? Surely not. Yet what was being asked of her was beyond the bounds of nature as she knew it. Hadn't everything she had experienced been of the supernatural? A man like Rev. McGill wouldn't entertain such notions, secure in his faith.

"Are you originally from this area?" she asked.

"No," he said, "I'm from the Borders. You're from further south than that, by your accent. What brings you up here?"

"I'm staying with a friend," said Brigid. "Her husband's the minister at Kirkton of Aberfoyle."

"Ah, one o' the Episcopal chaps," said Rev. McGill. "I'm Church of Scotland myself." He sighed. "I would like tae offer ye a lift back, but my petrol ration won't run tae it this week, I'm afraid. I'll take ye to the bus stop, though. Just when ye're ready. Feel free tae use the facilities an' freshen up. Can ye manage tae walk, or would a wee bandage help wi' support?"

Brigid stood and tried to put weight on her foot. Her ankle was tender and she winced, afraid of turning over on it.

"I'll strap ye up," said the old minister.

His touch was so gentle, his manner so kind, she almost wished she could stay there in the Jane Austen atmosphere of Balquidder Manse with her uncomplicated host, and forget everything.

#

When she limped back into Kirkton Manse late that afternoon, Susan was in the kitchen with Ria. "Whatever happened to you?"

"I tripped and fell."

"Oh, you poor darling! Where? Did you have to go to hospital?"

Brigid had wondered how much of the truth she should tell. Word could easily get back, so she decided to be honest about where she had been, if a little economical with the true reason why she had been there. "I was in Balquidder," she said. "I like Sir Walter Scott. Rob Roy's grave is there. Luckily, the minister was passing and he came to my aid – his manse is nearby." She couldn't look at Ria as she said it. She felt the woman's stare burning into her.

"Well, thank goodness for that!" said Susan. "Ria's found something interesting in the smithy," she continued, "and I was just saying to her that it reminds me of…there! You have it on. Do you see, Ria?"

The two women peered at Brigid's brooch, pinned to her cardigan.

"I've noticed it before," said Ria, "and I thought it looked old, as I said. I found this in the loft o' the smithy." She held out a small knife, fashioned of iron like Brigid's brooch, but in much poorer condition. Rust bloomed over the thistles and ash leaves engraved on both blade and hilt.

"It does look similar, the way the leaves and thistles are worked," said Brigid. She reached out to touch the knife, but Ria snatched it away.

"Funny combination, isn't it? Thistles and ash leaves," she remarked.

Brigid shrugged. "I've never thought about it. The brooch belonged to Mam, as I told you, Ria. She's Irish and Dad's Scottish – ash for Ireland, thistles for Scotland. That's what it represents for me."

"Did your mother bring it from Ireland?" asked Susan.

"No – it belonged to Dad's great aunt, from Callander."

"Well, isn't that a coincidence!" cried Susan, delighted. "They could have been made by the same person!"

Ria smirked. "It's strange that the brooch is in such good condition. Not a bit of rust. And isn't it a coincidence that wee Brigid just happens tae turn up here wearin' it?"

Brigid glanced at her and felt a jolt of knowledge. She saw a challenge in the blacksmith's eyes. "It's an even bigger coincidence that you just happened to find the knife," she said.

Susan looked from one to the other and frowned, puzzled. "Ria thinks it's a ceremonial or ornamental piece," she said. "It's a dirk – a traditional hunting knife from these parts – but much smaller, of course, and fancier. This was never meant to be used as a weapon. Isn't that right, Ria?"

"Aye. It's far too wee an' fancy." Ria wrapped the knife carefully in a cloth and placed it in her bag. "I've done what I can tae restore it, but that's the best I can dae. What's yer secret, Brigid? That brooch is too good tae be true."

Brigid shrugged. "You're the metals expert, surely, Ria," she said. "As I told you before, I don't know. I really don't know why it's in such good condition. Was the knife wrapped in that cloth when you found it?"

Ria shook her head. "No."

"What was it wrapped in?"

Ria hesitated. "Newspaper."

"What was the date?"

"What does it matter?"

"It might give a clue to how long it had lain there before you found it." Now the challenge was in Brigid's eyes. She knew very well it was no recent discovery.

Susan sensed something in the atmosphere. She followed their exchange, still looking puzzled. "That's true," she said. "It would have been interesting. I mean, it's odd that none of your forefathers ever found it. It's a wonder you didn't think of that, Ria – don't tell me you threw the newspaper away?"

"I have to be going," said Ria, already heading for the door.

When she had gone, Susan shrugged. "Interesting find. Very peculiar, it matching your brooch so well."

Brigid's heart was beating wildly beneath the weight of the brooch. She had felt heat creep into the old iron whenever she had set eyes on the knife, and now it was burning into her. She put her hand over it as if to calm it, to cool it.

"Ria doesn't look as if she belongs here," she said.

"Her ancestors certainly didn't come from here," said Susan. "Or one of them didn't, at least. But the smithy has been handed down from father to son for generations until…well, to Ria. To the first daughter."

"Then what do you mean by her ancestors not coming from here?" asked Brigid. "Where did they come from?"

"Suriname, at an intelligent guess," replied Susan, "and somewhere in Africa before that."

"Africa?" asked Brigid, astounded.

"Yes," Susan smiled wryly. "The MacKendricks owned estates in Suriname in the late seventeenth century, sugar plantations. They brought slaves from parts of sub-Saharan Africa to work there. It's fascinating, but people prefer not to speak of it."

Brigid frowned. "Her skin's quite tanned-looking, even in winter – I thought maybe Italian or something – but she isn't black!"

"Well, no, dear. She's been watered down. A master taking advantage of a slave woman, probably, then marriages down the centuries. It can suddenly show up even after generations, you know. It has with our Ria here. But you should see her brother – ginger and pale as any Scotsman!"

Brigid stared at her friend. "You mean there were slaves here in Scotland? Away up here? And they bore white men's children?"

"Oh, the MacKendrick lands were much further north, around Inverness. Don't look so shocked. You must know some of our greatest cities were founded on the backs of slaves, even not so far from here. Glasgow, for a start, with its tobacco lords." She paused and contemplated the glowing tip of her ever-present cigarette. "London was full of slaves, of course. I'm sure my own ancestors were no better than my husband's in that respect. And yes, masters used slaves for all their needs. Slaves often took their masters' names, especially ones sired by them."

"I never thought about it," said Brigid.

"I didn't give it much thought myself until I met Ria here and saw the evidence," said Susan. "Not just her skin tone, but her bone structure and lips, her eyes…the genes have shown up after all these years! Then I started to do some reading, some research, and found out about my husband's – and Ria's – ancestry, and discovered slavery was linked to the MacKendrick name. I've no doubt Ria's line was forged on the wrong side of the blanket. Anyway, let's get you a nice cuppa and a sit down, and you can tell me about your day out and your mishap."

#

As soon as she could, Brigid escaped to her room and pulled her copy of "The Secret Commonwealth of Elves, Fauns and Fairies" from her carpet bag. She riffled through it and skimmed pages eagerly until she found what she was looking for.

"Say to Duchray, who is my cousin as well as your own, that I am not dead, but a captive in Fairyland; and only one chance remains for my liberation. When the posthumous child, of whom my wife has been delivered since my disappearance, shall be brought to baptism, I will appear in the room, when, if Duchray shall throw over my head the knife or dirk which he holds in his hand, I may be restored to society; but if this is neglected, I am lost forever."

It was the second legend to spring from Robert Kirk's death; the first, that he hadn't died at all but had been taken to Fairyland, and then this, a vision supposedly experienced by a relative – that he could be freed by the throwing of a knife over his head when he magically appeared at his posthumous child's christening. The man Duchray had been so stunned by the sudden appearance of Robert Kirk, so the legend went, that he had failed to throw it. Brigid sat back on her bed, her heart pounding. She felt as if every hair on her body was standing on end. The sensation of being watched – which she managed to shake off most of the time – had returned stronger than ever. She thought she saw movement in her peripheral vision, and feared to turn round.

She had believed her baby had to be born here in Aberfoyle for his own sake – that it was to do with his destiny, that he had a purpose. She knew it was connected with Robert Kirk. She wondered if her son was to carry on his work, to reveal things about the fae, about this Otherworld, the reality of which she had come to believe. That was why she was determined to stay, to see her child brought up here and fulfil his destiny. Today, however, in Balquidder, she had known the truth without any doubt. Her son's birth was linked to freeing Robert Kirk from the world that lay beyond the portal which was Doon Hill. It was another chance, another bid from the captive clergyman after all these years. Ria's knife had confirmed it; and along with what Susan had said about the blacksmith's ancestry, an image came to Brigid's mind – her birthday, in the kirkyard here at Kirkton of Aberfoyle, the earth tremor – and a dark face at one of the attic windows.

Chapter Twenty

May 14th, 1689

Margaret had summoned Molly the wise woman under the ash tree the previous day, and had returned to meet with her as was their arrangement. The fae woman was already there as she approached, beneath the tree, spinning wool. Margaret was annoyed.

"Why are ye makin' a display o' yerself?" she demanded. "Anybody would know what ye were! Nae mortal would drag a spinnin' wheel oot here!"

Molly looked taken aback, but quickly recovered her composure. "It's such a bonny morning. I love the light in your world. My world was gloomy and my wee cottage is dark." She had set up home in an abandoned hovel of which Margaret knew, but was forbidden to visit.

Margaret gazed at the thread upon the spindle, finer than anything she had ever seen. "What are ye plannin' tae make wi' this?"

"A blanket for your son. If you don't know it yet, Margaret, I do — you are with child, as I promised."

Margaret blushed. "I knew it at once. And my courses haven't come."

"So, are you not delighted?" beamed Molly.

"Aye. Thank you for yer help. But…" Margaret licked her lips, seeking the right words. "He only lay with me that night because he thought I was Isabel!" she blurted. "Never since. Was that what yer potion was meant tae dae — make me seem like her?"

Molly dropped the thread she held. Her lips opened uncertainly. "No! My intention was that he should have his heart's desire, as I conjured for you with the green unction! What man does not want sons?"

Margaret stared at her in disbelief. *"After what I told ye aboot his love for his first wife? I think ye know less of men than I do myself!"*

It was Molly's turn to blush. *"I am very new to this world!"* she cried. *"I only recently passed through the veil."*

"Am I the first ye've tried tae help in this way?" asked Margaret. She knew Molly had been delivering babes, but had she ever aided the conception of one before?

"Yes. What I did, I have only done for you, because of the danger in which your good husband stands." There were tears in her eyes.

Margaret was on the verge of tears herself, with panic. *"Tell me the truth – ye're certain the danger my husband faces is from the fae, an' not mortal men? Because there is fearsome strife in this country! William an' Mary have been handed the throne o' Scotland as well as that o' England now. Catholics are detested, Episcopalians are suspected an' scores o' clergy have lost their places! Those who support King James are takin' up arms an' callin' themselves Jacobites. Are ye sayin' my Robert is safe amongst all this? That it's his pursuit o' the fae that could harm him? For he thinks it will be our salvation!"*

Molly took up the thread again, but her hands trembled. She was young, so young, Margaret noted. How did those who chose to leave the Otherworld step through the veil? What price did they pay?

"There's no greater danger than falling foul of the fae," the wise woman replied. *"No hardship on this earth, no worse downfall a mortal could suffer. They will bind you to them after death. You believe in Hell, but God's fallen angels could not torment you more."* She swallowed. *"His danger is all from the fae. I swear to you. I am sorry for the effect the potion had. But Margaret, I say again – look to your strengths. Isabel is dead. You live, and you carry his son. If you fail to heed my words, three years from this day will be his reckoning."*

#

That evening, Robert went out. He hadn't been gone long when the earth shook. It was much stronger than other incidences Margaret had felt in this area, more akin to tremors she had experienced in Comrie. She ran to the window and looked for Robert among the shadows of evening creeping over the fields, but she couldn't see him. He must be on Doon Hill already, chasing the fae as he had done, tirelessly, since their night of love on the parlour hearth rug. He had barely looked her in the eye since; she knew he blamed her for keeping him from his research on a most auspicious eve,

Beltane, when he was on the brink, he said, of making the greatest discovery of all. Margaret knew what that might be, and had wanted to keep him from it by any means. She thought he suspected her of some women's meddling – she had her ways with herbs like any woman, of course. Whatever would he say if he knew she was intimate with one of the fae, and together they were working to keep him from his objectives? This shifting of the earth, like a living thing, and him on Doon Hill, was therefore a bad omen.

Margaret tried to keep herself busy with embroidery, but she lacked concentration. She turned to some simple mending instead. Robert's oldest pair of britches were holed at the knees again. She wished she could say it was because of prayer, but he had a liking for wearing them on his walks, and she had only recently discovered why they had worn away at the knees – he was kneeling on Doon Hill and peering into all the hollows of the hill and among the roots of trees in his quest for hiding places of the fae. They came in all shapes and sizes, these hidden folk, as anybody who lived in the vicinity knew. Some were more solid in appearance than others, and many could change their shape. You never knew what you were dealing with.

Margaret thought of Molly – had she always looked as she did now, or had she been some other type of being before she took on mortal flesh? And was she really mortal flesh? The wise woman wouldn't speak of passing through the veil, but Margaret had seen the sadness in her eyes and guessed that while she retained magic beyond any mere mortal, she had lost much in the transition. As for that veil itself – well, it didn't really exist, of course. It was just a way to describe the boundary between worlds. There were doorways and passageways which could be anywhere, although the fae favoured certain places, especially mounds like Doon Hill; but any portal was a way into the Otherworld, something no mortal would recognise, and few were those who had blundered through one and returned to tell of their encounters.

Many were the tales of meetings with the beings who had crossed into the world of human beings, however, and Robert had been busy since his days in Balquidder gathering as many as he could – to add to his own. Margaret shuddered to recall the experiences he had shared with her, despite her own meetings with Molly. The fae midwife was strange enough for Margaret – she wished to have no more dealings with her kind, benevolent or not. How was she supposed to heed her warnings and keep Robert from wandering? It was too soon to tell him of the child.

He burst through the door after dark, when she had fallen asleep in her chair. His long greying hair was disordered, damp, with twigs in it, and he smelt of earth and roots and – she couldn't help thinking it – he smelt of the grave. Decay surrounded him like an imperceptible mist, but he was grinning, wildly happy. His excitement at least reassured her that he himself had come back, and not some co-walker in his place, a double conjured by the fae to dupe her – for such a one would have lacked the sheer joy animating Robert. He had been there, he said; he had passed through the veil, found a doorway, a portal. He had visited the Secret Commonwealth, and returned to tell the tale, and to share the findings of his research with the world! Margaret knew then that Molly had spoken true – there was far more danger in this than anything mortal man could do to him. She placed a protective hand over her belly.

#

Brigid woke in a cold sweat as the old grandfather clock in the manse hallway chimed one in the morning. It was now May 14th, the anniversary of Robert Kirk's death in 1692. Two hundred and forty-nine years had passed, yet they were somehow linked. She lay under the same roof and she felt an increasing sense of oppression within the house. The ceiling above her head creaked. She hadn't been sleeping well, and she was sure this creaking was becoming louder. It was an old house and all houses made noises as timbers settled after the heat of the day, but to Brigid's mind this was the sound someone walking on the floor above might make. She had asked Susan about the attic – there was a door leading to it at the end of the upper hallway, which Susan kept locked. She said there were only a few old boxes up there, containing nothing of note, and the Christmas decorations.

Brigid took deep, calming breaths, trying to damp down the fires of her imagination. She had to think of the baby. She was relieved he wasn't due around this time. His birth coinciding with the anniversary of Robert Kirk's supposed death would have been deeply disturbing. He wasn't due for weeks, she told herself, as she tried to go back to sleep. Yet now that she knew her son was linked to Robert Kirk's bid for freedom, she was afraid. She told herself that he was a man of God like Rev. McGill, the present minister of Balquidder. Love of his land and its people had been the driving forces of his life, the reason he respected and wished to record their beliefs. Of course he believed the things he had written; after all, she, Brigid, believed them. He was a good person who had acted for all the right reasons. She had nothing to fear; so she told herself.

In the morning, Ria appeared at breakfast time and Susan smiled and said she had a surprise for both of them. Ria was wearing her usual boiler suit. Brigid had dressed in the cream frock she had worn in Balquidder, but Susan insisted she changed into something less fine. Puzzled, she came back downstairs and Susan led them out to the yard. She was carrying a torch and she produced a large key from her trouser pocket as she led them to the top of the cellar steps. Like the attic, it was always kept locked.

"I can't come down with you because of the babies," she said; it was what she called her two youngest. The older three had just left for school. "There's something down there to interest both of you. I only remembered it last night. It flashed into my mind when I was having trouble sleeping."

"Why couldn't you sleep?" asked Brigid.

"Noises above my head," smiled Susan. "Strangest thing, never heard creaks like that before. It was nothing, of course, just an old house doing what old houses do." She handed Ria the key. "It's filthy in there, I'm afraid, but I think you'll find it's worth it. Look for an old chest of drawers to the back at the left. The thing I want you to see is on top of it. I found it when we first moved here, but forgot all about it. I wouldn't mention it now, except for the fact that…well, you'll see."

Ria took the rusted old key and Brigid followed her down the steps. The blacksmith wrestled with the lock, and it finally gave with a loud clank. She had to put her shoulder to the door to push it open. "I wonder when anybody was last in here?" she said.

They peered into a black cavern whose extremities they couldn't even see. A waft of thick cobwebs drifted down with the opening of the door and hung in tatters over the entrance.

Brigid grimaced. "This had better be worth seeing," she said.

Ria flicked the torch's switch. They stared into the bowels of the manse, a large basement with some smaller areas to the sides divided by brick walls. The main part contained old furniture, thick with webs, dust and grime, a few pieces draped with tarpaulins.

Ria whistled. "Phew! By the look o' this lot, some of it goes back tae the Jacobites!"

Brigid shuddered. "What on earth does Susan want us to see in here?" It was dank and chilly in the cellar after the pleasant sunshine of the morning outside, and she was coming out in goose pimples. She also had a prickling sensation of another kind which was becoming more common – that feeling of being watched, that she was not alone, that they were not alone.

"Best foot forward, Sassenach!" said Ria, shining the torch beam ahead as she set off to the left around a pile of old furniture heaped like a bonfire in the middle of the oppressive space.

They found the chest of drawers, a Victorian piece by the look of it, hunkering at the back to the left as Susan had said, half-covered by a tarpaulin which draped whatever was on top of it. Ria handed Brigid the torch and hefted the ancient covering away with some difficulty, raising a great cloud of dust and setting two enormous spiders scurrying. There was an ominous wooden clunk as the object, whatever it was, seemed to tip sideways. They both jumped back, choking on dust. Brigid's skin was crawling. They found themselves staring at an old wooden cradle which the removal of the tarpaulin had set gently rocking. Neither spoke until it had come to a stop.

Ria looked angry. "Why would she think I would be interested in this?" she cried.

Brigid's throat felt constricted. It was the dust, she told herself. "Maybe because of the carvings?" Her voice was strained. Despite the tarpaulin, the cradle was dirty, but the profusion of wooden thistles which decorated the carved hood stood out. "There were thistles on the knife you found." She didn't add, *"and on my brooch, which matches it."*

"It's Scotland!" Ria exclaimed. "There are thistles on everything!"

"Alright, alright!" said Brigid. Really, it was an odd situation Susan had put them in, but it didn't merit quite as much anger from the blacksmith.

"Finely engraved metal is one thing," said Ria, "but any father-to-be in years gone by could have knocked this up!"

The carvings were a bit crude, not of the standard of the thistles on the knife and brooch. It was a tenuous link; and yet, Brigid knew in her heart that there was a link. The dark cavern seemed to spin a little. She grabbed Ria's arm to steady herself.

"What? Oh no! Dinna faint on me doon here! I'm no' good wi' that kind o' thing!"

Brigid gave herself a shake. "It's just the dust," she said. She reached up and touched the cradle, forced herself to take hold of it and pull it round. There, on the bottom end now facing them, they read the words "Love and Life". Brigid's mind flew back two weeks to the kirkyard in Balquidder, the lichen-covered headstone of Isabel Kirk. She stared mutely. Suddenly, Ria shoved her. She landed against the chest of drawers and set the cradle rocking again.

"Why did you really come here?" the blacksmith demanded.

Brigid stared at her in shock. "You know why! You know more than anybody else except Susan! She told you what happened to me in London!"

Suddenly, Susan's voice echoed around the cellar. "Halloo in there! Have you found it? It's very old, I reckon. Maybe as old as your knife, Ria, and your brooch, Brigid?"

Ria's eyes dropped to Brigid's chest. "Where is the brooch?" she hissed.

"I left it on the dress I was wearing when Susan told me to change!" cried Brigid. "Ria, please, what's the matter with you?"

"What's going on in there?" Susan called.

Ria stepped back. "Nothin'," she answered her kinswoman. "Just wondered why ye sent for me first thing in the mornin' tae see a cradle – I'm hardly the maternal type!"

Brigid headed for the door. Her throat still felt constricted, and she tried to keep it that way. There were words forcing their way out in spite of herself. She wanted away from the cradle. Ria was just behind her as they mounted the steps into daylight, where Brigid took great steadying gulps of air. She couldn't stop herself, however – the words spilled out in spite of her absolute reluctance, her efforts to stop them.

"I would like to have it for the baby."

The other women stared at her in disbelief.

"But you're getting my children's cot," said Susan. "I had it sent from Edinburgh – it was the finest of its day!"

Brigid fingered her tight throat. Behind her, in the dank darkness of the cellar, she was sure she could hear the cradle still softly rocking.

#

Kirkton Manse, May 1689

Margaret Kirk didn't know what her strengths were; Molly had told her to discover them and own them, but she was still looking. She knew she was a good wife; she managed the household well. Her kitchen garden flourished, her pantry was well stocked with preserves, there was always good food on the table. She carried out her parish duties with genuine care and concern. It didn't seem to be enough for Robert, though. He was paying her scant attention. Now that he had been in that Otherworld, that Secret Commonwealth, he wanted nothing except to return there.

She told him about her condition sooner than a wife normally would, to try to keep him with her more, to keep him from Doon Hill. He was pleased and excited about the baby. He kissed her and held her as if she was made of glass and looked upon her as if she was a marvel, a wonder. Maybe Molly was correct, and a new child would put him to rights, when he was born. Maybe motherhood would be her strength, and she would be such a paragon that he would fall in love with her at last, and his little family would be enough to make him happy. Maybe he would think better of his involvement with the fae, in order to protect their son.

It came as a blow, therefore, when he produced the cradle from the cellar. Oh, she knew of it; she had seen it down there, and she had seen her stepson in it as a babe in Balquidder. It was Robert's own handiwork; but it had been made for his son with Isabel. Margaret was fond of Colin. He was an intelligent and appealing ten-year-old, and he was her blood relative as well as her stepson, Isabel having been her cousin. He hadn't been an only child, though — his younger brother William had died in that cradle. That wasn't really the problem, however; babes died, sadly, and heirlooms lived on. It was just such a personal object, carved as it was with those words "Love and Life", which Robert later engraved on Isabel's headstone with his own hand, and paid to have inscribed on the bell he bequeathed to Balquidder Church. Margaret had never asked the significance of those words, but she imagined them toasting each other by the fire as they murmured them, love shining in their eyes. Maybe Colin had been conceived after such a toast.

"It...it's beautiful," she had stuttered, "but..."

"But what, my dear?" He looked genuinely puzzled.

"I thought we might make a fresh start," she managed to say. "With our baby, you know — the child of our marriage."

"Oh," he said, looking as if the idea had never occurred to him, which it surely hadn't.

"There's ample time tae carve another, dear Robert," she said gently. "Perhaps wi' some words o' endearment special tae us?" Yet even as she said it, she knew there had never been any. She could have bitten her tongue. "Or a wish, a blessing, for our child?" she added quickly.

He looked crestfallen. "I spent a long time upon this, you know, Margaret. And the words are a blessing, a thanks to God for the love and life of a child and an entrusting of that child, be it Colin or my lost little William, or our new babe, to His care."

He looked so innocent, no guile in him, that Margaret felt ashamed. "Of course, Robert, of course," she said. "'Tis but a woman's fancy. I'm sorry. Thank you."

He smiled. "Well, then," he added, content with the situation now, "I'd best be gettin' on. I have a lot to do. Many reports tae write up, and another walk upon Doon Hill this evening."

Margaret bristled inwardly. "Robert — I thought we might celebrate. Such lovely weather — we could take wine together in the garden an' discuss our good news."

He frowned slightly. "You know the importance of my work, dear, not just to me but perhaps to the nation — and certainly to the fate of Christianity and the peace of Gaeldom. Our brethren continue to be evicted. There will be war between Catholics and Protestants. I aim to astound all and restore faith and perspective by revealing another world and a new order from which we can learn!"

Margaret bit back her anger, her bitter disappointment. "Of course, Robert." She forced a smile. If a wife wasn't to be a nag and a scold, what more could a woman do? He went out that night, and he achieved his objective again. He came in, grass stains on his clothing and even a green tinge to his skin, and that wildness in his eyes she was coming to dread.

"What happened, Robert?" She was impelled by curiosity, though scared.

"Such beings!" he cried, as he washed his face at the bowl on the stand and prepared himself for bed, where she had been for a long time already. "Such creatures! They are not like us, my dear! Not flesh and blood, although they mimic it well! They can mimic many forms, for they can change in the twinkling of an eye! They're made of congealed air, and can shift shape and thereby move between worlds with ease and go anywhere they please!"

Margaret shuddered. "Are such creatures to be trusted?"

Robert didn't consider her question relevant. "My dear, having the ability to do these things, of course they will do them. Wouldn't you, to go anywhere and be anything you pleased for a time? Of course they amuse themselves by so doing. They follow their nature as we follow ours. My point is, that they are of a substance somewhere between flesh and blood and angelic spirit – a race between man and angels!"

"Some angels are fallen, Robert. Legions of them."

He sighed and climbed into bed. "My dearest Margaret, you misunderstand me yet again. I am not commenting on their morality. I am expressing a scientific opinion as to what they are made of."

"But you also alluded to how they behave!" cried Margaret.

"Yes, maybe so. But that was also a scientific observation based on the fact that a creature's nature will determine its behaviour."

"Well then – you admit they are not to be trusted. I fear for you, husband, that is all. I am carrying your child. I am your wife!"

He looked at her kindly. "I'm grateful for your solicitude, Margaret. Truly I am. Do you not see I have a parallel purpose with these fae, parallel to the education of our fellow human beings? Margaret, I mean tae bring them tae faith in God! They already have some knowledge o' the Bible. I mean tae teach them the truth o' it, an' thereby change their behaviour, as savages have been tamed by bein' saved! I saw the *evidence myself in London, wi' Mr. Boyle's slave."* He kissed her swiftly on the cheek, turned and snuffed the candle.

Margaret lay in the dark, awake long after Robert, exhausted from his wanderings, was softly snoring. She was hot and thirsty. Eventually, she gave in and padded down to the kitchen for a glass of her own home-brewed beer, candle in hand. She had to keep up her strength, after all. She heard noises and thought there must be mice in the cellar again. The household cats kept it clear most of the time, but vermin always crept back. What a pity they had never set their teeth upon that cradle! The sounds became louder, and she feared it was rats rather than mice. Then she heard a groaning and grunting that came from no rodent she had ever known. She fled back upstairs and shook Robert awake.

"Robert! Did ye lock the cellar door after you brought the cradle up?"

He was as concerned as she was. They crept downstairs. The noises had stopped by the time they reached the kitchen. Elsie, the maid, had heard them stirring and came into the kitchen behind them. Robert put a finger to his lips, armed himself with a large meat knife and a lantern and walked silently out the back door. The women followed behind, waiting at the top of the steps. He descended and threw open the cellar door.

"Who goes there? Show yourself! If it is only shelter ye seek, ye have nothin' tae fear." He held the lantern aloft and kept the knife behind his back.

The light picked out an astonishing sight. Two faces, one so dark it almost blended into the black hole of the cellar, and one white, but filthy, crowned by a disordered nest of dirty hair, stared out at them. The woman's skirts were raised and the man's britches were lowered; he looked terrified, she merely laughed.

Robert turned to Margaret and Elsie, blocking their view. *"Leave some food an' refreshment in the kitchen an' get back tae bed."*

"But Robert..." Margaret whispered, the candle shaking in her hand.

"I'll be fine. It's just two lost souls," he said.

"But..."

"Go, Margaret! Now!" His eyes were blazing.

She turned and nudged Elsie, whose mouth was as wide open as her eyes. They walked shakily into the kitchen and Margaret ordered the maid to fetch bread and cheese and a jug of beer. She sat at the kitchen table and rested her head in her hands, wondering. She had never actually seen a black man before. There were none that she knew of in these parts, although the gentry had slaves in the cities and she had heard talk of them being kept on grand estates.

Elsie was babbling with excitement. "What a thing tae turn up, Mistress! A black man! An' the state o' his wumman!"

"Now, Elsie!" Margaret reprimanded.

"Can we wait until the master brings them up? Tae see them better, like?"

It was tempting. "No," said Margaret. "Rev. Kirk said we were tae get back tae bed, an' we will."

Elsie's face fell. "But they'll be gone by mornin', Mistress. The master will feed them an' send them on their way, an' we'll not get a good look!"

"Whoever they are, they are not things to be stared at! They are human beings, no matter their appearance or behaviour," said Margaret. She rose. "Come, Elsie. Bed."

Margaret had her suspicions regarding Robert's treatment of the pair, and she was correct. They were not gone by morning, and Elsie would have plenty of time to stare at them.

#

Susan watched Brigid through the kitchen window. Her household help, or lodger, or friend – she didn't quite know what to call her – had hosed down the old cradle and was now washing it thoroughly with disinfectant. Ria had looked daggers at both of them as she had hefted the ancient crib up into daylight for the first time in generations. Then, while Brigid set about her work with a pained expression which didn't convey the gratitude she claimed, Ria had rounded strangely on Susan.

"What dae we really know aboot her?"

Susan had been surprised. "We know plenty, Ria!"

"I dinna think she's told us everythin'!"

"She's told us things she could have kept hidden," said Susan. "What are you getting at?"

"I think she's one o' the Robert Kirk crowd."

Susan smiled. "She's never once mentioned him. You're quite mistaken!"

"I warned her ye wouldna take her in if she was one o' that lot," hissed Ria. "She knew tae keep her mouth shut!"

Susan rolled her eyes. "Even if she was – or is – interested in Kirk, she's had more important things on her mind. Like expecting a baby and staying safe from a predatory landlord and his deranged wife! I told you all about it!"

"But ye wouldna have taken her in!" insisted Ria.

"Not if she had knocked on the door asking questions about Robert Kirk like all those damned folklorists or the nutters who actually believe in fairies, no – but even if she does know about him, Ria, that was not her purpose in coming here."

"So she says!"

"What's got into you, Ria?"

The blacksmith had shaken her head angrily then, lips pursed, and had stomped out the door.

Now Susan looked around the kitchen. It was needing a good clean. Brigid had been slacking the last couple of weeks. She had been distracted and at times a bit distant. A heavily pregnant woman couldn't be expected to keep up with the work of such a large household, and Susan had always known that. Brigid had simply managed to get under her skin. The young widow had a certain vulnerability about her, yet she had hidden strength. Susan shrugged. She didn't know what was wrong with Ria, why she had never taken to Brigid. The shenanigans of a long-dead minister certainly weren't uppermost on the young woman's mind. In any case, Brigid's future would be decided when her mother and the midwife came. She really didn't expect her to stay long after the birth.

Susan set about washing the breakfast dishes, keeping an eye on Brigid in the yard. When the cradle stood gleaming, having been polished until it shone in the sunlight, she went out and stood beside her.

"You've done a good job, Brigid," she said. "It really is rather beautiful. But I still don't see why you would choose this over my cot!"

The look on Brigid's face suggested she didn't know, either. She looked quite bewildered.

"Would you help me take it upstairs, please, Susan?"

"Of course, if that's what you want."

Neither of them was as strong as Ria, and it was heavy. They managed it between them, with Susan bearing most of the weight. Brigid was most particular about where it should be placed in her bedroom. Susan was puzzled at first, then increasingly irritated, as Brigid insisted on the crib being positioned just so on a spot in the middle of the room.

"Why do you want it there? Surely it should be beside your bed!"

Brigid's eyes flared. "Ah! It's the bed that's in the wrong place – we'll have to shift the bed!"

Susan stared at her. "Really, Brigid, this is ridiculous! What is wrong with everybody this morning? I can't move the bed by myself, and you can't help me. If you want to rearrange the room, you'll have to wait until your mother arrives!"

Her harsh tone seemed to bring the young woman out of whatever strange mood she had fallen into. She sat on the edge of the bed and swiped a hand across her pallid face. "I'm sorry, Susan. I don't know what came over me."

Susan looked at her. "Pregnant women take odd notions, I suppose," she shrugged. "You've been a bit off for a couple of weeks, if I'm being honest." As she said it, her eye fell on the inscription carved at the foot of the cradle. "Love and Life." Of course – that's what had triggered Ria's suspicions. They were Robert Kirk's words, engraved on his first wife's headstone in…Balquidder. Brigid had gone to Balquidder two weeks ago. She dismissed the thought as quickly as it flitted across her mind. It was mere coincidence, surely…but that cradle was old indeed, and very interesting to some, if linked to the Fairy Minister. No wonder Ria had been annoyed – she hated any mention of her town's most famous former resident. Susan thought about asking Brigid if she had heard of him, but she had left the children alone downstairs long enough.

"I'm just feeling tired. I'm not sleeping well," said Brigid.

Susan nodded briskly. "Well, there's nothing unusual in that at this stage of pregnancy," she replied, already on her way out of the room.

#

Kirkton Manse, May – June 1689

Robert insisted that the pair found in the cellar marry, and he performed the hasty ceremony himself. The man, MacKendrick, tried to say he was a Catholic, had converted to be like his master who had, in fact, sired him and named him for himself; he should not marry the woman on religious grounds, he said, and certainly not by the hand of a reformed minister. Robert knew he was only trying to escape his duty. It didn't matter to Robert that he claimed the woman had seduced him, it didn't matter what kind of woman she was. MacKendrick had been happy to enjoy her at least twice in the manse cellar, according to the mischievous creature (who truly had no shame), and therefore, if they were to stay, they would be married. He offered too good a proposition for MacKendrick not to accept, and he was determined to keep the woman, too.

"Why?" Margaret had cried. "She is not the kind to have in a manse!"

Robert looked at her strangely. "So you do not mind that we house a vagrant negro, but you object to a poor misguided woman?"

Margaret fought to find the words to explain herself. "We are agreed on slavery, Robert! MacKendrick has been through things we can't imagine. I'm glad he's been given his freedom, although the reason is dreadful!" She shuddered.

The young man's father was a laird near Inverness, who had made a fortune in the sugar trade. He had brought his natural-born son home from the plantation as a footman for his house, a novelty which his wife had requested after a stay in London. However, she discovered her husband's relationship to the slave and demanded he be sent away. The laird had granted him his freedom and dismissed him with only the clothes on his back and a small sum of money, which was soon gone. He had been unable to find work; nobody would employ him, fearing his appearance, which favoured his mother's heritage. He had little of a Scottish laird about him.

Margaret sighed. It was all so unsavoury. "But her, Robert!" she continued. "She's no better than a whore! He doesn't want her. He was just being a man and following his baser nature. He sees the error of his ways."

Robert stared at her. "And what if I say she was just following her baser nature? Women have desires also, I think?"

Margaret knew there was a challenge in his words. She wrapped her arms round her belly, although the baby wasn't showing yet. She would not be ashamed for wanting her husband and his child. To her satisfaction, it was Robert who looked embarrassed.

He straightened his back and assumed a different expression. It was his pulpit face, and his pulpit voice followed. "Think of the women of ill repute in the Bible. Think of our Lord's work with Mary Magdalene, and with the woman caught in adultery. We have a duty to save her from her sins, as our Lord did."

Margaret was wretched. "But Robert, can it not be done by some other means? Send her somewhere else, find them both a position some place more suitable? We have Colin tae consider, an' a bairn on the way!"

"Who would take MacKendrick on? He has tried. The matter is decided!" *said Robert.* "He stays. Aggie stays."

#

The man preferred to be known as Mac. He said he was not proud of his sire's name, which was his only name. Margaret set him and Aggie to clearing and cleaning one of the attic rooms to use as their quarters. There were three rooms with fireplaces up there; it was meant for servants, although she and Robert had so far kept only Elsie, who slept in a box room at the end of the hallway. Robert did not like to live in a grand way, and Margaret, who had been used to a finer household in Comrie, had often lamented this. When she complained again of Mac and Aggie, he simply reminded her of her previous requests for more servants. Now she had them, he said.

She didn't stipulate which of the attic rooms they should choose, but the creaking above her head on their first night in residence, the night after they had been discovered in the cellar, told her that they had lodged directly above her bedchamber. She listened to their feet padding back and forth, Mac's sturdy boots and the clatter as he threw them off, the softer footfall of Aggie who had arrived barefoot. She sighed; she would have to clothe the slattern adequately. Margaret turned over in bed and tried to sleep, but she was tense. Robert wasn't yet in bed, and she was over-aware of the strange couple in the room above her. She flushed as she thought of the noises she had heard coming from the cellar the night before, animal sounds alien to her experience, and she pulled the covers up over her ears. Nothing would have blocked the rumpus which erupted above her head, however; the screeching of the woman, the shouting of the man. She couldn't make out what they were saying, although there were none of those awful grunts and groans she had expected to hear. The pair were obviously arguing; and so it continued for several nights. At last, Robert heard it, too, and said she should speak with them – managing the servants was her domain.

By this time, Margaret had guessed what the problem was, and was embarrassed to confront them. She sent Elsie to tell them they were to come to the morning room when they had finished their first tasks of the day. They appeared before her. She mustered her dignity and told them quietly but firmly that they must cease their quarrelling at nights; that she and the Reverend could hear them. Mac stared straight ahead, his eyes empty, his expression veiled, his face a mask; it occurred to Margaret that he was behaving like a slave, like the slave Robert had seen and examined in London with Mr. Boyle. Aggie stared straight at her and simpered in that annoying, defiant way she had. Margaret lamented Robert's morality being such that he had insisted on the marriage. They should not have kept the slut Aggie. Mac, it seemed, now wanted as little to do with her as possible. That's what the rows in the attic were about; he was rejecting her advances. The woman was a liability, for who knew where she might take her lust if her husband wouldn't have her? She was also clumsy in her work, and there had been several "accidents" which Margaret suspected — but which Robert waved away when she said it — were deliberate. She simpered around the house, eyes glittering strangely, her expression hovering between mischief and malice.

As they turned to go, Mac's eyes fell on the two lumps of meteorite which Margaret had taken from the drawer while she was waiting for them. She often turned to them in times of distress — gifts from the stars, as she thought of them, and a happy memory from childhood. The man's face transformed, the mask of a few moments ago dissolved, and a fierce light filled his eyes.

"Sky iron! Gifts from the stars!" he cried.

Margaret gasped. "You know of such things?"

"I was apprenticed to the blacksmith on the plantation, Mistress," he said. "The magic was in my blood — my mother told me of my grandfather and his father before him, all our ancestors, all men who were what you call blacksmiths, who work magic with fire and metal. Iron which falls from the sky, blazing like a star, carries special magic."

Margaret put a hand to her heart. Her eyes met the young man's. She felt the stirring, new to her, of recognising a kindred spirit. She turned and held the fragments out to him, and he took them from her hands, wonder in his eyes. It was then that she noticed Aggie. The smirk had been wiped from her face and her eyes were narrowed. She had taken a few steps backwards towards the door, and suddenly she turned and fled the room.

"I did not dismiss you!" Margaret cried after her.

"I apologise for my wife. I will speak with her." Mac bowed and handed the lumps of meteorite back to Margaret. *"If ever you wish something fashioned from one of these, Mistress — a trinket to wear, perhaps — I could do that for you, if I had access to a forge. Such a thing would offer great protection."*

Margaret took a breath to steady herself. *"Against what?"* she asked.

"With respect, Mistress," Mac replied; *"I know what is happening here."*

His mask had disappeared. There was knowledge in his eyes, and something else — complicity. What exactly did he know? She could not encourage it. One did not engage with servants in this manner.

"Thank you, Mac," she said loftily. *"That will be all."*

Chapter Twenty-One

Susan was becoming increasingly concerned about Brigid. The young woman was languid and dreamy – but not in the way one would expect of a mother-to-be. As the time drew nearer to her due date, she was disinterested in the coming baby rather than weary of pregnancy, detached rather than concerned about the birth. Her eyes seemed to be focussing beyond her surroundings sometimes, as her gaze roved the middle distance. Purple patches from sleepless nights stained her delicate skin, and she jumped at shadows, the slightest noise or movement in the room startling her from her reverie, recalling her from far away.

Susan knew that her mother and her midwife friend planned to arrive a week before the baby was due. They had rented a cottage not far over the bridge, in the Clachan. Their arrival was still over a fortnight away. She paced the floor one day when Brigid was out, thinking it over, then she took a deep breath and went up to Brigid's bedroom. She looked around at the surfaces – the dressing table, the chest of drawers, the bedside table – but she couldn't see what she was seeking. She was looking for a book which might have Brigid's home address on the inside cover, or even a letter which would reveal it, breach of privacy though that would be. She peered inside the wardrobe, staring at the bottom of it; nothing but a sunhat and the carpet bag Brigid had been carrying when she arrived. Maybe the bag would have something in it. She opened it and saw some books. "The Lady of the Lake" was on top – Brigid had said she liked Sir Walter Scott. Below that was "The Celtic

Twilight", by W.B. Yeats – of course, Brigid's mother was Irish. Then she saw it – "The Secret Commonwealth of Elves, Fauns and Fairies", by Robert Kirk. A shiver ran down her spine. This book had been written in what was now her home, two and a half centuries ago, by a minister of religion who had believed in a hidden realm of fae creatures.

Neither Susan nor her husband had known anything of the man and his legendary reputation when they moved here. Tom MacKendrick's branch of the family had been born and bred in London for three generations, and it was an ancestral whim which had brought him back to Scotland, to minister in the church in Aberfoyle where only three living relatives remained – his Uncle George, his son who was named after him, and his daughter, Ria, vaguely remembered from a childhood visit. They hadn't lived in the manse long when the first Robert Kirk fanatic came to the door. Most of them were interested in folklore, either reading it or recording it. They had a passion for keeping it alive, but more as a genre than anything. Annoying as they could be, the ones Susan had come to dread were those who believed the Fairy Minister had never died, that he was captive in Fairyland – apparently, the interior of Doon Hill teemed with fairies – and that one day, he would be released. They clamoured at her door desperate to see inside his house, his study, his bedroom – was there anything still there that had belonged to him, they wanted to know?

Susan swung round and stared at the cradle in the middle of the room. "Love and Life." Could it be that he had made this? If so, it would be the first thing from his life there of which she was aware. There might well be other pieces of furniture in the cellar, but who could prove their ownership? She glanced at the book in her hand. Why had Brigid kept it hidden, along with the others which clearly revealed her interest in folklore – an interest she had never mentioned. Susan recalled Ria's words. *'I warned her ye wouldna take her in if she was one o' that lot.'* No, she probably wouldn't have let her stay more than the one night, since she found Kirk enthusiasts so disturbingly fanatical, but she was still puzzled at Ria's over-reaction – and now, at Brigid's secrecy.

Still, she had to admit she had seen another side to Brigid these last couple of weeks. The children were beginning to notice, and really, the young woman was not her responsibility. She flicked open Robert Kirk's book and found Brigid's Birmingham address written inside. Hurrying along to her own room, she copied it quickly and returned the book. As she did so, she saw something sticking out of the lining of the bag. It was a banknote. She put in her hand and pulled out a wad. There was a fair sum of money here. Susan was surprised. She had never charged rent, of course – their arrangement was bed and board in return for household help and a small remittance – but it hadn't been a fair exchange lately. Even given her condition and the need for lighter duties, Brigid had not been pulling her weight. She stuck her hand further inside the lining. More money. Susan frowned. Where had a poor young war widow got all this? A horrible suspicion flitted across her mind. Had Brigid robbed the Johnstones before she fled? Or had they paid her in advance for the baby – had she made an agreement with them? Was anything Brigid had told her the truth? Susan's hands trembled with shock. Her discoveries bolstered her resolve and absolved her guilt at prying in her lodger's room. She slid the money back into its hiding place, returned the books to the bag and left it as she had found it on the floor of the wardrobe. Then she went to the study, sat down and began to write.

'Dear Mrs. MacKenzie,

We have not yet met, and I was looking forward to making your acquaintance in the near future. However, I am concerned about Brigid's well-being, and wondered if you and Mrs. White might come sooner than arranged? I do not think there is any danger to Brigid or the baby, but I am worried about her state of mind. As we both know, Brigid has been through a great deal since last summer, and I fear it may be catching up with her. She is very withdrawn as the time approaches for the birth. I think it can only do her good to have her mother nearby – in fact, maybe to accompany her home – and would be obliged if you would consider my request. I have not told Brigid of this letter, because I do not wish to distress her further.

Yours sincerely,

Susan MacKendrick.

#

Molly had let it be known that she was retiring soon, in a mortal sense – going to Cornwall to live with a niece, she said. When she showed herself at church and around the neighbourhood, people were shocked at her appearance, which she wasn't taking as much care as usual to disguise. *"Cancer,"* they whispered behind her back, *"Not long for this world."* Offers of help came pouring in, for hadn't she helped so many? Molly was secretly delighting in these last few weeks, making gifts of the contents of her rented house, keeping only clothes and a few precious things to take with her. Of course, what nobody but the MacKenzies knew was that she was bound for Aberfoyle. She and Mary had hatched a plan to travel separately to London then meet up and take a train to Scotland.

When the letter arrived from Susan, their plans had to be brought forward. Molly pondered the matter, scrying in the flames of her range, and felt a shudder of apprehension. She still had no idea why Brigid's Midsummer baby was of relevance to whatever forces were afoot; the mother-to-be had mentioned nothing in her letters, except a strange comment recently that she was finding her surroundings menacing; even the hills and glens unsettled her, she had said. Mary had believed it was homesickness, but Molly wasn't so sure. Walter assured them that the Trossachs were breathtakingly beautiful, and Molly mutely agreed. The women had left him in ignorance of the truth of what was happening with his daughter. Now this request from Susan upset the flow of their arrangements and caused Molly great concern. She told people that she had decided to go earlier; looking at her ravaged face, they expressed their sorrow but understood.

With her cat Seamus in a pet carrier, two of her more affluent clients drove her to the station and took her to the platform to catch the London train for the first leg of her supposed journey to Cornwall. Molly allowed them to install her and her baggage on board, and waved at them until the train chugged clear of the platform. They, like others, had made noises about keeping in touch; but none of them, seeing the emaciated old lady, expected it. It was better to see her going, happy and smiling, and to imagine her in Cornwall, without knowing whether she was still in this world or not.

Molly sat back in her compartment and felt renewed strength with the beginning of her journey. In London, she sought not the train to Penzance, but the toilets, where she slipped a phial from her handbag, drank it down and emerged from the cubicle quite a different woman. Molly's magic was growing weaker every day, but she had been saving some dregs of it for this purpose, to renew herself for Aberfoyle; she was plump and twinkling again, her white bun a soft halo around her head and the scent of lavender surrounding her like a mist. She squared her shoulders and strode purposefully; she knew she was about to go full circle, back to where it all began; to the place where she had left unfinished business, at the opposite side of the wheel of the year, so long ago. She would meet Mary later, and together they would travel to Aberfoyle.

#

Kirkton Manse, December 1689

Mac was a fine young man, and had proved to be an asset. The Kirks kept some cattle and sheep on the glebe, and he knew well how to manage them. Robert took him to the smithy in the Clachan and introduced him to Wullie the blacksmith, who was intrigued and allowed him to use his tools. It was clearly his calling – he wielded the tools like an artist, and struck up a friendship with the elderly smith. Margaret, passing one day, saw him at the anvil and felt her breath taken away, seeing him there amidst the sparks and steam in the glow from the forge, like a man from another world. She found she liked having him around, especially when Robert was off on his rambles and research. It was galling that he was less and less interested in domestic matters now, being determined to have his manuscript ready for publication the following year; and midwinter was approaching fast. No doubt he would be off to Balquidder again, despite the bairn in Margaret's belly.

She was proved right – he told her of his intention, then looked at the floor as he said Aggie would be accompanying him. Margaret suffered the most painful thoughts then, of betrayal of a kind worse than still worshipping a first wife. "Why, Robert?" she asked helplessly.

"She can help me," he said, still avoiding her eyes.

"With what, Robert?" *Margaret folded her arms around her body, as if to hold the child close and prevent him hearing.*

"With my research. I've never passed through the veil there as I have here at Doon Hill, and she is from Balquidder."

Margaret tried to catch at fragments of thought as they drifted across her mind. It was the first she had heard of Aggie coming from Balquidder. "What veil dae ye speak of, Robert? The one between this world an' the next, or that Otherworld ye visit, the realm o' the fae?"

He looked at her then with a quizzical expression and laughed. "What would I be doin' tryin' tae see beyond the veil that separates us from the dead, Margaret? That would be heathen, pagan!"

She was more confused than ever. She thought they had had this conversation, or something similar, before. "Tae seek Isabel, Robert." *She whispered it as if it was a deadly secret. It was spoken at last.*

He stared at her. "My interest in Balquidder has never been to disturb Isabel's spirit," *he said.* "I have always been in quest of the fae. How long have you had this terrible thought in your head?"

She couldn't speak, choked by tears. It was good to hear him deny it, but it didn't change how he felt about Isabel, and it didn't explain why he was taking Aggie.

He started suddenly, as if the thought had just struck him. "Ye surely dinna suspect me o' any impropriety wi' Aggie?"

Margaret was miserable. "I don't know, Robert. But I wouldn't trust her with any man, an' that's the truth! You are a good man, and can be naïve in matters o' the world, husband. Think on yer reputation, please!"

Robert began to pace the room. "I thought maybe ye had realised, Margaret," *he said. He sat down next to her on the wooden settle. He took her hand and caressed it gently while marshalling his words.* "She's one of them," *he said.* "One o' the fae. She wants tae live in this world, be a midwife from some ancient order they have, but ye've seen what she's like. They won't have her. I thought maybe she could be of the brownie type, work in the hoose. But she isna much good at that, either, I know."

Margaret's head swam and a wave of weakness swept through her body. She thought she might slide off the settle. She could only stare at her husband in horror. Of course she knew about fae midwives, only too well; and of course she had heard of brownies, those fae who chose to live with mortals and help around the house; but neither turned up in your cellar with their skirts round their waists, like the sordid, filthy humanity you would find in any whorehouse. This creature was in no way like Molly – she was the kind whose mischief and malice among mortals benevolent fae like Molly sought to redress.

Robert spoke again as if reading her thoughts. "She means well, really she does. She's not malevolent, just…mischievous. She's a mischief."

Margaret tried to find her voice. "You kept her here, knowing what she was? With your son in the house, and our new child on the way?"

"I mean it, my dear, she's harmless. I hoped she might be expectin' her own bairn by now."

"Why ever would you wish that?"

"Because the offspring o' a fae creature and a black African - would that not be somethin' for my research, for science? Mr. Boyle would be so very impressed!"

Margaret couldn't answer him; bile rose in her throat at the horror of the workings of her husband's mind. Yet his eyes shone with enthusiasm, his expression as innocent as she had ever known it.

"Robert," she said, "I fear for you." She didn't add that she feared for herself, too.

After he had gone to Balquidder, Mac came to her as she sat by the fire, sewing for the baby. "I have seen you under the ash near the bottom of Doon Hill, Mistress."

Margaret started at his words. "What have ye seen?"

"Your friend, the fair one. The good one. The one who is so unlike my wife in every way."

Margaret's heart skipped a beat. "What do ye know, Mac?"

"I have learned a great deal from Aggie. Her kind are afraid of iron, you know. It repels them. They cannot have their way where it is. You remember how she fled from the room when she saw the sky iron. I must thank you for our iron bedstead, Mistress. She sleeps on the floor." He looked away, smiling, while Margaret blushed. "Your sky iron is very powerful, Mistress."

Margaret locked eyes with his. "What do ye have in mind, Mac?"

"A brooch," he said. "A talisman, to wear as protection for you and the babe."

#

It was a hot, airless June afternoon. Susan wiped her brow with her forearm, smearing it with dirt – she had been working in the vegetable garden at the side of the house. She heard a car coming up the road. Not many vehicles passed that way. She listened as it stopped, engine running, at the end of her driveway. A few moments later came the sound of the heavy door knocker Ria had made for her, as the car's engine revved and receded into the distance. She tutted. Who would come here in a car, and be dropped off? Whoever it was, they would have wakened Brigid from her nap, pounding the door like that. The mother-to-be was so nervous and jumpy these days that she was unsettling company, and Susan was happier for all their sakes when she was resting in her room. As she thought of Brigid, it crossed her mind that the caller might just be a Robert Kirk fanatic. She would see them on their way. She pulled off her gardening gloves and brushed herself down, noting the dirt on her arms and sighing at the soil clinging to her blouse. Her clothing, as always, was elegant, and would have been perfect for snipping a few roses, but not for the heavy work wartime "digging for victory" demanded.

She walked round to the front of the manse. There, in her porch, were two respectable-looking elderly women. They didn't look like believers in fairies, mused Susan. That type was usually a bit eccentric or Bohemian in appearance. These were probably literary folklorists, she guessed. After all, Robert Kirk, despite all the daftness surrounding him, had influenced not only Sir Walter Scott but Jules Verne. Oh, she knew the man's work had merit – and he had been a learned scholar – but the legends which had grown up around him had, as far as she was concerned, belittled and made an embarrassment of him. She still hadn't broached the subject with Brigid.

The old ladies turned at the sound of her footsteps. Susan fixed her clergyman's wife smile in place. "May I help you?"

The smaller of the women spoke. She wasn't as well dressed as her companion, and her face was lined and careworn. "I'm Mary MacKenzie," she said in a soft Irish accent. "I'm Brigid's mother."

Susan felt wrong-footed, flustered. Mrs. MacKenzie hadn't replied to her letter. They had obviously just decided to pack and leave for Scotland on receiving it. "Oh!" she exclaimed. "I wasn't expecting you!

Forgive the state of me, I've been gardening…and this must be Mrs…er…and have you brought a cat?"

The other woman stepped forward, holding out her hand. "I'm Molly White," she said. "Please don't concern yourself with your appearance! We came on the Paddy – the overnight Irish mail train – and I assure you we feel crumpled and stained!"

Susan took in the woman's lilac suit and her perfect bun with not a white hair straying from it, and she felt as if she was in the presence of a person to be reckoned with, a force of nature. A hint of lavender wafted on the summer air. Despite her surprise, her discomfort at their unannounced arrival, a sense of reassurance crept over Susan. This woman would take charge. She would take Brigid off her hands. "I'm very glad to meet you both," she said, shaking Molly's hand, then Mary's. "Please come in. You must need some refreshment."

She opened the front door and gestured for them to step inside. Molly White hesitated a moment, a shadow crossing her face.

"Your cat is very welcome, too," said Susan. "I'll find something for her – or is it him? – to eat, and you can let the poor creature out."

Molly smiled politely and stepped into Kirkton Manse.

#

Kirkton Manse, January – February 1690

Mac returned to Margaret in the New Year, 1690, with the brooch he had fashioned from one lump of her meteorite. It was an iron circlet of thistles and leaves – ash leaves for her, he said, and thistles to represent the master. It was simple, but well-executed, and it delighted Margaret. She had been thinking.

"Mac, would you be able to help me in another way?" She explained what she wanted. He nodded and said she was wise, and that his blacksmith friend would agree – for there were many murmurs about the master now, he told her, and his wanderings on Doon Hill, and the beings whom he might be disturbing. There were demons and strange spirits in the far-flung lands from which he came, he told her. Maybe they were different, but in all places and at all times, creatures from worlds beyond had broken through to this one; and some from this world had gone to theirs, but had rarely fared well from it.

#

A few weeks later, on the eve of St. Brigid's Day, Margaret's pains came on with dawn. Molly the midwife had anticipated this — it had been part of the charm she had used in conjunction with the potions she had given Margaret. She set out to make her first visit to the manse, the only occasion they had met anywhere except under the ash on Doon Hill. She was nervous, eager to please but apprehensive because of the presence of Aggie, of whom Margaret had told her at Midwinter. To Molly, she sounded like the worst of her kind, the sort to create mayhem with no thought but to please and amuse herself.

Margaret had assured her she would be kept well away from the bedchamber. She had moved into another room so that Robert would not be disturbed while she gave birth and recovered. The cradle upon which he had insisted stood ready beside the bed there. He would stay away until after the birth; it was no place for a man, and Margaret wanted as little contact between him and Molly as possible. She had told him of the new midwife; indeed, Molly had delivered several babies in the neighbourhood by this time; but he had never met her, and Margaret feared he would know her for what she was. Molly now took the precaution of pinning her hair up severely and wearing the dullest clothes, as she had learned was best for her station in this world. Really, it would be better to be plainer and older, but these were things which would come with time. She called herself Mistress White.

Elsie admitted her to the manse. She found Margaret in a state of agitation, sitting on the chamber pot. The pains were coming and going and she had awakened to find the bed wet; a trickle of fluid had begun and would not stop.

"It's your waters breaking slowly," said Molly. "It happens this way sometimes. Women expect a sudden flood, but it can be like this. Perfectly normal, don't worry." She gave Elsie orders and saw to it that the rags Margaret used for her monthly periods were made into pads to catch the fluid which had surrounded the growing baby for nine months, and helped her patient into bed. She didn't express her concern that Margaret's severe pains were not yet proper contractions. This did not bode well.

After a few hours, Margaret's waters had drained away. There had been no pains for some time. Her back ached, though, and she became agitated. She had been awake for hours and was tired. Molly fetched a sedating draught from her bag and said Margaret should sleep now.

"Why would I dae that?" cried Margaret. "Am I not just about tae give birth?"

"I'm afraid not," said Molly. "There'll be a lot more pain before that. You need to gather your strength. Take the chance to sleep while you can."

"No!" Margaret batted her hand away, and the phial slipped from Molly's grasp and smashed on the floor.

"Oh! I don't have any more with me!"

"I have no intention of taking it!" Margaret was defiant in her exhaustion.

Molly bent over her, mopping her brow, enfolding Margaret in the aroma of lavender which always hung about her person. "It won't make the baby come any sooner if you don't sleep now, and it won't make the birth any easier. I'll leave you with Elsie while I run across the fields to my cottage and…"

Margaret's hand seized her wrist like a vice. "You will do no such thing! Ye'll stay here an' help me like ye said ye would!"

Molly saw the fear in her eyes. "I am trying to help you," she said gently. She leaned closer, sat on the bed and cradled Margaret's head, caressing her soft brown hair from her brow to the tip of the plait in which it was woven. She willed a slight intensifying of her lavender scent; not enough for Elsie to notice, but sufficient to make Margaret relaxed and drowsy. That was when she first felt it – a barrier between her and her patient, invisible, but there. Her magic was not working. Margaret was not responding; she was becoming more agitated and beginning to writhe with the pain coming from her back. Molly knew the cause of this – the babe lay in a dry womb, his spine against Margaret's. It was going to be a long, hard labour and birth.

Molly thought quickly. "If you won't sleep, Margaret, I'll give you something for the pain, but I would rather save it for later. You can have just a little now."

She rose and reached for her bag.

"I won't take it! How do I know ye're no' tryin' tae make me sleep?"

"Because I just told you, I have no more sleeping draught with me."

"I thought a midwife like you would make things easy," she said, trying to convey her meaning without alerting Elsie.

Molly turned to the maid and asked her to go and fetch some beer for her mistress. She sighed and spoke to Margaret when she had gone. "I have things to ease labour and birth which a common midwife does not," she said. "My medicines are more potent and I am more skilled in the knowledge of what is happening, and with the delivery. But I can't make a baby pop out like magic. It's sleep you need now, Margaret. Your birth pangs proper are yet to begin."

Margaret began to cry. "And yet ye helped me tae get in this condition, and promise a boy? How can ye dae sae much, and yet not other things?"

Molly shrugged. "It's the way it is. The things you call magic are common amongst my kind. We are made differently, we are skilled in different ways. I do what I can. Margaret – I feel a barrier between us. Is this bed all of wood?"

Margaret Kirk uttered a startled "Oh!" and looked at the midwife as if something had just occurred to her. "I didna think it would affect you!"

"What is it, Margaret? What have you done?" Molly groaned inwardly – she had guessed already.

"I had Mac put iron strips under the bed, an' under the cradle – tae repel his wife, an' any other harmful fae. You are not of that kind!"

Molly sighed again. If Margaret stopped being so difficult, she could work round the deterrent. Time spent in this world, especially time well spent doing good, meant that the effect of iron was growing weaker, but she hadn't been here so very long. "It doesn't affect me so much as our relationship," she said. "We're a team, bringing this child into the world. Everything will be fine as long as you heed me well and do as I say. You must trust me, Margaret, and oblige me in this." As she spoke, her glance fell on the brooch Margaret wore pinned to her nightgown. "Your bonny brooch is also of iron, I think?" She knew the answer. There might be strips of iron under the bed, but the brooch, she realised now, was the main source of her discomfort. It threw a force field around her patient; it was more potent than anything she had yet come across.

"This is special," Margaret replied. "It's made from sky iron – iron which fell blazing from the stars."

Molly sighed. This was powerful magic indeed. "We would work better together if you removed it and put it away – well away from me. I could do more for you then."

Margaret gazed at her through narrowed eyes. "No," she said. "I will not!"

"Surely you do not mistrust me, Margaret? When I helped with the babe's conception?"

"How dae I know what your purposes were, now it comes tae it? I would wish you gone this minute if I had anybody else tae help me! I wish I had never had truck wi' your kind!"

"Then you diminish the help I can give," said Molly. "I swear my intentions in this world, with you and any other woman, are only good."

"Just do what ye can for me! It will be enough."

Molly nodded, but labour hadn't even begun properly, and she despaired. Matters did not go well. When the pains began in earnest, Margaret refused to turn over on to all fours to ease them, saying she would not behave like an animal. She also refused, later, to get out of bed and pull on the rope Molly had tied to one of the posts, to let gravity take some of the strain. She fought Molly off at every turn, screaming that she had expected ease and dignity from a fae midwife, and Molly sent Elsie away, saying her mistress was fevered and raving. She would accept nothing from Molly's hand to help her, and Molly was kept by the presence of the brooch from doing anything to coax the medications into her mouth. Margaret lay on her back, writhing. Unlike the peasant women whom Molly had aided in her first year amongst mortals, this gentlewoman knew nothing of labour and birth and was totally unprepared.

At sunset, Rev. Kirk himself appeared, rather than sending Elsie for another report. He was ashen faced from hearing his wife's screams all day, and asked if the matter was not nearly over. No, said Molly, for the baby had turned and was lying across Margaret's body. Eventually, she had Elsie return and hold her mistress's shoulders down while she pitted all her will against the effect of the brooch and tried to bring the infant's head back to the birth position, but instead he went the other way and was breech, his feet coming out first. Molly's hands were small and adept at such births, but Margaret's lack of cooperation and Molly's need to fight the force field of the brooch were exhausting. Finally, just after one in the morning on St. Brigid's Day, Robert Kirk junior entered the world.

Margaret hadn't the strength to hold him. While she drifted in and out of sleep, Molly quietly asked Elsie to remove the iron brooch — for the baby's sake, she said, lest it jag him — and unbutton her mistress' nightgown. She supported the mite, who was healthy and hungry, at his mother's breast. When he had guzzled his fill, and been washed and swaddled by Molly while Elsie bathed and changed Margaret, Molly turned to find the new mother glaring at her with loathing.

"This was not what I expected. I would not have had truck wi' your kind had I known it was tae be like this."

Molly swallowed. *"It wouldn't have been, but for the brooch,"* she said. *"But I understand why you did it. You didn't know all the implications."*

"Is the cradle protected?"

"It is."

"Then that's all I want tae know from you ever again," said Margaret. "Stay away frae me an' my family!"

"But you have the son I promised," said Molly, "and now, for your husband's sake, you must…"

"Try tae keep him wi' me? Aye. We have another o' your kind livin' here now, at his invitation. So what good can keepin' him away frae Doon Hill dae? It's too late." She turned her face into the pillow.

"The one who lives here does not sound as if she has intentions like mine!" protested Molly. "I came into this world to serve mothers and babes. Your fae maid sounds as if she stumbled here on a whim." She was bone-weary. "I still say it's best to keep Mr. Kirk away from Doon Hill. That is where the danger lies. That is what I have foreseen. But seeing a thing in the future does not mean it has to come to pass. It is still possible for it to be changed."

Molly collected her belongings and left the room. It was past four in the morning now; she had sent Elsie away because she was falling off her feet with exhaustion. Rev. Kirk had retired for the night after greeting his new son with joy, but he had said there would be refreshments left for her in the kitchen when she was ready, and the bag of coins she had named as payment.

The manse was large, but she crept downstairs and followed the long passageway towards the back of the house, where light spilled from beneath a doorway. This must be the kitchen. She opened the door gently so as to make no sound, but uttered a cry, soon stifled, at what she saw there. By the light of a candle, the creature who called herself Aggie sat reading the Bible. Molly recognised her, although she knew her by another name – just as she herself had not been called Molly in the world from which they both came. Aggie had been Deire, a servant in her father's house, a drab who had to be scolded regularly and who had a habit of following her around. Molly had been Sherene, the precious eldest daughter of the house, and she had never been sure whether the slatternly maid admired her or was making fun of her; mischief and causing discomfort to everyone she could had been her way. Molly had ignored her with all the dignity of one born to her high station, as if she did not exist.

Aggie turned to look at Molly, holding the thin leaf of the Bible page between finger and thumb as if it might contaminate her, her face in a grimace which suggested a bad smell. The fae had little use for scripture, except to twist it against mortals. Molly understood that. As a midwife, she had to pass as human and so had begun attending church, realising it was necessary to her reputation, but she paid little heed. She had chosen another, not Rev. Kirk's, and she was glad of it now. She wondered what Aggie was up to, for the frown left her face when she saw Molly in the doorway, and a malevolent smile lit her eyes.

Molly turned immediately. She would go without refreshment. She would not be alone with this creature. The long hours in this house had gone badly enough.

"Is the lovely Sherene afraid o' little me?" Aggie taunted.

Molly turned back to face her. "No, Deire. But I fear for this good family."

They didn't hear Robert Kirk padding barefoot down the passageway until the light of his candle spilled around them and he spoke. "Ah, Aggie, you've stayed up tae see tae our guest. And doing a little study while you waited, I see! Good, good. Well done! Come in, Mistress White, ye have more than earned your refreshments before ye go."

Molly turned back into the kitchen. Aggie wore only a nightgown, a cast-off of Margaret's, which had worn thin and was almost transparent in the flickering candlelight. Her ebony hair was loose and tousled but clean and shining, tumbling down her back. She looked better than she had within the realm from which they came. Molly used the last of her strength to will a protection spell on Robert Kirk beneath her breath. Aggie would use everything at her disposal to have her way, including the curves on display below her nightgown and her dark pools of eyes where a storm of malevolence could be changed in moments to the false calm of enticing waters.

Molly allowed herself to be gently steered into the kitchen, where Robert pulled out a chair and poured some beer for her. He invited her to help herself to the food on offer, and told Aggie she could go to bed now. To be polite, Molly forced herself to eat, although she had lost her appetite. They made small talk. He was a good man, a genuine man, she could tell that. He was also naïve. She had always known that, and she feared for him, and for this family. Well, she had done her best. She ate and drank a little, then thanked him and rose to leave. He picked up the pouch of money lying on the table and held it out to her.

"Thank you, Sir, but I will not take it. Your wife is dissatisfied with my service."

"I'm sure that's just because she's exhausted," said Robert. "And you are, too. Ye have more than earned this. My wife, I think, was a most difficult patient. I did not hear such cries and complaints from the first Mistress Kirk!"

"It was a very difficult labour and birth. You would be as well not to say such a thing to your wife, Sir," said Molly. She could imagine that he would, with no guile or ill will. He just wouldn't think. It would simply be an observation, but it would twist the knife of bitterness in Margaret's soul with consequences no-one could measure. Perhaps her work with Robert Kirk here in the kitchen would earn her some redemption this dark morn. He pressed her to accept the pouch of coins, looking puzzled at her refusal. She took it, with the intention of putting all of it in the church collection before she left Aberfoyle. It seemed fitting.

Back in her cottage, which she had beautified with her arts, she knelt before the blazing fire where bunches of dried herbs spilled over the mantel and filled the air with fragrance, and she requested another posting. She beseeched the Goddess, the Mystery, to send her onwards. She had made mistakes, but she had learned much. Margaret was the only person she had told of her origins, and she would not do that again, nor concern herself with any affairs other than childbirth. She would veil her beauty even more in subsequent postings, and through time, through generations of mortals being born and passing on into whatever Mystery was theirs, she would mature and age and do good, until the time came when she had to disguise her great age and state of decay in order not to disgust.

#

In Brigid's bedroom, Molly White glanced at the cradle and recoiled at the memories it sent flooding into her tired brain. She looked better than she felt after travelling for more than a day, and she was going to have to rest and renew herself if she was to aid Brigid. This room didn't help. It was the one Margaret Kirk had used for her lying-in, the old-fashioned term for labour, birth and recovery.

Brigid lay on the bed, her mother sitting holding her hand. Her other hand clutched the brooch Mary had given her for her wedding – Molly hadn't been able to recall it clearly and grasp its significance when first she had seen it, but now she knew. It had been part of the protection Margaret had arranged with her black servant, and no doubt it had been fundamental to Brigid's summoning to Aberfoyle. Molly had been in this world so long that not even sky iron bothered her now, but she was wary of the brooch because she didn't know the forces who were using it, and what their intentions were. It was in remarkable condition for a piece so old made of iron, which suggested magic of some sort had been worked upon it. She wondered how it had come into the MacKenzie family. Callander, where Walter said his ancestors had lived, wasn't all that far away.

When Brigid hadn't appeared downstairs, Mary had asked if they might go and surprise her. They had found her lying awake, but far away, her eyes roaming the room, although she had focussed when she realised who was there. She had cried with joy and relief.

"How long have you been feeling not quite yourself, dear?" Molly asked now.

Brigid's eyes were still brimful of tears. "Oh, Mrs. White!"

"I know all about it, Brigid," she said. "I'm sorry I didn't see it from the start, but I'm old, very old, and not so quick these days. I've come to help you. What do they want of you – whoever called you here? Do you know who they are?"

Brigid shrunk away from Molly. "How do you know such things? Are you a witch, Mrs. White? There's an old hag here who calls herself a midwife, but I think she's a witch!" Brigid was sobbing, her words punctuated by gasps for air.

Molly swallowed at the reference to a hag. If she didn't have access to a fire and her herbs and potions soon, she would revert to being an old hag like none Brigid had ever imagined. "You're knowledgeable about folklore, Brigid, so you know there are many types of fae with many motives and intentions. You can be sure of me, though. I turned my back on my own world long, long ago. I'm a fae midwife. I abhorred seeing babes brought in, stolen from their mortal mothers just to be an amusement to my kind. Or good mothers taken captive to nurse fairy children. I'm here to help you. Now, tell me why you think you're here, of all places. I need to hear it from you."

Brigid took a calming breath. "I always thought there was something different about you, Mrs. White."

"I suspect you've inherited some intuition, a leaning towards such things from your mother – and maybe even your father's side, too, coming from these parts – but whatever happened that night in the Blitz has opened a window in your mind, a window in your soul, maybe. Anything can use that window. You know you've never seen me do anything but good. So, why are you here? Start at the beginning, on that night in London."

Molly listened as Brigid told it all. She half-wished she could give the explanation any doctor surely would, especially a psychiatrist; that Brigid had been injured and unconscious after a bomb blast; that she had been raped; that she had turned to her favourite books in her trauma, and that she had imagined everything, an explanation for the child growing in her womb, a child she loved and wanted despite the circumstances of its conception. However, Molly had good reason to believe her.

"In what manner is your baby to free Robert Kirk?" she asked gently.

"I don't know," said Brigid. "I think it might happen when I lay him in the cradle at Midsummer, when he's born, when the veil between worlds is thin."

A fear, unspoken by any of them, hung in the air. Had Brigid been summoned to give her son in exchange for Robert Kirk? Molly remembered the kindly cleric she had met just once. How could that guileless man do harm to anyone? He would wish to be free, but never at the cost of anybody else. Not Rev. Kirk. Yet the cleric had also been dangerously naïve. Why, though, had Brigid been chosen for a fae conception? It didn't make sense, this breeding of a child to exchange for a captive. It was not the way things were done – a fully human child, a normal babe, would have been sought. A fae conception was for a child who would walk between worlds, a seer with a purpose in this human world, bearing the gifts of the fae. She didn't voice her thoughts to Brigid.

"So," she said, "you've seen things and known things and sometimes, since coming here, you've had glimpses of the past. What is going on in this house now, Brigid? What are you seeing?" The young woman's troubled eyes had been roaming the room as she spoke; they were rarely still in the calm, serene way Molly remembered.

"I keep seeing movement out of the corner of my eye," she said, "and for a long time, even before this started happening, I felt as if I wasn't alone at times. As if I was being watched. I sometimes hear noises in the attic above me – I told you about the earth tremor when I was in the graveyard, and the faces at the windows."

Molly knew to whom these faces belonged – her first patient, Margaret Kirk, and her two servants, the former slave whom she had never met and his awful wife whom she knew only too well. "I don't believe this house is haunted by those people, dear. You had, as you said yourself, a glimpse of the past. On some morning a long time ago, those three people all happened to be looking out of the windows. Perhaps something in the kirkyard had caught their attention, but it wasn't you." She was satisfied in her own mind that the three former residents she had known were long gone.

"But somebody or something is watching me!" Brigid protested. "Something is getting inside my head!" She pulled her hand away from her mother and wrapped her arms around her head as if to block whatever it was she feared.

"What do you mean, Brigid?" Mary MacKenzie's voice trembled.

Brigid glanced fearfully at the cradle. "I didn't want that. I don't want it. But something made me say I did!"

Molly frowned. This matter was becoming more complex by the minute. "Well, there's a quick solution to that, dear. We'll take it away! Where did you find it?"

"In the cellar," said Brigid. "It's where it's meant to be, but the bed is in the wrong place, and I don't know why I wanted it or how I know these things!"

"Hush now," said Molly. "Mary, can you help me get rid of this old thing? We'll go and speak with Mrs. MacKendrick, Brigid, and I'll bring you a sleeping draught from my case."

Molly stepped towards the cradle, remembering the one and only time she had seen it before. Margaret Kirk hadn't wanted it, either – she had felt obliged to have it because Robert wished it. It was surely a cursed object. Mary MacKenzie kissed her daughter and took hold of one end of the cradle, and the two elderly women shuffled out of the room with it. They carried it downstairs with some difficulty and followed the sound of voices through to the kitchen.

The MacKendrick children turned and stared as they came into the room and lowered the cradle to the floor. They were kneeling around Seamus, Molly's cat. He looked half-afraid and half-indignant at the attention. They laid the cradle down.

"He's rather anti-social," said Molly. "He isn't used to company." Neither, she thought, was she, not to live with.

Susan appeared from the pantry. "Has Brigid changed her mind about the cradle? That's a relief. I only gave in because of her strange mood, her insistence. How did you find her?"

Molly hesitated, choosing her words, glancing meaningfully at the children. "I laid down the law about the cradle," she said, voice full of professional authority she didn't feel. "Not the best thing for baby. Not nowadays. Brigid requires a lot of rest. It's as you said. I have something in my case that I can give her to help. I'll take it up to her now." She had noted that their luggage was still in the hallway.

The minister's wife also seemed to be choosing her words. "Perhaps it would be best if Brigid were to move into the cottage with you? She would have more peace and quiet there. Unless, of course, you think she would be better to go home?"

Mary MacKenzie opened her mouth to speak when an unearthly wail came from upstairs. They all paled at the sound, and the younger children fled to their mother and clung to her legs. Mary ran from the room. Molly followed her, telling Susan to stay with the children. They found Brigid huddled in a corner of her bedroom, sobbing and hardly able to breathe.

"Brigid! What is it?" Mary dropped to her knees beside her daughter, gathering her into her arms.

Brigid raised glazed eyes and stared at her mother. "Angry…so angry…whoever it is…like in Balquidder, but worse…they're angry about the cradle!"

Mary looked helplessly at Molly. Molly shrugged. She was increasingly at a loss, and exhaustion was taking over. "Let's get the cradle back for now," she said. It would silence whatever force had Brigid in its grip. They would not leave Brigid to sleep in this room, however. They helped her to her feet and they all hastened down the stairs.

Susan MacKendrick and her children turned shocked, concerned faces towards them as Mary pulled out a chair for Brigid and the young woman slumped into it, resting her head on her arms on the table.

"What happened?" asked Susan.

"We'll have to put the cradle back," said Molly. "I'm sorry, Mrs. MacKendrick, but it's necessary to Brigid's well-being." She glanced at the children. "However, I don't think she should sleep in that room."

A beat fell. "As I was saying before you had to run upstairs," Susan said, "it would be best if Brigid were to go home with you if she's able, or move into the cottage if not. I really can't justify her being in my employ any longer."

Brigid raised her head from the table and looked around at the three older women as if something had just occurred to her. "Why have you come, Mam?" she asked. "Susan, did you send for Mam and Mrs. White?" When Susan met her eyes and nodded, any colour she had fled from her face. "How did you find the address?"

"There were books in your bag in the wardrobe, Brigid. It was written in one of them."

Unspoken words hung in the air between them.

Mary MacKenzie spoke hesitantly. "I phoned the owner of the cottage before we set out," she said. "I'm afraid there are holiday-makers in it now. We can't have it until the time arranged."

"And my professional opinion is that Brigid cannot make the journey home," Molly added.

There was an uncomfortable silence. Susan's face hardened. "Then I suppose you'll all have to stay here. For now."

Chapter Twenty-Two

Molly had never lived with anybody before, and if any time in her long, long life – her many incarnations – was inconvenient, it was now. The others were all early risers, which meant she had to be up and fit to be seen before they were. This required fire, and potions. It was summer. No fires were lit in the manse. She had asked Susan if she might have a small one in her bedroom from time to time, pleading old age. This was enough for the small pot she had concealed in her suitcase.

The dried ingredients which Molly had brought with her were proving insufficient for her growing needs of restoration and concealment. Fresh botanicals were easy enough to obtain in the garden, fields and hedgerows at this time of year, but she had to exhaust herself by taking walks to pick them. The MacKendrick children were smitten with her and often came after her, so she had begun slipping out of the house at three in the morning, a headscarf pulled low on her brow, hiding her emaciated face. She was sleeping in Brigid's room; Brigid and her mother shared the twin room which Susan had grudgingly offered until they could go to the cottage. Molly had tried to summon whatever had plagued Brigid in that room, but it left her undisturbed, for which she was glad. Things were hard enough. She sighed as she hobbled from the house once more, acknowledging the fact that the herbs and flowers she sought were more potent plucked at this hour; and indeed, she was far more energetic once she had taken her peculiar medication, with its fresh ingredients, than she was after using dried herbs and other preparations.

Molly felt a frisson of déja-vu every time she left the manse at this eerie hour. It was grey with the coming of dawn, rather than pitch black as it had been on that first occasion in 1690, but it still reminded her of that desperate day and night when she had pitted her will against Margaret Kirk to try to deliver her son safely into the world. She disliked the manse because of the memories, and was ill at ease there. However, she had to stay to help Brigid, without understanding what was happening here; try as she might, scry in her meagre bedroom fire as she had, she could not work it out. The legend of Robert Kirk's supposed death and abduction hadn't surprised her when she had researched it before coming – the foolish, naïve man had meddled far too much in matters of the fae. He had suffered the fate she had foreseen, the one of which she had tried to warn his wife, in order to attempt to save him. Yet why Brigid had been chosen to free him, and how, was beyond her.

"Good morning."

Molly froze, her hand outstretched to pluck a flower from the hedgerow. She daren't turn to whoever had spoken – a voice she didn't recognise – for she couldn't show her face, a visage which belonged in a coffin.

"Ye needna fear tae look my way. It'll be like lookin' in a mirror. Comes tae us all."

Molly turned then and gasped. Another of her kind, unmistakable, stood in the road, skeletal teeth bared in a rictus grin. She tried to keep a quaver from her voice. "We are few and far between. I am merely visiting. I did not know of another such in these parts." Was she trespassing on another fae midwife's territory? The only midwife Brigid had mentioned was the one she said was a hag, a witch, merely descriptive terms, for of course she was talking about an old woman and no true fae midwife could be described thus, no matter how old she was. Molly was living proof of that; their gifts and potions ensured it.

Oh...the awful knowledge came as she looked into those eyes, glittering with insolence despite the decaying flesh around them. "Deire! Or is it still Aggie?"

"I've gone by the name o' Agnes long ages past," the woman replied. "More dignified."

"But you're not a midwife…"

"Not accordin' tae the likes o' you, *Sherene or is it Molly*, but I'm a survivor. I made my way regardless. I've brought generations intae this world."

Molly shivered. "And how many have you swapped in their cradles, imposter? How many handed over to the fae? How many mothers with good milk have you enticed to that Otherworld?"

Agnes laughed and made a dismissive gesture. "What brings ye back now? I think I know, but I want tae hear it frae your lips. How much have ye worked oot, Clever Clogs?"

Molly stared at her. "What made you stay in these parts? How did you manage it? If indeed you have always been here. And how come you retain your memory of all these years?"

"I've been here and hereaboots," said Agnes. "I canna travel far, but I can remember everythin', unlike you and yer kind. Two hundred an' fifty years is a heavy weight o' rememberin'. It's a punishment for slippin' oot o' oor world on your coat tails. Yer fine mother didna grant permission for either o' us tae leave, but you were protected by yer profession. No such luck for me. Ye havena answered my question."

Molly was dumbfounded – so that's what had happened. Aggie had followed her, Sherene as she had been then, just as she had done around her family home and everywhere she went when she was a servant in the fae realm. "I brought the lass staying at the manse into the world, and I'm here to help her," she said.

"Oh aye. Goody Two-Shoes Brigid. Just your type. Well, she'll need yer help right enough."

"What do you know about this matter? Tell me!" cried Molly, with all the imperiousness of Sherene.

"Me? What would I know, an' me such a misfit anywhere she goes, not much skill o' any kind, not even a good servant in a fae hoose? What could I possibly know?"

Molly glared at the glittering eyes, the cocky tilt of the head. Aggie hadn't changed. "I've got what I came for," she said. "I'll be getting back."

"Aye," said Agnes. "Likewise. Back tae drink a draught o' youth. Not that I can work the magic like you – I've seen ye wi' yer smooth skin and white hair. It disnae work the same for me. Still – by the look o' ye at this minute, we're both due for retirement, I think. Not that I'll be granted it. Funny that we're both just collectin' hedge-browse, like a pair o' auld cattle treatin' oor ain ills, reduced tae the same in the end. Ha! They've forgotten that, in this modern world, the hedge-browse for coos an' humans alike. And oor kind. Medicine for free, in the wild. Ye'll be lookin' forward tae retirement, I suppose?"

Molly didn't reply. She turned slowly and walked away, aware of Agnes staring at her still. She couldn't believe this dark vestige of her past had survived. She almost respected her for it, except that it could not have been done without dark arts. Now she knew Aggie – Agnes – was involved, she had to act to foil her. No doubt she was awaiting the baby's birth at Midsummer; it was good that her arrival and taking charge prevented any possibility of Agnes being present at the birth itself. There was a dried ingredient Molly had brought thinking she might need it. She had laid the ground for its use by saying the other day that Brigid would never carry full-term, that she was small for so big a baby. It was Dried Raspberry Leaf. It was time to start treating the mother-to-be to a special tea – something to strengthen her, she would say. It would ensure the child was not born at Midsummer. Molly intended that the innocent mite should enter the world sooner, and be spared whatever was afoot – even if Robert Kirk remained trapped because of it. He wasn't blameless in the matter of his captivity, unlike this infant who had been called into being, it seemed, like an animal to be farmed for its usefulness – although Molly didn't know how, or by whom, for Agnes hadn't that power. She was working for someone, something else. Only a powerful force could have homed in on that iron brooch and sought out Brigid in London.

\#

Brigid went into labour on June the twelfth. Molly had hoped it would be a few days later, once they had moved to the cottage, although Brigid had been resisting that. Molly was annoyed at herself for making the special tea too strong. She had prepared Brigid for the fact that she "might" give birth early, but the young woman was distraught, still under the influence of whoever or whatever had summoned her. Molly had thought removing her from the manse might weaken that influence. Brigid was in the grip of something dark, and this early birth would be a victory over it and maybe free Brigid from it. She twinkled at Brigid now as she helped her to walk up and down between contractions, her smile a reassurance but brooking no nonsense; babies came when they chose to, she said, and this one was well on its way.

"But Molly!" Brigid pleaded. "You know why I'm here! You understand! Midsummer was meant to be the time, it was important!"

"I don't fully know why you're here, my dear," said Molly, "but if the little one is coming early, it's for a reason. Nature has decided he needs to be born now." She knew that she had given nature a helping hand with Dried Raspberry Leaf Tea and a few more ingredients, but she was convinced she was right to have acted as she did.

"But what about Robert Kirk?" cried Brigid.

What indeed? thought Molly. The more Molly had thought about it, the more she had come to doubt that Robert Kirk was involved at all, but that some evil force was; some force which had used his legend and the brooch to summon Brigid. She hadn't told Brigid about her meeting with Agnes, or her prior knowledge of the woman.

Labour progressed smoothly, so unlike the last time Molly had helped to birth a child in this house. She thought of the little boy she had delivered all those years ago. Her potion had guaranteed both the conception and the sex of Margaret's child. True to her word, she had never meddled in such a way again. She offered nothing to barren women but her sympathy, and suggested nothing which might mean control over the baby's sex; such things were old wives' tales, she told those who sought her advice. You had to take what God gave you. She didn't know in advance whether a mother would produce a boy or a girl;

the mother's instinct was often right, though, she had learned. Brigid, of course, was certain that she was having a boy, and Molly had no reason to doubt her. It would seem to be an essential element of the summoning the young woman had received, whatever and whoever was behind it; just as long as he was not born at Midsummer, thought Molly, and never laid in that old cradle. She realised that might be the next difficulty with Brigid, for although she detested the sight of the cradle, she was afraid not to use it. Molly would be adamant; she had to foil whatever trickery was afoot.

In the end, another matter threw them into confusion and the cradle was forgotten. At ten past seven on that grey and drizzling June evening, Molly delivered Brigid of a daughter. Brigid gazed in shock at the squalling infant and said this wasn't right, none of it was; where was her little boy that she meant to call Will, who should have been born into the Midsummer dawn? She was well – the birth had been easy – and she was fierce in her fury. She reminded Molly of Margaret in her attitude, but the midwife was more perplexed than ever. A girl, when Brigid had been so sure. What did any of this mean?

#

June 1691

Margaret had read and sung to young Robert, and tucked him in bed. He was a handful now he was walking, and she was tired in the evenings, but not as much as her husband. He had aged in the last couple of years. Jacobite battles had been fought, the first at Killiecrankie two years ago, the cause a banner to all Catholics who wanted to see King James the Second (and Seventh of Scotland) reinstated. Their Catholic friends were oppressed, and there were moves to suppress the Gaelic tongue; despite this, the distribution of Robert's Gaelic Bible had gone ahead without hindrance; the Presbyterian love of God's Word above all else no doubt meant they saw it as a good thing in any language, something which might tame the Highland savages.

Robert's research into fae matters contributed to his exhaustion. He still walked out at times when the air was thin, and as if sensing the trouble among humankind, the earth shifted relentlessly and drew back the veil more times in those days than usual. Margaret and their son had been unable to deter him, to bring his interest back to family matters. He insisted on keeping Aggie, observing her and continuing to lament the lack of offspring between her and Mac. He had not dared write to Mr. Boyle of the pair lest the letter fall into the wrong hands, but he planned to visit London again sometime soon and tell him. He would take him his manuscript, which detailed his research, and which was progressing well – except that his eyesight was failing. Margaret had offered to scribe for him, in an effort to have some role in his life other than keeping his house and raising his children.

He was difficult to work for. He looked for perfection, kept going back and forth and altering words, phrases, whole paragraphs. He read a lot of scientific papers, not just for the knowledge they contained, but to achieve the right format and tone for his own work. "The Secret Commonwealth of Elves, Fauns and Fairies" was a serious study, not written to entertain. He hoped it might be presented at the Royal Society, and stand as a bastion against the rising tide of atheism, for it revealed anew the existence of a creator responsible for more dimensions of creation than anybody dreamed. He demanded the highest standards of Margaret. She kept failing him.

Tonight, he referred to the fae as the "lychnobious people". Margaret had never heard of the word, and had to stop him to ask how to spell it and what it meant. He had been impatient with her. It meant they lived by lamplight and candlelight in that other realm, where a half-light, a kind of twilight, reigned permanently. Margaret shuddered. "Might this not be affecting your sight, Robert, you being among them and your eyes growing dim?" He was angry at her again. Another time, she had questioned the way he spoke of the Good People. It was common to call them this by way of respect – and out of fear – to keep them happy. Like everybody else, she knew the word "good" was mere lip service.

That wasn't what she questioned. It was this – did he really see them as "people" at all? He spoke of them at times like animals in a scientific laboratory, and she had seen how he observed Aggie. Margaret still had no love for their slatternly servant, but she knew the fae woman had a soul and was a person, even if of another world. She wasn't sure Robert understood that. He continued to defend Aggie and her "mistakes" and "accidents" as just being according to her nature, but there was something sinister in his attitude, no actual concern for her; she was like a wildcat that he kept and whose feral nature he observed with total objectivity.

Margaret was glad when the session was over and she could go to bed. Yet despite her fears and frustrations over her husband, despite her exhaustion, she still loved him, and she wanted him. He hadn't turned to her in a long time, not in the way *that mattered. Margaret wanted another child. Maybe a second one would achieve what the first had not, especially since she could play on how ill she had been bearing wee Robert. She could appeal to him to cease his activities so as not to stress and endanger her and their unborn child; and maybe it would be enough to save him, if she acted now. Yet how was she to manage it? The midwife who called herself Mistress White had long since departed the area, and had never been heard of again. Margaret regretted her behaviour to Molly; she would have sought her many times in the past year.*

#

Susan was sitting in the kitchen, smoking and staring into space, when she heard the tramp of the workman's boots Ria habitually wore. Her kinswoman appeared clutching a present for Brigid's baby.

"Hello stranger," said Susan. They hadn't seen much of each other since the day she had sent her down to the cellar to see the cradle. "You heard, then?"

"Aye. Katie told me yesterday. Are they still here?"

"The midwife's gone to the cottage they rented. Brigid's mother is still here with her and the baby. I can hardly insist they move, even just down the road, until she's recovered a bit. She's not getting much sleep. A week in bed, says the midwife. She's here a good few hours of the day, too."

"Regrettin' takin' her in now, are ye, Susan? I'm sorry I brought her here."

Susan sighed and shrugged. "I was sure that she'd sort things out with her parents and be on her way long before the birth. I was certain she'd get homesick. Heaven knows, I did when I first arrived from the big city, but I had to stay, no choice – she had nothing here to hold her."

A beat fell. "Maybe she did, though – have something to hold her," said Ria.

Susan blew a last stream of smoke into the air and stubbed out her cigarette. "Oh, don't start all that again, Ria!"

"She's called the bairn Ellen?"

"Yes. Lovely name."

"It's from *The Lady of the Lake*, by Sir Walter Scott. He discovered the legend o' Robert Kirk when he was here writin' it, as you know."

"So? It's one of her favourite books. Nothing odd about calling a child after a character in a book. Anyway, I don't understand why you're so bothered that she's into folklore – you don't believe this Fairy Minister nonsense any more than I do!"

"I never actually said that," said Ria.

Susan stared at her. "But you get annoyed at all the tourists who come sniffing around – you even warned Brigid! You laugh at the legends!"

Ria hesitated. "Maybe there's good reason we all laugh an' try tae put the tourists doon."

Susan was tired, irritable. "Whatever do you mean?"

"You dinna come frae these parts, neither you nor my cousin. Tom wasna brought up here, like me. The locals – we just prefer it never tae be mentioned."

Susan frowned. "I know that – because it's silly and it disparages the memory of a man who was actually a fine scholar."

"Not exactly. What ye say is partly true, but…we dinna want tae stir them up again."

Susan reached for another cigarette. "Stir up who? What are you talking about?"

"The fae. The Sith. The creatures from that other world who can cross into this one. Doon Hill is a gateway. So's Balquidder. An' if they have Robert Kirk, we dinna want tae disturb him, either, after all this time."

Susan paused, a match half way to her cigarette, which drooped in her lips as she tried to take in what Ria, sensible, practical Ria, was saying. "You're not serious?"

"Right after Brigid arrived, there was an earth tremor an' she had a funny turn. She tried tae cover it, but I saw it an' I should have known then. Some folk can see things when the earth moves – she's one o' them. She went tae Balquidder an' came back injured. Rob Roy's Grave? Runnin' for a bus? Ha! She was at Isabel Kirk's grave, an' somethin' happened. It's another thin place, ye see. Then she went strange the minute she saw that cradle. Robert Kirk made that for certain. You know fine she hasna been right ever since. Katie says she's not very happy because the bairn's a lassie and born too early. She wanted that bairn born here at Midsummer for a reason. She or whatever summoned her here."

Susan stared wide-eyed. She recalled her surprise at finding the books hidden in Brigid's bag. She thought of her odd behaviour. She frowned as she recalled the secrecy which seemed to envelop the three women who had ended up living with her. Mrs. White and Mary MacKenzie whispered in corners, broke off conversations when she came near and plastered false smiles on their faces. Brigid was well, apparently, but showed little joy in her baby. Mary MacKenzie was nervous and evasive, the midwife - that perfectly coiffed and scented paragon of respectability, Mrs. White – was reassuring and concerned to the point of being nauseating. She had had enough of all of them. Now Ria was talking mumbo-jumbo; she didn't know what had got into her.

"Really, Ria, I do not know what the matter is with everybody! Kindly never utter such frightening nonsense when the children are around!" She was becoming increasingly concerned for her family. She missed Tom and wondered what he would make of all this. He was glad she had some pleasant company, he had said in his last letter. So much for that!

Ria reached into her bag and brought out a package wrapped in brown paper. "This is for you," she said to Susan. "I don't know why, but I think ye might need it. It's the knife, the one that matches Brigid's brooch. I've always known aboot it – it's been in my family for years, made by an ancestor, so the story goes. A freed slave." She smiled at Susan's open-mouthed stare. "Oh aye, ye were right aboot ma looks. Maybe aboot the rest as well, Suriname an' all that, who can say? But if he made this, he also made that brooch, an' Brigid turnin' up here wearin' that is more than a coincidence. The family legend is that this knife has somethin' tae dae wi' Robert Kirk. There's the tale o' how he was tae be freed, of course, a dirk thrown over his head when he appeared in a vision at his child's christening. I hope that's no' why ye need it now. We've always kept quiet aboot it, like aboot everythin' else.

Things best forgotten. But Brigid has brought it all back. God knows what she's stirred up."

Susan stared at the package on the table. She was a Londoner, a modern woman. Sometimes she found it hard to believe the things her husband preached from the pulpit, never mind all this talk of fairies and brooches and knives and this cleric who had lived in her home so very long ago. Yet there were goosepimples on her bare arms despite the heat of the summer day.

"I'll leave ye tae think aboot it. Take care, Susan, for I don't believe whatever's at work here hasn't made use of you, too."

Susan found she was, for once, lost for words, as Ria rose and left the kitchen.

#

Kirkton Manse, September 1691 – May 1692

Margaret paced the parlour in a state of agitation. How could this be? Should she send for Mac and hear the truth of it? She didn't trust the word of his wife. If it was true, it wouldn't be his…Aggie had disgraced herself and brought shame upon them all by throwing herself at Robert's cousin, the local laird no less, on his last visit to the manse. Graham of Duchray had rebuffed her and reported her to Robert, and Margaret had to reprimand the slut. Heaven knows how many others there had been, since Mac continued to refuse her. She was forever creeping out and wandering in the wild at night. Glancing out of the window, Margaret saw Mac on the glebe. She drew her shawl around herself – she would go and speak with him, make it look as if she was simply out to take the evening air.

Her legs were shaking as she approached him. "Mac!" Her voice was unnaturally bright. "I hear you are to be a father. My congratulations!"

He looked at the ground. She waited for him to deny it, or to deny the child was his. The two of them shared secrets – they understood each other well. It felt like a slap in the face, therefore, when he mumbled, "Thank you, Mistress," without raising his eyes.

"You do not have to hide the truth from me," said Margaret, while a cold shiver ran down her spine. "In any case, it will soon be out when the child is born, for it is bound to be as white as she is!" She desperately wanted this to be the truth.

"She tricked me," Mac said helplessly. "The child is as like to be mine as any other man's. She put something in my beer when she brought it to the smithy. It was the best beer I had ever tasted, begging your pardon, Mistress. I was so hot and thirsty…"

Margaret maintained her dignity with difficulty. "Very well, Mac. I had to establish the facts. We shall see what happens, and if…well…let's just say we shall be happy to welcome your child into the manse." *If it obviously wasn't Mac's, she thought, she would use it as an excuse to be rid of Aggie, finally. However, magic had been wrought, and she knew what that meant.* She swallowed hard, admitting that the babe was likely to be his after all.

"Thank you, Mistress. You have always been kind, so very kind."

Margaret nodded and walked on, tears blinding her vision. She was afraid of what this child, this half-fae, would mean for them all. No doubt Robert would be delighted that his experiment, his ultimate piece of research, was to bear fruit at last.

She made a circuit and came to the river, walking in the direction of Doon Hill. Robert was busy with a meeting in the church; she supposed she should tell him the news before anybody else did. She paused at the foot of the hill. She could see up the pathway to the great ash under which she used to summon Molly, and she wished she could do so now. Margaret needed another child, for her own comfort as much as anything else. She couldn't bear to watch that slattern's belly grow big.

Suddenly, a figure emerged from the undergrowth. Margaret gasped; it was Aggie. There was no doubt she was blooming; she had never looked so well. Her clothes were as drab and disordered as ever, but she had an air about her…she was pleased with herself. She knew her power, she had harnessed it.

"Come away, then, Mistress," said the brazen woman. "Come away below the ash tree an' I'll see what I can dae for ye."

"I need nothin' from you!" said Margaret, her hand straying to the brooch Mac had made her, as it so often did in Aggie's presence.

"No? Well, if you won't take that trinket off an' let me help ye, I'll drop a potion in the master's beer, or his tea. Same as I gave Mac. I'm only tryin' tae help."

"I wonder why I find that hard tae believe, Aggie?" cried Margaret.

The woman, who belonged in two worlds yet fitted into neither, came down the hill towards her, ample hips swaying, so unlike Molly in every way. "Suit yersel'. But I'll *dae it anyway. Ye can try tae resist him if ye like, but I dinna think ye will. Ye want another bairn, an' ye want him."*

Margaret flushed with embarrassment and fled the scene as fast as she was able to walk with dignity. The misfit creature was an affront to nature and respectability; she was beyond endurance.

Yet she had spoken the truth. Before long, there was another pregnant woman at the manse. This time, Robert was attentive in every way – to both of them. He compared and measured and asked personal questions, noting everything for his research. Margaret shuddered; this was not the kind of attention she had craved. She was exhausted and stopped taking dictation for him. He shut himself away and drew up the final draft of his manuscript. His experiment with Aggie and Mac would not feature in this paper; this great matter he would discuss in confidence with Mr. Boyle at a future date after the hybrid child's birth, and take his advice on how to proceed. Unwilling now to spare time away from home, he posted his manuscript of "The Secret Commonwealth of Elves, Fauns and Fairies" to Robert Boyle, and eagerly awaited his response. There was none. After a few months, Robert made enquiries and received a letter from Mr. Boyle's solicitor in the grey light of a January day which threatened heavy snow. The previous month, December 1691, he read, both Boyle and his sister the esteemed viscountess had died, one week apart.

Robert sank into grief and misery for his patron and his book – without Boyle's backing, there was little chance of "The Secret Commonwealth" being published – and his country needed it now more than ever, when Gael was against Gael, divided along lines of politics and religion, and the old beliefs were dimming into the darkness of forgotten obscurity. His research could help reunite them, and restore faith.

#

The year sixteen hundred and ninety-two had a nightmare quality to it from the beginning. Margaret often felt she had gone to sleep and become trapped in a dark dream from which she couldn't wake. The manse itself was a prison of tension and imaginings, as her belly rounded with the babe procured by Aggie's help, and she watched the fae creature herself grow large like a seed about to burst deep in the earth and sprout who knew what oddity; it couldn't be wholesome, that was for sure.

Robert was lost in his grief for Boyle and the viscountess and equally, Margaret believed, for the London society now lost to him. Nobody was interested in his scientific paper on the commonwealth of the Sith. He had copied a few manuscripts for friends who had been polite, but everybody had much more important matters on their minds. The owl which roosted near the manse shrieked long and loud during that time, merging with Margaret's fevered dreams.

The country was rent asunder, deep cracks of politics and religion widening every day; and here on the edge of the Highlands, the earth shook frequently as if to remind them there was no stability, nothing they could be sure of, the very ground beneath their feet shifting and leaving them shaken in more ways than one. In such times, the lawless took their chances; the previous year, the Wild MacGregors had raided all the barns in Kippen, stealing every beast belonging to the villagers. Then, in the middle of a freezing cold and snow-bound February, word emerged from the Highlands of the terrible treachery in Glencoe, where some thirty members of the Clan MacDonald had been slaughtered in their beds by men commanded by Campbell of Glenlyon. It turned the downward spiral of Robert's spirits into a rapid drain which stole all cheer and perspective from him. That fellow Scots could entrap their own countrymen in a glen, where some of them had been billeted and partaking of MacDonald hospitality, was obscene. It was an outrage, an atrocity of inconceivable magnitude. The Campbells involved were not of Margaret's branch, although there would have been links if looked into closely, but it gave Robert's distorted mind even more cause to be annoyed with his wife, that Campbell was her maiden name.

Margaret clung to the thought of the child growing in her belly to cheer her. She thought of the babe as uniquely hers; she gave up all hope of Robert's interest in it, for he barely acknowledged his sons, not even Isabel's Colin. She still loved her husband and longed for him to return to himself, praying fervently for his release from the melancholy which had claimed him. His obsession with the fae increased as his state of mind deteriorated. He remained interested in Aggie's unborn child, which was galling.

On a cool March day at the time of spring when day and night are equal, she returned from the fields carrying the bairn, which she had birthed all by herself in the woods; Mac told them that she had insisted upon it when her pains came on. Margaret suspected malice, thinking that she had gone to bear her brat and exchange it for a human babe; but the bundle she presented to them contained a child so obviously kissed with Mac's colour, and blessed with his great dark eyes, that she had to be the offspring of them both, the creature Robert had longed to bring into being. Despite her misgivings, Margaret took to the little girl Mac named in her honour, although they shortened it to Meg. Robert was thrilled with the outcome of his experiment, only lamenting that he couldn't share his findings with his deceased mentor Mr. Boyle. He observed the infant with the eye of one who had bred a prize horse or cow, taking measurements and peering into her eyes and mouth, watching for signs which heralded her worth. He had helped to bring a creature half-fae, half-Negro into the world, and at times he seemed half-crazed with the knowledge.

He boasted of his many visits to the subterranean commonwealth, where he had reported the birth of Meg with glee. Of such importance was the news that he had finally been taken to meet the Fairy Queen, he said, on a night when he had sensed the ground hold its breath before a major tremor, and he had rushed out and over the fields in his nightshirt.

"What is she like, Robert?" Margaret had asked, unable to contain her curiosity, her voice trembling.

"One minute she's air and wings, the next she's solid dimpled flesh. She's young and old, beautiful and ugly as the shadows pass across her and through her…she radiates light, she becomes the darkness. Margaret, she is a terrifying creature!"

"And what did she have to say aboot baby Meg?"

"That she would dearly like tae dae her ain research into her!" Robert beamed.

Margaret shuddered. "Robert, this is a threat, not a compliment! Can you not see that, husband? They would never give her back! She's a being born of both worlds, but a human being, Robert — never forget that! It would break Mac's heart. Maybe not her mother — I'm not sure Aggie feels for the bairn what she should. Ye must not tell them this!"

Robert rubbed his hand over his stubbled chin, pondering. "I have thought long on the matter. The babe would be Aggie's pass back tae the Otherworld, and you are right, she does not display the maternal instinct I hoped for."

"What dae ye mean, her pass back tae the Otherworld?"

"Aggie cannot return. She's tried. I hoped she might give me safe passage at Balquidder, as once I told you, but she could not. She is barred for deserting her mistress."

Margaret felt the blood drain from her face. "And would any bairn suffice tae gain her way back? I took measures tae protect wee Robert, an' I'll dae my best for this one in ma belly, but…" Her words trailed off. She couldn't tell him that Aggie had helped in the conception of their unborn child. Throughout their marriage, Robert had reached for her so rarely that he hadn't given thought to the fact that it had been their only encounter in many months. He had been so preoccupied with Aggie's pregnancy, the death of the Boyles and the Massacre of Glencoe, and his obsession with seeking out the fae, as always. She was afraid now that Aggie had helped in the breeding of her unborn bairn for her own ends.

"No," Robert said calmly. "She tried that, too, in the early days after she left her world, before she came here. Remember the hue an' cry when the MacTavish bairn went missin'? Then it turned up under a tree, an' they blamed a neighbour that had a grudge for tryin' tae give them a fright? That was Aggie, stealin' the bairn tae try tae buy her way back in. Robert was always safe. This one will be, too. But her own child…that's a different matter. I stand tae lose them both."

Margaret fell back against her cushion, her mind reeling. "Ye've let me fear sae much, husband!" she cried. "I would dearly like for Aggie tae be gone! But not at cost tae that innocent babe's life, an' the heartbreak it would bring tae Mac. Robert, what has become of you? You terrify me!"

There, she had said it. He merely regarded her quizzically, shrugged and left the room. His sudden wanderings in his nightshirt became commonplace after that. Margaret's pleading with him was to no avail. The time was approaching when Molly had foretold that he would pay for his intrusions into the realm of the Sith. Margaret couldn't see any way to hold back the tide which was about to engulf them. On the fourteenth of May, a date she had dreaded for three years since Molly's warning, Margaret watched Robert pacing all evening. He had been distracted since Beltane, when he had spent a fruitless night trying to gain admission to the Otherworld via the gateway Balquidder offered. Since coming home next morning, he had remained in his nightshirt, unwashed, for two weeks, bent over his books in his study until dusk fell, when he set out for Doon Hill and wandered all night. Margaret covered for him, let it be known that her husband was ill, arranged for a neighbouring clergyman to fulfil his most urgent duties.

Robert was mad with impatience, desperate to be back in the realm of the fae. Despite her pleadings, he set off as usual across the fields, pink-tinged in the sunset of a warm evening which was ominously still. This was no time to go wandering on fairy hills, except for someone like Robert, who wanted to meet the Sith, who yearned for it more than he longed for anything else in life. His family forgotten, cast aside, he *stumbled from the manse, a man half-crazed by lack of sleep and obsession, a man doomed.*

The earth trembled as Margaret knew it would, and she fell to her knees at the window where she beheld Doon Hill, grieving already. She sent Mac to seek his master. She didn't know if, on the whole of Doon Hill, there would be anything to find; but Mac found him, or some semblance of him. Other men of the parish joined in carrying his body home, but all said it was not him. They believed the Sith had taken their minister and left his double dead in his place, the co-walker spoken of in myth and legend. Margaret agreed with them. They said the Fairy Queen must have taken him for her own chaplain, an honour; but they only said it to comfort her. They all knew he had inquired too closely into fae affairs, the final affront being his efforts to publish his findings to the world. The Sith had claimed him as their captive.

Chapter Twenty-Three

The longest day of 1941 dawned in a sheet of red-tinged gold radiating over half the sky. Even in her exhausted state, having been up most of the night with Ellen, Brigid appreciated it although with a shiver of regret born of confusion and anxiety – surely she should have had a son, born today? She was trying hard not to doubt her sanity. Even if she had borne a boy on Midsummer morning, what did the Sith have in mind for him? What would have become of him? Yet still, she felt as if she had failed somebody – Robert Kirk, presumably. Overwhelming feelings of despair washed over her every so often, but – and this she couldn't explain at all – they seemed to come from outside herself. Her mother and Mrs. White said they believed her, but they looked at her with concern and pity; and Susan, despite not knowing the real reason she had come here or why she was behaving as she did, wouldn't look in her in the eye at all.

She had remained in the manse after her mother followed Molly to the cottage despite Susan's coldness, because she felt this was the one place where she might find answers. She had pointed out to Susan that moving all the baby things she had borrowed would be an upheaval, and it would only be for a little while longer; Susan had acquiesced, being in a strange mood and not keen to argue with Brigid, or speak to her much at all. This morning she had given up trying to settle Ellen and had put her in Susan's Silver Cross pram to go for a walk, hoping the rocking of the shiny carriage on the great sprung chassis might send her off to sleep.

It worked. An hour later Brigid wheeled the pram through the yard and stopped at the back door. She was exhausted, but Ellen was sleeping soundly at last. She didn't have the strength to manoeuvre the pram into the house, so she decided to leave her sleeping in the back yard. She made sure she was well tucked in and fixed a fine net over the hood as protection against insects out foraging – a breakfast of fresh human blood would be nectar to some of the flying beasties around here. Then she dragged herself through the house and upstairs and fell into bed.

Away from her child, Brigid sighed and relaxed. She had moved back into her original bedroom, against Molly's advice – she wanted Brigid and the baby to leave the manse. Brigid was convinced that if she was to find closure anywhere, though, it would be in this room, in this house. The veil which had been drawn aside several times, allowing her to see or sense a magical world, had fallen back into place and left her stranded in the very real world of single parenthood, and Brigid couldn't be at peace. For now, however, body and mind exhausted and at ease with some respite from the baby for a while, she fell asleep.

#

Susan had risen to use the toilet before Brigid went out. She saw her lodger leaving with the pram, and sighed at the thought of the day ahead and how she should handle matters. No doubt Brigid's mother and the midwife with her cloying lavender scent would be here by mid-morning, hanging around most of the day. Today she would ask them all to decide their future plans – plans which did not involve her home or family. Despite Ria, she hadn't mentioned Robert Kirk – it was all too ridiculous – and she hadn't told a soul about the money hidden in the lining of Brigid's bag. She feared the Johnstones turning up on her doorstep to demand the baby they had "bought", or worse – the police, accusing Brigid of theft.

Susan was stressed in her own home now. There was an oppressive atmosphere; she felt both watchful and watched. The three women who had shattered her peace of mind had to go. She washed and dressed while Brigid was out, and now, having heard her return and go straight to bed, she made her way down to the kitchen and outside to see to the livestock. Ellen was asleep in her pram. Susan smiled down at the bonny baby. She couldn't comprehend why Brigid was moping around and seemed less than delighted with her child. She sighed and went about beginning her day.

#

Brigid woke with the sun streaming into her room. For a few blissful moments, she forgot she was a mother. She had enjoyed more than four hours' sleep, the most at a stretch since Ellen was born. She had been dreaming of life before motherhood, when her breasts weren't full of milk and the flesh of her empty stomach left sagging. She wanted her body back, and for a few seconds after she woke this morning, she thought Ellen had never happened. Then reality and responsibility hit her hard in the chest, and she struggled up thinking Ellen was bound to need a feed. Her breasts were painful with the swell of milk they contained. It was a wonder she hadn't heard her baby crying – she was sure they could hear her in the Clachan when she did. Brigid groaned and flopped back on her pillows briefly. Then she swung her legs over the side of the bed, sighed and squared her shoulders to go downstairs and face Susan. She glimpsed her in the study as she went past, and thought she had managed to avoid her; but Susan called her back, squinting at her over the top of her reading glasses.

"I've checked on Ellen from time to time. She hasn't stirred. It may be that she's going to begin settling better now, sleeping longer. Still early days, though." Her voice was level, devoid of emotion. She turned back to the letter she was writing.

"Thank you," said Brigid, trying to match her polite, neutral tone. She walked to the kitchen and out the open back door to the pram. She peered inside and did a double take. Ripping the insect net off, she pulled at the covers and gasped in horror. Ellen wasn't there; one of Katie's dolls was in her place, Ellen's hat on its head, which was turned sideways and the covers drawn up closely around it. Brigid looked frantically around. "Katie!" she called. She ran back inside repeating her name, checking the parlour and dining room as she went, her feet pounding on the flagstones. She headed upstairs.

Susan came out of the study, calling after her. "Brigid? Is anything wrong?"

"Katie's playing a trick! She's taken Ellen!" she cried.

"But Katie isn't..." Susan ran upstairs after her, reaching the room her daughters shared just behind Brigid, who was ashen. The bedroom was empty.

"I know she's the oldest and used to looking after the others," gasped Brigid, breathless, "but Ellen's so tiny! And she doesn't have her hat on! Where are they?"

"I was just going to say, they went out earlier," said Susan. "It'll be fine, don't worry. She shouldn't have taken Ellen. I'm sorry." She went over to the window and saw her brood playing on the glebe. "There they are," she said. There was no sign of the baby, though. "She'll have put the pram in the shade somewhere. She's very responsible. She won't have forgotten her."

"But the pram's still here!" cried Brigid. "Ellen's gone! Katie's left her doll in her place, wearing Ellen's hat!"

"Oh!" said Susan. "I see. Well, she probably got bored waiting for you to wake up and discover the joke. It doesn't excuse her behaviour. I am sorry. She'll have laid her on the ground on their cardigans or something..."

"Laid her on the ground? With the horse in the field?" Brigid turned and fled for the stairs.

Susan followed her, a stream of chatter trying to ease Brigid's panic and her own sense of guilt. "We'll go and get her back. She'll be fine. No doubt she needs changing. It's a wonder she hasn't cried for a feed." As she said it, she realised how long it must be since the baby had been fed. Katie would have brought her back if she had cried, and yes, Cherry was in the field with them. Her older children were used to playing near the docile mare, but a newborn baby on the ground...

They hurried over to the glebe, calling Katie's name. The little girl came running. She knew nothing of Ellen's whereabouts; she had left her doll in the kitchen – she hadn't played any trick, she hadn't touched the baby. She stopped protesting her innocence when she saw the panic on the adults' faces. Brigid and Susan stood for a second, stunned and helpless. Then they looked at each other and spoke at the same time.

"Agnes Clay!"

"We need to ring the police immediately!" said Susan.

"I'm not waiting for them to get here!" cried Brigid. "I'm going to get Ellen back!"

"Will you be alright on your own?" asked Susan.

"I've never been scared of her – I just didn't want her near me or my baby. Only Ellen matters now!"

Susan stepped forward and pulled Brigid into a fierce hug, mumbling against her hair. "I'm going to call the police anyway. I'll send Katie to fetch your mother and Mrs. White from the cottage, then I'll follow you. She's waited a long time to have revenge on me, and I'm sorry she's taken it out on you!" She released Brigid. "I'm certain she won't harm Ellen. She's never harmed anybody that I know of. She's just abrasive, oddball and lacking in personal hygiene. But she's not getting off with this! Off you go, fast as you can! I'll catch up!"

Brigid looked at Doon Hill hunkering in the near distance. She had only been to Agnes' railway carriage home once. She decided to take a more direct route this time, climbing the fence and setting off across the fields. She was still recovering from the birth, with loose flesh which dragged as she ran on the uneven ground, while her full breasts were painful and weighed her down. It was too much. She had to leave the fields at a tangent and join with the beaten earth track. Finally she arrived, breathless and panting, at the railway carriage, sweat streaming down her face, dress sticking to her back. It was sticking at the front, too, where her breasts had begun to leak. She threw herself at the door and hammered her fist against it, screaming Agnes' name, trying to open it, but it was locked. There was no reply. She climbed down the steps and stood back, peering at the windows. She picked up small stones and began to throw them at the glass.

"I know you're in there! Give me back my baby!" She picked up a rock the size of her hand and prepared to lob it.

Just at that moment, a voice called to her. "I wouldn't do that if I was you, Miss! It's a criminal offence."

Brigid dropped the rock and stared at the local police officer, Sergeant MacAllan, who had ridden up on his bicycle. "She took my baby! It's her you should be threatening!"

"We don't know that, Miss."

"It's Mrs! Mrs. Watkins. And yes, we do know. She has a grudge against me and Susan MacKendrick, and her manner towards me has been threatening! Who else would take her? Nobody steals anything around here, let alone babies!"

The policeman propped his bicycle against the carriage and ascended the steps. "Open in the name of the law, Miss Clay!" he shouted, knocking loudly and pausing with his ear to the door. When there was no reply, he surveyed the windows as Brigid had done.

"Aren't you going to break the door down?"

"She isn't here," the man replied. "You develop an instinct for these things. There's nobody here. She isn't hiding from us, Miss…Mrs. Watkins."

As Brigid sagged and sat shakily on the steps, exhausted, there was a clatter of hooves and Susan arrived riding Cherry. She rode bareback, clinging to the horse's mane. Her eyes and cheeks blazed. "Well?"

"She's not here," Sergeant MacAllan repeated, staring up at the imperious woman. "And you've made a huge allegation. But of course we'll look for the baby. I'll put word round all the local stations and arrange a search party. Please come with me now and make a statement, and think of anybody else who might have taken her, and anywhere they might have gone…"

"Doon Hill!" shrieked Brigid. Her mind had been racing as the policeman spoke. Sunset to sunset, Midsummer…she had expected her pains to begin after sunset on Midsummer's Eve, and for the baby to be born at dawn; but it was still Midsummer until the sun set today. She looked up at the wooded slopes behind the railway carriage. "It's Midsummer, the veil is thin! Agnes is behind all this, all of it – I should have known! She wanted my baby, but I don't know why!" Renewed strength coursed through her limbs. She jumped to her feet and scanned the hillside helplessly, looking for a pathway.

Susan urged Cherry over to her and bent down, holding a hand down to her. "Sergeant MacAllan!" she cried. "Please help Brigid up! Come on," she said to Brigid, "I know a trail we can use!"

"But you don't believe any of this!"

"No, but I'll bet Agnes does," said Susan. "Take my hand and grip my arm. Sergeant, please assist my friend!"

"But I've never…" said Brigid.

"Do you want to look for your baby or not?"

The policeman had removed his helmet and was scratching his head. "Ladies, this is dangerous folly…"

"Help her up, man!" Susan ordered.

Uncertainly, he stepped forward and gripped Brigid's waist, lifting her as Susan pulled and Brigid swung her leg over Cherry's back behind her. Before he could utter another word of caution, the horse and the women were already away in a swirl of dust.

#

Kirkton Manse, May 1692

Aggie simpered as she approached Margaret in her kitchen garden, where she sought solace continuing the tasks which needed doing. Her household still required feeding, after all. She had to remind herself to eat for sake of the babe in her belly, although everything stuck in her throat. Robert's funeral had taken place the day before. Nobody believed it was Robert they had actually buried.

"Mistress," smiled Aggie; that smile which made everybody wary, for you never knew what was coming next. "I know how we can get the master back."

Margaret sighed. "And how would you know that, Aggie? It seems tae me ye have little influence wi'…them." She hardly dare call them any of the names they went by; she hardly dare mention them at all.

"The master appeared tae me yesterday," she said. "He told me what must be done. I still have some powers, Mistress, as you of all people should know." She nodded to Margaret's swollen stomach.

Margaret dropped her garden fork and turned to face her. "You saw him? He spoke to you?"

"Aye. He said he could be freed at the wee one's christening, which should take place at Midsummer. He said his cousin Graham of Duchray must be the one to do it. He'll need a dirk, an iron dirk, an' he needs tae throw it over the master's head when he appears."

"Robert will appear at our child's christening?"

"I swear to ye, Mistress. He'll be like a ghost, but when the dirk is thrown he'll be freed an' return tae flesh an' blood."

Margaret struggled to understand. "But why does it have tae be Duchray?" She frowned, still painfully embarrassed by the episode when Aggie had tried to seduce the laird.

"That's what the master said, Mistress. It has tae be his cousin, the laird. But ye must tell him some man saw the master, not me. Nobody listens tae women's tales."

Margaret flushed with emotion. "If there's any chance we can get him back, I'll do it!" she said.

"One more thing, Mistress. It canna be just any dirk. It needs tae be of ancient iron. The finest iron. The finest this world has tae offer. Or that any other world has tae offer."

"Sky iron!" whispered Margaret.

"Only the best can break the spell and free him, Mistress."

Margaret nodded and wiped her hands on her apron. She went straight to the drawer where she kept her treasured possessions. She would entrust the remaining lump to Mac. It wasn't big, but a representation of a dirk would do, she was sure. It was the gesture and the metal which mattered, surely? He would fashion just what was needed, a talisman and a weapon to strike the air - an assault of iron from the stars on a Secret Commonwealth and a secretive people of air who had taken her husband.

#

Susan urged Cherry up the steep, winding path as fast as she could go. Brigid's legs clung to the mare's body, her arms clamped around Susan's waist. She had never ridden before, and only in films had she seen anyone ride bareback. When they reached the top, they stopped and looked around them. Brigid managed to slither off the horse's back, racked with pain. She stood, arms wrapped around her body, breathing deeply and trying to get her legs to stop shaking. Susan jumped down beside her. They were standing beneath the great tree people called "The Minister's Pine". One of the legends stated that Kirk's soul was trapped within it, other versions said he was bodily captive within the hill itself, or the Otherworld to which Doon Hill was a portal.

"Agnes!" Susan yelled. "Agnes Clay, come out with that baby and stop your nonsense! Give her back to her mother!"

"Whatever you have planned, Agnes," screamed Brigid, "it won't work! I had a girl – it was a boy that was wanted!" She put her hand to the lapel of the dress she wore and gasped. "My brooch! I'm not wearing my brooch!"

Susan rolled her eyes and shook her head. Then, however, she opened a bag she had strung across her body, and showed Brigid the contents. "Since Agnes is obviously a believer and some kind of witch, I thought this might…I don't know…impress or frighten her in some way. Ria gave it to me recently. She said I might need it."

Brigid looked and saw the rusted miniature iron dirk. She had realised weeks ago that Ria, despite her protests and disdain, knew the truth of the things which happened around here. The blacksmith had given herself away that day in the cellar. She shivered, despite the heat. Silence surrounded them. They turned in a circle, surveying the undergrowth where not a leaf, not a bird or even an insect stirred. It was eerie. Something was afoot. The sun was high in the sky now, beating relentlessly down on the clearing around The Minister's Pine, the sky a bleached blue-white. They were the sole unquiet creatures on Doon Hill. Even the horse stood still, head raised as if spellbound. Brigid's gasp as premonition dawned at the last second caught in her throat. She had felt this sensation before, the earth holding its breath, then… Everything shook. It was a stronger tremor than the previous ones she had experienced. Cherry shied suddenly and bolted. Reaching for her mare helplessly, Susan fell and landed painfully. Brigid, too, stumbled and fell. She looked up. The Minister's Pine above them was shuddering as the earth continued to shift, the whole hill shaken by the force. The tree reared and shook like a great angry beast of the forest. Brigid crawled over to Susan and grabbed her bag, pulling out the iron dirk. It blazed in the palm of her hand and lodged itself there, heat searing up Brigid's arm. She closed her eyes as images began to play on the black voids behind her closed lids.

#

Ria arrived at the manse shortly after the earth tremor. Simon had been sent by Mary MacKenzie to fetch her, and such had been the urgency of the hastily-written note he carried that Ria had jumped on her motorbike. The tremor had been strong enough to make her pull over until it was past. It didn't bode well. She hadn't heard that Ellen was missing until Simon arrived, having just returned from discussing some work with a local farmer. She found Mary white-faced in the kitchen, watching the older children in the yard while the younger two played at her feet. Her words took her by surprise.

"Mrs. White has been taken seriously ill," she said. "Could you take the children away? Just down the road to the holiday cottage."

"I'm sorry to hear that," said Ria. "Have ye sent for the doctor? What's wrong with her? And is there any news of Ellen?"

"No news," Mary replied. She was trembling. "I really have to stay with Molly."

Ria stared at her. The old woman looked terrified. "What's going on, Mrs. MacKenzie? What's really going on? Ye might find I'm able tae believe more than ye think. I come frae these parts. It's Midsummer. Things happen."

Mary stared back, weighing her up. Then she glanced at the children and beckoned Ria to follow. She led her to the sitting room. "Just give me a moment," she said, opening the door a crack. "Molly, dear, Ria is here. I think she might be able to help us."

"She can help by taking the children away!" The voice which issued from the room was dry and rasping.

Ria grimaced. There was also a stench which accompanied the voice, seeping out the door and into the hallway. "Let me in there!" she said, shouldering Mary aside.

There was a figure huddled over a meagre fire lit in the grate, wrapped in blankets. Molly White tried to shield her face with the blanket over her head, but Ria stepped forward and pulled it back. She would have screamed if the sight before her eyes hadn't been so ghastly it drove her voice back into her throat and invoked instead a strangled gagging from the bile rising in her stomach. When she could speak, her voice came out in a tremulous whisper.

"What the hell is goin' on? What has Brigid brought here?"

She didn't wait for an answer. She ran from the room, scooping Susan's youngest two from the kitchen and calling the others to follow her, and she marched them down the road to the rented cottage Mary and Molly shared.

#

Brigid tried hard to grasp what she was seeing. Her eyes were still closed, the searing force of the knife burning up her arm and holding her in its thrall. Other tremors had caused her to glimpse a moment in the past with open eyes, but now she saw a sequence of images flickering across her mind's eye like a speeded-up film reel. There was a young woman in old-fashioned garb with dark hair tangling around her shoulders – she was kneeling where Brigid had fallen, beneath The Minister's Pine, and she was wailing and beseeching. Wisps of mist began to curl from the roots of the tree and from the surrounding undergrowth, forming into living creatures. Some remained transparent and ethereal, while others took on solid form, mostly human in appearance. They mocked the woman. They called her a misfit and a useless lump of low-born scum, unwanted in any world. They were vicious, pitiless.

Time seemed to pass. Brigid beheld the woman returning again and again, dressed in different kinds of clothing, skirts growing shorter, beseeching the creatures as she grew older, greyer, frailer, until…Brigid recognised Auld Agnes Clay with a jolt, but the nightmare didn't end there. Agnes continued to age until she was truly a hag, a skeletal bag of bones, eye sockets with stretched skin barely holding her still-glimmering orbs in place. Brigid tried to cry out; all at once, she knew that Agnes and Molly were the same kind of creature, that they shared their origins in that Otherworld reached via the portals of Doon Hill, and Balquidder, and Tower Hill, and all those fabled hills of myth and magic.

Suddenly, the images cleared and Brigid's vision spiralled down like a bird in flight, swooping low over the fields and the Avon Dhu between Doon Hill and the Clachan, to a bus stop. Auld Agnes was waiting to board a bus. The woman in front of her was boarding already, a baby cradled on her shoulder. Brigid's voice tore from her throat.

"ELLEN!"

#

Kirkton Manse

Margaret had an easy birth this time. Aggie and Elsie assisted. Aggie had told her not to be ridiculous – she knew about birthing babies. Did Margaret not trust her now she had helped with the conception of the bairn, and had a plan to bring the master back? Margaret was surprised to find that although she was still wary of Aggie, she was coming round to Robert's view of her – she was a mischief, a stirrer, her moods were mercurial and she certainly wasn't a doting mother to wee Meg, but – she wasn't malicious. She hadn't tried to take Meg away, to offer as her pass back to the Otherworld, after all. She performed her duties as clumsily as ever, but she did perform them.

Margaret didn't exactly trust her, but she knew she meant no real harm. It was a burden off her shoulders to find herself thinking this way. Even Mac seemed happier with his wife. She called him and had him remove the iron strips from under her bed. The cradle was another matter. She did not need to please Robert by using it. If the plan worked and he returned, she would stand up to him about that and other issues. Things would have to change. She instructed Mac to remove the cradle to the cellar.

Therefore, she allowed Aggie to assist in the labour and birth, and all went smoothly. Aggie tried to take the credit and make comparisons with Molly, but Margaret knew there had been none of the complications with which Molly had to contend, and she had been a compliant patient this time. True, Aggie had some skills with herbs and her medicines helped; her manner had been brusque and not holding back, though, shorter on sympathy and much less gentle than Molly, but somehow it worked and Margaret had felt safe in her hands. When Aggie handed her newborn daughter to her, there had been a light in her face and a pride in her manner such as Margaret had never seen before.

"Why could ye not be a midwife like Molly?" she asked.

"I'm from servant stock. Rough and ready. Not yer lady born like Molly." Aggie shrugged. "Our world is no more equal than yours. It's just as unkind, just as unfair to its own."

Margaret arranged the christening for a week later, at Midsummer, as Aggie had said it had to be. A locum minister had replaced Robert temporarily; Margaret had been granted time to have her child and recover before she must vacate the manse for the new minister and his family. If all went according to plan, that need never happen. She sent a note to Robert's cousin the laird, Graham of Duchray, inviting him to visit. He was a man with the blood of Gaeldom running in his veins, and he had absorbed belief in the fae like mother's milk, as all raised in these parts did. She decided not to involve anyone else in the matter; she took it upon herself to lie and say Robert had appeared to her. He would believe her word; she was his cousin by marriage, after all. She would never mention the involvement of her slatternly maidservant whose improper advances had so affronted him.

Mac had fashioned the iron dirk from the lump of meteorite, and such a dirk it was, with the thistles Robert loved and the ash leaves he associated with Margaret engraved around the miniature hilt and blade. Margaret sewed a leather pouch for it and showed it to Graham of Duchray. He handled it with awe. His hands trembled slightly. Of course, he told Margaret, if the Rev. Kirk had asked for him by name, he would do it. It was an honour, although he could not think why he had been chosen. They assembled in the kirk for the private christening, a small party still in mourning for Robert. They had met in the manse first, where Aggie and Elsie had served refreshments. Duchray partook liberally. The dirk was a weight in the pouch hanging from his belt and a burden on his mind, he told Margaret; he could not wait to dispatch his duty with it and be done! The bravado in his speech didn't reach his eyes. Margaret felt for him. It was a frightening thing to stand against the fae in any way. Would they fight for Robert? What was going to happen?

The locum baptised little Marjorie. She was a discontented baby who fought against her swaddling and had seemed to be in ill humour since she was born. Margaret struggled with her, trying to placate her, as prayers followed the act of baptism. Duchray, of course, did not once close his eyes, watchful for his cue. Suddenly, he cried out. The minister's words faltered on his lips and everybody's eyes snapped open. Duchray stood transfixed, staring at a spot behind the minister's shoulder. His *face was a mask of terror. Margaret could see nothing, but she didn't doubt that he could.*

"The dirk!" *she hissed.* "Throw the dirk!"

Duchray fumbled with the pouch on his belt. He pulled the dirk out and dropped it; it clattered to the floor. He bent to retrieve it, but his hand groped uselessly and he stumbled as if from too much whisky and lost his balance. Margaret had always joked behind his back that he was round as a prime cock pheasant and just as vain, but all pride and pomposity deserted him then as he rolled on the floor at the foot of the christening font. He looked up and gave another cry as he beheld the apparition of Robert Kirk dissolve into thin air. He had missed the moment.

Only Duchray had seen the former minister of Kirkton, and only he, Margaret and Aggie had known of the plan. To the others present, the laird was drunk and had disgraced himself. He would later spread the truth of what he had witnessed to try to save his reputation, and he slipped silver and gold into the hands of others present to say that they, too, had seen Robert Kirk that day; but Margaret knew a different tale. Aggie had spiked his whisky with a potion. She had worked a charm to ensure he would see what he believed he was going to see. How she had laughed when confronted by Margaret later, when she shamelessly told her mistress the truth; she had waited long for her revenge on Duchray.

"It was even better than I thought it would be!" *the woman cackled, wiping tears of glee from her eyes.* "I thought he might nearly take the minister's eye oot with the dirk, but lyin' there like a barrel, rollin' aboot the floor! I thought I would pee mysel', Mistress!"

"But what aboot me, Aggie?" *Margaret had cried.* "Ye made me believe it! I thought I would get my husband back!"

Aggie shrugged. "He's deid, Mistress. I canna raise the deid any more than I could get him oot o' Fairyland, as ye call it, if he was there!"

"But he is! Everybody says so!"

"Well, I think he's deid. I don't really care, Mistress. He did little for me. He made me marry Mac an' kept me here as his wee experiment. He tried tae make me take on his religion. I care nothin' for him."

Margaret clutched the brooch Mac had made her. "And what aboot me? I thought ye had grown tae respect me!"

Aggie threw back her head and laughed. "I didna mind helpin' get ye a bairn an' birth it. It stopped ye bein' like a cat on hot coals aroond me. But I've wasted enough time here. There's been some laughs, but I'm off now."

"Off? Where?"

"Hame, hopefully. If not, or not yet, then I'm a survivor, I'll get by."

Margaret gaped, horrified. "What aboot wee Meg an' Mac? Ye're not takin' that bairn tae try tae get back tae the fae! I'll dae whatever it takes tae stop ye!"

Aggie shook her head dismissively. "Dinna fash yersel', Mistress. I'm not all bad. I wouldna dae that tae Mac, or the bairn. They wouldna be kind tae her. He can keep Meg. I'll find another way back eventually."

"If you leave this house, you leave with the clothes on your back and nothing else!"

"Of course. I telt ye, Mistress, I'm a survivor."

She marched out the back door after that, and Margaret never saw her again in her life. No longer the lady of Kirkton Manse, no longer with any right to live there, she was preparing to return to her family in Comrie, taking her stepson Colin and her own two children. Elsie would come with her, but she couldn't employ Mac. Wullie, the blacksmith, had offered to take him on as his assistant; Mac was skilled and a hard worker, and Wull was growing old and had no children. It looked as if the former slave was set for life. Margaret was delighted for him. He said he hoped to find a proper wife, a good mother for Meg – more than one of the local maidens apparently had no problem with the colour of his skin. When Margaret pointed out that he was still married to Aggie, whether she was here or not, he laughed.

"Married to a fae creature, Mistress? To a woman who doesn't exist on any document in this world? There were no witnesses and no record made. This only dawned on me recently. I wasn't acquainted with the laws of this land at the time."

Margaret blushed to think the legality of the marriage had never occurred to her. Robert would have known. It had been a cruel and unethical thing he had done. Yet she grieved for him sorely. She had worshipped him from afar when he was wed to her cousin, and despite everything that had happened, she still loved him and his brilliant mind – as it had been before it was misted by pursuing the fae in the names of science and religion, before those grand men in London turned his head.

Chapter Twenty-Four

When Brigid opened her eyes, Susan was holding her by the shoulders and shaking her. She heard someone screaming her baby's name over and over, and realised it was herself.

"Susan, I saw Agnes Clay getting on a bus! She's got an accomplice – another woman was carrying Ellen. They're going to Balquidder, I just know it!"

Susan was ashen. "Brigid, you were having some kind of fit – I think you must have banged your head when you fell!"

"No, Susan, no! You've got to believe me – the things people say about this place, about Robert Kirk, they're true! I see things, Susan, I know things! I was summoned here!" She scrambled to her feet as she spoke, and Susan rose slowly from the ground.

"Who was the other woman?"

"I don't know – I could only see her back, and she was wearing a headscarf. But she had Ellen!" She gulped as she pictured her baby's innocent face snuggled into the neck of a stranger, her tiny head supported against the woman's shoulder.

Susan frowned, her thoughts racing. "Tell me one thing, Brigid – did you have any financial arrangement with the Johnstones for your baby?"

"What? No! What's that got to do with anything?"

"I discovered money hidden in your bag when I found the books. You've never been entirely honest with me. You came here chasing nonsense about Robert Kirk. What am I supposed to think?"

"That money was Mam's and Will's first, then mine by right!" cried Brigid. "And it isn't nonsense! You said you would help me – you even brought the knife! When I held it, I saw things! Agnes and this other hag or whatever she is, they're taking Ellen to Balquidder, to where Molly and Agnes came from!"

"Mrs. White is from Balquidder?"

"Yes, she's the same kind of, of…creature…as Agnes! I know it now! They're both fae, and older than we could ever imagine! Please, Susan, where's Cherry? We have to go!"

Susan cast her eyes frantically around the clearing and saw her horse returning, trotting up the hill and through the trees towards them. There was intelligence in the animal's eyes, knowledge. Susan recognised it and the hairs on the back of her neck stood on end. The mare had returned as if by a sixth sense – Susan trusted it in animals, especially her beloved horse, although she laughed such notions to scorn in humans. She thought of Molly, her perfection, the lavender mist surrounding her, the whispers in corners… She noticed the iron dirk lying on the ground, retrieved it and put it back in her bag.

"Let's go, then!" she said, helping Brigid mount then pulling herself up behind her this time, squashed against her friend as Brigid held the mare's neck and Susan grasped her mane.

They streamed downhill like a shot from a bow, Cherry taking the main pathway where the trees encroached less than other trails. Susan would never usually have attempted this with another person on the horse's back, but she felt both held and compelled, held by some force beyond her understanding and compelled to carry out its objectives. Brigid felt it, too, but to her it was familiar, the way she had felt most of the time for months. Now Susan was involved in the slipstream of whatever or whoever was guiding matters around Doon Hill. They arrived, sweating, at the manse, to see Ria running up the road towards them. Susan jumped from the horse's back.

"Dinna go in there! The bairns are safe at the holiday cottage!"

"Why? What's happened?" asked Brigid, slithering to the ground.

"Yer auld midwife's shown her true colours!" replied Ria. "I'm sure you already know what she's really like. Ye've stirred up things that should hae been left alone, ye meddlin' wee Sassenach!"

Susan was stroking Cherry's muzzle, her face like flint. "What's Molly done? Are you looking after the children?"

"She's in there decayin' like somethin' in a grave! She's no frae this world, Susan! I've tried tae keep everythin' frae the bairns but what they need tae know!"

"Thank you. You were right, Ria – things happen. It's not nonsense. We know where Ellen has been taken. Agnes Clay and an accomplice have taken her to Balquidder. Agnes is the same as Molly – you didn't spot that, did you? Please see that Cherry is wiped down and watered, will you? Is that your motorcycle I see parked there? Have you filled the tank lately?"

As Ria nodded, dumbfounded, Susan called to Brigid to come on, and she found herself mounting the bike behind Susan. The key was in the ignition; nobody secured anything here, which had astounded city-bred Brigid at first. The only thing she had known to be stolen was her own baby.

She had never been on a horse until that afternoon, and she had never ridden a motorbike, either. Susan screamed instructions about keeping her feet up and leaning into the bends. Brigid clung to her waist, eyes wide with panic as they swung round sharp corners and roared up and down hills, skirting lochs. Shutting her eyes didn't help, as she felt sick and disorientated. She choked on petrol fumes and dust. As they approached their destination, Susan slowed and pulled in to the side of the road a good way short of the steep dirt track which led up to the two churches on the hill – the dignified ruin which had been Robert Kirk's first charge, and the Victorian one higher up which had replaced it.

"I don't want to give warning," Susan said. "Let's creep up on them."

"As long as we go quickly," Brigid replied, dismounting shakily. "Susan – thanks for believing me!"

Susan pushed the motorbike on to the grass verge and they began to run. They came to the broad path leading up to the churches and moved as stealthily as they could. They both knew the old church was their goal. Built in 1631, it had replaced an even older chapel founded in 1250 on top of the grave of St. Angus, who had brought Christianity to the glen in the eighth century – but worship here was far, far older. Four thousand years of archaeological finds attested to that. The ancients had recognised that the air between worlds was thin here.

The two women broke off the path and began to wind their way through the sinking graves and haphazard headstones which littered the grass. They paused at Rob Roy MacGregor's grave, close to the doorless entrance to the church where the small tower built to house the bell which Robert Kirk had donated stood empty to the air over the roofless ruin. His first wife's resting place lay not far away. Trees stirred in the breeze, their fluttering leaves casting shadows over the ancient walls, and deeper shadows within embraced the presence-filled silence which was the spirit of the place. They couldn't see anybody through the doorway, so they skirted the walls to the back.

Lurking in a corner, where a graceful, glassless window looked from darkness into light, to the Midsummer sun dappling the fresh green leaves of nearby trees, they saw them. Ferns sprouted from the window ledge and a yew had taken root within the ruin, dwarfing the two women who stood there, one clutching a baby and the other facing her, a bag at her feet. Brigid gasped in horror. Of all the things she thought she might find, this had never entered her head.

It was Doreen Johnstone who held Ellen, over by the window. She was not the Doreen Brigid had known. She was emaciated, her eye sockets shadowed where her unnaturally large eyes were smudged with fatigue. Yet she wore lipstick, her usual bright red, which had smeared and bled around her mouth. Her headscarf had slipped; her curly hair was longer, a wild bush around her head, and her clothes tattered and dirty. She looked crazed.

Brigid made to rush forward, but Susan held her back. She slipped the dirk out of her bag and whispered to Brigid to walk slowly in case they made a run for it. They approached unheeded, the two women within seeming to be deep in conversation. When they were a few feet away, Brigid spoke.

"Give me back my baby!" Her former landlady turned to stare at her. "I don't know what this old hag has told you," Brigid continued, edging forward, glancing at Agnes, "and I don't know what she stands to gain. But Ellen isn't hers to give away!"

Agnes uttered a small cry. "I've looked after the bairn half the day waitin' for you tae show up! This waste o' space canna change a nappy, nor had she a thing for the mite, no' even a drop o' Carnation Milk! Lucky I had just been tae a birthin' an' had my supplies wi' me!"

Brigid looked at Agnes in confusion, but she couldn't wait a minute longer. She launched herself at Doreen. "Hand her over!" she cried.

Doreen hunched away from her, holding Ellen in the shadow of the wall. "She's mine! We made an agreement!"

"You held me prisoner!"

"You killed my Fred!"

"What?" Brigid's arms fell to her sides.

"Her man died in an air raid," said Agnes. "I told her that was nothin' tae dae wi' you."

"He never drank!" screeched Doreen. "They said he must have been drunk! I think you had more of those pills, you murdering bitch!"

Brigid blanched, the strength going from her legs. She couldn't speak.

Susan pushed forward, brandishing the iron knife. "Hand that child over now!"

As Doreen turned towards the window, raising Ellen, who began to squirm and cry, Susan threw the dirk. It sailed over Doreen's head and out of the window as she had intended, but it distracted the woman enough for Brigid to rush her and grab Ellen. Doreen crumpled against the ancient wall beneath the window as Ellen wailed and Brigid rained kisses on her baby's head.

Susan slumped with relief, breathing hard. "Now what do we do?" she asked. "How do we get the baby home and what do we do about *her?*" She was staring at Doreen Johnstone and talking more to herself than anybody, trying to take charge of the situation.

"First things first," said Agnes. "That bairn needs another feed. I had some diluted Carnation Milk in a bottle, left from the birthin' I'd been at – fifteen that wee lassie was, scared stiff, I knew nae milk would come – but Ellen's had every drop." She looked at Brigid's chest, where damp patches bloomed on her dress. "Looks like ye've a full load there, lass. Get busy. Best thing for both o' ye."

As Brigid sank down in the grass beneath the yew tree and unbuttoned her dress, Agnes bent and pulled a knife from her bag.

"It's for cuttin' the cord," she said. She nodded at Doreen who stood with her back against the wall, eyes roving as if she had no idea where she was or how she had got there. "She may as well hae it tae kill hersel'. That'll be one less problem." She casually held the knife out to Doreen.

"NO!" Brigid and Susan cried in unison.

Susan hit Agnes' arm away. "You can't do that!"

"She'll not want tae live withoot the bairn an' her man," said Agnes. "It's been the only thing keepin' her alive, the thought o' gettin' here tae claim Ellen. It makes perfect sense tae let her take her life. It's many a year since I've had tae advise it, but it's for the best in this case."

"NO!" Susan and Brigid screamed again, looking at her in horror. What kind of creature was she, from what kind of world, to reason like this?

Brigid's head was spinning. She didn't look in the direction of Doreen, who was now regarding her and the baby hungrily and muttering incoherently. "So you didn't take her, then, Agnes?" she managed to say.

"No. Why would I? I dinna like bairns. I like birthin' them, that's all. Very satisfyin' work."

"And you would suggest a crazed woman should kill herself? You've done it before?"

Agnes shrugged. "Aye. It's for the best, when they've nothin' tae live for an' they're just a waste o' space."

Brigid shuddered. She tried to calm herself for the baby's sake. "Why are we here? Why did you bring them here, Agnes? If you didn't take Ellen, what happened?"

"Well, I saw them between the Kirkton an' the Clachan. A wumman in that state carryin' a bairn wrapped in a pram blanket, nae wee hat – it wisnae right. She was passin' the bus stop when up came the bus an' she went tae get on, so I queued behind her. An' then she had nae money an' looked half daft, but I still wisnae sure if the bairn was hers or no', so I asked where she was goin' an' she said London. So I winked at the driver an' paid her fare here. This is where I come frae. I brought her here tae get the truth o' the matter an' see tae the bairn. I knew ye would turn up lookin' here sooner or later. As for her, she's mad an' miserable an' would be better off deid!"

Silence fell. Then Doreen began to bang her head on the stone wall behind her, moaning distractedly. Agnes gazed dispassionately. Brigid and Susan averted their eyes in pity. Brigid hunched Ellen away from her. They heard the whine of an engine and the crunch of rubber tyres on the grit of the dirt track, and pounding feet announced the arrival of the police.

The officers took in the scene, flinching with embarrassment at the sight of Brigid sitting in the grass with her baby at her breast, and staring in horror at Doreen. They glanced uncertainly at the other two women.

"We were told Agnes Clay abducted a child," said one of them. "Which one of you is Agnes Clay?"

"She's innocent," Susan said, before Agnes could speak. "Did my relative, Ria MacKendrick, call you? We thought Agnes had taken Ellen, but in fact she was trying to rescue her. She realised this poor woman here had abducted her. Her name is Doreen Johnstone and she was Brigid's former landlady. She and her husband kept Brigid captive in London, and she had to escape from them. She isn't in her right mind."

The policemen looked at Doreen in bewilderment. She was now shaking her head from side to side, quickly, like an automaton whose mechanism had gone wrong. "Madam, you'll have to accompany us to the station," said the older officer. Doreen didn't respond; her staring eyes didn't even take them in. They approached her, knelt down and peered at her. Then they gently began to raise her. As they walked her towards the car, her feet lifted off the ground and made a rapid cycling motion in mid-air, her head still flicking from side to side.

"Better off deid!" muttered Agnes.

One of the officers stayed with Doreen while the other returned to take garbled statements from Susan, Brigid and Agnes. He said his colleague had radioed for another car. When he had finished, Susan went to retrieve Ria's motorbike and roared away, desperate to see her children. Agnes disappeared outside the ruin, watched warily by the young constable, who began to follow her. Brigid, standing rocking Ellen, glanced out of the window and saw her searching the grass, pushing tussocks aside with her foot. She picked up the iron dirk and waved it at Brigid with a wink before hastily concealing it in her jacket as the policeman strode up to her.

"What did you just pick up?" he asked.

Agnes sighed and rolled her eyes. "A big juicy dock leaf tae wipe ma fanny, son," she said. "I need tae pee. Ye can watch if ye like."

Brigid laughed out loud while the young constable turned, face flaming with embarrassment, and headed for the safety of the patrol car. This was one call-out he would be only too happy to forget. The news his colleague conveyed to him, having radioed a report to headquarters, restored him somewhat; they had a patient who had absented from a psychiatric hospital on their hands. An escaped lunatic made for a proper crime. He sighed with relief. They weren't just dealing with a bunch of strange women fighting over a baby, after all.

When they were safely in the back of the second patrol car and the engine whining uphill, Brigid whispered to Agnes: "Thank you, Agnes. I've been mistaken in you. I thought you meant to use Ellen somehow, to free Robert Kirk."

"He's deid," said Agnes.

"Is he?"

"Aye, long years since."

"How do you know for sure?"

Agnes grinned. "I was there. Nothin' tae dae wi' me, though!" She clutched her chest and grimaced dramatically, falling sideways, mimicking a heart attack.

Brigid shuddered. "Why does it not entirely surprise me that you were there? The dirk, Agnes – how come you can handle it?"

"Ach, I'm more like Molly than ye give me credit for. I've been here centuries workin' for the good o' mothers an' bairns. I may be more rough an' ready an' hae different ways, but I've had few complaints. I've earned my resistance tae iron. It canna fash me any more."

Brigid sighed. "Well, I'm glad all this is over."

Agnes shifted in her seat, turning to stare at her in surprise. "What dae ye mean? Of course it's not over. Ye were summoned, lass. We'll get rid o' the boys in blue an' get this finished once an' for all."

Brigid stared back in consternation. After today, she would have been happy to have been proved wrong all along. She had borne a girl, after all – she had been mistaken in that – and at the wrong time, so why shouldn't she just have imagined the whole thing? She didn't care any more. She just wanted to go home with her baby.

#

The police dropped Brigid and Agnes off at the manse, reminding them they would have to attend the station tomorrow to make formal statements. Mary MacKenzie appeared at the front door and Susan came running up from the holiday cottage.

"Now then. How is Mrs. White? *What* is Mrs. White?" She looked from Mary to Agnes and Brigid. Her voice had steel in it.

"I only found out she was fae when she came here," said Brigid.

"And she told me just a few months ago," gulped Mary.

"Aye, she comes frae the other world next tae this," said Agnes in a matter-of-fact tone. "She wanted tae be a midwife in this world, tae make up for what some o' oor kind get up tae – stealin' bairns, or swappin' them for fairy brats, or takin' your women captive tae suckle wee fairy bairns. I wanted the same thing, but I'm no' as good as Molly. Never was. Bit o' a mischief, me, bit o' a meddler, an' no frae the right stock. So it didna work oot, but they wouldna let me back, ye see. I'm a mistfit, no' wanted anywhere." She shrugged.

Brigid remembered the vision had seen on Doon Hill when she gripped the dirk. "Well, you've saved Ellen," she said. "Mam, what's wrong with Molly?"

"The magic stopped working," said Mary, wringing her hands. "She suddenly started to shrivel and shrink and…oh, I knew it happened, she had told me, but it was terrible to see, terrible!"

"She needs her retirement," said Agnes. "She'll get it when this is done."

Susan stared at her. "What precisely do you intend to do in my house?"

"Lay a restless spirit," said Agnes. "Your house will be all the better for it. If not, there's a chance it could happen again. Next year, or maybe in a hundred years, but it will."

"This better not be useless mischief, Agnes," said Susan. "I'm going back to the cottage to explain to Ria, tell her to keep the children away until this is sorted out. Don't begin anything without me!"

She stalked away down the road and the others slipped inside.

#

When Susan returned, Ria was with her. She insisted the iron dirk was hers and she was a native of this place – she had a right to be present. She had managed to keep the children unaware of anything except Ellen's abduction, and assuring them that the baby was safely back home, Susan said they had to stay there for now. There were a few groans, but they accepted it.

In her sitting room, Susan retched at the stench despite Ria's warning. She stared in horror at the hunched bundle of bones which had been the pristine Molly White. "What do you need to do, Agnes?"

"I need tae finish what Brigid started by comin' here," she said. "If her bairn had been born this mornin' an' laid in the cradle made by Robert Kirk's hand, wi' the other elements present, it would have been fixed."

"But I had a girl," said Brigid. "I was meant to have a boy."

"Ach, thinkin' ye were havin' a boy was just your fancy," said Agnes. "It wouldna have made a difference either way."

Molly's voice came out in a strangled rasp from beneath the blanket she kept over her head. "But I took steps to prevent matters coming to a head! Forgive me, Brigid – I induced an early labour for you so that the baby wouldn't be born at Midsummer. I don't know what was meant to happen, but I didn't believe it was anything good for you or Ellen – quite the reverse. I have my suspicions about a couple of things," she said. "Beware of Aggie, or Agnes, or whatever she calls herself! You think she's saved the day, but I still don't trust her!"

"Ye never did give me a chance, did ye, *Molly or whatever-you-call-yourself?* Not when we were in oor ain realm, nor in this one." She addressed everybody. "Molly an' me go back a long way. A long, long, way – many lifetimes. But until recently, we hadna met since 1690." She paused at the collective intake of breath which followed this statement. "The last time we met was in this manse. Molly had delivered a bairn tae the minister's wife. Her name was Margaret, second wife o' a certain Robert Kirk." This time there was a gasp. "Aye, the Fairy Minister himsel'. He knew what I was – he had found me an' kept me for his research – but he never recognised what Molly was. Margaret knew, an' she was disappointed at the hard labour an' birth she had. Tae be fair, it wasna Molly's fault, an' Margaret later regretted speakin' sae harshly. But a few words was all it took tae send this one askin' tae be moved on. That's the way o' it, see – fae midwives leave their realm and serve their time in different places. This was Molly's first, but she gave up very easily. Never liked criticism, did Molly, or Sherene as she used tae be called. Always needed tae be petted an' praised, needs tae be liked."

"How dare you?" cried Molly, collapsing in a fit of choking coughs.

"As for me, I had little choice but tae stay hereaboots. I wasna a midwife, see, much as I wanted tae be. I had left my ain world withoot permission fae Sherene's lady mother. I walked oot, trailin' in the shadow o' Sherene, or Molly, as you know her, when she embarked on her great career. I was her servant, back when she was a lady born. She never took any notice o' me. I managed tae follow unseen – she knew nothin' until she saw me here in this hoose. I managed tae keep ma heid doon an' hae some fun among humans til then, a wee bit mischief here an' there…but anyway. I couldna be posted elsewhere like her ladyship here, an' I couldna go back tae my ain world. Her grand family wouldna have me. When I say I was a servant, I mean unpaid and tied for life – a slave, really. Which is funny, given that I took up wi' thon Mac, son o' a laird and a slave wumman…aye, Ria, your ancestor! But never mind that now…"

Ria's mouth fell open. "But…but…"

Agnes raised her hand to silence her. "Aye, we might be related, but we can sort all that oot later. The thing is, I was stuck in this hoose until I got mysel' movin', which I did after the Rev. Kirk died. That legend as they call it noo, aboot the dirk an' Graham o' Duchray? That was me, all my idea. I made it up. The minister was deid. I was on Doon Hill an' I saw him fall, clutchin' his hands tae his chest. He was exhausted. He wasna a well man. His mind was disturbed. His heart gave oot."

It was Brigid's turn to exclaim. "But I was summoned, he called me, showed me things…"

"He did no such thing! He's at peace, wherever he's gone. He hasna troubled these parts in two hundred an' fifty years, an' I've been here for all o' them. I left the manse, but I couldna go far. I was always someplace between here an' Balquidder. The Hill o' Fire there an' Doon Hill marked the boundaries o' how far I could go. Folks took me for a hedge witch, a healer, a wise woman. Simple folks, who were glad o' me." She looked pointedly at Susan and Brigid. "They protected me in times when one such as I might have come tae a sticky end. An' all the time, Madam Molly here was forgin' on makin' a name for hersel' an' growin' wise in the ways o' this world so she could pass hersel' off as one o' you lot, in any company. She was allowed tae forget things as she moved on, but my punishment was that I remembered everythin', an' had tae stay."

"So what brought me here, then, Agnes?" asked Brigid, perplexed. "Who summoned me? I didn't imagine it!"

Agnes smiled. "No, dear, you didn't. The minister's wife called you here. Not Susan MacKendrick an' her wee advert for a help. She had her ear whispered in, too. Just because she didna believe in such things doesna mean she wasna influenced, livin' in this hoose. I'm talkin' aboot a bitter, restless spirit grown powerful. I'm talkin' aboot Margaret Kirk."

Chapter Twenty-Five

Margaret grieved quietly at her father's estate in Comrie, outside the village which hunkered deep among the hills — hills which also trembled, as the earth beneath them shifted. Her children were her only solace. She thought of Robert, her foolish, naïve man, whom she still believed was held captive in that strange realm, that Otherworld of which few had good tales to tell, if they ever returned from it and remembered. Not many did. Some who had been lost were found in time, confused and with no memory of where they had been or what had befallen them, but everybody knew. She had grown up with such knowledge, but had never thought one of her own would be taken.

A new century dawned and Queen Anne came to the throne; in 1707 the English and Scottish Parliaments were united, as the Crown had been for over a hundred years. There was still turmoil, Protestant against Catholic, England and the Lowlands alike regarding the Highlands as a savage and troublesome place, but it didn't stop the Jacobites plotting for their cause. Margaret took little interest in any of it. She brooded instead on another realm entirely, and took to questioning her father's servants and local peasants about their beliefs and encounters with the fae, trying to think if there was any way to bring Robert home.

Then one day, an elderly man called and asked to see her in private. She met with him in the morning room. He was poorly dressed in a tattered plaid and his copper red hair and beard were wild, his skin weathered like old leather; but his green-flecked hazel eyes were clear and intelligent. His voice, when he spoke, was cultured, commanding, and at odds with his appearance.

"Mistress Kirk," he said with a bow, "My name is Angus Innes. I believe ye have a missing husband."

Margaret fingered the simple cross she wore on a ribbon around her neck, sat to steady herself and asked what he knew. He had heard the whole story; the fame of it was spreading across the land, he said. He also said he could help her.

"What qualifies ye to offer help in this matter?" asked Margaret.

"Lady," he said, "I am one such as many years ago was known as a Druid. Oh, I know – we are not supposed to exist any more, and in name and numbers we do not. But there are those of us who retain the beliefs and practices in isolation."

Margaret swallowed hard. "Such a thing cannot be Christian, Sir."

"Neither are those whom I call upon for wisdom and aid. For power. The very ones your husband sought and found, to his cost."

Margaret stood shakily. "I think it best if you leave, Sir. My husband's motives were other than yours."

The man had the audacity to sit on the nearest chair. "And much good it did him," he said. "I know how to deal with the fae," he continued. "I know what it will take to free your husband."

Despite herself, Margaret had to hear him. She sat and listened as he named the deeds required, and his terms. When he had finished, she drew a deep breath and spoke seven words: "I will do it, God forgive me!" She fled the room and his overpowering presence, calling to a manservant to see Innes out.

So it was that Margaret arranged a journey for the first time in years that June, taking only Elsie and telling her family that she wished to visit her stepson Colin in Edinburgh, where he now worked. They were pleased to see her with a purpose and a plan for some enjoyment for herself. The women didn't go directly to Edinburgh. They stopped in Aberfoyle, where Margaret had promised Elsie she could visit her family in the Clachan overnight. She had arranged lodgings nearby and intended to call on old acquaintances.

First, however, Margaret went to the manse, her old home, saying she had come for sentiment's sake and to pay her respects to the present incumbents. She was welcomed by the minister's wife, a talkative woman who apologised for her husband not being home and offered her refreshments. As Margaret already knew, and as was obvious from her appearance, this young woman was heavily pregnant with her first child. As soon as was polite, she brought the conversation round to her hostess' condition and casually mentioned the cradle lying in the cellar.

"I'm so sorry I didn't take it for Marjorie!" she exclaimed. "The sight of it was a hurtful reminder of my husband's death at the time, but I later regretted leaving it. Marjorie should have spent the first months of her life in it."

"Oh," said the minister's wife, "ye're welcome to take it now. I could have it cleaned and sent to your lodgings…"

Margaret waved her hand dismissively. "It is not practicable, when I am travelling on tae Edinburgh," she said. "And I have no use for it now. But you could use it, Mistress MacKenzie! It would please me sae much tae think o' a new bairn in Kirkton Manse in the cradle the dear Rev. Kirk made!" She gazed intently at her companion.

Mistress MacKenzie hesitated a moment. "That is a kind thought," she said. "I will think on it."

Margaret waited for her to say more, but she had gone quiet. "It would dae my heart good tae see that cradle again," she said. "Might I go an' take a look, my dear?"

Mistress MacKenzie gave a slight shrug. "Of course, but ye'll forgive me if I dinna accompany ye. I'm near my time and won't risk the steep steps these days." She stood and reached for the bell pull to summon her servant.

The maid came and accompanied Margaret outside, pausing to light a candle in the kitchen. At the top of the cellar steps, she took the candle and the old key she remembered so well and dismissed the girl, saying she knew her way and would manage fine on her own. She descended and opened the door, glancing around for the place where Mac had deposited the cradle fifteen years ago. She located it near the back, covered by an old dust sheet which she cast aside. Robert's carving danced in the shadows cast by the candle, "Love and Life" leaping out at her.

"My Love, my Life," she whispered. "The love of my life! Who would have guessed that this object I hated could be the salvation of you?"

When she returned to the house, Rev. MacKenzie had come home. He and his wife abruptly ceased their conversation as she entered the parlour. Her hostess looked flushed. She stayed only long enough to be polite; conversation was stilted with the reverend in the room now. He regarded her with a wary eye, and Margaret was glad he had not been in when she arrived. His wife had been so much easier to manage. Margaret was sure of her success with the young woman.

As a parting gift, she took the brooch she wore on her jacket and pinned it to Mistress MacKenzie's dress. "To wish ye well, my dear," she said. "It was a gift tae ensure a safe birthing for me. This goes with it." She had a pouch secreted within the folds of her dress. Reaching in, she withdrew the iron knife, causing the minister and his wife to shrink back, open-mouthed in shock. She laughed reassuringly. "It is a ceremonial piece, an ornament," she said. "No cause for concern. It has never known violence, never drawn blood."

The other calls she made in the district were briefer. She visited the handful of people to whom Robert had gifted copies of his manuscript, "The Secret Commonwealth of Elves, Fauns and Fairies"; and she simply requested that she might be given them to pass on to others, his children and other close family members. All but one were readily returned to her; one was missing, and her shame-faced host admitted it may have been thrown out at some time. Margaret was gracious in telling him not to worry, while secretly hoping he was right. She did not call on Mac, who had taken over the smithy in his own right now; something held her back. His great dark eyes would prise the truth of her visit from her, she knew.

Safely installed in Colin's house in Edinburgh, she threw all but one of the manuscripts in her possession into the flames in her bedroom fire. Angus Innes had instructed that all should be burned, but he would never know that she kept one back. This one she poured over, and took her quill to every mention of her husband's own encounters with fae creatures, and his journeyings into their secret realm. By the time she had finished, the manuscript was a document of local beliefs in the fae, claims which others had made, that was all. That night she and Colin sat together in his study. He was now a man of twenty-eight years, trained in the law, with all the intelligence of his father and none of the naivety. He was only too glad to do as his stepmother requested, and copy the manuscript according to her edits.

"I can't bear to burn all of your father's hard work, his research," she told him. "But the world is changing. The things which we know to be true, others would scorn. What remains in this manuscript is harmless enough, and he will agree with me when he returns."

"But how will we explain his return?" asked Colin. "If indeed this man Innes speaks true, mother?"

"I have no reason to doubt him," she said. "The child is due at Midsummer, when the air is even thinner on Doon Hill. Innes will be there to meet your father, and will *convey him directly to Comrie, where we will live quietly and none will know he has returned except my family."*

"But the child...if this is true...which I'm not sure..."

"*Enough, Colin! Your father's life and eternal life are at stake! He will never die and go to Heaven if left among them!*"

"But the child..."

"*Just do as I say! It is all in motion now.*"

Colin turned from her and committed Robert Kirk's last remaining original manuscript to the flames, the doubt and concern on his face hidden from his stepmother – whose eyes, he noticed, were bright with the light of obsession, just as he recalled his father's had been.

#

Midsummer was drawing to a close, shadows lengthening towards sunset. Agnes said now was the time. Susan had let the children come home and tucked them safely in their beds; they had been allowed to see baby Ellen, and Molly was hidden away from them. Ria retrieved Robert Kirk's cradle from the cellar yet again and carried it up to Brigid's room. Mary used a pram pillow to line it. Agnes laid the iron brooch and the iron dirk side by side on the hood. The elements in the charm were the cradle, the dirk and the brooch, and one other thing – a newborn child laid in the cradle at Midsummer. These were the elements Angus Innes had declared necessary to Margaret Kirk, in order to free her husband.

"Now, Brigid lass," said Agnes.

"And you're sure she'll be alright?" asked Brigid.

"She will be," said Molly, who had been very quiet since Agnes took charge. "I have a feeling this is meant to be, after all. I shouldn't have meddled."

"I have every confidence," said Ria, who had always championed Auld Agnes.

Susan shivered, arms clasped around herself. "Let's get on with it, then."

Ellen was swaddled in a shawl Mary had knitted. Brigid laid her gently in the ancient cradle.

"Mistress?" whispered Agnes. "It's me, Aggie. Show yerself, Mistress. Everythin' is ready."

Everybody held their breath. They gasped in shock as the pale shade of an elderly woman appeared at the foot of the cradle. Brigid bent instinctively to grab Ellen back, but Agnes stopped her.

"Ye see, Mistress, it's all here. Everythin' Angus Innes said was needful tae bring the master back. But he's no' comin' back, Margaret. Ye were tricked. He died on Doon Hill. He's at peace. It's you that's been kept frae yer rest, waitin' for this charm tae work. Angus Innes was the worst o' his kind. He lied tae ye – he would have taken that wee MacKenzie bairn for a sacrifice all those years ago, an' his part o' the bargain would never have been fulfilled! He had a grudge against Rev. MacKenzie, who believed he was a Druid like he said he was, and preached against him. But he was fae, Mistress, the worst kind. It was never goin' tae work. Ye've been in search o' the brooch an' the dirk an' another bairn for the cradle all these years for nothin'! It's time tae go an' leave this place in peace!"

Brigid's mouth fell open. "MacKenzie!" she exclaimed.

"Aye," said Agnes. "She gave this brooch tae the next minister's wife here. Must have been some ancestor o' yours. She left the dirk as well, but they had heard the story an' guessed what it was, an' they returned it tae Mac. They never brought the cradle frae the cellar."

Margaret Kirk's wraith stared at them all. She bent down and gazed at Ellen. She stood back up and looked directly at Brigid. "I'm sorry," she mouthed. It was as if she spoke through a thick glass window, her voice distorted and barely audible, a cracked whisper which sent a chill throughout the room. Her face was anguished. Then she suddenly went rigid, throwing her arms out and her head back, and she flew backwards with a shriek as if she had been grabbed by the waist from behind. Her cry resounded in the room, gripping them all with dread, but she had gone. Brigid reached for Ellen, and Agnes didn't stop her this time.

"What's happened to her?" asked Molly.

"Not for me to say. You know that," Agnes replied.

"What do you mean?" asked Mary, crossing herself. "God rest her soul!"

"She sold her soul tae the devil when she had truck wi' Angus Innes!" cried Agnes. "What has become o' her noo is not our business. She would have given an innocent bairn tae the fae tae try tae bring Robert Kirk back, an' she knew it!"

"Is there not forgiveness?" whispered Mary.

"There may be," rasped Molly. "But we don't know for sure. It's all part of the Mystery. I hope her case will be heard in some higher court – she suffered a lot because of her husband. Agnes, I'm sorry. I misjudged you."

"Did you really misjudge her, though? I don't know what to think!" said Brigid. "She wanted Doreen Johnstone to kill herself! I'm grateful to you for saving Ellen, Agnes, but you scare me!"

"The ways of our world are not the ways of yours," said Molly. "I've adapted – been softened – by yours. Our laws are harsh, most of your kind might say. Mine – they would say they were realistic, for the best, maybe. Doreen Johnstone probably has little to look forward to in life."

Brigid hung her head. "I did put pills in Fred's tea," she said.

"You were saving yourself and your unborn child!" her mother cried. "It wasn't your fault the house took a direct hit! I'm sorry, Brigid, we thought it best to keep it all from you. Doreen Johnstone was in hospital last we heard - we didn't see any threat from her!"

"Life is hard," said Agnes. "Long an' hard. I've needed my wee bits o' fun along the way." She looked drawn and faltering, as if she might begin to disintegrate like Molly.

Molly took a deep breath. "Perhaps it's time for us to test the Mystery, Agnes. See what is in store for us in retirement."

"That's not available tae me," said Agnes. "I just have tae plod on. That's the curse they laid on me, your lady mother an' the others. No retirement, no rest."

"No," said Molly. "Not if we go together. I will plead for you." She held out her skeletal hand, decaying flesh hanging from its fingers.

Agnes stepped forward and took it lightly in her own gnarled hand. "I thank ye, Molly," she said.

"Well," said Susan, lighting a cigarette and taking a long draw, " this reconciliation is delightful, but I do hope you're not going into your version of retirement directly this minute? Because I can't stand any more strange goings-on in my house! And Agnes, you have a witness statement to make at the station tomorrow! And you, Brigid Watkins, will say nothing about bloody pills! You will never mention them again. Fred Johnstone died in an air raid, and good riddance!" Her practicality was bizarre in the atmosphere of the room, where only a few minutes ago a wraith had appeared, and where Molly in hag form huddled in blankets on a chair by the window. She turned and glanced at her. "Agnes, do you not have something you can give this poor woman? How's she supposed to go away to her retirement? She can't even leave the house in that state!"

Suddenly, the others glanced at one another and began to laugh. Susan's stating of the practical aspects of the situation was too funny. Hysteria broke out then, a release of the tension which had gripped them all day, as they giggled uncontrollably for several minutes. Only Susan herself didn't join in.

"Mrs. White?" said Brigid into the silence which followed. "If I wasn't summoned here by Robert Kirk, or the fae, but by Margaret Kirk's spirit – how did I become pregnant? If it wasn't a fae conception, after all?"

They were all very still. "That, too, is part of the Mystery, my dear," Molly said, her voice a gentle whisper. "Some things may never have an answer."

Mary spoke. "Don't think on it, Brigid. It doesn't matter. Never think on it again. Ellen is perfect, and that's all that matters."

Brigid nodded. "My Blitz bairn," she said.

\#

Ria ran Agnes back to her railway carriage on her motorbike, the old woman cackling with glee at her first trip on such a machine, an incongruous sight in her threadbare tweeds behind Ria in her boiler suit. They fetched back a restorative draught for Molly, so that she had the strength to return to the cottage again and reappear briefly at the manse next morning to say her farewells to the MacKendrick children. They were delighted with her parting gift to them – Seamus, her cat, who had settled well into country life. Susan, Brigid and Agnes went to the police station to make their statements, then Agnes returned to the holiday cottage for Molly. They left together and walked away in the direction of Doon Hill, carrying not so much as a bag.

Susan was bewildered. "Where are they going? What about Cornwall?" She had been listening as Molly spoke to her children.

Brigid gave her a despairing glance. Susan had witnessed more than her mind could cope with in the last twenty-four hours; she had seen with her own eyes, heard with her own ears, but she was never really going to be able to understand or accept it. "That's just a cover story," she said. "They're going to commune with the Mystery, or the Goddess – they don't really know themselves, I think. Do any of us know what's going on, how many worlds there are, if anybody or anything is in control of it all?"

Susan shuddered. "So they don't know what awaits them?"

Mary had tears in her eyes. "It's the end of their lives in this world and the one they came from," she said. "Their kind live long. But they've both had enough."

"So…?" asked Susan.

"So they're going to their deaths," said Brigid. "You saw the state Molly was in when her magic ran out."

Susan's mouth fell open. "And do they have hope of an afterlife, as we do? Of Heaven, of resurrection?"

"I don't know," said Brigid. "Do any of us?"

Mary crossed herself. "Brigid!"

Susan swallowed hard and cleared her throat. "I'm not immune to doubts. I question things. But I live in this world, and I'm the wife of a clergyman and the mother of five children. I hope God is in charge and I dearly want there to be redemption, and Heaven, and resurrection. You are a very fine and brave woman, Brigid, but my husband is coming home on leave next week, and my family needs the manse to ourselves.

We've suffered enough disruption. I would be grateful if you would make alternative arrangements."

#

So it was that Walter MacKenzie travelled to the country of his birth to help his wife, daughter and grandchild home. They didn't tell him anything that had happened. He was besotted with Ellen at first sight, overcome with emotion to see Brigid again, and expressed his sorrow that he had missed Molly before she set off for Cornwall. Susan, Ria and the children accompanied them to the station to wave them off. As they waited for the train, Brigid unpinned the iron brooch from her dress. She handed it to Ria.

"I think this belongs here," she said quietly. "My family have had it long enough."

Ria smiled. "I'll keep it safe," she said. "Thank you, Sassenach."

"It's just an ordinary brooch now," said Brigid. "It's beginning to look a bit duller already. Molly said some sort of magic surrounded it before."

"I'll see if I can conserve it somehow," said Ria. "It'll be good tae keep it wi' the dirk. They're part o' my story – they help me understand who I am and why I'm different. I'm so glad Auld Agnes could tell me aboot Mac."

Walter had been speaking to Susan, thanking her for her hospitality to Brigid and his wife. He turned round. "Is that Great Aunt Flora's brooch?"

"I gave it to Brigid for her wedding – something old," said Mary. "She can do what she likes with it. It didn't bring her much luck."

"The past is past, Dad," smiled Brigid. "We're looking to the future."

The train arrived in the station with clouds of steam and the grinding of great wheels. Brigid averted her eyes from Doon Hill as they chugged away from Aberfoyle. She kept her gaze on Ellen, who grizzled contentedly as the mountain crags and lochs of the Trossachs disappeared into the mist of an overcast morning.

EPILOGUE

Margaret Kirk

They banished me frae the manse, Aggie an' the latest ones tae live there. It didna matter. I saw my last hope had gone and I had become a wicked creature. In fact, I came tae understand that I never really had any hope o' gettin' Robert back. Angus Innes wanted the Rev. MacKenzie's babe for his own nefarious purposes. He never had any power tae free Robert. I didn't know that when I watched and waited all those years for a bairn born there tae be laid in the cradle wi' the dirk an' brooch nearby. The brooch was taken from the manse in time, and I fastened my will upon it as it went. The power of my undying love for Robert preserved it. My spirit awoke each time it was worn anew, no matter where it travelled – but I needed tae call it home tae Aberfoyle.

I had been watchin' that young bride since her weddin' day. She was my best hope in years – she even had Robert's book. His fame had spread. After my death, Colin returned the edited manuscript o' *The Secret Commonwealth of Elves, Fauns and Fairies* tae Kirkton Manse, asking that it be placed among the records kept there as a piece o' research intae the beliefs an' folklore o' the area. By that time, I think he had convinced himself that's all it was. He was an Edinburgh lawyer, shuttin' the door on the happenings of his childhood, as so many do.

I tried callin' to the young bride Brigid. I sensed her yearnin' for her father's homeland. When she lost the baby which had brought about her marriage, I despaired. Then she turned up again at the thin place Robert knew in London, Tower Hill. She wore the brooch as a talisman, and it called me. She was a fey young woman, her mind on other worlds, I had recognised that. She conceived that night. Never mind how. I could scarcely believe my luck, an' I summoned her as she lay stunned in a *trance on the sacred ground o' Tower Hill. I showed her the length and breadth of that Secret Commonwealth as I had come tae understand it, and she heeded me well...*

Where am I now? I am not at rest, for I have not found my Robert. But now I know I never will, I am accepting o' my fate. I bide in Comrie where I was born and where I died. My spirit strides the hills as they shift and I watch for shooting stars to rain pieces o' sky iron upon them. I have no power now. Sometimes a lonesome walker feels a sudden chill from nowhere, or an unearthly cry startles their reverie. They catch these senses of my presence, but they shrug them off as natural; as indeed, they are – to those who have understanding of the many layers of reality, and the many ways of being in them. My Robert did.

#

In July 1941, the *Times* newspaper carried two short reports, buried deep among the more important news of the day.

The first concerned the strange case of a Mrs. Doreen Johnstone, who was reputed to have faked a pregnancy after making an arrangement with a young woman to raise her unborn child as her own. Mrs. Johnstone was certified insane after her husband, Mr. Frederick Johnstone, a well-respected local council worker and ARP Warden, was killed when their house was destroyed in an air raid at the end of January. Mrs. Johnstone had been out of London staying with her sister at the time. The death of her husband plunged her into serious mental incapacity, and she required treatment in a psychiatric institution. In late May, she managed to escape from the asylum and made her way to Scotland, where she traced the pregnant woman to her new address and abducted her newborn infant. Local police arrested Mrs. Johnstone, who was found to be criminally insane and committed to an institution for life. The child was returned to its mother unharmed.

The second report concerned the good news that attacks by a suspected serial rapist around the area of the Tower of London seemed to have ended. Police had maintained silence on most of them because they had concerned prostitutes and other women of unsound character, although there were common factors with some attacks perpetrated upon decent women returning from nightshifts in factories or hospitals.

However, no new rapes had been reported since January, and it was assumed the rapist had perhaps been killed in an air raid, as he seemed to stalk the area around the Tower of London at such times.

#

The Last Word – Robert Kirk

They all have a point, you know. I did die of a heart attack. I am well and truly dead to the world in which I was born. It was my own earthly remains they buried, not a double conjured by the elves, fauns an' fairies o' the Secret Commonwealth. None o' them wanted me there. Yet here I am, for they cannot be rid o' me. My spirit entered the portal on Doon Hill just as my body was about to when my heart let me down. My shade went where my earthly body could no longer travel.

Should I not be in Heaven, a man o' the cloth like me? But this is my heaven! To gaze ever upon the fascination these creatures in this hidden realm, this Otherworld, this Secret Commonwealth, provide. I am neither their chaplain nor their prisoner. I am their tormentor, ever following, questioning, badgering them like a child wi' the thirst o' my insatiable longing for knowledge aboot them.

Are there still those who dream o' freeing me? They waste their time. Leave me be, an' leave THEM be, too. The Sith. For not everyone can look upon the sights I have seen an' remain sane. I, of course, am perfectly sane. I always preferred their world to my own.

THE END

Historical Note

(or where fact blends with fantasy!)

The known facts about Rev. Robert Kirk are intriguing enough, but basing some speculation upon them is utterly absorbing and is what led me to write this novel. Kirk was an academic and linguist, and he did indeed spend eight months in London supervising the translation and production of the first Gaelic version of the Bible. This was financed by Robert Boyle, known as the Father of Chemistry, who was a founding member of the Royal Society. He was an Irishman of noble birth who shared Kirk's belief in the fae of their similar Celtic heritage, as well as being a pious Christian. It was common at the time for people in certain places to retain belief in fairies alongside belief in God without any difficulty, although on the cusp of the Enlightenment, this view was being challenged. It was part of Kirk's intention in writing "The Secret Commonwealth of Elves, Fauns and Fairies" to prove that the hidden realm of the fae not only existed but was also part of God's creation.

Kirk's manuscript is written in the manner of a scientific paper, and I have speculated that he was influenced by his time in London when he worked with Boyle on the Gaelic Bible. I don't know if he actually stayed with Boyle, who lived with his sister Viscountess Ranelagh in her grand house in Pall Mall, but it is known that Boyle often had people living as guests while they assisted him, so it's reasonable to speculate that he did. Boyle had a laboratory in the house, and his sister was also an eminent scientist – there's no doubt she was a leading figure in the field of medicine, but the conventions of the time dictated that she hide her light behind men. Kirk's scientific manner of expression and his references to the study of nature and to the revelations of microscopes show that he was definitely influenced by the discoveries of the times in which he lived.

A shadow hanging over Boyle, whose contribution to science was immense, is his involvement with research into skin colour and race. He approved of the slave trade and of empire, and seemed to think tobacco and sugar were of such benefit that the "indigents", as he called them, had been created for the purpose of toiling at producing them for the more advanced parts of the world where they could be put to best use. At least, unlike most contemporaries, he believed that the "indigents" were created by God as part of the one human family, although low in the hierarchy. He tried (unsuccessfully) to push for better rights and conditions for those slaves who converted to Christianity, and no doubt thought himself a generous and pious man for this, although nowadays we recoil in horror.

I don't know if there were slaves in the house in Pall Mall, but it seems likely, so I speculate that Robert Kirk was influenced by that, too. Nobody has any idea what he actually thought about the issue of slavery. However, I draw upon another aspect from Boyle's writings to influence the views I attribute to Kirk: despite Boyle's assertions that "indigents" are part of the human family, it's been noted that he never seems quite certain whether he's speaking of people or animals, and something of that comes across in Kirk's writing about the inhabitants of the Secret Commonwealth – are they "people" or "animal" in nature? He likens their behaviour to birds and animals who behave as they do because they follow their natures and cannot help it. I have tried to reflect this in Aggie / Agnes. Mac, the freed slave son of a slave owner, is a figment of my imagination, but I based his background on the MacPhersons of Inverness, who had sugar plantations in Suriname at the time, worked by slaves from sub-Saharan Africa.

Although it was a scientific body, the Royal Society when it was founded was interested in investigating what we would call supernatural phenomena such as second sight, and the famous diarist Samuel Pepys thought it might be of military use to the nation. It's known that Kirk met with Rev. Stillingfleet (who later became Bishop of Worcester) while he was in London, and it's been suggested that it was at his wife's instigation that he wrote The Secret Commonwealth of Elves, Fauns and Fairies (Stillingfleet himself being interested but expressing reservations as referred to in this novel). In fact, Kirk had begun collecting accounts of fae encounters while minister of Balquidder and continued on his return to Aberfoyle, to the very manse near Doon Hill where he had been raised as the seventh son of the then minister; in 1685, he replaced a successor of his father. As a seventh son, it is believed he had the second sight himself and that The Secret Commonwealth originally contained his own experiences, even of entering the Otherworld itself, but that someone (probably his eldest son, Colin) later edited these out, fearing for his father's reputation.

Kirk married relatively late, when he was thirty-four. He was in a position to have married far sooner, so I wonder if he was perfectly absorbed with his books and ministry until he met Isabel Campbell? I like to think it was a true love match; he is believed to have engraved her headstone himself when she died. Among the words on the inscription are "Love and life", which he also paid to have engraved on the bell he donated to Balquidder Church. The cradle, brooch and dirk in this novel are my inventions, although the legend concerning Graham of Duchray did involve the throwing of a dirk. (I could find no information about the character or appearance of this gentleman, so hope I have not maligned him if he was actually a thin, reserved paragon of sobriety!)

It seems to have been a few years before Kirk married again, so perhaps Isabel was hard to follow, and it is on this that I base my speculation regarding his second wife Margaret, about whom we know very little, not even the year of her birth or the date of their marriage; she was, however, born and raised in Comrie. As there were no children born to her and Robert until 1690, it's reasonable to guess he may have remained single for several years after Isabel's death in 1680. Margaret was Isabel's cousin; we will never know why they married, but for the purposes of my story I imagined a woman who had loved Robert from afar, only to be disappointed as a slighted and neglected second wife who never measured up to the charms of the first. As is sadly common with records of women at the time, we know little about either of them.

The manse of this novel is an invention. The house in which Kirk was born and to which he later returned as minister was rebuilt in the 1730s; therefore, although Sir Walter Scott is said to have written "The Lady of the Lake" in the manse in 1810 when he is said to have discovered Robert's manuscript (this is a commonly held belief), it wouldn't have been the same house. I found financial records detailing building work in Robert's manse, which makes me think it was perhaps showing wear and tear by the 1680s. The ruined church near Kirk's grave in Kirkton graveyard is the one which replaced the church in which he and his father served.

Isabel's grave in the kirkyard at Balquidder still bears the stone engraved by her grieving husband, but it can barely be read. The bell commissioned by Kirk is on display in the Victorian church which replaced Robert's church, which is now a graceful ruin; the setting is beautiful, and the area has been a place of worship, pagan and Christian, for four thousand years, widely acknowledged as a "thin place". The kirkyard is also famous for the grave of Rob Roy MacGregor, romanticised by Sir Walter Scott, a place of pilgrimage for members of Clan MacGregor. In Robert Kirk's lifetime, the lawless family were known as the Wild MacGregors, and they did indeed raid Kippen in 1691 as I mention in this novel. However, Rob Roy came into his own later in life when his crops failed and he took to full-time raiding and running a protection racket. Balquidder Kirkyard is also a place of pilgrimage for members of Clan MacLaren, whose chiefs lie buried within the Old Kirk; the MacLaren Trust and Historic Scotland paid to have the ruin stabilised and conserved in 1997.

The Trossachs region is where the Scottish Lowlands merge with the Highlands, a geological difference created by the Highland Boundary Fault Line. There are earth tremors in the area, and there have been occasional small earthquakes, most commonly around Comrie, birthplace of Margaret Kirk. There is a theory that seismic activity can release clouds of gas (known as earthquake lights or earthlights) which cause people to hallucinate; could fae sightings in this area (and others such as the Pennines or Iceland, for example) be explained by this? I don't know, but I used the idea to facilitate Brigid's time-lapse experiences. There is no evidence of increased seismic activity in the periods of which I have written.

I based Margaret's meteorite on a spectacular incident in 1917 when a huge fireball exploded over Perthshire and parts of it landed around the Strathmore area. While refreshing my memory, I discovered reports of other meteorite activity in the vicinity, and also of UFO activity over Comrie in recent years. The theory of earthlights is also said to account for some UFO sightings, and indeed some accounts of fairy sightings from past centuries sound remarkably like alien visitations described in the space age of the twentieth century. All of this adds deliciously to the magic and mystery of the area and creates a feast for a speculative writer!

The importance of the years 1688-1692 cannot be underestimated. It was a period of religious and political turmoil known as "The Glorious Revolution", and it can't have failed to affect anybody who lived through it. Robert Kirk seems to have been a studious and sensitive sort of man, deeply interested in his books, his country and his people, whatever their religious persuasion. I therefore speculate that he was greatly affected by the rising tide of strife in these years, and particularly by the Glencoe Massacre three months prior to his death. It is indeed said that he had taken to wandering Doon Hill in his nightshirt as I portray, and that his wife feared for him, so I speculate on his mental health – perhaps it was declining in the face of the religious and political conflict of the times, and he was a man driven by obsession at the end. It's assumed he died of a heart attack. His death was preceded by those of Robert Boyle and his eminent sister Viscountess Ranelagh, who died within a week of each other in December 1691; I speculate that this, too, had an effect on Kirk.

In 1943, the folklorist Katharine Briggs recorded that she had met a pregnant woman in Methven, who spoke of her wish to give birth in the manse at Aberfoyle. She apparently said there was a chair there which had belonged to Robert Kirk, and she believed he would be freed from Fairyland if her baby was born and baptised there, and a dirk thrust into the chair. No further information exists and nobody is sure who the woman was; it's thought she may have been a military wife visiting the area. This was the inspiration on which I very loosely based the story of Brigid Watkins. From Sir Walter Scott through Jules Verne to, most recently, Sally Magnusson and Philip Pullman, writers have been fascinated and influenced by Robert Kirk and have based their own speculations upon him and his work. I believe he was a brilliant, sincere and well-meaning man who died of a heart attack due to stress, but who may – who knows – have been on to something. I would like to think so. Quantum physics has revealed that the nature of reality is far more complex than we ever imagined, and other worlds – or universes – may not be so very far away, in places where the "air is thin".

Finally, if you liked the sound of Megan and Rab the Raven, and want to know how she got on with her new life, you might like to read "The Water Bailiff's Daughter", which was my debut novel in 2020.

Yvonne Hendrie, May 2022

Acknowledgements

Inspiration

The Secret Commonwealth of Elves, Fauns and Fairies by Robert Kirk. Various editions exist, with introductions from different eras and additional material.
The Lady of the Lake by Sir Walter Scott
The Celtic Twilight by W.B. Yeats
If interested in the theories of earthlights and timeslips, I recommend *Time Storms* and *The Pennine UFO Mystery*, both by Jenny Randles.

Guides And Articles

The Enchantment of the Trossachs by Louis Stott (Loch Ard Local History Group ISBN 978-1-9999487-0-2)
The (Super)Natural Worlds of Robert Kirk: Fairies, Beasts, Landscapes and Lychnobious Liminalities by Lizanne Henderson, The Bottle Imp Issue 20 www.thebottleimp.org.uk/the-supernatural-worlds-of-robert-kirk-fairies-beasts-landscapes-and-lychnobious-liminalities/
The deep-rooted racism of science, Elizabeth Yale
www.qz.com/637284/the-deep-rooted-racism-of-science
The man who taught us to believe in fairies by Marina Warner, New Statesman, www.newstatesman.com/the-secret-commonwealth-robert-kirk-fairy-lore
My thanks to VisitScotland Aberfoyle iCentre, whose friendly staff provided directions in 2019 and additional information during lockdown, and where you can discover the best way to explore the sites associated with Robert Kirk.

Fiction

Robert Kirk has been the inspiration for many writers, from Sir Walter Scott to the present day. Most have taken his descriptions of faerie and his idea of many worlds as the inspiration for their fiction without reference to the man himself, but a few, like me, have tried to imagine the gaps in his story. I recommend *The Ninth Child* by Sally Magnusson and *The Secret Lives of Elves & Faeries* by John Matthews.

Other novels, novellas and short story collections available from Stairwell Books

Pandemonium of Parrots	Dawn Treacher
The Electric	Tim Murgatroyd
The Pirate Queen	Charlie Hill
Djoser and the Gods	Michael J. Lowis
The Tally Man	Rita Jerram
Needleham	Terry Simpson
The Keepers	Pauline Kirk
A Business of Ferrets	Alwyn Bathan
Shadow Cat Summer	Rebecca Smith
Shadows of Fathers	Simon Cullerton
Blackbird's Song	Katy Turton
Eboracvm the Fortess	Graham Clews
The Warder	Susie Williamson
The Great Billy Butlin Race	Robin Richards
Mistress	Lorraine White
Life Lessons by Libby	Libby and Laura Engel-Sahr
Waters of Time	Pauline Kirk
The Tao of Revolution	Chris Taylor
The Water Bailiff's Daughter	Yvonne Hendrie
O Man of Clay	Eliza Mood
Eboracvm: the Village	Graham Clews
Sammy Blue Eyes	Frank Beill
Margaret Clitherow	John and Wendy Rayne-Davis
Serpent Child	Pat Riley
Rocket Boy	John Wheatcroft
Virginia	Alan Smith
Looking for Githa	Patricia Riley
On Suicide Bridge	Tom Dixon
Something I Need to Tell You	William Thirsk-Gaskill
Poetic Justice	P J Quinn
Return of the Mantra	Susie Williamson
The Martyrdoms at Clifford's Tower 1190 and 1537	John Rayne-Davis
The Go-To Guy	Neal Hardin
Abernathy	Claire Patel-Campbell
Tyrants Rex	Clint Wastling
A Shadow in My Life	Rita Jerram
Rapeseed	Alwyn Marriage
Thinking of You Always	Lewis Hill
How to be a Man	Alan Smith

For further information please contact rose@stairwellbooks.com

www.stairwellbooks.co.uk
@stairwellbooks